The Soul Collectors

CHRIS MOONEY

NGUIN

PENGUIN BOOKS

UK | USA | Canada | Ireland | Australia
India | New Zealand | South Africa

Penguin Books is part of the Penguin Random House group of companies
whose addresses can be found at global.penguinrandomhouse.com

First published 2010

007

Copyright © Chris Mooney, 2010

The moral right of the author has been asserted

Set in 12.5/14.75 Garamond MT Std
Typeset by TexTech International
Printed in Great Britain by Clays Ltd, St Ives plc

A CIP catalogue record for this book is available from the British Library

ISBN: 978-0-141-04950-2

www.greenpenguin.co.uk

For Mari Evans,
editor extraordinaire

pity this busy monster, manunkind . . .

Dear Coop,

By the time you read this, chances are I'll be either missing or dead. Whatever you do, don't come looking for me. Making people disappear, as you already know, is what they do best. They're experts at hiding things: the living and the dead . . . the truth. They've been doing it for at least a hundred years – longer, if Jack Casey is to be believed, and I have no reason not to believe him. Not any more.

This is what I know for sure. They're known to strike in daylight but more often they wait for darkness, like vampires. They work in pairs. If they come for me – no, not *if*, it's a matter of *when* – *when* they come for me, I'm sure they'll bring a small army. They won't kill me. They want to bring me back to that place they call home.

It's where I belong, they say, to atone for my sins.

I'm writing you this letter on the back porch of a rental home in Oguinquit, Maine. It's remote and private here. The salty air blowing off the water feels unnaturally warm for this first week of December. Maybe it's the Irish whiskey. I'm drinking Midleton, your favourite, and as I look out over the porch railing, at the setting sun, I can't stop thinking about how we're only given one life.

How there's no second or third act, just this messy and imperfect one we've been handed, and it's up to us how we choose to live it.

You were right, Coop. I should have chosen you when I had the chance.

I've included the key for my condo, just in case you no longer have the copy I gave you. The condo, everything inside – it's all yours now.

You need to know everything that happened. I want you to know the truth about what I saw. About what happened to me and Jack Casey.

The first time I met him, Casey told me about his early career, his days working as an FBI profiler in what used to be called the Behavioral Science Unit. He called it the Monster Factory. He told me there are creatures lurking around us, doing things that the human mind doesn't want to, or maybe can't, comprehend.

I thought he was being overly dramatic. Now I know Casey was speaking the truth. I've witnessed what lives behind their masks.

I'll tell you one other thing I know for certain:
Casey?
He's the only one who believes me.

PART ONE

The Good Thief

I

When the helicopter began its rapid descent, to the now defunct Pease Air Force Base in Portsmouth, New Hampshire, Darby McCormick shifted her gaze out of her window and saw, courtesy of the bright searchlight blazing from the copter's belly, a big white van parked on the quiet stretch of dark and empty tarmac far below. She spotted a turret on the roof and then, a moment later, could make out the black gun ports along one side. Not a van but an Armoured Personnel Carrier, a brick shithouse of a vehicle meant to withstand both gunfire and explosions. The thing could roll over a landmine without suffering so much as a dent.

Darby rubbed her fingers across her dry lips, thinking. An hour ago she'd been sitting in her living room, finishing off a Heineken and watching the final minutes of the Celtics game (Boston was giving the New York Knicks a well-deserved and highly enjoyable ass-kicking), when the phone rang.

She had hoped it was Coop calling from London. He'd been moved there three months ago, and because of the different time zones – London was five hours ahead of Boston – they were constantly playing phone tag. She had called him earlier in the day to thank him for the gift – an antique hardcover copy of her all-time favourite book, Jane Austen's *Pride and Prejudice*.

The gruff voice on the other end of the line introduced himself as Gary Trent, SWAT senior corporal for the Portsmouth and Durham areas of New Hampshire. He told her she was needed up north immediately and that someone was already on his way to take her to Logan Airport.

Darby told him she didn't store her SWAT gear at home, just her tactical equipment. Don't worry, Trent said. All the arrangements had been made. Then he hung up.

The man's abruptness or his failure to explain why she was needed didn't surprise or shock her, as SWAT never spoke over an unsecured channel. She shut off the TV and went to her bedroom closet to gather the things she needed. Five minutes later, when she heard the buzzer for her condo, she grabbed her duffel bag, locked up and headed down the winding set of stairs to the building's front door.

Her escort, a skinny, puppy-faced Boston patrolman she didn't know, looked like a teenager dressed up as a cop for Halloween. He said his name was Tim and informed her he'd been ordered to bring her to Logan, where a private helicopter would take her directly to New Hampshire. Clearly Timmy had been given the word to step on it. Lights flashing and sirens wailing, the car made it to Logan in record time.

Darby wondered how the Boston brass felt about her being called in to assist in a SWAT operation. Three months ago, Boston PD had suspended her, with pay, from the Criminal Services Unit, the department's special-ized group that dealt with violent crime. CSU had been dismantled temporarily – maybe even permanently – in the wake of the murder of Boston Police Commissioner Christina Chadzynski.

Seated inside the helicopter, it came back to her again, that night inside the abandoned auto garage with the two cops who had kidnapped her. One was a federal agent, the other a Belham detective, a man she had known since childhood – Artie Pine, a close friend and confidant of her deceased father – and they had planned on torturing her. Darby killed them both and on her way out of the garage found Christina Chadzynski waiting in an adjoining room, the woman sitting at an old desk holding a shotgun, the police commissioner's hands covered in latex gloves. Darby remembered the momentary flash of surprise on the woman's face at being discovered. *You're supposed to be dead*, that look said, and then the woman said, *I have a way out of this for you . . . If you play your cards right, you'll come out of this looking like a hero.*

Darby didn't have to worry about Chadzynski any more – or Internal Affairs. Darby had told the IA officers that Artie Pine had killed the police commissioner. She had staged the crime scene, and, after hearing the recording of Chadzynski boasting about her skilful corruption methods, IA had cleared her. Now she had a more pressing problem: the Boston Police Department. The brass believed she had committed the one mortal and unforgivable sin: airing the department's dirty laundry in the press. That was the real issue at work here, why the suits were taking so long deliberating her fate. If she was reinstated – her lawyer had an almost unwavering confidence that this would, in fact, happen – the powers that be would find a

7

way to punish her. Probably kick her back to the lab and make her process rape kits or feed old DNA samples into CODIS. Drown her in mind-numbing work given to a first-year forensic tech.

The helicopter made a hard landing on the tarmac. Darby unbuckled her seatbelt, grabbed her heavy duffel bag and opened the cabin door, crouching underneath the steady *thump thump thump* of the spinning blades. Once she cleared them, she hoisted the bag over her shoulder and ran through the brisk late-September night air, heading for the SWAT officer, dressed head to toe in black assault gear, standing by the APC's rear doors.

Darby climbed inside, quickly found the empty spot on the edge of the right bench mounted against the wall and sat. A SWAT officer banged a gloved fist twice on the wall, the signal to get rolling. The APC lurched forward, and just before its rear doors slammed shut she caught sight of the copter taking back off.

Six SWAT officers, all men, in heavy black assault gear and with black greasepaint on their faces, crammed the benches. Her attention locked on the seventh man – a big white guy standing near a partition behind the driver, looking away from her and his men. He held on to one of the metal handles installed on the ceiling while he talked on a phone connected to an encryption pack. He stared down at the floor listening to the person on the other end of the line, his jaw muscles bunching as he bit down hard on the wad of gum wedged between his front teeth. He appeared to be in his mid-to-late forties, and in the dim interior light she could make out the stubble on his shaved head, the webbing of fine white lines around his narrowed eyes.

Has to be Trent, she thought, tying her hair behind her neck using one of the elastics she always wore around her wrists. She could feel the stares coming from the black-painted faces. They were trying to size her up.

SWAT was still strictly boys-only. It didn't matter if she could shoot the balls off a flea or that she could go head to head with any one of these bozos and have him on his knees sobbing in less than a minute; right now they couldn't see past her tits. They were probably wondering how she'd be in the sack. The Puerto Rican-looking guy sitting to her right – a dead ringer for one of her favourite Red Sox players of all time, Manny Ramirez – held a gas grenade launcher between his knees and had no problem checking her out like she was a piece of meat.

Darby turned to him, grinning, and said, 'Something on your mind, cowboy?'

He licked his lips, and she expected him to say how she looked like Angelina Jolie. More than one person had said they had the same lips and eyes, but Darby didn't see it. She had auburn hair, for one, and green eyes; and, unlike Mrs Brad Pitt, she had a permanent scar on her left cheek, courtesy of being hit by an axe that had fractured her cheekbone. The surgeons ended up removing the bones and installing something called a MediCor implant.

Instead, the Manny Ramirez-looking guy said, 'You the same Darby McCormick who was involved in that shootout at the garage with the Boston police commissioner?'

She nodded, knowing where this conversation was headed.

'That recorded conversation between you and Chadzynski, where she admits to all of her foul deeds?' He whistled. 'That broad was one cold and cunning bitch. She sold her soul and for what? To protect that Irish gangster prick Sullivan – and a serial killer to boot. Damn smart of you using your cell to record that conversation.'

Darby had a captive audience. She saw the grins and nods from the other men seated around her, leaning forward to listen to her every word.

'Lucky you that conversation got leaked to the media,' he said. 'Otherwise, no one would've believed that shit.'

'I'm assuming you have a point here.'

'Got some friends at Boston PD.'

'Congratulations.'

'Word is you released that recording to the press.'

Darby shook her head and chuckled softly. Amazing. The cops she met now didn't care about Chadzynski being exposed for the corrupt and cunning bitch she was; how the woman had, over the course of her career, orchestrated the murders and disappearances of several dozen state cops, federal agents, Boston patrolmen, undercover detectives and eyewitnesses. With a phone call, she had removed from the earth anyone who had tried to expose Frank Sullivan's horrific methods. Thomas 'Big Red' McCormick had been one of her victims. Yet the only thing every cop wanted to know was whether she had been the one who had leaked the Chadzynski tape to the media.

'Wasn't me,' Darby said. Technically, that *was* true. Coop had been the one who had released it to the press. She had only forwarded him a copy.

Manny Rameriz leaned in closer. She could smell his stale cigarette breath.

'You'll have to forgive me for asking this, but me and the boys here are wondering if you're recording this conversation right now?'

'What do you think?'

'I think I should pat you down just to make sure. Nobody here wants to be on the news. You know how reporters can slice and dice things to make you look bad.'

Darby smiled. 'Touch me and you'll be picking your broken fingers out of your ass.'

Manny seemed to be seriously considering making a move. He opened his mouth, about to speak, when a wail of sirens cut him off. The APC had picked up a police escort – several of them, judging by the multiple sirens.

The big white guy standing at the end shouted into the phone: 'Tell him we're on our way, ETA ten minutes.'

The gruff and raspy voice belonged to the man she had spoken to earlier. Gary Trent slammed the phone back against its cradle, walked down the APC and took a seat across from her.

2

'That was the command post,' Trent shouted over the sirens. 'CP said the subject is threatening to start killing the hostages.'

Darby leaned forward, propping her elbows on her knees. 'How many?'

'Four. He's got them tied up in this bedroom right here.' He turned slightly to point to a whiteboard showing a layout of the house. 'He's drawn down the shades on all the top-floor windows, so there's no way we can get a clear shot.'

'You already got a sniper in position?'

Trent nodded. 'He's on the roof across the street. It's the only place offering a clear view of the bedroom. Spotter's using a thermal-imaging scope, so we can make out their heat signatures pretty clearly. One hostage appears to be tied to a chair; the other three are on the floor. At the moment, everyone's alive, but this guy's getting edgy, threatening to kill them. I'm hoping he'll hold off until you get in there and talk to him.'

'I'm not a hostage negotiator.'

Trent flapped a hand. 'I know that. But you know the family. Mark and Judith Rizzo.'

The name triggered a flood of memories and mental snapshots. There was one that stood out from the others:

that overcast morning she'd spent in the couple's kitchen of their Brookline home, a place where the greatest threat to kids was getting hit by a car. The previous day, on a late October afternoon with the sky beginning to grow dark, their youngest child, their ten-year-old son, Charlie, told his mother he was going down the street to visit a neighbourhood friend. The mother told him to be careful and to ride his bike on the sidewalk, not on the main street, and returned to making dinner. Charlie hopped on his blue Huffy and vanished.

In her mind's eye Darby could see Mark Rizzo, a man with thick, bushy black hair and olive skin, sitting at the kitchen table next to his wife, Judith, a curvy, pale-skinned Irish Catholic eleven years his senior; could see the parents staring down at a mess of photographs sprawled across the blood-red tablecloth, both unwilling to touch them, terrified that by picking one to run on the TV and in the newspapers they'd seal their son behind it, imprison him someplace where they'd never see or hear from him again.

And they never did, Darby thought, returning her attention to Trent. The APC was driving fast now, the engine's low, deep rumbling vibrating through the metal bench and climbing through her limbs. The air, much warmer than before, reeked of gun oil.

Trent shouted, 'The kid disappeared over a decade ago, right?'

'Twelve years,' Darby shouted back. Charlie Rizzo's abduction had been her first field case.

'You ever find his body?'

Darby shook her head, a part of her still thinking back to that morning in the Rizzos' kitchen. Standing behind the parents were Charlie's older sisters, blue-eyed curly blonde twins named Abigail and Heather, tall for their age and wearing tight Abercrombie & Fitch T-shirts stretched over curvy frames still holding baby fat. Abigail, the one with the Cindy Crawford type of beauty mark near her lip, swiped a shaky hand over her wet and bloodshot eyes and then reached over her father's big shoulder.

This one, Abigail said, picking up a photo of a gap-toothed kid with dark black hair and olive skin, his rolls noticeable under the white *Star Wars* T-shirt with Darth Vader. *This one's the most recent picture of Charlie.*

Trent shouted, 'When was the last time you spoke to the parents?'

'Back when they were living in Massachusetts – in Brookline. Must've been . . . maybe two years or so after Charlie vanished. They came to ask me about some private investigator who offered to help them. The father was thinking of cashing in some of his retirement account to pay for it and wanted to know if I knew this guy, what I thought. I told them to save their money.'

'They hire him?'

Darby nodded. 'Nothing came of it. No new leads. I think they hired another guy who specialized in missing kids, but I don't know for sure. When did they move to New Hampshire?'

'When their girls got accepted to UNH. They're finishing up their final year. They're living at home, not at the college. After what happened to the boy, I guess the parents wanted the girls to stick close so they could keep an eye on 'em.'

'You need a hostage negotiator.'

'Already got one. Guy named Billy Lee. He's already made contact.'

'So why am I here?'

'Person holding the family hostage, he's demanding to speak to you – won't speak to anyone *but* you.'

'What's his name, do we know?'

Trent nodded. 'Guy's saying he's their kid – their son, Charlie Rizzo.'

3

Darby stared at Trent. Stared at him for what seemed like a long time.

'You heard me right,' Trent shouted. 'Guy said he can prove it too.'

'How?'

'He won't say. This guy – let's just call him Charlie, keep it simple – Charlie says he won't speak to anyone but you. Said that if we can get you to come up here and talk to him, alone, face to face, he'll release the hostages. I'm not buying it. He's already shot someone.'

'Who?'

'Don't know the vic's name; he didn't have any ID on him. He's a white male, bald, somewhere in his fifties. Charlie shot this guy in the back. Twice. Ambulance arrived at the house before we did and found the vic lying in shrubs. Last report is this guy's still alive but unconscious. He lost a lot of blood.'

'How do you know Charlie shot him?'

'He called 911 and told the operator.'

'*Charlie* made the call?'

Trent nodded. 'He identified himself by name to the dispatcher, then told the woman about the shooting and dumping the body out the window – told her *exactly* where it was lying. Then he said he's holding the Rizzo family hostage and – get this – the son of a bitch *requested* a SWAT team. Said he wouldn't release a single hostage unless a SWAT team was brought to the house along with some sort of bulletproof vehicle. Oh, and the body dumped in the shrubs? He told the dispatcher it was a gift. For you.'

Darby shifted in her seat. 'Those were his exact words?'

Trent nodded, checking his watch.

'He say why he asked for me?'

'No. You have any ideas?'

She shook her head. 'Has he asked for any other demands besides wanting to talk to me?'

'No, just you.'

Darby took a moment to digest this. Not for one second did she believe Charlie Rizzo was alive and waiting for her at this house; but *someone* had summoned her, and this person's actions and choice of words were unsettling, to say the least.

Trent shouted, 'I talked with your former SWAT instructor.'

'Haug.'

Trent nodded. 'He gave you nothing but high praise. Said you're one of the best shooters he's ever seen, that you know how to handle yourself in close-quarter combat. He called you Rambo with tits.'

That sounds like something Haug would say, Darby thought, grinning. The man was without a filter. Haug called it like he saw it and didn't give two shits about political correctness. He had no shades of grey in him. You always knew where you stood with him. She wished there were more people like him in her professional life.

17

Trent said, 'He also told me you've had some experience in hostage situations.'

She had, but her first one hadn't ended well. She had tried negotiating with a frightened thirteen-year-old named Sean Sheppard. The boy had somehow managed to smuggle a revolver into his hospital room. Instead of surrendering the firearm, he shot himself in the head.

Darby didn't see any need to inform Trent about this. The news about Sean Sheppard, along with her paid suspension following the murder of the Boston police commissioner, had been plastered all over the New England papers and TV for several weeks. Even if Trent hadn't read about it, Haug would have told him.

The sirens stopped wailing. A voice crackled over the wall-mounted speakers: 'ETA, three minutes.'

Trent said, 'I'm going to have you go in alone, but we'll mike you so we can hear, and you'll be able to hear either me or the hostage negotiator with this.'

He handed her a small wireless earpiece. She doubted Charlie would notice it. If he did, he wouldn't care, as he had been the one who had requested a SWAT team. Odd.

No, not odd, an inner voice cautioned. *It's bizarre, like he's already got some endgame in place.*

'As for gear,' Trent said, 'I've got you a full assault suit. What size are you?'

She told him. She didn't need boots; she was already wearing the extra pair she kept at home.

Trent stood up in order to grab her gear. Darby fitted the earpiece into her right ear – it went in smooth and easy – then reached into her duffel bag and removed a pair of Hatch protective arm sleeves. The thin layer of Kevlar would protect her arms, wrists and hands (but not her fingers) from biting and sharp object like knives and razors.

Trent came back holding a tactical vest. 'I already installed a mike on it,' he said, taking the seat opposite her. 'In case you're asked to take off the vest – and it has happened, believe me – I want to place a second mike on you, someplace where he's not likely to look. Or touch.'

'You got the mike on you?'

Trent opened his hand. Resting in the centre of his rough, callused palm was a tiny wireless mike around the size of a pencil eraser. She knew the perfect place for it.

Darby pulled off her long-sleeve T-shirt, catching Trent's look of surprise. She didn't feel embarrassed. She had been the only female cadet during her SWAT training and hadn't asked Haug for any special treatment, sleeping and eating with the boys, even sharing the single locker room – albeit on a separate row to allow her some semblance of privacy.

Trent's gaze lingered on her bra for a moment. Then he realized what he was doing, forced his attention to the ceiling and pretended to be studying the turret. Some of the other men examined their weapons or checked their tactical equipment while she went to work clipping the mike to the centre of her black lacy but padded bra.

The Manny Ramirez-looking officer to her right had no problem staring down her cleavage.

'They're a 34C,' Darby said. 'Satisfied?'

'Very,' he replied. 'Nice abs too.'

'Thank you.' She looked at Trent and pointed to the

mike hidden in the centre of her bra. 'How much juice does this thing have?'

'Battery's got two, maybe three hours. Same with the one in your vest.' Trent looked down the row, to the short SWAT officer holding the padded end of a headset against one ear.

'Loud and clear,' he told Trent.

From the duffel bag she removed a nylon sheath holding a tactical knife with an eight-inch blade. She strapped it underneath her left forearm, resting the handle, with its dual-pronged grips for quick and easy removal, near her wrist. She put her T-shirt back on and rolled the baggy cotton sleeve over the knife. Perfect. Charlie wouldn't see the knife, but he'd find it if he patted her down.

Trent had good taste in equipment. He had given her a Blackhawk Tactical Float Vest. Good Kevlar protection and multiple side pouches with ALICE clips. One side pouch held three empty slots for extra ammo. The bigger one contained a brand-new gas mask, a top-of-the-line model with a wide transparent polycarbonate visor and a military-grade filter positioned on the right side so it wouldn't interfere with her vision. The mouthpiece also had the new voice-amplifying system.

'Where'd you get the funds for all this equipment?' she asked, dipping into the duffel bag again for the tactical pouch holding her sidearm. 'You guys hit the lottery?'

'In a macabre way, yes, we did,' Trent said. 'After 9/11, the state got a massive influx of cash to upgrade all our gear and weapons, and there was enough money left over to buy the Bear.' He tapped the wall of the APC. 'What are you packing? Looks like a SIG Sauer.'

'P226,' Darby said, strapping the sidearm against her right thigh.

'Nice choice, but our guy's probably going to have you dump it. You're going to need a backup piece and some-place to hide it. I'd sug—'

'I've already got it covered.' She rolled up her jean cuff and showed him the weapon tucked beneath the lip of her boot — a compact SIG Sauer P230 in an ankle holster.

She slipped on the tactical vest, zippered it up and found, strapped to the right front, a black piece of metal shaped like a baton. It had a trigger.

'What's this?'

'Netgun launcher,' Trent said. 'Two rounds, though you only need one. Wraps the person in a web. It's electrified, gives the person a slight jolt. And it's made of this sticky shit, so there's no way you can tear it off. I'm not a big fan of the non-lethal gadgets, but this one shows a lot of promise.'

Darby started transferring the extra clips of ammo from her duffel bag. 'What's the plan? You going to drive the APC up to the house?'

'Our boy Charlie requested it. I'm going to park it right in front so he can't miss it.'

'I want you to keep your men in here until I give the order to breach.'

'He asked for us, remember?'

'Understood. But if you want me to go in there and talk to him, I'll be the one giving the orders.'

That hit a nerve. Trent's gaze narrowed in his stony face. She knew the senior corporal was about to launch into a lecture about how this was a tactical operation and, as such, *he* would be the one calling the shots.

'I don't know anything about this guy's mental state,' she said. 'For all I know, he's a schizophrenic. If he sees your men standing around the house, armed, it might set him off. He might start shooting.'

'All the more reason why my men should be positioned in and around the house.'

'I can handle him. And I'm going to get him to walk out of there alive. If we carry him out in a body bag, we won't know why he's holding the family hostage.'

'And if I say no?'

'Then you can go in and try talking to him.'

Darby removed her SIG, clicked off the safety and jacked a round into the chamber. She slid her weapon back into the holster, clipped the strap and leaned back against the wall, waiting for Trent's answer.

The APC came to a jarring stop.

Darby didn't move. Nobody did, everyone waiting for Trent to speak.

Finally, he did.

'Nobody moves or takes a shot until McCormick gives the word.'

Darby thought she caught a look of admiration flash across his eyes before he turned to his men. 'Everyone clear?'

Nods all around.

Now it was her turn to address the group.

'If I say "blue", that's the signal to breach the house. If I use "red", have one of the snipers take Charlie down. Any questions?'

There were none.

Darby opened the back doors to a rush of cold air and flashing blue and white police lights.

4

Darby stepped into a crowded police blockade. She didn't see any homes or streetlights, just a long, double-wide road paved through densely packed woods that seemed to stretch for miles in every direction. Country living at its finest. A city girl, she could never understand why anyone would choose to live in such an isolated setting.

The air crackled with police radios. She followed Trent, weaving her way through the blue-uniformed bodies and plainclothes detectives, almost every one of them talking on a cell phone. A strong breeze rattled the tree limbs and shed autumn leaves that had already started to turn – deep orange, yellow and red colours that danced in the wind and were lit up as they blew across the road by all the flashing police lights.

'Press here?' she asked Trent.

'Not yet. When they arrive – and God knows they will – they won't get close. We've got patrols on every street. The whole area is sealed off.'

But not the air, Darby thought. Once word got out – and she was sure it had – there'd be more than one news copter hovering close to the Rizzo home.

The command post, a plain white vinyl-sided mobile trailer, was parked to the side of the road between the two police blockades. Trent walked up a set of collapsible metal stairs and held the door open for her.

Inside, she found a good amount of space, all of it strategically designed and organized. The shelving carried almost every type of conceivable surveillance equipment: a microwave receiver for the trailer's roof camera, tactical audio kits and a stereo accelerometer that could be used to pick up voices through windows, walls and floors. The warm, stale air smelled of coffee and it triggered memories of long nights she'd spent at the lab, dry-eyed and desperate, fighting to stay awake while combing through notes, files and evidence with the hope of finding something that had been overlooked, something that would break a case wide open. It reminded her of that adrenalin-fueled feeling of racing against the clock. Of desperation.

It also reminded her of Coop. How deeply she missed him and how badly she wanted him standing here beside her. Now he was living in London and working for a firm that specialized in fingerprint technology, his area of expertise. Instead of going through crime scenes with her, he was now a consultant for Britain's Identity and Passport Service, a government branch that was currently attempting to create a fingerprint system that could be integrated with the world's largest biometric fingerprint database, IAFIS, owned and maintained by the American FBI.

The man she assumed was the hostage negotiator sat in front of a workstation set up on the wall behind the driver. Trent quickly introduced Billy Lee, a slight man with angular features. She had Lee pegged as being somewhere north of fifty. Dressed in a sharp charcoal-grey suit and tie, his grey hair combed and carefully parted, he looked more like someone accustomed to sitting on a board of directors. When she shook his hand and felt his dry palm, she had the feeling that Lee shared the same attributes as Gary Trent – precise and certain with his words, an alpha male accustomed to playing all forms of mental chess – and winning. That desperate feeling drizzling through her chest didn't evaporate, but it did ease back a bit.

'What's the latest?' Trent asked, pulling a seat out from another workstation.

'Still quiet,' Lee said. 'I'm sure he'll be calling any moment.'

'You don't want to call him, tell him we're here?'

Lee shook his head. 'I have something he wants now,' he said, pointing to Darby. 'I'll wait for him to call me.'

She turned her attention to a flat-screen computer monitor showing five bodies glowing with bursts of white, orange, yellow and red. One body appeared to be sitting in a chair; three were on the floor, one lying sideways. The fifth paced the room. Charlie.

The monitor next to it showed three different angles of the house, courtesy of a multiplexer unit that allowed the command post to view four cameras simultaneously. Trent had set up three remote-controlled cameras around the perimeter of the house – front, side and back – to give him real-time feeds. A date and running time was on each screen. Each video, she noticed, was being fed into a separate DVR to record every second.

'Nice resolution,' Darby said.

'Cameras are using a 24 para-digital lens,' Trent said.

'We can rotate them 360 degrees, and we got infrared capabilities in case —'

A phone rang.

Trent scooped up a pair of headphones from his desk. Lee calmly picked up a pair with an attached mike as he swivelled around in his chair and faced the monitor set up on the desk.

'Hello, Charlie,' Lee said brightly, as if he were speaking to a personal friend. 'Dr McCormick just arrived. She's here with me right now. Would you like to speak to her?'

Darby couldn't hear Charlie's response, but she could read the words filling the screen. Voice-recognition software had converted his speech to text:

'I want to speak to her inside the house. Alone.'

Lee glanced up at Darby. She nodded.

'Okay, Charlie,' Lee said. 'Dr McCormick has agreed to come inside and meet with you. Alone. I delivered on my promise; now you need to deliver on yours. Release your family.'

Charlie's response appeared on the screen:

'She needs to see them first.'

Lee's brow creased in thought, but he didn't seem rattled or concerned.

'You gave me your word,' the hostage negotiator said, his tone sounding neither confrontational nor impatient. 'You need to show the police that you're willing to cooperate — that you have no intention of harming your family.'

Charlie responded: 'I told you I won't harm them. I gave you my word on that.'

'I know you're agitated,' Lee said. 'And I sympathize with your frustration at having to wait for Dr McCormick to arrive. But she had to come all the way from Boston. We ordered a private helicopter to get her up here as quickly as possible. I delivered on my promise, and now you have to deliver on yours. You don't want me to look bad in front of my boss, do you?'

Lee spoke in a relaxed way, his tone amazingly empathetic, as though he was connecting with a long-lost relative.

'I need Dr McCormick to bear witness,' Charlie responded.

Lee said, 'To what?'

No response.

Darby glanced to the screen holding the heat signatures. The man pretending to be Charlie Rizzo appeared to be holding something against the ear of one of the hostages. A phone? A gun?

She sidled up to Trent and whispered, 'What's he saying?'

'Don't know,' he said, keeping his voice low. 'We didn't install a mike in the house. I was going to have one of my men install a parabolic while you were in there talking to him so we –'

'Keep your men back until I give the order.' She moved back to Lee, reading the words scrolling across the computer screen.

'Please,' Charlie responded. 'We're running out of time.'

'That's the fifth time you've mention that,' Lee said.

'Please tell me what you mean so I can help you, Charlie. Everyone here wants to help you through this. We don't –'

Lee stopped talking to listen to Charlie.

Darby watched the computer screen. 'I'll tell her. Dr McCormick. Alone,' Charlie had responded. 'Have her go through the front door. No escorts, no tricks. And remember to park the bulletproof van or car or whatever it is you brought – I want it waiting for me near the front of the house. After Dr McCormick has heard what I have to say, she'll arrest me and bring me out. You have my word on that. Do what I ask, and I'll release everyone as promised. But if you don't do what I ask – if you try to trick me – then I'll kill my family and then myself. I can't survive the wheel again.'

'Tell me about the whee—'

CALL TERMINATED flashed across the screen.

Lee took off the headphones.

'What's the wheel?' Darby asked.

'I don't know,' Lee said. 'You?'

She shook her head.

Lee rubbed the bridge of his nose. 'Charlie has placed a call to me every five minutes inquiring about your arrival. Each time his voice has vacillated between agitation and panic. When I was on the phone with him just now and confirmed that you were, in fact, here, he sounded relieved, even . . . well, hopeful.'

'Has he given you any indication as to why he asked for me?'

'No. I've asked, and each time he's refused to answer – and

he stubbornly refuses to talk about the person he shot and dumped in front of the house. Any time I broach either subject, his voice changes. I can tell you this much: he's afraid.'

'Do you think he's suffering from a schizophrenic disorder?'

'That was my original thought, but he's not showing any signs beyond his delusion that he's really Charles Rizzo. His speech is coherent. He doesn't stop midsentence and start jumbling together meaningless words. His thoughts are organized and he can follow a conversation.'

That didn't mean he wasn't schizophrenic. There were varying degrees, varying symptoms. She wouldn't know until she spent time with him.

Lee said, 'Do you know the first rule of hostage negotiation?'

'Form a bond.'

'Yes. That's your primary goal. Always remember that. When you go in there, let him think he's Charles Rizzo. Don't fight him on it. Listen to his grievances. If he believes you really *do* care about his pain, cause, whatever, he'll be more receptive to releasing the hostages, which is our goal. Remember to always be working on that bond. We'll be listening in and speaking to you over an earpiece. That's all I have.' Lee glanced to Trent.

'The APC will take you in,' Trent said.

'And SWAT won't move in until I give the order?' Darby said.

'Until you give the order,' Trent repeated. 'You have my word on that. But at the first sign of trouble, I'm ordering my men to breach.'

The APC had built-in ladders on both sides of the back doors to allow a sniper quick access to the roof. She didn't want to ride inside or in the back. She had all of her equipment, and the fresh, cold air was keeping her head clear.

Darby extended one of the ladder's rungs, climbed up and knocked on the side of the APC. The driver looked in his rear-view mirror, saw her standing on the back, then put a hand out of the window and waved.

The engine came to life, rumbling, and the APC started crawling towards the house.

5

Darby mulled over the cryptic conversation she had just heard between the hostage negotiator and the man calling himself Charlie Rizzo. *I need Dr McCormick to see them first*, Charlie had said. *I need her to bear witness.*

Bear witness to what? Killing the family? And what the hell did he mean when he said he couldn't survive the wheel again?

Another police blockade had been set up on the far end of the street. She spotted three cruisers, their flashing blue and whites lighting up every inch of the neighbourhood, a place far different from, and light years beyond, the Rizzos' former Brookline address with its multimillion-dollar McMansions and professionally landscaped lawns and gardens, high-end BMWs and Mercedes parked in two- and three-car garages. A real-estate agent would call these three New Hampshire homes – the only ones here on this long stretch of woodlands – either 'cosy' or 'fixer-uppers'. No garages, just driveways with small, dependable economy cars. Living here in the Granite State gave you plenty of land and privacy. The houses were spaced far apart from each other, and each one looked like it had been dropped in the middle of the woods. No streetlights either.

She caught two remote cameras set up on tripods on the front lawn and driveway of a small colonial with white-chipped paint and dark green shutters – the new home of Mark and Judith Rizzo. The windows, at least the ones she could see, were dark, the shades on the top floors drawn, just as Trent had said. Two cars were parked in the driveway: a white Jeep Cherokee and a maroon Honda Civic. She could make out stickers for the 'University of New Hampshire' on both back windows.

Darby glanced to the ranch house across the street. It took her a moment to spot the sniper. He was lying on the flat roof, staring down his target sight. His partner, the spotter, knelt behind a chimney and stared at the Rizzo home through a thermal-imaging scope.

The APC came to a stop. She stepped off and moved up the leaf-covered walkway.

Please, Charlie had said, *we're running out of time.*

Darby walked up the front steps and gripped the door-knob. It turned without a problem.

She stepped inside alone, as instructed, but didn't shut the door behind her. The flashing police lights coming from opposite ends of the street were bright and strong enough to part some of the house's interior darkness, and it gave her a chance to take in her surroundings.

Hardwood floors and directly in front of her, a set of stairs carpeted with a dark burgundy runner. To her left, a living room with a sectional couch and a small flat-screen TV. Modest furnishings. The Rizzos' Brookline home had had Ethan Allen furniture in large, spacious rooms. *They were probably forced to downsize after blowing that money on private investigators*, she thought. *They probably moved here so the kids could get in-state tuition fees.*

'Shut the door and lock it.'

The screechy, breathless male voice came from somewhere upstairs.

'*Hurry. We're running out of time.*'

We, she thought, easing the door shut. She locked it, hearing the bolt slam home, and moved to the bottom steps. She couldn't see Charlie up there. Too dark, but she could hear him panting.

'Are they listening?' he asked.

'Who?'

'The police. Did they send you in here with some sort of microphone so they could listen to us?'

She thought about how to reply, recalling Charlie's response to the hostage negotiator: *I want to speak to her inside the house. Alone.*

Lee whispered over her earpiece: 'Tell him about the mike strapped on your vest. It will be a show of good faith, a way to build trust with him.'

Darby said, 'There's a mike strapped to my vest. It's in the front.'

'Good,' Charlie said. 'Will they be recording our conversation?'

'Yes.'

'Good. Very good.' Sounding excited and, as Lee had said, hopeful. 'Please fold your hands on top of your head. When you reach the top of the steps, turn left. The bedroom is directly at the end of the hall. That's where I want you to go. Keep your hands on the top of your head until I tell you otherwise.'

Darby followed the instructions, clasping her fingers

together and folding her hands on top of her head. She climbed the stairs thinking about the excited tone in the man's voice. She wasn't imagining it.

'Tell me about the man you threw out the window.'

'It was a gift,' he said. 'For you.'

'What's his name?'

'He doesn't have one. None of them do.'

Darby was about to ask what he meant by that when it hit her, an intense, sour smell that reminded her of the homeless people she'd sometimes pass on her way to work during the hot summer months in Boston, that putrid stench of body odour mingled with soiled clothing.

She stepped on to the second floor, gagging. She couldn't see Charlie in the nearly pitch-black darkness, but she *could* hear moaning coming from down a hall. Moaning and muffled voices.

Breathing through her mouth, she started walking, bumping into a wall full of hanging pictures. She knocked over one, hearing glass shatter against the floor. She kept walking, coming to a stop when she made out a door. Her eyes had adjusted to the darkness and she could see it was cracked open. No light coming from behind it, just sounds – crying and a dull thump. And that goddamn odour – she could feel it coating the back of her throat.

Keeping her hands on her head, Darby used her foot to slide open the door.

6

The bedroom shades were drawn, but the police lights flickering around the edges allowed Darby to make out the frightened faces.

She saw Mark Rizzo first. Dressed in boxer shorts and a tank top spotted with what had to be blood, his swollen head hanging over his lap. He was the only one tied down to a chair.

Judith Rizzo, wearing a white flannel nightgown and rollers in her grey-white hair, lay sideways, most of her face pressed into the carpet. Her ankles had been tied together with what appeared to be electrical tape. Hands tied behind her back, mouth taped shut.

The woman's single, visible eye shifted to her daughters. They had been taped in the same manner as their mother, but the twins – thin and tall now, wearing tight boxer-type shorts and T-shirts – had managed to get themselves into a sitting position. Their backs rested against the foot of a king-sized bed, their knees propped up to their stomachs. They shook in fear but didn't appear hurt. Darby didn't see any blood on them.

'Everything will be okay,' Darby told the girls, quickly taking in the rest of the room. A black goosedown jacket lay across the bed's tangled sheets. One of the nightstands had been tipped over. 'Just try to stay calm.'

Darby saw the twin with the beauty mark above the lip, Abigail, turn her head to the door. Darby was about to move when she felt the muzzle of a gun pressing against the back of her skull.

'Don't turn around yet,' Charlie said behind her. 'Just stay right where you are, okay?'

Darby hadn't heard any footsteps and wondered if the man had taken off his shoes so he could slide undetected through the darkness.

'This is just a precaution,' he said. 'I only want to make sure you do what you're told. This is important. I don't want to hurt you or anyone else.'

'Then why did you shoot your friend?'

'That . . . *thing* was *not* my friend.'

'Who was he?'

'I'm hoping you'll find out. That's why I gave him to you.'

The man reached across her thigh and fumbled for the holster strap holding the SIG. As he worked, keeping the muzzle pressed against her skull, she carefully slid the fingers of her right hand underneath the elastic fabric of her shirtsleeve . . . there, she felt the handle of the tactical knife. To pull it free and grip the knife properly would take no more than four seconds; but to use the blade effectively, she needed him to face her.

He pulled the sidearm from her holster. She heard the SIG land somewhere in the hall.

'I just want to talk,' he said.

Darby waited. He didn't pat her down for any other weapons. Yet.

'I don't want to hurt anyone,' he said again. 'Please believe me.'

A part of her did believe him. She could hear the hope in his voice, the excitement, as if a gift he had longed for was about to be realized. And he was speaking too clearly and coherently for a schizophrenic.

'The people listening to us right now,' he said. 'I want you to tell them to stay away from the house until you've heard the truth. We're all going to talk, that's it. After we're done, I'll release the hostages, and you can arrest me. I'll cooperate. Did you bring something to transport me?'

'It's parked right out in front of the house.'

'What is it?'

'An Armoured Patrol Car.'

'Is it bulletproof?'

'It can withstand rocket fire.'

'Thank you.' His voice caught, strangling on tears.

Judith Rizzo moaned.

'Thank you,' he said again, more clearly now. 'Tell the people listening to us I won't harm anyone.'

'They heard you.'

'I want you to tell them. I want them to hear *you* say it.'

Darby's gaze had cut sideways. Judith Rizzo had rolled on to her back. Blood dribbled from her mouth and broken nose. A dark, wet pool was on the carpet.

'It was an accident,' Charlie said. 'She tried to run while I . . . She fell and hit her head on the edge of the bureau. Now talk to the SWAT people and tell them what I just said, word for word.'

'I will if you release your mother.'

'Not yet. She has to stay here.'

'Why?'

'We'll get to all of that. Now tell the SWAT people, *hurry.*'

Darby said, 'Charlie Rizzo has asked for SWAT to stay away from the house. All he wants to do is talk. After he's done, he'll release the hostages. I'll arrest him and then transport him to the assault vehicle.'

'Ack—' Lee began, interrupted by a coughing fit. 'Acknowledged.'

Darby expected Trent to pipe in and add his two cents. Much to her surprise, he remained silent.

Charlie said, 'Dr McCormick, I'd like you to please turn slowly to your right . . . Okay, stop. Stay right there. Don't move.'

Behind her she heard the scratch and hiss of a match being struck. The room lit up with a faint orange glow and now she could see the terror etched on the twins' faces, their cheeks shiny with tears.

Charlie said, 'My mother told me someone named Detective Kelly was in charge of trying to find me. Stan Kelly.'

'That's right.'

'What happened to him? I called the Boston police and was told there was no one there by that name.'

'He retired.'

'Retired,' Charlie repeated. 'That means . . . that's when a person leaves a job, right?'

Darby blinked in surprise. *Is he being serious?*

'That's right,' she said.

'When did he die?'

'Why do you think he's dead?'

'Never mind, it's not important.' He was speaking quickly – too quickly, she thought. *He's panicking.* 'My mother also said you helped look for me. Said you're a good person, someone worthy of trust.'

Judith Rizzo blinked dully in the candlelight. Her pupils appeared dilated.

'You can turn around now.'

Darby didn't move. Up until this point, she had cooperated. Now it was time to push back a little, to try to turn the tables.

'Release your mother and I'll turn around.'

'She needs to hear the truth first,' Charlie said. 'She needs –'

'What your mother needs is medical attention. Let me bring her outside. There are people waiting who can take her to an ambulance. I'll come back upstairs and we can talk.'

'No.'

'If you really are Charlie Rizzo –'

'I am! I *am* Charlie Rizzo, and I'm going to prove it to you!'

'Careful,' Lee whispered over her earpiece. 'Don't push him too hard.'

Darby said, 'If you really are Charlie Rizzo, you'd want your mother to get help. She's suffered a serious head injury. Accident or not, she'll die unless you let me bring her –'

'*TURN AROUND*,' Charlie roared. '*You turn around*

right now or you'll never know the truth about what happened to me, what I'm doing here. I'm giving you a GODDAMN GIFT so you turn around RIGHT NOW or we'll lose EVERY-THING!'

She did, slowly, her hands folded on top of her head.

A small votive candle had been placed on the foot of the bed, and in the flickering candlelight Darby got her first look at the man claiming to be Charlie Rizzo and felt the blood drain from her limbs.

7

Darby's gaze flashed inward, away from the man claiming to be Charlie Rizzo and seizing on a memory of herself at thirteen, lying on her stomach underneath the bed in the spare bedroom of her childhood home and watching, in mounting horror and fear, a pair of soiled work boots moving slowly across the carpet towards her – the serial killer she would later come to know as Traveler, a real-life Michael Myers dressed in greasy blue coveralls and wearing a mask of stitched-together flesh-coloured Ace compression bandages, the holes for the eyes and mouth hidden behind strips of black cloth.

The mask covering Charlie's face was made of *human* skin.

The areas around the mask's eyes and mouth had been cut away, and in the candlelight she saw black non-absorbable sutures crisscrossing their way around the mask's eyeholes and dark leathery flaps of dried skin around Charlie's neck. The curling, cracked edges of the mask's mouth had been sewn into his healthy lips. There was no sign of blood, or of swelling or infection, on the lips or along the healthy, living skin around the sutures. This . . . procedure had been done some time ago, and Charlie's skin had healed.

Darby swallowed drily, the candlelit bedroom taking on a surreal quality, as though by turning around she had stumbled through some portal and straight into one of Stephen King's creepy horror stories.

Charlie stood behind the chair holding Mark Rizzo, whose head was still slumped forward. With the aid of the light, she now saw that Rizzo's face was swollen, the skin split in several places – Christ, the skin around his left eye was a bloody mess. Darby thought Rizzo had been beaten unconscious; he didn't stir or make a sound when Charlie placed a hand on the man's shoulder.

She saw dirty, callused nubs of scarred skin. No fingernails. They had been removed.

'I didn't do this,' Charlie said, pointing to the mask with the revolver.

She believed him. There was no way he could have done that to himself – or *by* himself. The sutures had been sewed and tied off with a neat, orderly precision. Someone else had sewn the mask to his skin – someone with a skilled, patient hand.

'Who did this to you?'

'One of the twelve,' he said. 'He sewed it on to my face as a reminder.'

'For what?'

Charlie grinned. 'You'll see. First, this.'

He removed his hand from Rizzo's shoulder and began to work furiously at the buttons of his long black shirt. *No, not a shirt*, she thought. *It's one long piece of black material, like a robe or a tunic.* It seemed to belong to some past century, some ancient and now dead culture. It brought to mind European castles, a time of fiefdoms and serfs.

'I was born with a specific genetic condition,' he said,

moving his bent and crooked fingers with their missing nails to work on the next button. 'Do you remember what it is?'

She did. And she easily recalled the odd-sounding name because the condition was so bizarre and unusual.

'Athelia,' she said. 'It's when a child is born without one or both nipples.'

'Yes.' Charlie grinned, pleased. '*Yes*. It's very rare. Dr Adams – that would be my family doctor – he told me there were something like two hundred thousand cases worldwide. This was back in '97, when I was taken. Do you remember how many nipples Charlie Rizzo was missing?'

'Two,' Darby said, staring at the dark rat's nest of unwashed hair secured to the mask.

Not a mask, she reminded herself. *He's wearing another man's* face.

'Come closer,' he said, training the gun on her. 'I want you to see this . . . That's far enough.'

Darby stopped about a foot away from the chair. If she could just move closer, she could bridge the gap and get into fighting range.

Charlie undid the last button. With his free hand, he pushed the fabric aside and let it drape across his shoulder to give her a full view of his naked body.

His chest, wasted thin and so pale it seemed to glow in the candlelight, was covered with a mess of thick, raised scars. Some were white, others pink and red; some were fresh welts, crusted with blood. Both nipples were missing. She also saw that he'd been turned into a eunuch.

Darby stared at the thick white scar left where his genitals had been and felt a cold place in her stomach, her skin slick underneath the heavy tactical clothing.

'Being born without *both* nipples,' he said, excited, 'that would put me in a rather exclusive club, wouldn't you agree?'

She did, but, given the thick scarring, it was impossible to tell if his nipples had been removed. Given the long, deep and jagged grooves – they seemed to cover nearly every square inch of his chest – she suspected it had been done with a carving knife.

'Now do you believe me? That I'm Charlie Rizzo?'

'Yes,' Darby said, not sure what else to say – and goddamn if some part of her hadn't turned over to the possibility that the man standing less than a foot away was, in fact, Charlie Rizzo. *And the lattice pattern covering his chest and legs – why does it seem familiar?*

'The mask,' she said. 'Whose face is it?'

'That's an *excellent* question,' Charlie said. He shrugged back into the tunic, quickly fastened a single button and then grabbed a tuft of Mark Rizzo's hair.

The man let out a yelp of surprise or pain as his head was yanked backwards. His daughters made frightened mewing sounds from behind the tape, but Mark Rizzo's single, good eye didn't look at them. Darby watched Charlie, her fingers, still tucked underneath her shirtsleeve, tightening around the prongs of the knife handle.

Come on, give me an opening . . .

'Now, Daddy,' Charlie said, looking directly at her. He had moved back behind the chair, the gun's muzzle pressed against Mark Rizzo's temple. 'I want you to tell Dr McCormick why I'm here.'

Mark Rizzo opened his mouth. Blood dribbled on to his chin. He licked his swollen and cut lips, then tried to speak.

Darby couldn't hear him – and she kept breathing through her mouth instead of her nose. The stench coming off Charlie had reached a nauseating pitch, making her eyes water.

'Speak up, *Daddy*. Don't be shy. Start with the day I was abducted.'

Rizzo's single eye rolled around in its socket, dazed.

'Charlie,' Darby said, 'why don't you tell me –'

'*NO*,' he roared, pointing the gun at her. '*NO. I've been waiting for this moment for ever – it's the only thing that's kept me alive all these years!*'

Darby stared at the gun hovering a few inches from her face. Adrenalin was pumping through her limbs, urging her to fight. She had to remind herself to keep her voice calm.

'Tell me what he did to you,' she said. 'Tell me and I promise I'll –'

'*We're not going* ANYWHERE *until he confesses! He needs to say it. That's why I brought you here! You need to hear it from the monster's own lips. I want the world to know* WHAT HE DID TO ME!'

Charlie, trembling with rage and watching her closely, leaned against Mark Rizzo's ear and hissed: 'Tell her, *Daddy*. Tell the nice lady about the day I was abducted – tell her *why* they took me.'

Mark Rizzo's single eye locked on her. 'This . . . *thing*,' he croaked. He swallowed, tried again. 'He's not . . . my son.'

Charlie pulled the gun away. Darby watched in slow motion as he pointed the gun to Mark Rizzo's leg, saw her window of opportunity and took it.

8

Darby lurched forward on her left foot, keeping her right planted firmly on the floor. Switchblade quick, she clutched Charlie's wrist with her left hand. Twisted it, surprised to feel bones snapping underneath her grip, and pulled him off balance as he squeezed the trigger.

The sound of the gunshot was no louder than a firecracker. The round splintered the headboard as she yanked Charlie's arm, pushing him up against Mark Rizzo's shoulder. Held on to his wrist as she pivoted her body and squared her shoulders, throwing all her weight behind her right fist and shattering his nose. His head snapped back. She heard the tumble to the floor. Before his knees gave out she gripped him by the throat, the dried leathery flaps of the skin mask hard underneath her palm and fingers, and smashed the back of Charlie's head against the wall.

Charlie didn't fight – didn't have the strength or the inclination. She tossed him over her leg and threw him against the floor. Turned him on to his stomach and then dug her knee into the small of his back, pinning him to the carpet. She had the pair of Flexicuffs in her hands and he continued to lie still, gagging on the blood pouring down his throat and into his mouth. She yanked his arms hard behind his back and then he screamed when she heard bones snapping and breaking.

'*Subject is down,*' she yelled into the chest mike, tightening the pair of Flexicuffs around his wrists. '*I repeat, subject is down and the house is secure.*'

'Promise me,' Charlie gagged, spitting out blood and teeth on to the carpet. 'Promise you won't let them take me.'

One of the bedroom windows shattered. Darby heard a whistling sound above her head and then a *thud*. A tear gas canister had hit the far wall and was now rolling across the floor, hissing smoke. Trent had heard the gunshot and ordered his men to breach the house.

Another pane of glass exploded, another tear gas canister hit the wall and then tumbled across the floor near the bedroom door.

Thick clouds of white smoke were quickly filling the room. Darby shut her eyes and, holding her breath, found the side pouch. She ripped it open, grabbed the gas mask and fitted it over her face.

Charlie had rolled on to his side. She had knocked out most of his front teeth. He stared at her, his wide, frightened eyes blazing from behind the ghoul mask.

'Lock me away,' Charlie said between gagging. 'Lock me where they can't find me.'

Darby jumped to her feet as the front door was knocked off its hinges.

'*Others,*' he screamed.

Smoke was quickly spreading through the room. Darby grabbed Judith Rizzo by the arms.

'*Promise me –*'

Charlie started coughing, hacking and wheezing from

the tear gas filling his lungs. She dragged the mother into the hall, and heard Charlie's last words: 'Get the others.'

Two armed SWAT officers were rushing to the foot of the stairs.

'Stand down,' she yelled, pleased by the strength and clarity of the mask's voice amplification system. She guided the woman's head to the floor. 'I repeat *stand down.*'

The front officer stopped running and stood in the middle of the stairwell. Darby moved to the top of the steps.

'Subject is down and cuffed,' she said. 'Bring the ambulance around, we have a –'

The SWAT officer raised his shotgun and fired.

9

BOOM and Darby felt the round hammer against the centre of her chest.

Her breath exploded from her chest, and she stumbled backwards. She hit the back wall and tumbled, her legs giving out. Her hands gripped the air, seeking purchase – *BOOM* and a second shotgun blast took out a chunk of plaster from the wall where her head had been just a moment ago.

Splayed against the floor, and making harsh and painful gasping sounds behind the gas mask, Darby turned on to her side. The armour plating had saved her life, but her ribs were broken, maybe even fractured. Blinking, she saw the two SWAT officers disappear through the smoke. It was drifting into the dark hall, and over the ringing in her ears she heard more footsteps pounding their way up the stairs.

Then she caught the figures of two, maybe three SWAT officers (*not Trent's men – they have to be someone else but who are they?*) turning left at the top of the stairs. They disappeared behind the smoke, their footfalls fading as they ran towards the bedroom.

Four, possibly five men were inside the house. More could be waiting downstairs or outside. They would head back this way and someone would see her squirming on the floor and keep pumping rounds into her until she was dead.

Sucking in hot air and trying to get her lungs to work, she reached for her sidearm and felt the empty holster. Charlie had ditched her weapon. She had heard it land somewhere out here, and she began frantically to search the floor –

BOOM and the shotgun's muzzle flash jumped in the white smoke from the bedroom.

BOOM and two SWAT officers emerged from the smoke hauling someone by the hands and feet – Charlie Rizzo, she thought. They rushed down the steps –

BOOM.

Darby fumbled for her ankle holster, where the compact SIG was hidden. The .32 ACP rounds didn't offer much stopping power, even at close range. They'd be useless against tactical armour. She'd have to try for a headshot. The gas mask's polycarbonate visors were scratch resistant but not bulletproof.

First, she had to find a vantage point.

Dizzy, she pushed herself up on to her knees. One, possibly two men left in there. Using the wall for support, she got to her feet and immediately stumbled, dropping to her knees and sucking in air. She had to wait and couldn't wait.

From somewhere outside she heard tyres skidding across the pavement.

Now heavy footsteps were coming her way and she knew the SIG wouldn't put a dent in him, so she dropped it. With one hand she grabbed a flash-bang grenade from her vest, while pulling the netgun launcher from its holster with the other.

The SWAT officer emerged through the smoke with his shotgun raised. He saw Judith Rizzo, stopped, and then placed the muzzle against the woman's head and fired. Darby pulled the pin and tossed the flash bang across the hall floor.

The grenade went off and the SWAT officer was stunned by an explosion of noise, the white light blinding him. Darby pulled the netgun's trigger.

There was a pop and hiss as the net hurled through the air, expanding into an electrically charged web. It wrapped itself around the SWAT officer's chest and face, tangling him in the sticky strands. Sidearm back in hand, she heard the man's squeal of surprise and pain as he stumbled and fell to the floor, writhing around like some insect caught in an actual spider web.

Darby staggered to him while holding the banister, her breath coming back but her ribs still burning, muscles growing stronger with each step. The web had him locked up. She kicked the gas mask off his face. He tried to reach up to put it back on but his fingers got caught in the sticky webbing. Her boot came down on his hand, breaking his fingers. He screamed. She kicked him against the side of the head and he slumped back against the floor.

She hadn't knocked him unconscious; she could hear him choking on the smoke. The web had locked him up but he had conveniently dropped the shotgun on the floor next to him before it had done so.

Standing with the shotgun, her lungs straining, burning as though they were on fire, she raised it at the man's head, about to fire when an inner voice cautioned her to wait.

You need him alive, the voice added. Darby turned and stumbled to the bedroom.

The drawn shades flapped in the wind blowing through the two shattered windows. Smoke was everywhere, curling like snakes across the walls and ceiling, and she got a good, clear look at the bedroom: a SWAT officer kneeling on the floor next to the bed, his back facing her; the headless remains of the twins and Charlie Rizzo – they had been shot at point-blank range like Judith Rizzo. But there was no sign of the father. Mark Rizzo had been cut free from the chair. Taken alive.

Four quick steps across the carpet and the SWAT officer turned to look over his shoulder. She didn't shoot him. She dropped the shotgun and, grabbing him by the head, twisted violently. There was a snap as his neck broke and he collapsed on the floor.

Sitting on the floor was a small device. It had a timer. And wires.

Wires connected to six sticks of dynamite bound together with electrical tape.

The timer's numbers flashed a glowing red in the thin, blowing curtains of smoke:

1:26.

1:25.

A quick glance over her shoulder and out the window: the APC was still parked out front, its back doors hanging open.

1:23.

You can do it. You've got time.

Darby grabbed the shotgun and started counting down

as she ran back into the hall, where the SWAT officer lay still. He appeared to be roughly her height, maybe two hundred pounds with all the gear.

1:19.

Another solid kick to the man's head, just to be sure, and then she knelt down, propping the shotgun against the wall. She grabbed the man by the feet and hoisted his legs over her shoulder. He wore black trousers and a pair of heavy winter boots. Definitely not one of the SWAT officers; they had all worn the same TrainMark footwear and tactical trousers.

1:08.

Wrapping her right arm around the back of the man's legs, she stood, screaming in pain, her lungs and chest burning. She grabbed the shotgun with her free hand.

58 seconds.

Her head pounded, and it hurt to breathe, and now her stomach was roiling from the exertion of carrying the man down the stairs. Darby stepped over the broken front door lying on the floor and raised the shotgun as she moved past the doorframe, coming to a sharp and sudden stop on the steps outside.

I O

The Manny Ramirez-looking SWAT officer who'd had no problem admiring her boobs was lying on his back on the walkway.

Darby saw the man's still, unblinking eyes. They stared up at the tree branches shaking in the wind. Vomit splattered the walkway and it covered the front of his tactical vest, his gloved hands and shirtsleeves.

More vomit-covered bodies were sprawled across the street. Some had been stripped of their tactical vests and jackets. Some wore gas masks. Those that did had pulled them aside to throw up before passing out and dying.

Darby whisked past the SWAT officer lying on the walkway and saw a thick, white frothy mixture bubbling from his mouth and dribbling down his chin and cheeks.

Has to be some kind of poison, but what kind – and how the hell did it get inside the APC? How could –

A flash of movement across the street and she raised the shotgun.

A SWAT officer stumbled across the neighbour's front lawn, his gloved hands clawing at his throat. Over the rustling branches she could hear him gasping for air.

He vomited and then collapsed on the grass, starting to crawl.

Not poison – whatever it is, it's airborne.

Nerve gas?

40 seconds.

Darby reached the back doors of the APC. Inside she found two more of Trent's team slumped against the floor and wall, the same white foam covering their mouths. One man was still alive. Barely. He blinked dully at her as she dumped the prisoner in the back.

She didn't have time to secure his wrists. She swung the heavy doors shut and secured the handles with a pair of Flexicuffs.

35 seconds.

Darby opened the driver's side door and found the APC driver slumped against the wheel. He had been shot in the head. She grabbed the man's blood-soaked jacket collar and yanked him out of his seat.

Seated behind the wheel and with the door shut, she slammed her foot on the gas. The APC jerked forward, the Bear, as Trent had called it, picking up speed.

Trent. The SWAT senior corporal hadn't spoken to her over her earpiece – only the hostage negotiator, Lee. She remembered hearing him coughing and now, nothing, not a single word from either man. Were they dead? Had anyone survived?

'This is Darby McCormick. Anyone listening, I order you to stay away from the Rizzo home. I repeat, *stay away from the Rizzo home*. SWAT team is dead, exposed to some sort of nerve gas. I have no idea what chemical was used or how long it takes to dissipate – it could still be lingering in the air. Call and warn the local hospitals to prepare their decontamination units.'

Her earpiece remained quiet.

She had to call 911, tell the dispatcher what had happened and alert all units to stay clear of the area – they needed to be warned before their men walked into a chemically hazardous situation. The same held true for area hospitals. Victims exposed to the gas would rush through the emergency room doors complaining of nausea and difficulty breathing. They needed to be decontaminated before receiving treatment. And if hospital personnel weren't dressed in hazmat gear, they too would be risking exposure.

To use the phone now, she'd have to take off her gas mask. She'd be exposing herself, and if this shit was lingering –

You've already been exposed. It's clinging to your clothes and your skin right now.

A new thought occurred to her: her prisoner wasn't wearing a gas mask. She had locked him in the back with the other sick officers and right now he was breathing in whatever had killed them. She'd have to find a place to decontaminate him.

The blockade came into a sharper view. The cruiser lights were still on, pulsing bright blue and white flashes, and the first person she saw was a patrolman slumped against a cruiser's front bumper. Scattered across the ground was a tangle of arms and legs wrapped in jeans and jackets – detectives and possibly some of the residents who had ventured outside their homes. No movement. No movement at all.

Dead, they're all –

A loud bone-crushing *boom* of thunder rumbled through her chest as the house exploded behind her, lighting up the dark, starless sky.

Tearing down the road, Darby spotted a house glowing with lights. The homeowner, an elderly man dressed in light blue flannel pyjamas, stood in his bare feet on the brightly lit front steps of his tiny ranch home, a dazed but alarmed expression on his wrinkled and craggy face as he stared down the dark street, looking in the direction of the explosion.

His gaze turned frightened when the APC came to a jarring stop near his lawn. Darby stepped out with the shotgun, catching sight of the fire blazing no more than a mile away, thick smoke blowing through the woods, over the tops of the tall pines.

Gripping a wrought-iron banister, the elderly man cautiously made his way down his front steps. 'What's in blue blazes is going on?' he barked. 'My wife and I were sleeping when we heard all these police sirens, and now I just heard –'

'Stay right where you are, sir, don't come any closer. What's your name?'

'Arthur Anderson.'

'Mr Anderson, I'm ordering you to go back into your house. I want you to make sure your windows are sealed shut. Do you understand?'

A fearful nod as he licked his lips. 'I understand what you said, but I don't –'

'*Listen to me.* I need you to get inside your house right now, no questions. Then I want you to get on the phone and tell all your neighbours to stay inside their homes and make sure their windows are sealed shut. Do it now. You got a hose out here?'

He pointed to the west side of the house. 'Water's still on, I haven't turned it off yet.'

'Get me a bucket and a scrub brush and a bottle of dish soap. Throw it out on the front lawn. Get moving.'

After 9/11, Boston police started to carry decontamination kits in their squad cars. Darby rooted around the front of the APC, searching all the console compartments, even under the seat. No decon kits – just a First-Aid box attached to the wall behind the driver's seat. She opened it. The supplies inside weren't ideal, but she'd have to make do until the proper equipment arrived. She grabbed what she needed and ran to the lawn.

She ripped open several packages of gauze pads, set them up on the grass and doused them with alcohol.

She wiped down her cell phone first, then her gloves. She threw the used pads to the side, then took off her gas mask and used the remaining pads to scrub down her face, mouth and ears until they burned. She called 911, cutting off the female dispatcher who answered.

'My name is Darby McCormick. Don't talk, just listen. Senior Corporal Gary Trent of SWAT summoned me earlier this evening to a home in Dover.' She quickly gave the woman the address and said, 'Do you have a list of area fire departments?'

'People have called about a fire, so engines are already en route to –'

'You need to warn them about a possible chemical attack. They are *not* to approach the bombsite unless they have gas masks with military-grade filters. Make sure whatever hazmat gear they're using has a Biosafety Level 4 rating. Now repeat back what I just said.'

'Hazmat suits,' she said, her voice cracking over the words. She was clearly in over her head. 'Masks with military filters.'

'Bio*safety* Level 4 rating. If they don't have that equipment, they're not to approach the bombsite under any circumstances. I have no idea what chemical agents were used. Your job is to limit the contamination as much as possible. After you call the fire departments, get on the horn to all the area hospitals. Have them seal the front and emergency-room doors to give their people time to access their hazmat gear. Tell them they're looking for victims showing signs of nausea and difficulty breathing, foaming at the mouth.'

A pause, and then the woman said, 'Are you saying there's been some sort of biological attack?'

'That's *exactly* what I'm saying. The hospital staff will know what to do, they've all had training.'

'Okay. Okay, I'll call them right –'

'Hold on. I also want you to make sure that you have people guarding the shooting victim – the guy the EMTs picked up from the front bushes of the Rizzo home. What's his status?'

'He's gone,' the dispatcher said.

'He died?'

'No. I mean, I don't know. The ambulance never showed up at the hospital.'

Darby glanced over her shoulders at the APC's back doors, listening to the woman's frantic tone. 'Union Hospital called and told us. They've had no contact with the ambulance in question. We sent out a patrol but haven't heard back from them. I also informed Senior Corporal Trent of the development and we haven't heard from him either – we haven't heard from anyone except residents calling about a fire and what they think was some sort of explosion.'

'What local agency do you call in case of bio-attack?'

'We, ah . . . I, I don't know, we haven't ever faced –'

'Where's your emergency protocol sheet?'

Darby heard shuffling of papers, things being moved.

'Where's the nearest army base?'

'We don't have one stationed here any more,' the dispatcher said.

'What about the Pease base in Portsmouth? The air force still has someone stationed there – they could mobilize one of their Air Mobility Command Units to –'

'They've been shut down. Budget cuts. And the hospitals in the area, I know for a fact they're not equipped to deal with multiple contaminated patients. Maybe two or three at a time, that's it, but if it's something as large as you're saying, we'll –'

'Boston University has a new Biological Agent Research Lab,' Darby said. 'They have people equipped to handle this, and you'll need trained people here anyway to identify the type of gas or chemicals used. They're in the South

End, about an hour away. I'll make the call and brief them. Call the fire department first, then the hospitals.'

Darby hung up without giving her cell number – no need since her number had been captured on the dispatcher's computer system.

At the beginning of the year, BU had opened their brand-new 1.6 billion-dollar research lab, courtesy of funding from former president Bush's Project BioShield, created to increase the US's response to bio-terrorism. The BU lab had a Biosafety Level 4 rating, the highest security classification, as it dealt with the world's most infectious and incurable pathogens. It also had, in conjunction with the army, a specialized Crisis Response Unit that could respond to any biological attack or catastrophe on the East Coast.

The public didn't know about the unit, but police and federal law enforcement agencies did. Every Boston cop and lab technician had been given the hotline number with strict orders to programme it into their cell phones. Her temporary suspension had forced her to turn over her badge and laminated ID card that gave her access to almost every area inside the Boston police department. She'd also had to turn over her beeper but not her work cell. She found the hotline number quickly.

The man who answered the phone identified himself as Sergeant-Major Glick. Darby gave her name and then explained who she was and what had happened in New Hampshire. She told him about the number of dead SWAT and police officers and Glick asked her several in-depth questions about the symptoms.

Glick said, 'Are you showing any symptoms?'

'Not yet.'

'The person you captured, where is he right now?'

'In the back of the APC.'

'With the other dead officers,' Glick added.

'I didn't have much of a choice.'

'Understood, but you need to decontaminate him quickly.'

'I haven't found any decon kits, so I'm going to scrub him down the old-fashioned way, with soap and water.'

'Scrub yourself down while you're at it. If he tells you what gas was used, it will save us some valuable time. We may be able to treat on site. Otherwise, we'll have to wait for blood analysis.'

'He'll tell me,' she said and hung up.

After she shoved the phone in her pocket, Darby put on the gas mask and then moved to the back of the APC, sliding the tactical knife out from underneath her sleeve.

12

A quick jerk of the sharp blade and Darby cut the Flexi-cuffs binding the APC's door handles. She opened the doors and backed up, bringing up the shotgun.

Her prisoner, still wrapped in the net, had managed to push himself up into a sitting position. In the process he had somehow worked the gas mask back over his mouth, what little good it did him. He had already breathed in the tear gas, the chemicals coating the soft, sensitive membranes lining his lungs, throat and sinuses. His chest heaved as he hacked into the mask, trying to expel the fire.

Darby stepped inside. In the dim interior light she could see his mottled face, his bloodshot and watery eyes. They tracked her as she knelt next to the SWAT officer who had been barely conscious earlier. Now he was slumped against the floor in a puddle of vomit, a white, frothy mixture covering his lips and bubbling from his nose and mouth.

She pressed a gloved finger against the man's neck.

No pulse.

She grabbed the prisoner by the back of his collar. He didn't put up a fight or struggle, too weak and disoriented from the tear gas and the blows to his head. She lifted him easily to his feet and marched him to the opened doors. When he reached the edge, she shoved him outside.

His hands jerked up to try to cushion the fall. They got caught in the sticky webbing and he slammed sideways against the ground, the sharp, painful cry lost in his coughing fits.

Darby hopped out. She kicked him on to his stomach. When he tried to roll on to his back, she brought her heel down against his shoulder and kept it there, pinning him to the ground. Using her knife, she began cutting the net.

As she worked, the sharp blade slicing through the webbing, she found the source of his pain: he had fractured his wrist during the fall. It made her think of Charlie, how his bones had snapped when she'd grabbed his wrist and twisted. No doubt something like that could happen – and no doubt the force of being smashed against the side of the head with an elbow could dislodge a tooth or two. But she had knocked out *several* teeth. Charlie was painfully thin, covered in scars. She wondered if he had weak, malnourished bones from time spent in captivity.

Captivity, an inner voice questioned.

Yes. After his abduction, Charlie Rizzo had been forced to live somewhere, enduring daily beatings, torture, and God only knew what else.

So you're buying that he is, in fact, Charlie Rizzo.

A part of her did, she supposed. At the moment she didn't know what else to think.

Darby tucked the knife in her trouser pocket then prised the netting off the man's body, surprised at its sticky strength. She cuffed him, then helped him to his feet.

Knife in hand again, she cut the straps for the man's tactical vest, the same model as the ones used by NH SWAT.

66

The people entering the house were dressed as SWAT officers; they must have grabbed the vests and gas masks from the back of the APC, after the men had been poisoned.

That meant a plan had been put in place before her arrival. They had been near by, watching.

But why grab Mark Rizzo? Why not just kill him like Judith Rizzo and the twins, whose remains were now shredded into unrecognizable bits and scattered across the woods? Why did these people need the father?

Darby ripped the gas mask off the man's face. The fresh air would help clear the burning from his lungs, nose and throat. But not his eyes; she'd have to rinse them with water.

'Where has Mark Rizzo been taken?'

The man didn't answer, too busy hacking, but she felt him stiffen underneath her grip. His clothing was entirely black. Black trousers and boots; and the strange fabric of a heavy black long-sleeved shirt that resembled the one Charlie had worn. She wondered if his body had the same severe scarring as Charlie's.

The man's head certainly did. He was bald, and on the back of his head and neck she saw scars in all shapes and sizes. And a tattoo: words and letters written in the centre of his neck, the light blue ink so faint she couldn't read it. She needed light.

She grabbed him by the collar and pressed the tip of the blade against the back of his neck.

'We're going for a walk. Try anything and I swear to Christ I'll sever your spine and you'll spend the rest of your life as a quadriplegic, pissing and shitting into diapers.'

She gave him a shove and started walking. The elderly homeowner had placed a big white plastic bucket on the front steps. All the inside house lights had been turned on, and she caught shadows whisking behind the curtains. When she reached the bucket, she turned the man around to get a better look at the tattoo in the light.

Two rows of tiny letters and numbers:

ET IN ARCADIA EGO
III-XI-XXIV

Roman numerals. Latin words.

Darby picked up the bucket, finding a scrub brush and a bottle of Palmolive inside. The bucket had a big metal handle for easy carrying. She draped it around her arm and pushed her prisoner to the side of the house, finding the hose neatly draped over a holder. The window above it threw a square of light on a lawn covered with autumn leaves.

She dropped the bucket. Withdrawing the knife from his neck, she tossed him over her leg and pushed him face first against the grass near the hose. He screamed, blowing leaves away from his mouth. She dug a knee into the small of his back, pinning him against the ground, and reached for the tap. Over the sound of running water, she heard footsteps moving towards the lighted windows above her.

After she filled the bucket with soap and water, Darby rolled the man over. His bloodshot, weeping eyes kept trying to blink away the burning. She flushed them with running water, and for the first time got a good, clear look at the man's face, with its network of scars both deep and faint, his egg-white skin so pale it almost seemed translucent, as though it had never been exposed to the sun.

She took the brush with its hard bristles full of suds and water and began to scrub down his face, head and neck. He kept twisting underneath her, hacking and coughing up the soapy water running down his throat and nose. By the time she had finished, his skin was red and raw, and his hacking had subsided to deep, body-racking coughs.

She dropped the brush, picked up the knife and sliced the shirt right down the middle. When she pushed back the fabric, she discovered the same thick, latticed scars that had covered Charlie's emaciated chest. As if scoops of flesh had been carved out. This man had a little bit more weight on him but not much. She could see his ribcage bulging against the ragged, scrawny flesh as she scrubbed him down with the brush.

Then the scar pattern hit her.

'Who whipped you?'

He moaned an answer she couldn't understand.

'Say it again.'

He started coughing. She cut off the rest of the shirt and tossed the pieces to the side. Darby rolled him over so that she could see his back.

Dear God Jesus.

13

Positioned in the centre of the man's back, between his shoulder blades and sitting directly on top of his spine, was a black rectangular device the size of a matchbook. The device had grooved edges, and someone had sewn it into the man's skin. No redness or infection.

A small green light blinked steadily.

'What is this?' Darby asked, tapping the device with her finger.

He turned his head to the side and moaned. Soapsuds bubbled from the corners of his mouth. Or was it the poison? If it had entered his system, he'd go into respiratory distress at any moment. She'd have only a few minutes to question him before he died.

She grabbed the tactical knife. Out of the corner of her eye she spotted shadows crowding the window.

She didn't want witnesses, so she stood up, grasping the man under the armpits, feeling his wet, soapy body shivering in the cold as she pulled him to his feet. His legs wobbled, about to tip over. Grabbing his belt and the cuffs wrapped around his wrists, she pushed him past the side of the house and into the backyard. Then she marched him into the pitch-black woods where they'd have privacy.

Their heavy footsteps snapped the dry branches lining

the ground. In between coughs she could hear him fighting to breathe.

A moment later she found a suitable tree well away from the home's back windows. She cut through the cuffs and kicked his legs out from underneath him, pushing him into a sitting position. He didn't try to run or fight, just sat there slumped back against the tree. She pulled his arms behind the tree trunk and bound his wrists with a fresh pair of Flexicuffs.

Darby wanted a record of this conversation. She didn't have her digital recorder and didn't want to rely on memory. Her iPhone had a recording application, but it could store only about a minute or so of conversation, and that –

Darby stood, tucking the knife in her belt, and grabbed her iPhone. The colour screen came to life, parting some of the darkness as she moved around the tree dialling her home number. In the distance she heard what sounded like a helicopter engine – probably a news copter wanting to capture all the chaos and carnage.

'Question and answer time,' she said after hearing the *beep* of her answering machine on the other end of the line. 'Let's start first with that device attached to your back. What is it? What does it do?'

The phone's screen had gone dark. She held it close to the man's mouth. He tried to speak over the moaning but she couldn't make out the words.

She knelt next to him. 'Is it some sort of GPS device?'

A cough and then he moaned a word that, oddly, sounded like 'quiche'.

'GPS,' she said. 'Global Positioning System?'

71

Again the moan, followed by the slurred *quiche*-sounding word.

'Do you speak English?'

'*Aaaa-ho . . . na . . . ah-nah-ho.*'

He spoke like a man who'd had his jaw broken.

Darby placed the phone on his lap, grabbed the flashlight from her belt and turned it on, shining the narrow beam in his face.

The man's bright blue eyes were wild, feral-looking. The sides of his egg-white, veiny face were bloody and swollen from the blows, but his jaw appeared to be working fine. He coughed, spitting out blood mixed with the soapsuds or possibly poison, and when he tried to speak, letting out that deep, moaning sound, Darby discovered why she couldn't understand him. His tongue had been cut out.

14

Darby recoiled not so much in fear as in shock. Her head snapped back, as though this . . . *thing* might eat her.

She started to tumble backwards until her gloved hand found the leafy ground. She didn't fall but realized she had dropped her flashlight. She found it quickly, snatched it up and pointed the bright, narrow beam into the . . . what? Not a man's face. This . . . creature sitting less than a foot from her had human eyes, a human mouth and lips (*but no tongue because someone had removed it along with his teeth, he doesn't have any teeth either*) yet whatever had made him a man had died long ago. Now he was thrashing from side to side, howling, his eyes clamped shut and jerking his face away from the light. Then his scarred body started jerking. Convulsing.

He's infected.

The thing vomited, spraying her mask.

Darby fell this time, deliberately letting go of the flashlight. She wiped at her mask as she stumbled back to her feet and started running, the vomit, hot and wet, clinging to her scalp and skin. Not looking back, she sprinted out of the woods, feeling the vomit sliding across the edges of the mask protecting her eyes, nose and mouth. She pressed the mask firmly against her face to keep the seal tight. *He's infected and now whatever's killing him is lying on my skin.*

She reached the side of the house and clutched the hose's spray nozzle. She kept the mask pressed against her face as she lay on the ground and started spraying cold water over her face and hair. She could see the black sky, the dark outlines of the tall pines, and over the jet spray drumming against her mask she heard the man's ungodly howls coming from the woods.

The helicopter's engine was growing louder and louder. She jumped to her feet and started spraying down her vest, catching sight of a searchlight sweeping across the treetops in the distance. She also saw, crowding the lit window next to her, the frightened faces of the elderly man and a woman dressed in a pink bathrobe with white hair wrapped tightly in curlers.

The searchlight was now moving across the street, searching for the APC. Darby dropped the hose, her boots waterlogged and her soaked clothing clinging against her skin. She ran for the street, stopping near the APC and, shivering, looked up at the sky, waving her hands.

The searchlight switched direction. The bright beam whisked across the street, heading her way, and then stopped as the copter began its descent. The spinning blades kicked up leaves, small pebbles and assorted street grit and trash, blowing everything into the air.

The copter didn't have enough room to land. It hovered in the air so close she could make out the pilot.

The hatch opened. Ropes were thrown into the air and she watched, with a growing relief, as four people rappelled to the ground.

They all wore dark green hazmat suits with thick rubber boots and gloves tied off at the elbows, their gas masks connected to oxygen tanks strapped across their backs. They approached cautiously as the copter rose back into the air.

Darby started moving towards them and the one in the lead put up both hands, signalling for her to stop.

'Stay right where you are and keep the mask on your face.' The deep male voice had a mechanical echo over the mask's speakers. 'Where's Darby McCormick?'

'I am.' Darby heard the words in her mask but not over the voice amplification system. *The water must have shorted it.* She tapped a finger against her chest.

'We need to decontaminate you,' the same male voice said. 'Just stand there and stay calm.'

A spray gun was pointed at her. Foam, thick and white, sprayed across her chest. It covered her mask and when she went to wipe it away she felt hands grip her wrists.

'Stay calm,' the same man said, closer now. She wondered if it was Glick, the man she'd spoken to on the BU hotline. 'We're going to help you sit on –'

'The prisoner is in the woods behind the house,' Darby shouted, praying to God one of them could hear her over the hiss coming from the spray nozzle and the copter's dying but still loud engine. 'He's in the woods –'

Hands gripped her roughly. 'Stand still, we've got to cover –'

'*Listen to me.* The prisoner is in the woods behind the house, about twenty klicks north. He's tied to a tree, and he's infected.'

'We're going to help you to the ground.'

She let the hands guide her down, shouting, 'He's one of them – one of the intruders from the Rizzo house. He's our only link, you've got to see if you can treat him.'

Sitting, she felt a pair of rubber hands cradling the back of her neck.

'Lie back, Miss McCormick.'

'Did you hear what I said? You need to treat him.'

She didn't get a response. Rough hands pushed her back against the ground and then she couldn't see, as a thick, shaving-foam-like substance covered her mask. She couldn't move either, pinned down by all these arms and legs.

'Miss McCormick, can you hear me?'

She nodded.

'The hazmat van hasn't arrived yet,' the man said. 'I don't want to risk waiting, so we're going to have to undress you here and decontaminate you. I'm not going to lie to you, it's not going to be pleasant.'

Her boots were pulled off her feet.

Now her socks.

'Miss McCormick, I need you to keep your eyes and mouth shut. Nod if you understand.'

She nodded.

Hands lifted her up and she stood, shivering.

'Hold your arms out . . . Yes, like that.'

Someone unbuckled her vest. Another pair of hands worked the buckle for her tactical belt.

Come on, take off the mask so I can talk.

Her wet trousers were yanked down across her legs as the mask was pulled from her sweaty face. She spoke quickly, her eyes closed.

'The prisoner is in the woods behind the ranch home, and he's —'

A pair of gloved fingers prised her mouth open. She grabbed the wrist and tore it away.

'*He's infected,*' she screamed.

'Where?' The leader's voice.

'In the woods, about twenty klicks north,' she said, shivering. 'I tied him to a tree. Find him and treat him — he's our only link to what happened at the house.'

The man didn't respond but she heard footsteps running away.

Her long-sleeved T-shirt was pulled up over her head. Now someone gripped her bra and pulled it away from the skin. She felt the strap pop free; someone must have cut it. Another hand gripped the elastic band of her cheap Hanes boy-cut underwear and cut it free. She stood there, naked and shivering, and heard the hiss of the spray nozzle as foam shot across her bare skin.

The person who had prised open her mouth did so again, and even though her eyes were shut she could make out the beam of a flashlight.

'Miss McCormick,' a new voice said — feminine and clearly nervous. 'I need you to spread your legs apart, just a bit.'

Darby did as instructed, too frightened to be embarrassed. Her imagination was racing with all sorts of grisly scenarios as fingers pressed against the lymph nodes underneath her armpits, then her groin. Her mouth was opened again and this time she felt a cotton swab rub its way across the soft lining of her cheeks. They were collecting a sample to see if she was infected. If she was, and

77

if the toxin couldn't be identified in time, she'd soon be lying on the ground, convulsing and throwing up until her lungs finally stopped working.

Her eyelids were pressed open by thick, rubbery fingers and held in place.

'We're going to wash them out with saline,' the nervous woman said.

The fingers held her eyelids open as a jet coming from a bottle of saline washed out her eyes.

Then she was ordered to shut her eyes again. She did and now thick bristles moved across her skin with such force she thought she was being cut by razorblades. An angry voice ordered her to stand still. She gritted her teeth as the brush raked across her breasts and nipples.

When the brushes finally disappeared, the woman said, 'Keep your eyes and mouth shut. We're going to escort you to the side of the house to be hosed off.'

'Am I infected?' Darby asked.

'I don't know.'

15

When the BU Biomedical vehicles finally arrived – two vans and a mobile trailer, Darby saw, each one sleek and black and peeling down the street – she was sitting on the grass with her knees pressed up against her chest, her wet hair and naked, shivering body bundled underneath several towels and blankets courtesy of the home's elderly couple. They had offered to let her inside, but the hazmat team wouldn't allow it. The old man – deadly scared and barely able to speak – said there were plenty of old towels and blankets on the garage shelves and they were more than welcome to help themselves.

Hazmat members poured out of the vehicles. One of them was heading her way.

'Miss McCormick, please follow me.'

She stood, several of the towels sliding off her, and wrapped herself tightly in the blanket. She trotted in her bare feet behind the man, wincing in pain. It hurt to breathe. She didn't know if the pain was from the fractured ribs or if she was infected. Or both.

The man helped her into the back of the mobile trailer. Before the doors shut, Darby saw the frightened expressions of the old man, his wife and what she assumed was the couple's grandson, a toddler dressed in footy-pyjamas and clutching a stuffed animal, as they were helped down their front steps by a pair of masked and gloved men. A bullhorn ordered them to a waiting van to be decontaminated.

The heated trailer was packed with medical equipment, and also held three people dressed head to toe in hazmat gear. One was armed – state police, she guessed, maybe even army. He had an MP5 submachine gun strapped across the chest of his hazmat suit and he kept his gloved hand on the stock, his eyes watching her.

Syringes and vials glinted underneath the light. One of the unarmed people took a tentative step forward and said, 'You're having trouble breathing.'

She nodded. 'I think I fractured a rib. Shotgun blast.'

He helped her to lie down on a gurney. When he completed his poking and prodding with his gloved fingers and cold instruments – Darby nearly screaming when his hands touched her chest – he dropped a pair of scrubs on her stomach and told her to get dressed. She did, slowly, and after she finished he came back with a syringe. He didn't speak or answer any of her questions as he drew blood, filling numerous vials. She had stopped counting after six.

Next she felt a cold swab of alcohol on her upper arm, followed by the sting of a needle.

'What's that?'

'Something to help you with the pain,' he said. 'This way.'

Darby followed the man to the far wall, which held three doors. He pressed a code on the keypad and then she heard the hiss of the air-locked door opening.

It led to a stainless-steel room no bigger than a closet. A quarantine chamber, containing only a toilet.

Darby didn't move. The sight of any confined space made her uneasy.

The doctor, standing behind her, spoke for the first time: 'It's only temporary, until we know whether or not you're infected.'

'How long?'

'Until we know if you're infected? The blood work will take some time – it will go faster when we can isolate what, exactly, has happened here. Until then, we need to quarantine you. It should be only a couple of hours, then we can take you to the hospital.'

Darby still didn't move. The guard, sensing that she might put up a fight, had stepped up beside the doctor.

Finally she went inside. The door shut and she flinched when she heard the bolt slide home.

The space was warm, and she had a view, courtesy of the small, square Plexiglas window. One of the vials containing her blood had been placed in some sort of separating unit. She could see the device sitting on a worktop, and as she listened to the tiny whirl of the motor she watched the doctor, who was sitting with his back to her and typing on a computer keyboard. She could make out part of the monitor but was too far away to read the words on the screen.

She heard the sound of the heavy back doors swinging open. Footsteps thumped across the floor and then a masked face revealing only a pair of blue eyes and dark bushy eyebrows flecked with grey filled the tiny window.

Then the face moved away and Darby watched the man step behind the doctor. There was no talking – at least nothing she could hear. The man seemed to be consulting something on the computer screen. He stepped away, disappearing from her view.

A moment later she heard the ceiling speaker crackle.

'How are you feeling?'

The voice of the hazmat man she'd first encountered.

'So far, so good,' Darby replied. 'Can you hear me, Sergeant-Major Glick?'

'I can hear you fine. Any problems breathing?'

She nodded. 'I think I fractured some ribs.'

'We'll give you a chest X-ray and then treat them when we get you to our hospital. What about nausea?'

'No. What's the army doing at BU?'

'Consulting.'

'On what?'

'Various governmental matters that don't concern you.'

'Then maybe you can tell me about the man I left in the woods. What's his condition?'

'I wish I could tell you.'

Darby swallowed. Her eyes narrowed. 'If you want my cooperation, you better drop the bullshit and –'

'No, you misunderstood me,' Glick said. 'I can't tell you anything about it because we didn't find him. We didn't find *anyone* in those woods, Miss McCormick, not a single person.'

16

Mark Rizzo started to drift back from the darkness of his mind only to encounter a new kind of darkness, one that was pitch black and smelled dank and musty. Something cold and hard and flat pressed up against the bare skin of his chest, thighs and arms. Every inch of his skin felt cold. Then he knew: he had been stripped of his clothes.

He turned his hand and his fingers felt rough stone.

A stone floor, damp and dirty.

Chilly air.

Dark air that smelled dank and musty.

No . . . Oh dear God in heaven please don't let this be true.

Adrenalin shot through his weary heart, flushing his skin and then . . . then it died. His muscles were unresponsive, and, while his mind felt thick and clogged, his thoughts sluggish, he had memories, fragments of them, and he remembered choking on the tear gas filling his bedroom and watching SWAT officers rush in and thinking, *Thank God, oh thank God it's over*. But one of the SWAT officers had a syringe and he remembered feeling the needle sink deep into his neck. Remembered trying to break free of the restraints binding him to the chair when he heard the first gunshot –

Mark Rizzo blinked the image away. He knew who had

him now – and they were somewhere here in this pitch-black darkness. He could hear breathing.

A voice boomed through the darkness:

'Welcome home, Thomas.'

PART TWO

The Cross

17

Darby lay propped up in the hospital bed with her hands folded behind her head, staring across the room at the clear Plexiglas door. Beyond it was a small, square-shaped area of spotless white tile. It covered the floor, walls and ceiling. The door in there was made of steel.

Two doors, both locked, both secured by keycard readers. You needed a card and a separate code for each door. Each person who came in here had a different set of codes. Some punched in three numbers. Others had six. One doc had seven.

She had stopped thinking about how to mount an escape. Even if she managed to grab a keycard from one of the docs or lab technicians who came in here to draw blood and then pump a cruiser-load of dope into her system, there was still the issue of the codes, and even with those there was the problem of whatever lay beyond these two doors. The BU Biomedical building, where she was currently quarantined, no doubt had top-notch security. A stolen keycard (*and the codes, don't forget the damn codes*) would get her only so far; they wouldn't open whatever doors separated her from the outside world. Then there was the staff to deal with, and guards – army boys, probably.

Would they shoot her? Unlikely. Would they Mace her or use something like a Taser? Most definitely.

Escaping wasn't an option.

Her thoughts shifted to the reasons why she wanted to leave here: the staff refused to let her use the phone to call someone on the outside. They refused to bring her a newspaper (although they brought her celebrity rag mags in droves and said she could read anything she wanted; she had asked for, and was given, Jane Austen's complete *œuvre*). The TV in here had cable but they had blocked out all the news stations. They refused to tell her what she had been infected with and why they kept drawing her blood and shooting her full of drugs. Orders, they said, from the man sitting high on the mountaintop, Sergeant-Major Glick.

Even more infuriating was the fact that no one would tell her when she'd be released. She was still showing no sign of infection. No nausea. No problem swallowing and no problem breathing. Well, it *did* hurt to breathe, but that was caused by her ribs. There was a lot of talking about her lying down and resting, and for the first few days she had complied.

Not one single symptom and yet they were keeping her imprisoned here, and refusing to explain why.

She wondered what time it was. There wasn't a clock in here.

A lot of things weren't in here. A *lot* of things.

That was going to change. Right now.

Darby yanked back the rough white sheets and scratchy wool blue blanket, sat up and swung her legs off the bed. She didn't hop off, just sat with her fingers digging into the edge of the mattress, waiting for the dizziness to pass. It always took its sweet goddamn time about leaving, and when it finally did she had to deal with how her head felt afterwards, this throbbing cement block on her shoulders that kept screaming at her to lie back down – a side effect, she assumed, from the pain meds. The shotgun blast had fractured not one but three ribs, tearing a considerable amount of cartilage. Thankfully, the damage ended there. Her lungs and spleen had been spared.

The dope they were giving her, though, had another, more serious side effect: it clouded her memories. Some were fuzzy; others were, well, black holes.

She had no problem recalling the details of everything she'd seen and heard inside the Rizzo house. And she remembered, quite clearly, what had happened in the woods behind the old couple's home and what had happened after she'd been locked inside the mobile trailer's stainless-steel quarantine chamber, bumping into the smooth, cold walls when the trailer got moving, driving her, the elderly couple and their grandson all the way back to Boston's BU Biomedical lab. She remembered being escorted inside some sort of plastic-looking tube and into a painfully bright room of white tile, where two women dressed in biohazard gear stood by a gurney. One gave her another injection as the other informed her she had to go through a second decontamination process, this one more thorough. The sedative would make her relax and help with the pain. Both women removed her scrubs and strapped her down into the cold gurney. The last memory Darby had was one of staring up at the ceiling's humming fluorescent lights, watching as they whisked past her, blurring together, growing brighter and brighter.

Whatever had happened after that was lost.

When she woke up, alone, in the hospital bed where she now sat, the first thing she noticed was her skin. It had been scrubbed raw and gave off, along with her hair, some sort of medicinal smell that brought to mind the disinfectant and germicidal solutions used in funeral homes. Nasty odours used in treating the dead.

She wasn't dead, or even hovering close to it, and yet they were keeping her locked up inside this quarantine chamber straight out of a sci-fi movie: blue-padded walls, floor and ceiling; stainless-steel sink and a private toilet and shower stall. Anything that left the room – her hospital scrubs, magazines, food scraps and paper plates, cups and plastic utensils – was wrapped and sealed inside a bright red biohazard bag.

The dizziness, at least the worst of it, had passed. Darby slid off the bed and made her way across the padded floor in her bare feet, hearing the now familiar mechanical whine coming from the pair of security cameras turning to track her. These cameras monitored her movements, even at night when she went to use the toilet.

She reached the console and picked up the phone.

'Yes, Miss McCormick?' a male voice asked. She didn't recognize it.

'What time is it?'

'Almost noon. Are you hungry? I can bring you –'

'I want to speak to Sergeant-Major Glick.'

'I'm sorry, but he's unavailable right now.'

'I was told he would return today.'

'He did, early this morning. He came by but you were asleep.'

'Why didn't he wake me up?'

'Doctors' orders.'

'I want to speak to him. Now.'

'Sergeant-Major Glick is involved in –'

'In a matter that has required him to be out of the office for an indefinite period of time,' Darby finished for him. Everyone here kept reciting the same party line. 'He's carrying a cell phone with him, right?'

'I . . . well, I would assume so.'

'I want you to connect me to him.'

'I can't transfer your call. We don't have that sort of equipment.'

'Then bring a phone to me.'

'A cell phone won't work in here.'

'Then connect a landline.'

'I'm afraid your room isn't equipped. The phone you're speaking on right now is wired to come straight to the security console.'

'Fine. Have someone take me to a phone.'

'I'm sorry, but I can't do that until we know you're not infected.'

Darby felt an itch spark deep inside her head, right around the place where her spine connected to her brain stem. She squeezed the receiver, wanting to crush it.

'You and I both know I'm not infected.'

'These tests take time, Miss McCormick. We still don't know what you were exposed to, and until we do we need to monitor –'

'Who's your second in command?'

'Second in command? I don't understand what –'

'The army's running this place, right?'

No answer.

'I want to speak to someone in charge,' Darby said. 'Now.'

'I'll forward your request, but, as you already know, we're not allowed to speak to you about the New Hampshire incident. Maybe you should ask the FBI. I can call them for you.'

Darby had already spoken to the two agents sent over from the Boston office, a pair of Irish boys named Connolly and Kelly. They stood in the white-tiled room beyond the Plexiglas barrier, writing down her statement while asking questions through a two-way speaker. They claimed to have no knowledge of the investigation happening up north, in the Granite State, and promised to send along someone to answer her questions.

That was four days ago. Maybe five, it was hard to remember.

Darby switched the phone to her other ear. 'What's your name?'

'Howard.'

'And what do you do here, Howie?'

'Me?' He chuckled. 'I'm just a lowly medical technician.'

'Okay, Howie, I want you to pass along a message. The next person who enters my room is going to be carrying my medical file and all of my blood work results. Said person is going to hand those to me and then sit down and answer my questions – *all* of my questions, including everything that's happening in New Hampshire. If this doesn't happen, Howie, not only will this person not be getting any more of my blood, he – or she – will have to crawl out of here. Do you understand?'

'I understand your frustration – I honestly do – but you need to –'

'Do we have an understanding, Howie?'

'I'll pass your message along. Now, about lunch, would you like –'

Darby hung up and went back to lying on her bed, wondering just how long she'd have to wait until someone came to speak to her.

And what if they can't or won't answer your questions? What are you going to do?

Then she'd have to deliver on her promise.

Her thoughts shifted to the man she had cuffed to a tree in the woods – the thing with the veiny egg-white skin, missing teeth and tongue. There was no way he could have got loose by himself. Someone had cut him loose, either one of his buddies who had been near by, watching; or one of Glick's hazmat people. Maybe even Glick himself.

And that black plastic device I found sewn into his back . . . just what the hell was that thing? Some sort of tracking device?

It was maddening to wonder.

Now she saw the man claiming to be Charlie. Saw his mask of dried human skin with its cut-out eyeholes and mouth, the sutures attached to horribly scarred but healthy skin belonging not to a man claiming to be Charlie Rizzo but to Charlie Rizzo himself, the boy born with missing nipples who had disappeared all those years ago and who now, seemingly for no reason, had reappeared back in his family's house to hold them hostage.

No, there *was* a reason.

Charlie – and he *was* Charlie Rizzo, she could feel it deep in her gut – Charlie had called 911 and requested SWAT *and* a bulletproof vehicle. He dumped a body in the shrubs, and when she asked him who that man was, he said, *I'm hoping you'll find out. That's why I gave him to you.* Charlie wanted her to go inside the house alone so she could bear witness to his father's confession. What had Charlie said to his father? Here it was: *I want you to tell Dr McCormick why I'm here . . . Don't be shy, Daddy. Start with the day I was abducted.*

Mark Rizzo never explained – no, that wasn't true, he said, *This thing is not my son.* She took down Charlie and tear gas flooded the bedroom and then the people dressed as SWAT officers stormed inside the house. They hadn't come for Charlie; they killed him along with the rest of his family.

But not the father. They took Mark Rizzo . . . where? To the same place Charlie had been living all those years? And *why* had they allowed Charlie to remain alive all that time? What was the purpose?

You're assuming there is a purpose.

Maybe not a purpose, but there *was* a reason.

As it turned out, Darby didn't have to wait long. Her thoughts were interrupted by the sound of the steel airtight door hissing open.

18

The person standing outside her Plexiglas door, dressed head to toe in a thick white biohazard suit, wore the same accoutrements everyone else did when they came into her room: gloves that ran up to the elbows; an M95 gas mask that covered the face, ran over one shoulder and down the spine, and connected to a lithium-battery air purifier/respirator. It rested against the small of the person's back, on a belt.

At this distance, Darby couldn't see a face through the clear visor but she suspected her latest visitor was a man, based on the height and width of the shoulders. The man waved an ID card across the keycard reader, then punched in a code. A stainless-steel tray rested against his hip and was held in place by the other gloved hand. She saw a stethoscope, glass vials, empty tubes and needles covered by plastic tips.

A slight whine as the security cameras turned to the man entering her room. Darby crossed her hands behind her head and watched as he lumbered across like an astronaut navigating the terrain of a strange planet.

He placed the tray on the foot of her bed. The cameras' whine disappeared, replaced by silence. She looked at his respirator pack.

'How are you feeling this morning, Miss McCormick?'

The man had an effeminate voice and she detected a slight lisp. She looked up at his clear visor and saw the dark blue eyes underneath thick eyebrows that formed one big hairy caterpillar.

'Have we met?'

'No,' he said, uncapping the plastic tip of a needle. 'Any problems breathing?'

'Are you a doctor?'

'I am. Tell me about your breathing. Have you been experiencing any –'

'Do you have a name?'

'Dr Jerkins.'

'Like the hand lotion.'

'Yes. Now please, about your breathing.'

'My breathing is fine. My vision is fine. No nausea.'

'What about problems swallowing?'

'Now that you mention it, yes.'

He looked up from the tray, his eyes bright with interest. The human guinea pig had a symptom.

'I'm having trouble swallowing this bullshit about you people not knowing what I was exposed to,' Darby said calmly. It irritated her, having to maintain this calm pleasantness. She forced a smile, then added calmly: 'And please don't feed me the line about how you're still running tests. You've been drawing blood for days *and* you've refused to tell me the name of this sedative you keep injecting into my system. My head feels like it's gone a few rounds with Chris Brown.'

'Chris Brown?'

'Rihanna's boyfriend. You know, the pop singer. He beat the shit out of her. It was all over the news.'

'I'm afraid I missed it. In any case, that lethargy you're feeling is one of the side effects from the sedative we gave you to manage the pain from your fractured ribs, and to make sure you didn't go into respiratory distress.'

'Which brings us back to the original question, which I'll ask for the last time. What was I exposed to, Dr Jerkins?'

'It appears you were exposed to sarin gas.'

'Appears?'

'Your blood work is inconclusive, which is why we've –'

'What about the bodies in New Hampshire? Did you take blood samples?'

'We did. They died of sarin gas exposure. Sarin gas, Miss McCormick, is a nerve agent originally developed by the Germans as –'

'As a pesticide,' Darby finished for him. 'Sarin gas is clear, colourless and odourless. It can exist on a person's clothing for up to half an hour, which explains why I was immediately decontaminated. Exposure to the gas, or even a small drop of liquid on the skin, results in loss of consciousness, convulsions, paralysis and then respiratory failure.'

'In layman's terms, yes, you're correct. But, as I was trying to explain before you interrupted me, we keep drawing blood to make sure you haven't been exposed. And these tests take time, Miss McCormick. I know you believe we're stalling you, but I can assure you this is not the case.'

Dr Jenkins turned back to the tray. He picked up the uncapped syringe and stuck the needle into a glass vial.

Demerol, a narcotic pain medication used to treat moderate-to-severe pain. No wonder why her head felt like it had been beaten. She always had bad reactions to Demerol.

'I don't want a shot,' she said.

'You need it.'

'I can deal with the pain.'

'Yes, I'm sure you can. You seem to have a very high threshold. But we're more concerned about coughing. You've been coughing during the night, and if you cough hard enough, it could refracture one or more of your ribs. That's where the Demerol will help.'

He placed the syringe back on the tray and picked up an alcohol swab packaged in foil.

'I want to see copies of my blood work,' Darby said.

'Sergeant-Major Glick will have to authorize that. He's detained at the moment, but he wanted me to tell you he'll speak to you as soon as he arrives later this evening.'

'You spoke to him?'

'The man you spoke to over the intercom did. He promised to come here and answer all of your questions.' He removed the swab from the foil and then turned to examine her arms. 'I think we should use the right one this time. The left is looking rather bruised.'

'No injection until I see my blood work.'

'Miss McCormick, it's vital for your health –'

'And it's vital for *your* health, Dr Jerkins, that you stay right where you are.' Darby smiled politely. 'Touch me and you'll be wearing your balls as earrings. Might be a good look for you, since I don't know which way you swing – no offence.'

He studied her, trying to determine whether she was serious or blowing off steam.

'Be reasonable,' he said, with a small vibration in his voice.

He took a step closer. 'This will be over in just a moment.'

19

The doctor grabbed her wrist. With her left hand Darby grabbed his index finger and swiftly bent it backwards, breaking it at the bottom of the digit.

The man howled. He clutched his wrist and stared at the broken finger as he staggered away. He hit the wall and tumbled sideways to the floor.

An alarm sounded, loud and piercing. Bright red lights started blinking from the walls.

Darby hopped off the bed. The doctor was lying on his back, howling. She straddled him. He tried striking at her with his good hand. She slapped it away and grabbed him by the throat, pinning him to the floor.

'Exposure to any nerve agent, *especially* sarin gas, results in immediate symptoms,' she yelled over the alarm. 'If I had been infected, not only would I have shown symptoms by now, you would have remembered to turn on your respirator before coming into my room.'

She ripped the mask off his face and said, 'Tell me why you're keeping me locked up in here.'

He sucked in air, his face a mottled red. He said something but she couldn't hear him over the alarm.

'What was that?' she yelled, leaning closer.

'Orders,' he gasped.

'Whose orders?'

'Please,' he begged. '*Please*.'

Out of the corner of her eye she caught a flash of movement.

Darby looked up and saw two men, one tall and white with a blond crew cut, the other a burly Hispanic man with a shaved head, standing beyond the Plexiglas door. Both wore suits, ties and sidearms on their hips; she saw the slight bulge underneath their jackets.

Feds.

The tall white guy with the crew cut waved a badge in front of the keycard reader. Darby got to her feet. She started running as the door opened.

Crew Cut thought he could grab her and toss her against the floor. He came at her with both hands and she knocked them away, then raked him across the face with her elbow. She heard his nose break before his head snapped back. As his hands flew to his face, she planted her knee deep in his groin and turned to the Hispanic guy, who was reaching underneath his suit jacket.

Darby hit him once in the solar plexus, throwing all of her weight behind the punch. His breath caught in his throat. He tried sucking in air and when he turned she landed two solid shots to his kidneys.

Weeping came from behind her. She turned and saw the doc huddled in the corner of the room, staring at his broken finger. Crew Cut was lying sideways on the blue-padded floor, gagging up blood. It spilled down his chest, covering his shirt and two-dollar tie. He coughed and spat up blood. While she was dealing with his partner, Crew Cut had somehow managed to release his sidearm, a nine, and was pointing it at her.

Not a nine. The shape of the handgun was wrong, the magazine long and fat.

A puff of air and something sharp pierced her thigh.

A dart.

Darby pulled it free. The dart tip was gone, stuck in her thigh muscle, burning as it dissolved. He'd shot her with a tranquillizer, like she was some sort of unruly zoo animal.

Maybe I am, she thought, her knees starting to feel watery. *They've got to keep me tamed. They've been pumping drugs into me to keep me tame. They want to keep me here, they don't want to let me go just yet because . . . they . . . because . . .*

She suddenly became aware of her body, of her accelerating heart pumping the drug through her system, flushing her skin. Crew Cut was no longer interested in her. He had stumbled to his feet and now had the wall phone gripped in his hand, saying something about bringing a gurney around to the front – at least that was what she thought he was saying. The man's voice sounded garbled, as though she were listening to him from deep under water.

They're not wearing biohazard gear, she thought.

Then: *I'm not infected – I never was infected.*

The room's colours grew brighter, more intense. Darby saw Crew Cut swipe the back of his hand across his shattered nose. He examined the blood, bright red and gleaming underneath the overhead lights, and listened to whoever was speaking on the other end of the line as she tumbled against the padded floor, the room spinning her into darkness.

20

When Darby's eyes fluttered open, everything appeared blurry, as if her vision was coated with Vaseline. And her head, Jesus, her head felt as heavy as a sandbag, and it was hanging suspended over her lap. She had a vague sense of something biting into the skin around her wrists and ankles, of something wrapped tightly around both biceps.

It took a few minutes of blinking to clear away the filmy layer.

The first thing she noticed was the string of drool hanging from her mouth. She had collected quite a puddle on the lap of her hospital johnnies or scrubs or whatever they were. On the dark blue fabric covering her thigh she spotted a tiny hole from the tranquillizer dart and, surrounding it, a dried patch of blood the size of a half-dollar.

They had bound her to a wheelchair. Thick Velcro straps were wrapped around her wrists and biceps to keep her from toppling off her seat. The same straps, she suspected, were wrapped around her ankles and shins.

Lifting her head – *slowly*, she reminded herself, *do it slowly* – she heard popping sounds in her shoulders and neck. When she finally sat up, the muscles in her back and shoulders sighed in relief. Her right hand, though, was throbbing. Swollen and cut from punching the feds.

They had moved her into a new room, small, everything white, including the empty desk and chair.

No security cameras on the wall facing her. She looked over her shoulder, the muscles groaning in protest, and didn't see any cameras on the walls. Nobody stood behind her. No clock anywhere.

Darby stretched her neck and moved her shoulders to get the blood flowing. She wondered why she'd been placed in here and not back in her room.

The door clicked open behind her.

'Good, you're awake,' a man said. He had a smoker's voice, deep and raspy, and a slight European accent – Eastern Europe. Russian, maybe.

A squeak of footsteps as moved to face her. He looked like an older version of the Irish actor Colin Farrell; he even had the same black hair. He was trim and tall, hovering close to six feet, and wore army fatigues, boots and a short-sleeved olive T-shirt that showed off his repulsively hairy forearms.

A clipboard holding a thick stack of paper was tucked underneath his arm. He removed it and placed it on the desk. Stamped in bright gold on a corner of the top page was the logo for the US Army.

He leaned back against the desk and crossed his arms over his chest. He methodically chewed his gum while staring down at her with a cold, flat glare, trying to intimidate her. That kind of ability came naturally; you either had it or you didn't. This guy didn't. And he didn't have a badge or ID indicating his name or rank or what he did here.

'You keep staring at me like that,' she said, 'I'm likely to wet my pants in terror.'

'You broke a man's finger. Your *doctor*'s finger.'

Darby said nothing.

'And you attacked two federal officers.'

Darby said nothing.

'The first guy you hit is in the hospital,' he said. 'Shattered his nose, and his balls are going to be swollen for weeks.'

Darby said nothing.

Army Boy went back to chewing his gum, pausing, she guessed, to let the significance of his words sink in. His hair, while not excessively long, covered the tips of his ears. Not an army-regulation haircut. And he had two to three days' growth of beard, which was also against regulations.

'The other guy's also in the hospital,' he said. 'That gut punch of yours? He fell and cracked his head against the wall. Serious stuff.'

Darby said nothing, looking at the man's smooth biceps. No tattoos.

'Was all that really necessary?' he asked.

'All fights involve gravity and weapons.'

'And that's supposed to mean what?'

'When you fight, you don't do it half-assed. And you always assume the other person is armed, so you hit him to make sure he can't get up.'

'Those guys you hit are federal agents,' he said.

'Boston office?'

He shook his head. 'Washington. That little stunt of

yours cost you big time. You're looking at aggravated assault.'

No, I'm not. Nobody's going to do anything.

Another dramatic pause. More chewing. Darby wanted to hurry the charade along, have Army Boy get to the point. Instead, she kept quiet and waited.

He stopped chewing. Here came the politician's smile.

'I explained to these gentlemen that you're on a lot of pain meds due to your broken ribs. That you were feeling an overwhelming and irrational anxiety brought on by cabin fever, a normal reaction for someone trapped inside a quarantine chamber. I also told them you got your period, you know, mood swings, PMS, all that good stuff.'

'Clever,' she said.

'Thank you. In other words, I convinced them that you weren't in any kind of normal or rational state when you went all Rambo back there. Plus – and this is where you got lucky – I reminded your two victims that they didn't identify themselves as federal agents. If they had, you'd be in deep shit. You're welcome.'

Darby said nothing.

'Your blood work came back,' he said. 'You're in the clear.'

'Good to know, since the two feds who rushed into my room weren't wearing any hazmat gear. What are they doing all the way here from Washington?'

'They came to review a few things about your statement.'

'The feds carrying tranquillizer guns now?'

He shook his head. 'We are. They borrowed them. I'm Billy Fitzgerald, by the way.'

'And what do you do here, Billy?'

'I guess you could say I'm the second-in-command. When Glick isn't around, I run the show. More often than not I'm what you'd call a desk jockey. All I do is shuffle paper, like the ones attached to the clipboard.'

'Can I see some ID?'

'What for?'

'Polite thing to do when you're interrogating someone.'

Billy laughed. 'This isn't an interrogation.'

'Good. So let me speak to Sergeant-Major Glick.'

'He's unavailable.'

'Then make him available.'

He blew out a long stream of air through his mouth.

'Dr McCormick, let me explain the lay of the land to you. You're a civilian now. No Boston PD badge – not that it would make a lick of difference. Badges and fancy Harvard degrees don't hold much with me.'

He picked up the clipboard, removed the stack of paper and flipped through the pages. Then he held up three or four sheets.

'These pages are real important,' he said. 'I'm going to tuck them in the back, save the best for last.'

After he did, he stood and placed the clipboard on her lap.

'I'm going to unbind the cuffs on your right arm,' he said. 'You promise to be a good girl and not try any of that kung fu shit with me?'

She didn't answer.

He undid the cuffs binding her right arm, watching her

carefully, then he dropped a pen on her lap and returned to the desk.

'Read and initial each page,' he said, pulling out a chair. 'Sign your name where stated, and after you've finished I'll have someone drive you home. I'd suggest sticking around your place. The feds will still want to talk to you.'

'How goes the investigation up north?'

He smiled. 'That's classified.'

'Because the army is involved.'

'Army, FBI, ATF. It's a joint effort.'

'Have they found Mark Rizzo?'

'Couldn't tell you.'

'Then maybe you can tell me the army's interest in a private biomedical facility?'

'Look, we can keep going like this, you asking me questions I can't answer, and entertaining me with your snappy comebacks. Either way, I'm here until ten. Or you can sign the forms and you'll be on your way.'

Darby stared at the clipboard, thinking back to the day when the Boston FBI office sent two Irish boys to get her statement. They proclaimed ignorance about what was going on up north, so she gave them a vague rehash of what had happened that night and told them that if they wanted to know the particulars, they had better come back with someone who could answer her questions. The same pair returned the following day with no answers for her and took another shot. She ignored them until they finally gave up and left, frustrated.

Now her new friend Billy Fitzgerald had said the feds sent two bigwigs from Washington – the two bozos who had rushed into her quarantine room sans hazmat gear. She had assaulted two federal officers, put both men in the hospital, and instead of being cuffed and hauled away, Army Boy was telling her all she had to do was sign these forms and she would be free to go, no charges filed and no more questions.

Interesting.

Darby shifted in her chair, the other strap digging into her arm.

'What am I signing?'

'Medical release forms and some other things,' he said. 'Go on and give it a read. You're going to love it. It's a real page-turner.'

21

Darby flipped through the stack of sheets with her free hand. Fifty-two pages packed with fine print. She started to read.

The front part, the first fourteen pages, consisted of forms releasing the BU Biomedical lab from any medical liability. After that came page after page of confidentiality agreements that spelled out, in excruciating detail, all the legal ramifications: ten years in prison along with a multitude of fines that, if they were ever enforced, would successfully bankrupt her – if she should ever feel oh so inclined to share *any* information about what she had seen or heard here during her treatment.

The bulk of the pages, though, concerned the events of that night in New Hampshire. Lots of fine print crammed with that mind-numbing legalese that made her head spin. She kept seeing the phrase 'the USA Patriot Act' in almost every line. The Patriot Act, a law enacted by former president George W. Bush the month after 9/11, gave law enforcement agencies the right to search anyone's telephone, email, financial and medical records – any record, for that matter – without a court order.

She looked up and said, 'A little extreme, don't you think?'

'When it comes to matters of domestic terrorism and national security, you bet we're extreme.'

Especially when you're trying to hide something. Darby didn't need to voice this; it hung in the air between them. She looked at the man's cold gaze and wondered what, exactly, he was so afraid she was going to find.

'I need my lawyer to review this before I sign,' she said. 'There's a lot of legal language in here I don't understand.'

'Really? I think it's pretty straightforward.'

'I'd still like my lawyer to look at it.'

'Sure, we can do that. Might take, oh, a week or two before our guys can get to it. You know how busy lawyers are. While they're working it out, you're going to have to stay here.' He grinned. 'Liability issues.'

'Do I get copies after I sign?'

'We'll forward them to you after we get the appropriate signatures.'

'From whom? I don't see any names listed here except mine.'

'Make sure you read pages fifteen through twenty real carefully, as they spell out in great detail what will happen if we catch you poking that pretty little nose of yours into this matter. In simple terms, we'll have you arrested. That wouldn't go over too well with the Boston brass, given your rather, ah, *tenuous* position with them over that matter involving the police commissioner. You wouldn't want to deep-six any remaining chances you might have for reinstatement – or any future employment opportunities, say, in another state.'

Billy Fitzgerald's eyes were dancing, all bright and confident. 'In other words, the US Army owns that pretty little ass of yours.'

Darby felt her face flush with heat; her mouth was dry, tongue thick with thirst. She swallowed.

'You all right, hon? Want some water? A soda?'

She didn't want anything to drink. What she wanted right now was to get out of the wheelchair, lock the door and pound his face until his teeth turned to dust.

She started undoing the strap binding her left wrist.

Army Boy reached for his belt and came back with a tranquillizer gun. He put it on the table, pointing the muzzle in her direction.

'What's that for?'

'Just in case you decide to pull any of that Rambo shit,' he said. 'You can take that strap off but leave on the ones on your legs.'

'No need to worry, I promise to be a good little girl.' Darby winked at him and grabbed the clipboard with both hands.

She pretended to read through the pages again as she considered her options. It didn't take her long since she didn't have any.

She picked up the cheap Bic pen from her lap.

'That'a girl.'

She removed the thick stack of sheets from the clipboard and found pages fifteen through twenty. She placed them on the top of the stack.

'What are you doing?' he asked.

'I want to read these carefully, make sure I understand everything since my head's feeling, you know, a little thick.'

'Smart move.'

Darby read through the five pages again as Army Boy

watched, his hand still gripping the tranquillizer gun. He kept stealing glances at his watch. When she placed the clipboard on her lap, he watched as she signed her name.

She held up the signed sheet for him to inspect and saw some of that caged heat leave his gaze. She placed the page on the edge of the desk, signed the next one, held it up for him and then placed it on the desk. By the time she'd moved on to the third page, his shoulders had relaxed.

All five pages were now signed and sitting on the desk. 'Can I go now?'

'Not yet,' he said, leaning back in his chair. He kept the gun on the table, pointed at her, and crossed his legs. 'You need to initial the other ones to say you've read them. And don't forget to sign where stated.'

Darby picked up the loose pages from the desk. She shuffled them together and tucked them behind the clipboard resting on her lap.

She read the first page on the stack, initialled it and held it up for him. He nodded and she placed it on top of the desk.

Darby went through the same motion – reading each sheet, signing it, holding it up for inspection, placing it on the desk – for the next twenty or so sheets. Then she reached underneath the clipboard and placed her fingers on the pages resting on her lap – those five lovely pages that spelled out in great detail what would happen if she decided to poke her pretty little nose into this investigation – and pushed them between her thighs.

Her legs pressed together, she picked up the loose

collection of pages, shuffled them and then placed them behind the stack resting on the clipboard. She moved it to the side and glanced quickly at her lap, pleased to find that she couldn't see the pages tucked between her thighs.

'I'd like some water,' she said.

'I'll get you a bottle on your way out.'

'You're the one who made the offer. I'd like it now please. And I need to use the bathroom.'

'Then I suggest you hurry up and finish.'

She was about to sign the next sheet when she hesitated.

'There's nothing in here about your returning my tactical equipment.'

'Confiscated,' he said.

'When am I going to get it back?'

'You're not. It's evidence, part of our investigation.'

'Why is the army investigating this case?'

'Domestic terrorism. We're working in conjunction with the FBI and the ATF.'

Which meant they had most likely pushed the New Hampshire detectives to the sidelines. The government hated sharing information among themselves, let alone with state or local police.

'What about my clothes?'

'Incinerated,' he said. 'But you'll be happy to know we managed to salvage your keys and all the plastic stuff in that little leather wallet of yours. The wallet and cash we had to incinerate, but the rest of it we decontaminated, free of charge. Why do you carry a guy's wallet? I thought pretty ladies like yourself carried handbags.'

'I can stick it in my front pocket. What about my phone?'

'Don't know anything about that.'

'You going to reimburse me?'

'Talk to someone in New Hampshire.'

Darby looked up. 'I'm talking to *you*. I invested a lot of money in that equipment.'

'Take it as a tax write-off.'

'I need to use the bathroom.'

'Finish signing and initialling, and you'll be good to go.'

She did, making a dramatic show of being uncomfortable.

When the last page was signed, she picked up the clipboard. The pages weren't fastened underneath the clip, and when she went to hand the clipboard over, they fell and spilled across the floor.

'Sorry about that,' she said, and tossed the clipboard on the desk. 'I've got to use the bathroom now. I'm bleeding.'

Confused, he examined her arms and face.

'My period,' she said.

Now he looked disgusted. He sprang to his feet and then wheeled her out of the room and across a painfully bright white hall to a bathroom door with a handicap sign. Standing around the corner were two army boys dressed in fatigues, heavy jackets and caps. Both white males, both young and packed with muscle – and name tags. She saw them sewn into their jackets: Anthony and Weeks. The tall one with the doughy face, Weeks, had a submachine gun strapped across his chest.

'They'll take you on out after you're done,' Billy Fitz-gerald said.

Then he grinned and winked at her. 'Remember to behave yourself out there, missy.'

22

Darby glanced up at the ceiling, looking for security cameras. In a place like this she wouldn't have been surprised to find one peering down at her, but the white walls were bare. She removed the Velcro straps and tossed them into the metal trash bin sitting next to the toilet. Then she got to her feet, pulling the folded sheets free from her thighs, and locked the door.

Billy Fitzgerald's parting words with their smug tone echoed through her head: *Remember to behave yourself out there, missy.*

Don't worry, I will, she thought, about to rip up the sheets and flush them down the toilet when another thought, this one more pleasing and appealing, occurred to her: Billy Fitzgerald had touched these pages. She could run his prints through the automated fingerprint database. Military personnel and law enforcement officers were required by law to submit their fingerprints to IAFIS.

Is that right? Billy Fitzgerald asked in her mind. *And why, pray tell, are you going to do that?*

Because I don't believe you're in the army.

She didn't have any proof, just a gut feeling based on the military men she knew who had served in Iraq or Afghanistan. Almost every one of them had some sort of military tattoo proudly inked on a forearm or bicep. It was a rite of passage. Her father, a former marine, had ink on both of his meaty biceps: the USMC emblem in faded blue on his right arm, and on the left, this one more colourful and intricate, the classic USMC bulldog with the words *Semper Fi*.

Billy Fitzgerald didn't have any tattoos, and, while that wasn't necessarily odd – not every military man got tattooed – he didn't have a military-regulation haircut. And he hadn't shaved either. If he wasn't military, why was he pretending?

Darby folded the sheets into a small square. Wrapped them up in a paper towel and tucked that in the front of the big hospital granny-panties they'd given her. You couldn't see a bulge under the baggy scrubs. She kicked the toilet handle with her foot and then went to the sink to wash her hands.

Walking out of the bathroom, the GI Joe named Anthony barked at her to park her ass back in the wheelchair.

Darby rolled it out of the bathroom, thinking about how easy it would be to take both these young bucks down. The big ones packed with show muscle weren't used to getting hit, especially in the way she did, especially by a girl. Two punches each, maybe four, and she could have them on their knees, sobbing.

But this wasn't the time or place. She sat like a good little girl and then waited as Anthony's partner, Weeks, went into the bathroom to retrieve the straps.

Once she was bound again, Weeks approached her holding some black-foam material shaped into one of those eye-masks people used to block out light when sleeping.

'What is that?' she asked.

'A blindfold.'

'For what?'

Weeks didn't answer, just pressed the spongy material against her eyes. He held it in place for a moment, and when he released his hand the wheelchair started rolling.

Darby moved her eyes around, hoping to catch sight of something along the cracks. But the eye-mask blocked out all the light.

But she had her other senses, and she paid attention to her surroundings. Weeks and Anthony didn't speak – nobody did. Beyond the occasional squeak of a footstep moving across the polished linoleum floor, the only sounds she heard were buzzers followed by electronic steel locks clicking back. The wheelchair never stopped moving; it just kept rolling through what felt like an endless corridor of warm air smelling faintly of some sort of industrial-grade antiseptic chemical.

Finally, the wheelchair stopped moving. Doors slid shut behind her. The floor rocked slightly and then she was heading down, down.

Then the elevator stopped moving, the doors parted and she was being wheeled across what was probably an underground garage. Cold air and exhaust fumes. Echoing footsteps. Now the unmistakable sound of a car idling. The wheelchair stopped. Hands worked at the Velcro straps. Hands gripped her wrists tightly and lifted her up. She felt cold concrete beneath her bare feet.

'Walk,' Weeks said.

She did. The guy had a thick Boston accent. A local boy. Good.

'Stop,' Weeks said.

She did and a hand touched the back of her head and pushed it down. Inside a car now; she felt cool leather beneath her fingers, warm air blowing from vents. Using her hands, she got her bearings as the door slammed shut.

The car started to move. She touched the blindfold with her fingers. Thick and rubbery, stuck to her skin. She gripped an edge and began to peel it away, then clenched her teeth, hissing in pain.

'Shit,' she muttered as the car started to move.

'The blindfold stays on until we get to your condo,' Weeks said. He was sitting next to her. She could smell the cigar smoke baked into his clothes. 'Try to rip it off and you'll take off your eyebrows and a whole lot of skin.'

Darby sat back against her seat, fuming silently to herself as she wondered what was behind all of the cloak-and-dagger bullshit. She knew its location – *anyone* could find it with a simple Google search, thanks to all the publicity the controversial lab had received. Local residents and community activists had been up in arms when the news broke that Boston's South End was going to be the new site of a lab studying infectious diseases that came with a Biosafety Level 4 rating, a first for the city. Those same articles had described, in gruesome detail, what would happen if a worker suffered accidental contamination; if there was a building fire or a chemical leak. The protests kept going, but when the lab went operational, that was the end of the matter – at least in the papers, anyway.

She paid attention to the turns. Counted in her mind as the car travelled a stretch of road before turning again. The driver was trying to confuse her, taking sharp rights and lefts and then going back across the same ground. He didn't want her to know the location.

Had she been housed in a bona fide army facility? She didn't know of any in or out of Boston. If she had, in fact, been treated in an army facility, it was most likely classified, which would successfully prevent her from finding it through any normal channels.

The erratic driving continued. She stopped paying attention and instead spent the time counting seconds. Minutes stacked up.

The car stopped. The door to her left opened and shut. She made note of the time: seventy-three minutes.

Then her door opened. A rush of fresh air blew past her.

'I'm going to spray something to get that blindfold off,' Weeks said. 'Keep your eyes shut until I tell you to open them.'

The hiss of an aerosol can and the spray of a cool chemical across her face. He grabbed one edge as he kept spraying, and she felt the blindfold peel away from her tingling skin without any pain or discomfort.

Weeks grabbed her wrist and put something soft and damp in her hand.

'Wipe your face,' he said.

She did. Her skin still tingled. When she opened her eyes, she saw, directly in front of her, a black divider separating the back seat from the front. *Not a limo, more like a town car*, she thought. Tinted windows and lots of black leather.

Her door hung open to cold darkness. The streetlights were on, and she could see the familiar set of stone steps leading up to the front door of her building.

Weeks dropped something on to her lap and moved away. Her keys, a rubber band holding her licence and credit cards.

Darby picked them up and climbed out of the back.

'Thanks for the lift, soldier.'

Weeks climbed back inside. He shut the door as the car – a scratched, beat-up black Lincoln with a dented rear panel – pulled away from the kerb with a small screech of tyres. No back number plate. The Lincoln drove to the end of Temple Street and then, without stopping, took a sharp right on to Cambridge. A tiny white Honda slammed on its brakes. Car horns blared and then the Lincoln disappeared.

23

Darby stood on the cobblestone sidewalk, a few steps away from one of the antique-lantern streetlights that lined both sides of her one-way street, and twirled her key ring around a finger while pretending to stare after the Lincoln, as if she were shocked at being dumped out here.

Out of the corner of her eye she watched a vehicle parked at the end of the street where Temple met Cambridge. An SUV. From where she stood she could see only the front half. It looked like a Chevy Tahoe, dark blue or black. The windows were dark, possibly tinted. It was parked against the kerb directly in front of the sandwich shop that catered to the college crowd. She couldn't see the fire hydrant but she knew it was there.

During the day, sometimes a car would pull up against the kerb and someone would run inside to pick up an order. The store was closed now, and no one in their right mind who lived in Beacon Hill would park in that spot, because they'd be towed and have to shell out two hundred bucks to get their car back from the impound lot.

That parking spot, however, offered an excellent, clear view of Temple Street. Her building, one in a long row of a dozen hundred-year-old townhouses, all of them built of ageing brick, sat right in the middle of the street. If someone was sitting behind the wheel, he or she could watch her comings and goings, make sure she kept good on her promise to behave herself.

It was also possible someone had simply parked there for a few minutes, praying like hell they wouldn't get towed.

The wind blew against her back and Darby felt the cold on the cobblestone sidewalk biting the soles of her bare feet. After being cooped up for so long, she didn't want to remove herself from the crisp autumn air filling her lungs, but she had been standing out here long enough. And the few stragglers moving up and down the street were staring and keeping their distance. With her bloodied scrubs, her bandaged and bruised arms, her bare feet and messy hair, she knew she looked like some sort of escaped mental patient.

Darby turned and moved up the front steps. It was time to get to work on finding Mark Rizzo. And when she found him, the man was going to explain what he had done to his son.

The lobby was empty, but there was a party in full swing in the ground-floor unit. Loud music she didn't recognize throbbed and college kids laughed behind the closed door. The person who owned the place, the biggest condo in the four-unit building, lived in Chicago and rented the space for an ungodly monthly sum to well-to-do parents thinking Beacon Hill was a safer place for their college-bound kids than Allston or Brighton or somewhere else near downtown Boston.

Jogging up the long, winding staircase, Darby thought about the FBI. If the feds were, in fact, watching her, it was equally possible they had bugged her home, maybe even going so far as to install pinhole cameras. She wouldn't put it past them. And they could do it all without a warrant. The Patriot Act provided all sorts of wonderful legal loopholes.

After disengaging the alarm for her condo, she dumped her mail on the kitchen worktop, went to the bathroom and shut the door. She stripped down and then turned on the water to take a long and blissfully private (hopefully) hot shower.

Standing underneath the running water, she thought about what to do with the folded sheets now sitting on the floor inside her hospital scrubs.

Processing the papers for prints was a no-brainer. Spray the sheets with Ninhydrin, maybe boost it with heat for better clarity, then transfer the latent prints to a finger-print card for processing.

The problem was the fingerprint database. To access IAFIS, you had to enter your name and password. She hadn't stepped foot inside the Boston Police Department since her forced suspension, and she wondered if Leland or some other higher power, maybe even the acting police commissioner himself, had blocked her access to the lab as well as to IAFIS and the other databases she used.

There was only one way to find out.

Darby changed into jeans, a white tank top and one of her favourite items of clothing: a pair of dark brown leather harness boots. She grabbed a check flannel shirt from her closet, put it on and buttoned it up on her way to the kitchen. Her hair, still slightly damp, spilled over her shoulders.

The kitchen window and the three windows along the wall in the large space that served as her dining and living room overlooked Temple Street. She grabbed a bottle of Midleton Irish whiskey and a glass, poured herself a healthy shot, leaned the small of her back against the worktop and looked out of one of the middle windows.

The SUV was still parked at the end of the street.

Her phone sat at the end of the worktop, near the window. The red message light was blinking. She walked over to it and inspected it with her eyes, not her hands, just in case she was being watched. She sipped her drink, staring.

The phone had been plugged into the bottom outlet, not the top. And she found flecks of yellow paint on her white worktop. The flecks must have come lose when the wall plate was removed. The painters she had hired had done a sloppy job.

So had the person who had removed the wall plate. The feds should have hired someone more professional.

She wondered if it had been a last-minute rush job. Maybe that was the reason why the two GI Joes had zig-zagged all over the place. They had been ordered to buy the techs working inside her place some time to finish.

Darby picked up her mail and carried it with her to the living room. She plopped down on the couch, then leaned back against the leather cushion and propped the heels of her boots on the edge of the old wood steamer trunk that served as her coffee table. She sat there, sipping her drink, thinking about the listening device installed in her kitchen wall jack. There were probably more. Two bugs, maybe three, would've done the trick. Her two-bedroom, two-bathroom unit was just under a thousand square feet.

She already had a federal tap on her phone, thanks to her run-in a few years back with a man named Malcolm Fletcher, a former FBI profiler who currently held the number-three slot on their Most Wanted List. Because of her limited involvement with him – and the fact that she was one of a handful of people who'd seen the man face to face and lived to tell about the experience – the tap on her phone was a permanent one, in case he decided to contact her. He hadn't, so far.

If the feds weren't behind it, there was one logical option left: the men who had ambushed the Rizzo home had found out her name and where she lived, broken into her house, managed to disengage her alarm system and installed one or more listening devices. Disengaging an alarm system was a pain in the ass, but someone with the right technical background and equipment could do it. You could buy the necessary tools and devices on the Internet. The same held true for listening devices. There were thousands of websites selling state-of-the-art stuff, all of it perfectly legal.

She could unscrew the kitchen wall plate and examine the listening device. It would take only a moment to see if it was something the feds used.

No, not yet. She wanted some more time to think, to see if there was a way she could use this to her advantage.

If the feds had bugged her home, and if they were parked at the end of her street and watching her building right now, that meant they were using her as bait. That was the reason why they had released her. They were using her to lure one or more of the men she'd encountered at the Rizzo home out of hiding.

She wondered too if her computer had been bugged to monitor her email.

The phone rang. She let the machine pick it up.

'Darby, this is Leland.'

The familiar WASPy voice, cold and dry, belonged to her former boss, Leland Pratt.

'I'm pleased to inform you that you've been reinstated at the lab,' he said. 'Unfortunately, you've been reduced a pay grade, which means you'll have to take a cut in salary. Report to me tomorrow morning at eight o'clock and we'll go over the particulars before we meet with the acting police commissioner.'

Click and he hung up.

Well, there it was. After months of deliberation, the bureaucrats had finally come to a decision: they were going to dump her back at the lab, with a pay cut. *You're officially persona non grata, McCormick. When you come in tomorrow morning, remember to smile when you get down on your knees to kiss our asses. Oh, and don't forget to thank us in between each smooch for not giving you the boot.*

Interesting that the job offer came on the same day she'd been released from quarantine.

She polished off her drink, imagining the look of righteous indignation on Leland's face when she told him and the acting police commissioner where they could stick their job offer.

Darby pulled out the nearly empty liner bag from the trashcan and glanced out of the window. The SUV was still there.

Moving to the bathroom, she grabbed the scrubs and folded sheets of paper and dumped them into the bag. From her office she collected the cord holding her laminated ID/keycard for the lab, and from the hall closet her leather racer jacket. Then, carrying the bag with her, she left the condo.

24

When Darby reached the end of the stairs, she turned the corner for the ground-floor unit. She didn't knock yet. She had one small chore left.

She opened the cellar door and took the narrow set of steps. She reached the bottom and, ducking her head, moved underneath the exposed beams and pipes, past the community washer and dryer, to the end where the big plastic garbage cans that stored a week's worth of trash were kept.

From the bag she removed the folded sheets of paper wrapped in paper towels. She tucked them in her inside jacket pocket, snapped it shut and then dumped her trash.

Now she wanted to examine her jacket.

She had only two in her closet: this Schott leather racer, which she bought for her motorcycle, and a denim jacket Coop had somehow convinced her to buy, saying that they had come back into style. She spread out her jacket on top of the washing machine, where the light was the strongest, and started prodding the fabric and thick black leather with her fingers, searching for a tracking unit. They made them small now, about the size of a hearing-aid battery. A Massachusetts state trooper once told her about how they had used a tracking device to follow a Boston drug dealer supplying cocaine and heroin to the eastern part of the state. The dealer knew the troopers and local cops were following him, and so would drive to multiple parking garages to switch vehicles. It worked – until an undercover cop managed to get his hands on the long winter overcoat the dealer always wore, cut the fabric along the seam on the bottom of the coat where it wouldn't be noticed and slipped a tracking unit inside. The dealer could change cars as many times as he liked. The tracking unit sent out a signal to the laptops installed in state police cruisers. Where he went, they went.

She doubted she was being watched. Installing cameras down here would be a monumental pain in the ass. A listening device, maybe. This basement was small, and old, with lots of hidden cracks and crevices. Drop a bug and run. Cameras took time. First you had to find a place that offered the best view. Then you had to figure out where to hide it. Then you had to install it. That required moving things around. Drilling. Hooking up power packs or wiring the camera into an electrical system. Too much noise, too much commotion. Upstairs, inside her home, they'd have privacy, but not down here. Someone might decide to dump their trash and then the questions would start.

She had already searched the bottom half of her jacket and found nothing. Maybe she was being paranoid.

Maybe not. A quarter-inch of stitching had been removed on the right-hand corner of the Schott tag. You had to look closely in order to see it. Not a design defect. She had purchased the jacket, brand new, at the beginning of the autumn season.

She didn't have tweezers on her so she fished a finger inside, ripping more stitching, and felt something hard and cold. It took her a moment to wrangle it free.

Two small discs, each the size of a watch battery but thinner, like a wafer. A tiny green light glowed on one. The other one had to be the battery.

She tucked the tracking device inside her pocket for the moment, then went back upstairs to the lobby. She had to knock on the door a few times before someone answered.

The person who did was a tall and lanky blond-haired college boy who looked as if he had stepped out of the pages of a J. Crew catalogue: tight-fitting jeans, polished black oxfords and a white shirt underneath a dark blue cardigan – Tim something, one of the two guys who rented the place. Nice kid, shy. Spent a lot of time on his hair to give it that messy, bed-head look. He came from some small town in Colorado and went to Suffolk University, which was conveniently located right across the street.

He seemed stunned to see her standing there.

'Hey, sup there, Darby.'

She smiled. 'How's it going, Tim?'

'Great, just great.' Then his face grew serious. He stepped out into the hall and shut the door behind him to block out the music. 'Are you here about the noise? I didn't think anyone was home. Vin and Wendy said they were going to be gone for the month – Switzerland or something – and Sue upstairs, she said she wasn't going to be home tonight, so I invited some –'

'Relax,' she said, and smiled. 'I just wanted to know if I could borrow your phone for a minute. I lost my cell.'

'Sure, no problem.'

He dug into his front pocket. The music had turned mellow and moody, some guy pining away because of a broken heart and lost love.

Tim handed her his cell. She dialled 911 and gave the male dispatcher her name and address.

'There's an SUV parked at the end of my street, on the corner of Temple and Cambridge,' she said. 'Looks like a Chevy Tahoe, either black or navy-blue, and I think it has tinted windows. I keep seeing these college kids walking up to the car and exchanging money for tiny baggies holding what looks like heroin. Could you send a squad car over? . . . Great, thanks so much.'

She hung up, handed the phone back to Tim and said, 'The bedroom that faces the street? You mind if I go in there and watch the show?'

'No, not at all. That's mine.' He opened the door. 'A real-live drug bust. Cool. Haven't seen one of those before.'

He took her through a living room with beanbag chairs and hand-me-down sofas with dented cushions. The built-in bookcase shelves around the fireplace were bare, coated in dust. The party had moved to the kitchen, where a keg had been set up. A gaggle of preening college girls – there were five of them – either stood or sat at the table playing quarters with a guy she assumed to be Tim's room-mate, a smug pretty boy who no doubt coasted through life on his good looks.

The girls didn't like the way he shifted his attention away from them.

'Well, hello there,' he said, offering his hand. 'I'm Timmy's roommate, Gregg.'

'Darby. Nice to meet you.'

'I've seen you before.'

'I live upstairs.'

'Oh. I was pretty sure you were a model.' His smile was as perfect and charming as his face. 'You're definitely pretty enough to model swimsuits and stuff.'

'You've got me confused with someone else,' she said, and, looking back at Tim, nodded with her chin to get moving.

Tim's small bedroom was surprisingly neat for a college student, the walls stuffed with posters and photographs, some framed, of Boston Red Sox players and different ball parks from across the country.

'Ted Williams,' she said, pointing to a signed picture. 'You've got good taste.'

'Best there ever was and ever will be.'

Darby moved to the corner window. The SUV was still there.

'Can I get you a beer?' Tim asked.

'I'm all set, thanks. I won't be here that long.'

Tim lingered close by, looking anxious.

'You don't have to stay here,' she said. 'Go back to the party.'

'Nah, that's okay. Those girls are interested in Gregg, anyway.'

'He strikes me as sort of a douche.'

Tim chuckled. 'He sort of is. And the girls love it for some reason. The more he shits on them, the harder they fight.'

'That will change after college, trust me.' She couldn't see anything behind those tinted windows. How many people were in there?

'He's going to move to Hollywood,' Tim said. 'Going to be a famous actor.'

'He'll wind up doing soft-core porn. If he's lucky, he'll find some rich cougar looking for arm candy and shack up with her.'

'What's going on with that guy you hang out with, what's his name, the one who looks like Tom Brady?'

'Coop.'

'Right, Coop. Good guy. Where's he been? I haven't seen him around.'

'He moved to London three months ago.'

'You guys still, you know, dating or whatever?'

'We never dated,' she said, and the night he left flashed through her mind: Coop running back through the rain and kissing her. He called her later, from the airport, and he told her how he really felt about her. Now, each time they spoke on the phone, he didn't bring up what had happened between them.

You haven't either, a voice added.

A Boston squad car, lights on but sirens off, came to an abrupt stop in front of the SUV. Two patrolmen jumped out, leaving their doors hanging open as they drew their weapons. Another squad car pulled up alongside the SUV, blocking the driver's-side door.

Showtime. Darby moved away from the window.

'Thanks, Tim.'

'You taking off?'

She nodded. 'Got some work I need to do.'

'Before you go, I was wondering . . .' He swallowed, then swiped a hand across his mouth. 'I was thinking maybe we could grab a beer together, or something.'

Darby smiled. 'Tim, I'm flattered. If I was your age, I'd take you up on that offer in a heartbeat.'

The hope crumbled in his eyes, and his pale face reddened with embarrassment. 'I wasn't asking you, like, out on a date or anything. I thought we could, you know, hang out or something.'

'Hang out,' Darby said. 'Sure. Absolutely.'

Tim, ever the gentleman, walked her to the front door. Even held it open for her.

Darby said just loud enough for Gregg to hear: I'll call you next week, Tim, and we'll set something up.'

She gave him a quick hug and a peck on the cheek before leaving.

25

Darby stood on the stoop of her building. The steady pulse of blue and whites flashing from the rooftops of the two Boston squad cars lit up the corner of her street. She could see the SUV. It was a Chevy Tahoe. The passenger's-side door was hanging open. The interior light was on but nobody was inside.

Two men dressed in suits, their jackets buttoned, stood outside. *Feds*, she thought. The first guy was white and middle aged, and had sandy-blond hair and a crooked nose. He stood on the kerb with his hands on top of his head, arguing with a patrolman pointing a nine at him. There was lots of shouting but she couldn't hear what was being said, their words lost behind the wind and busy traffic on Cambridge Street.

The second guy was Italian or Greek, a Tony Soprano type with thinning black hair that had been combed back over his bald spot. He was taller than his partner, maybe six feet, and fatter. He leaned forward with his hands splayed across the front hood, the buttons of his suit jacket straining against the swell of his gut. He was being frisked. He wasn't speaking and he ignored the scene happening around him, his gaze locked on her building. On her.

Darby didn't recognize him or the blond man. Was

confident she had never seen either man before. She *did* recognize the patrolman shining his flashlight on the SUV's interior seats: Jimmy Murphy, an old flatfoot leftover from an era when the Irish made up the majority of the Boston police force. He was thick and jowly and had a fine network of spider veins covering his nose and cheeks from a lifetime of hard drinking. Darby headed down her front steps, making a mental note to give Jimmy a call sometime later that night or the next day, see if she could get the names of the two feds so she could pay them a visit.

Fat Tony kept eyeing her. She held his gaze for a moment, giving away nothing, and as she crossed the street, heading for the alley between the college and the oldest brick townhouse on the block, she saw Fat Soprano make a move for the car door. The patrolman frisking him pushed him hard against the hood. Lots of shouting and another patrolman pressed his nine closer to Tony Soprano's head. She caught the worried expression on Fat Tony's face just before she ducked into the alley.

Darby emerged on Hanover Street and then went through another alley and walked on to Joy. The one-way streets, jam-packed with parked cars, were dark and quiet. A few people were out, walking home or to one of the bars or restaurants that lined Cambridge. As she walked to the best place to pick up a cab – the corner of Cambridge and Charles Street, on the other side of Beacon Hill – she thought about Fat Tony's worried look.

The man's cover was blown. He was going to get his ass chewed out by his superiors. There'd be demerits, maybe even a possible relocation to some federal outpost. A natural reaction. She would have bought off on it if he hadn't first tried to go for the door. Like he needed to call someone and let this person know where she was heading.

Why? They had installed a tracking device in her jacket. It was now sitting in her jeans pocket and it was broadcasting a signal. Fat Tony shouldn't be worried. But he had made a move for the door, like he was afraid of losing sight of her. Like he had to radio for help or back-up.

Darby emerged on the end of Charles Street, looking for a cab. As she waited, she thought about the tracking device. The design was something the feds probably used – very high-tech, sent a wireless signal to a nearby computer – but the installation had been sloppy. The feds, generally speaking, weren't sloppy. They planned and prepared and executed their surveillance ops with an admirable efficiency. If the feds were behind this, they would have come inside her condo, taken pictures, made sure everything was put back together properly. They wouldn't have left the broken stitching in her jacket.

Maybe the feds weren't responsible for this sloppy work. Maybe someone else was, like one of the men she had encountered inside the Rizzo home. Men who knew she was alive and wanted to see where she would go, what she would do.

26

At a quarter past eight, Darby stepped through the Boston Police Department's revolving front doors for the first time since her suspension, and brushed the hair out of her eyes. It had been windy as hell out there and she had forgotten to tie her hair behind her head before leaving the condo.

The long, wide lobby of dark brown and yellow marble hummed with activity. The phones at the main desk kept ringing; and crowds of patrolmen and plainclothes detectives, plus a handful of lawyers she knew, had cornered themselves into small groups for private discussion. Lots of familiar faces here, and she caught more than one tired or bloodshot gaze shift her way as she made her way to the security checkpoint set up in front of the bank of elevators.

A pot-bellied blue uniform sat in a stiff chair. His name was Chet Archer, and he had manned the security checkpoint since the beginning of the year. Working this spot was a highly sought-after position for those patrolmen who had been injured on the job and didn't want to go out on disability. Working it this time of night was a cush-gig. Park your duff on a stool and look up every now and then to check the ID of some cop or lab tech, wave them on through and go back to reading a book or magazine – or, as in Chet's case, click the time away on a portable videogame.

'Playing anything good?' she asked.

Chet looked up from his game.

'Blackjack,' he said. 'I'm heading off to Foxwoods this weekend with the missus, need to brush up on my skills.'

Chet leaned forward in his chair, squinting as his gaze shifted to the laminated badge hanging from a cord around her neck. Darby unzipped her leather jacket and placed it on the conveyor belt for the X-ray machine.

Chet got to his feet slowly, wincing in pain.

'How'd the knee replacement go?' she asked.

'I just got the other one done.' He gripped the top of the X-ray machine for balance. 'What brings you by, Darby?'

'I'm coming back to work tomorrow, so I decided to swing by and catch up on a few things, take advantage of the peace and quiet.'

'Nobody told me anything about that.'

'Probably because Leland called me about an hour ago.'

'He's gone for the day.'

Darby had counted on that, since Leland had called her from his cell phone. Leland Pratt, ever the efficient administrator and state employee, always locked his office at 4:30 p.m., the time the lab closed for the day.

Chet said, 'I can't let you up there without his permission.'

'So call him.' She glanced to the phone hanging on the wall behind Chet.

'I don't have his cell number, let alone the one for his home.'

'No problem. I know them by heart. Let me know when you're ready.'

Chet shifted, grimacing. Leland was a pro when it came to kissing ass upwards but not downwards. He virtually ignored people he considered beneath him. People like Chet.

Right now Chet was wondering whether it was worth the risk of placing a call to King Leland's Brookline palace. Chet knew he had a good gig and didn't want any trouble. And a top pencil-pusher like King Leland could make a lot of trouble if he got pissed at being bothered at home.

'I'll call him,' Darby said.

Chet waved a hand. 'No, that's okay, I'll take your word for it. Go on through. And welcome back, Darby.'

Walking out of the elevator, Darby removed the cord from around her neck. She held her breath as she waved the laminated badge in front of the keycard reader that guarded the lab's twin steel doors.

The keycard's light turned green. The locks clicked back and she felt the trapped breath nearly explode past her lips, the tightness in her chest drizzling away.

Dim lighting hung over the empty desk where the lab secretary sat. Darby walked past it and then turned and looked down the hall. The doors for the two-person offices were open, all the rooms dark. The door for Serology, where she had spent most of her early adult working life, was dark. No one was here. It didn't surprise her. With the bad state of the economy, the department's budget had been cut, and the first thing to go was overtime. Nobody worked past 4:30 unless it was an emergency, and then the overtime had to be approved by Leland, who was all too willing to say no. Nothing excited the man more than staying under budget.

Darby turned around and walked down the hall to her corner office. Her name plate had already been removed, but the locks hadn't been changed. Her key turned without a problem.

Clicking on the light, she found that the few items she had hung on her wall had been taken down and placed into boxes. The wall behind her desk – her *former* desk, she reminded herself – was crammed full of Leland's framed diplomas and several pictures of him shaking hands with the mayor, the governor and new Massachusetts senator. There was a picture of him with President Clinton and one with Hillary Clinton. And Leland, through his Rolodex of political connections, had somehow weaseled his way into getting a picture with President Obama. The pricey frames had been strategically positioned on the wall so the person entering the office would know he or she was dealing with a man of *great* importance.

Of course he'd take over my office. It's slightly bigger than his and has more windows and a much better view. That's how pricks like Leland keep score.

Darby pulled out the chair behind the desk, sat and turned on the computer. Old and slow, it took a long time to boot up.

She entered her name and password and pressed the ENTER key.

ACCESS DENIED.

Shit. She was locked out. No way to access Charlie Rizzo's case file – and now no way to access the lab's fingerprint database. The same password worked on both systems.

Darby leaned back in her chair and stared out of the window, thinking.

The first problem – information on Charlie Rizzo's case – was easy enough to solve. The lead investigator was a Greek guy by the name of Stan Karakas, who had long since retired from the force. The question was whether or not he was still living in the city – or the state.

The Retired Boston Police Officers Association would know. They'd have contact information, address and phone numbers. Their offices were closed now, but she could call them first thing tomorrow morning. Better yet, she could drive over to West Roxbury and talk to someone in person.

Now the second and more pressing problem: what to do with the papers inside her jacket pocket? She could ask one of the lab techs to do it on the sly. Randy Scott would do it, no questions asked . . . but if Leland found out, the prick would go out of his way to punish Randy. Scratch Randy. Scratch anyone here at the lab, which left her –

Darby leaned forward and grabbed the phone.

27

Darby dialled the number, listening to the strange trans-continental double-ring for a phone on the other side of the world. Four of those double-rings and then Coop's voicemail message played.

'Coop, it's me. I need a favour. A big favour, actually. I'm going to FedEx you a set of papers. I need you to process them for prints – and here's the important part – I need you to figure out a way to feed them into IAFIS. I can't do it here – long story – but I'm hoping you can. Last time we talked, you mentioned that the feds had provided access to IAFIS's biometric data to test out the system on your end. Maybe you can use this as test data, I don't know. Call me and we'll talk. I lost my cell phone, so call me at home.'

She thought about adding *I miss you* and, instead, said, 'Charlie Rizzo, that kid from Brookline who disappeared a decade ago? I met him, Coop. He's been alive all this time, and I need to find out why. What happened to him.'

Darby hung up then grabbed the mouse and clicked the icon for the date and time. A clock and calendar opened: today was the 18th. She had been called to New Hampshire on the night of the 9th. She'd been locked up in that quarantine chamber for *nine* days. Nine days without showing any symptoms and they had kept her locked up and drugged.

Why?

She clicked on the Internet Explorer icon, relieved to discover she could access the web. At least they hadn't blocked that out.

She headed over to Google news. In the search box she typed 'Mark Rizzo' and 'New Hampshire'. A lot of links came back. She started with the first and most recent one, and it brought her to the website for New Hampshire's Portsmouth *Herald*. The article was only a couple of paragraphs long. She read through it quickly, then went back to the main page and clicked on the link for the *Boston Globe*. Read that article and then read two more before stopping. Each newspaper was spouting the bullshit about Mark Rizzo and his family being killed in a drug deal gone bad.

Deborah Collier, a special agent from the FBI's Boston office and acting spokesman for the Durham and Portsmouth police departments, had told reporters that Mark Rizzo, an accountant who had recently been laid off from a local NH firm, had turned to the lucrative world of methamphetamine manufacturing. Forensic agents from both the FBI and ATF reported finding traces of the highly addictive street drug on several debris samples recovered from the explosion. Special Agent Collier said that the remains of a fifth person recovered from the blast site had been identified through DNA analysis as belonging to Alex Scala, a 43-year-old meth user and distributor known to the FBI. Collier didn't have much information about Scala other than that the man's last known residence was in Dorchester, Massachusetts.

The explosion that caused the deaths of seven New Hampshire SWAT agents and five police officers, all unnamed, had been attributed to the release of phosphine, a deadly gas that can be emitted during methamphetamine production. Several local residents, all unnamed, had been treated at hospital and subsequently released.

None of the articles mentioned the 911 call placed by a man claiming to be Charlie Rizzo (although the *Boston Globe* article had briefly mentioned the boy's abduction in 1984, when the family lived in Brookline, Massachusetts). No mention of the unidentified man Charlie had shot and dumped in the bushes. No mention of the ambulance that had gone missing. And the *coup de grace*: not a single mention of the army's interest or involvement in the case.

With no new information released about the explosion, New England reporters had turned to churning out stories about 'the new and explosive growth' of homemade meth labs that were popping up all across the country in houses, apartments and mobile homes.

It was a great spin job – a *brilliant* spin job. The FBI spokesman had cleverly explained the explosion. Stories about methamphetamine were everywhere these days. The drug was cheap and easy to manufacture, provided the person knew what he was doing. More often than not, the labs were assembled by some meth-head who didn't have the first clue as to how to properly store highly unstable chemicals like anhydrous ammonia. If that didn't explode, they'd spill or mishandle some other volatile chemical and *boom*, the police had to wait for the deadly phosphine gas to dissipate before heading out to search for body parts.

The spin job had worked. The Rizzo story had been confined to New Hampshire and neighbouring Massachusetts. The surrounding states had their own problems to report about, along with terrifying the public with article after article on the swine flu pandemic that, if the quoted experts were to be believed, would turn the entire country into the same kind of apocalyptic landscape Stephen King had written about in *The Stand*.

Darby imagined Special Agent Collier and her PR cohorts standing inside her office. Imagined lots of back-slapping and self-congratulations for launching yet another successful spin that had pulled the wool over the public's eyes. *She probably corked a bottle of champagne for this one.*

Why had the truth been swept under the rug? Was it because sarin gas had been used? If that titbit of information had been made known, New Hampshire hotels would be doing brisk business trying to accommodate the swelling numbers of media outlets coming in from across the country to get the inside scoop on a chemical attack on US soil – the first, Darby suspected.

The real inside scoop, though, wasn't the sarin gas but what had happened inside the Rizzo home. Imagine if that story broke. *Ladies and gentlemen, we've received confirmation that the Rizzo family was held hostage by a man claiming to be their son, Charles, who disappeared without a trace twelve years ago. The only person who lived to see these horrific events transpire is*

Dr Darby McCormick, a former investigator for Boston's Criminal Services Unit.

Which, Darby suspected, was the reason why she'd been locked inside the quarantine chamber; the feds needed some time to work their spin job and feed it to the media. Nine days later, after she put up a fight, they agreed to release their only eyewitness, provided she signed a thick stack of legal forms that prevented her from speaking to anyone. She was the wild card, the only one who could derail the spin campaign.

And Charlie's 911 call, what had become of it? All 911 calls were recorded and copies were often made public. Not Charlie's. *The feds must have confiscated it.* The audio and video recordings from inside the mobile command centre – had those too been confiscated? She'd have to find someone in New Hampshire who would be willing to speak to her off the record.

Heading back to Google, she typed in the tattooed words she'd seen on that thing's neck. The phrase *Et in Arcadia ego* came back with pages and pages of hits. Most of the info underneath the links referred to a pair of paintings by a French classical artist named Nicolas Poussin. She clicked on one and found that the Frenchman, born in 1594, had created two highly influential pastoral landscapes in which shepherds come upon a tomb. The more famous of the two versions hung in the Louvre in Paris. According to several scholars, the tomb housed God.

Darby was more interested in the meaning of the actual words. There were more links, more pages and pages of information, some of it quite detailed.

She checked her watch. Fifteen minutes until the last FedEx pickup of the night. She shut down her computer and grabbed one of the flat FedEx mailers on her way out the door.

28

Darby emerged from the police station and managed to hail an empty taxi on Tremont Street. She hopped in the back seat, checked her watch and told the driver to take her to the Boston Garden. Then she remembered it wasn't called that any more. Fleet Center or TD Bankgarden North, she forgot which and didn't care. For her it would always be the Boston Garden, not the name of some bank which had paid for naming rights.

Twenty minutes later, when she reached Causeway Street, traffic slowed to a crawl, then came to a jarring stop, just as she suspected.

'Celtics game is over,' the driver said. 'We could be here a while.'

'They win?'

'By two. My boy Pierce dropped a three with ten seconds left.'

'They'll need to get Garnett and Wallace off the DL if they're going to go through to the playoffs.'

'True that.'

She handed the driver a ten, told him to keep the change and got out.

Darby took her time walking. She didn't bother trying to spot her tail. She had the tracking device in her jeans pocket, so they could afford to hang back and watch from a safe distance.

People were pouring out of the Garden, flooding the streets and packing the sidewalks. She slid her way through the bodies, taking her time as she made her way to Staniford Street, which would take her right back to the top of Cambridge. Once she'd crossed that, she'd be on Temple. She wanted the people tailing her to think she was heading home.

She slid the tracking device from her pocket, about to toss it on the ground, when a new thought occurred to her: use the tracking device to draw them out. She had no idea how many were watching her right now, but she needed to capture only one – so that he could tell her what had happened to Mark Rizzo.

Instead of making for home, she turned right and ducked on to William Cardinal O'Connell Way, the street named after the Archbishop of Boston who, at one time, had urged his priests not to give Communion to women wearing lipstick. Darby knew the deceased prelate by his more recent headline-grabbing accomplishment: he'd been one of the high-ranking clergymen who had helped shift well-known child-molesting priests to other Boston parishes.

The parking garage had a back entrance for those who paid for monthly spots. Darby unlocked the door and then took the stairs to the ground floor.

Her last car, a vintage forest-green Ford '74 Falcon GT Coupe in pristine condition that Steve McQueen would have been proud to own, had been stolen by one of Christina Chadzynski's henchmen on the night she'd been abducted from Coop's house and taken to the abandoned auto garage to be killed. With the car most likely dumped at the bottom of some river or quarry, and the insurance company's auditors haggling about the car's *actual* cost and not its *perceived* cost, Darby decided to make do with a beautiful, old-school motorcycle: a black 1982 Yamaha Virago 750. It had been well cared for by the previous owner, and she changed only one thing: the drag bars, preferring ones a little bit lower for a more comfortable ride.

The parking spot offered a decent light, but she removed her flashlight and began a thorough inspection of her bike. It didn't take long. She found the tracking device mounted underneath the hugger, secured to the steel by a tiny adhesive Velcro strip. At least the person who did this had taken the time to spray-paint it black so it would blend in with the paintjob.

She left the device where it was, then put on her helmet and hopped on her bike.

Darby hooked a sharp right and turned on to Moon Island Road, the mile-long stretch of causeway that ran over Quincy Bay and led to the 45-acre island sitting smack dab in the middle of Boston Harbor. As she drove she could make out, in the distance, the dark silhouettes of boats rocking lazily on the calm water. The road was pitch black, and the only source of light came from the single lamp set up on the desk inside the security guard shack.

She stopped in front of the gate and, leaning her foot off the bike, followed the protocol: took off her helmet so the guard and the single security camera mounted above his sliding glass window could see her face; unzipped her jacket, picked up the laminated badge hanging around her neck, held it up to the camera and then showed it to the guard.

He ducked his head back inside his shack and entered her name into the computer to see if she was authorized to enter. She doubted she'd be turned away. During her suspension, she had logged a lot of time at the shooting range and practised SWAT exercises during odd hours of the night without a problem or complaint – unless Leland had decided sometime during the day to call here and get her privileges revoked.

He hadn't. The gate lifted, and Darby drove a few feet along a stretch of dark road. She stopped, parked her bike and left her helmet on the seat. From the small trunk she removed a pair of field glasses and jogged back through the dark to the gated security post.

She found a spot and, leaning back against a tree, checked her watch and recorded the time. Then she watched the causeway through her field glasses. There was no light source down there, but her eyes had adjusted to the darkness and she could make out the road, the shape of the trees. She would be able to see movement.

When it came to counter-surveillance, the first law was never to assume anything. If the people following her were from out of town and didn't know this area, there was a chance her tail might make the mistake of trying to drive across the causeway. The posted no-trespassing signs were visible only *after* you turned on to the road.

She kept track of the time, counting the seconds off in her head. Four minutes and twenty-two seconds later, a car turned slowly on to the causeway.

29

Darby zoomed on the car, which had come to an abrupt stop.

Must have seen the signs, she thought, catching sight of the BMW hood ornament as the car backed up. It was black or a dark blue, and the tinted windows prevented her from seeing whoever was inside the car.

She watched as the BMW drove down Border Street and slowly turned right into Bayside Road. *They look for a place to wait, then follow me after I leave.* The red brake lights glowed on the dark road and then the car took another slow turn into Monmouth. The BMW's head-lights went out but she could still see it, watching as it did a three-point turn. It came to a stop in front of a house near the end of the street, and looked like just another ordinary parked car. That spot offered a clear, unobstructed view of the causeway, the only way off Moon Island.

A moment later she saw a white glow coming from inside the BMW. *Too bright to be the light from a cell phone screen*, she thought. A laptop, maybe.

Darby walked back to her bike. She started it up and drove through the dark stretch of road that led to the shooting range. The floodlights were on, illuminating the grassy, empty field. There were no lights on inside the small one-floor building where she housed most of her tactical equipment. She parked her bike and took her keys with her to access the building.

From her locker she grabbed the spare sidearm she had recently purchased at the urging of her SWAT instructor: an MK23 SOCOM, the same tactical sidearm commissioned by the United States Special Operations Command. The .45 calibre pistol had a great sound and flash suppressor, but what had impressed her most was its high accuracy – even without the use of its laser-aiming module.

Next, she grabbed the spare nylon shoulder holster she used for SWAT exercises. She slipped it on and adjusted the straps, tightening them to the point of being uncomfortable. The MK23 wasn't much good as a concealed weapon, especially with this snug jacket. She zipped it up and could see and feel the handgun bulging against the leather. She could live with it for now. She could have used a smaller handgun but it wouldn't have the MK's one-shot stopping power. She needed that for the moment when one or more of her new friends decided to make a move and try to get close to her.

Now, the final item: the duffel bag. She couldn't carry it with her, and she could only fit two or three pieces of tactical equipment inside the motorcycle's small trunk box.

She placed the duffel bag on the bench. Unzipped it, removed each item and placed it on the long piece of wood. Hands crossed over her chest, she stood over the bench examining each item, thinking about a strategy.

The person or persons sitting inside the BMW had to

have brought others. She didn't know this for a fact but it would be a smart tactical move to do so. These people might just want to follow her for a while, but at some point they would want either to grab her or to take her down.

Darby stood in the locker room's cool and musty silence, thinking. She had all night, could stand here for as long as she wanted. And she wanted to make them wait. Let them sit there and wonder what the hell she was doing. They didn't have the answers, but they would keep turning the question over and over in their minds, and it would make them anxious. Nervous. They might decide to do a rush job, which would cause a tactical mistake.

Before leaving Moon Island, she used the computer at the front desk to log on to the Internet and map out the quickest route to the Rizzo home – the blast site.

30

Darby reached the highway and pushed the bike past eighty, weaving across the four lanes and keeping a close eye on both rear-view mirrors, on the alert for the BMW or any vehicle that decided to get too close. If these people wanted to take her out, this would be the time to do it. Driving across a dark highway virtually free of traffic, they could easily knock her off her bike. One good push and she'd lose control and be bouncing and skidding across the pavement. By the time she came to a stop she'd be a mess of broken bones, unable to get up or move – and unconscious, if she got lucky. That was the best-case scenario.

Forty minutes later, Darby reached the Portsmouth exit. Her new friends had decided to keep a safe distance – at least for the moment. Maybe they wanted to see why she'd decided to head to New Hampshire. Hopefully they'd hang back. Her plan depended on it.

Downtown Portsmouth hummed with activity. People bundled in coats walked along sidewalks lined with green store-front canopies. They entered and exited bars. They examined the restaurant menus displayed in glass windows and doors. Too many witnesses here for her friends inside the BMW to try anything.

Three miles later the neighbourhoods grew quiet. Ten miles later, coming up on the spot where the APC had first dropped her off, the streets grew dark and then pitch black. Another mile or so and she came to the spot where the mobile command trailer had been parked. It was gone now, but in the bike's single headlight beam she found a wide and deep tyre impression in the soft dirt. Saw the deep grooves the tyre had left as it was moved off the soft dirt shoulder and hauled away. She drove up the road, the same route she had taken while standing on the back of the APC.

Up ahead she saw police tape hanging over the street, strips and strips of it creating a flimsy yellow barrier that shook in the wind. She looked to her right, at the house where Trent had placed the sniper and spotter. The explosion hadn't knocked the house off its foundations, but it had torn off most of the front, exposing upended furniture inside the rooms that were visible.

When she reached the police tape, she kicked the heel of her boot to release the kickstand. She took off her helmet and breathed in the cool air still carrying the faint odour of charred wood.

A big steel dumpster, the kind used on construction-job sites, had been set up just beyond the tape and blocked access to the street. She spotted another one further down the road. The street was bare, clean. During the time she spent quarantined, the debris had been cleared away. And whatever had remained of the Rizzo home had been bull-dozed. Nothing left but a black hole in the ground, a few dumpsters and a collection of burned trees, mostly pines, neatly stacked and awaiting removal.

The entire perimeter of the blast site had been cordoned

off by police tape, so why wasn't there a cruiser parked here? In Boston, it was standard procedure to keep watch on a blast site to make sure no photographer, reporter or local yahoo ended up tripping on the debris and bumping their head, only to turn around and launch a multimillion-dollar lawsuit against the city for negligence. It had happened too many times in Boston, and they all had been settled out of court with taxpayer dollars. Maybe the Dover police had a different policy. Maybe this place was so remote they didn't have to worry about someone stumbling along and getting hurt. Or maybe, like every other law enforcement agency, they'd been hit by budget cuts and forced to do without things like patrolling a blast site where there was nothing left to see. Darby killed the engine. The headlight went off and she was plunged into a near pitch-black darkness. No stars out tonight, no moon. A soft but biting cold wind rattled through the trees and shook the branches as she took what she needed out of the trunk box. All her pockets were stuffed, so she had to carry the night-vision goggles and tactical belt. She ducked underneath the tape, estimating that the BMW was about five minutes behind her. She had to find a vantage point.

During her drive, she had thought about using the house across the street. The roof would offer the best tactical advantage. First problem: how to access it. She couldn't rely on finding something like a ladder in the garage, and searching for one would eat up too much time. Using one might arouse suspicions. She couldn't use a flashlight either: someone might see it. And now that she had viewed the condition of the house, she knew she couldn't stumble around dark rooms, kicking and tripping over debris – making all sorts of sounds as she searched for a way to access the roof.

The second, and more important, problem was her choice of weapon. The MK handgun tucked in her shoulder holster was an excellent close-quarters combat weapon, but it lacked the long-distance accuracy of a scoped sniper rifle. So she had scratched the roof. And the trees: a good watching point, but, again, the problem was a matter of shooting accuracy. Plus, she'd have to climb high to find decent cover. If they spotted her, she'd be a sitting duck. With no room for her to manoeuvre, it would be like shooting fish in a barrel.

That left ground cover, either a spot in the woods or one of the three dumpsters set up near the blast site, which was where she wanted to draw the occupants of the BMW. They might decide to come in for a closer look. They might decide to pounce. Either way, she'd be ready.

Her eyes had adjusted to the darkness, and when she reached the edge of the crater, she looked down and found a basement of broken walls half buried by debris and dirt. She removed the tracking device from her pocket and tossed it into the wide hole, hearing a *plink* as it bounced off a piece of metal.

Now she had to find a dumpster.

Three here, but the one parked at the end of the driveway fifty feet or so away from the crater offered a good view of both the blast site and the woods. She jogged to the side, grabbed the edge and hopped up on the dumpster's small ledge. Looking inside, she found it almost full.

Lots of charred and splintered wood. Burned furniture and clothes. Perfect.

She looped the tactical belt around her shoulder. The straps for the night-vision goggles were sewn into a black wool cap. She put the cap on, leaving the goggles off her eyes for the moment, then unzipped her jacket and climbed into the dumpster. She scooped up all the dark-coloured clothing she could find, then discarded them when she hit the jackpot: a set of burned sheets and a comforter.

Wood and whatever else was beneath her palms and knees creaked and moaned as she crawled to the edge of the dumpster. Working quickly and methodically, she cleared some of the debris away, mostly wood, until she had enough room to lie down. She stopped working and examined the space. Good enough. She transferred the tactical belt to a spot where it could be accessed easily. From her jacket pocket she removed a silencer and placed it, along with her handgun, on the lip of the dumpster. Darby rolled sideways into the small space and covered herself with the bedding, making sure she had enough of the comforter left to wrap around her head. Now the final part: transferring the splintered and shattered boards and other assorted debris on top of her body.

Covered, she did a slow roll on to her stomach and kept her weight propped up on her forearms. Grabbed the MK, threaded the silencer and then wrapped the burned edge of the smoke-smelling comforter around her head. She put all of her weight down on her stomach. A few hard edges poked her legs, and her ribs, still in the process of healing, groaned in protest. Discomfort but not pain; she would manage.

The split and shattered ends sticking up from the edge added additional cover. She flipped the night-vision goggles down on her eyes. The ambient green light parted the darkness. She could see the street and every inch of the surrounding woods. She reached for the handgun, gripped it in her hand and waited.

The cold air remained silent except for the occasional stirring of the tree branches from the wind. Quiet, remote and dark, this place was the perfect spot for them to make a run at her. If they didn't do it tonight, they would sometime soon. The sole survivor, they believed she had seen and heard too much – that could be the only reason why they were following her.

She thought about numbers. The BMW driver would have brought along help. She needed only one alive; figure out who the leader was, then make a plan to take down the others as fast as possible. Take the survivor and make him talk about Mark Rizzo.

It was also possible she'd be forced to put them *all* down, as a matter of survival. *Maybe take them all out at once*, she thought. *More bodies, more evidence, more avenues to explore.*

The wind stirred the trees again. Something shattered and fell.

The sound came from across the street.

She couldn't turn and see the house. Had the wind caused that?

She waited and heard nothing.

Had to be the wind, she thought, and went back to waiting.

Sometime later, in the distance, she heard the crawl of car tyres crunching against the road. The sound came from the east, somewhere past the woods.

Using her thumb, she clicked off the safety.

The tyres stopped moving. She could make out the sound of an idling engine. A moment later, it stopped.

Darby waited, listening and watching.

Here they come.

Darby counted three men – at least she assumed they were men, given their height and clothing – standing stock still, like mannequins, on the northern edge of the woods. The threesome stared into the woods as if waiting for something to happen.

Or waiting for the word to move ahead, she thought.

Had they already sent someone in as a spotter? Maybe a small group who were making their way to her right now?

Hidden underneath the blanket and debris, Darby slowly moved her head to the right, past the group, to do a visual sweep of the woods and the road. She moved her head as far as she could.

No other people in the woods or on the road, and she couldn't see any vehicles. The trio could have been dropped off and the vehicles parked somewhere east or south of the dumpster. No way to check unless she stood up.

Now a slow turn back to the threesome.

Still standing, still waiting.

She moved her head to the left, doing a slow, methodical visual sweep of the woods while keeping track of the road. It curved around the woods and then turned on to the main street. The only thing she saw was her bike parked a few feet beyond the fluttering yellow strips of police tape. If a spotter or spotters had been sent into the woods, they were well hidden. She couldn't see *or* hear them.

Back to the threesome. No change.

What the hell are they waiting for?

Darby took in a slow, deep breath, smelling the charred wood as her left hand reached up and grabbed the lens control for the monocular tube. She turned the knob slowly, zooming in on the tall person standing in front of the others. Boots, dark trousers and a dark hooded sweatshirt.

She zoomed on the face next, waited for the lens to focus.

The person's face – his true face – was covered behind the same stitched mask of leathery flesh she had seen on Charlie Rizzo. The lip of the sweatshirt's hood covered part of the forehead but not the eyes. They seemed to be staring directly at her, and she could see his lips moving. Speaking.

Darby adjusted the lens to see this person's two companions.

They hadn't moved. They stood slightly behind him, staring and waiting. Looking back to the face, Darby saw, hovering near his right cheek, what looked like the microphone end of an earpiece.

Probably one of those wireless headsets that allow the person to speak over a cell phone, she thought. You used it to keep your hands free, to keep your attention focused on a task. *Is he listening to someone? Or is he the one giving orders?* If he was giving orders, then some –

Blurred movement flashed in front of the lens.

Someone had stepped into her line of vision.

Darby didn't move, remained absolutely still.

The lens control was still pinched between her fingers. She turned it slowly, not making a sound, and zoomed back to the blast site to get a closer look at who or what had dashed in front of her.

A bald man with a severely scarred head was crouched on the ground, his toes hugging the edge of the crater as he looked down into the dirt where she'd thrown the tracking device. Clutched in the deformed fingers of one hand and held high in the air was an odd-shaped billy club.

A spring clicked free and the club turned into a telescopic baton with metal plates crackling with electricity.

A telescopic stun baton. They hadn't come here to kill her. They wanted to capture her. Alive.

The man, realizing she wasn't inside the crater, looked up and around the area. His face had also been horribly scarred, possibly from a burn; the thick, twisted dark meat along one cheek had, after it healed, contracted and pulled back the lips into a permanent sneer, exposing crooked and blackened teeth. His right eye darted back and forth, but the left, a sightless white orb, didn't move.

Ghoul. That was the first word that flashed through her mind. A ghoul dressed in modern clothing – dark baggy sweatpants and a half-zipped sweatshirt that revealed a scarred chest with skin stretched tightly across knobs of deformed bone, like Charlie Rizzo's. She saw the skin stretching across the ribs as the ghoul breathed, wheezing plumes of air that evaporated in the cold night.

The ghoul – she didn't know what else to call it – jumped into the crater as scattering sounds came from the woods. She looked towards the northern edge of the woods and saw the trio still standing there, watching and waiting.

They sent this thing in to knock me out and then drag me away.

To where? The same place where Mark Rizzo was being held?

Smashing sounds and then a howl of pain roared from inside the basement.

Two more figures had moved to the edge of the crater.

Like the ghoul rooting around in the scorched dirt, this bone-thin pair were dressed in ratty clothing and had shaved heads and scars. They both held telescopic stun batons. One of the pair was crouched low to the ground, looking around the woods and street like a hunter.

Not looking, she thought. *Guarding*. The other stood ramrod straight, its back facing her. She could see the tattoo on its neck: *Et in Arcadia ego*. Even in Arcadia, Death exists.

The thing turned, sniffing the air in front of her.

Darby clutched the MK23. If this thing came at her – if it discovered her – she'd put it down with a headshot, then turn to the other two in the crater before dealing with –

Snapping sounds and then she saw the ghoul scurrying up from the basement. The thing's face was darkened by soot and dirt, and she saw a bright red gash on the side of its head. Its mouth opened as it looked up to the singed tree branches.

'*Ka-kah! Ka-kah!*'

Silence. The three ghouls had turned stock still, waiting.

Incredibly, she saw the end of a small, wireless earpiece protruding from the ear canal of the one standing closest to her.

Take them down, she thought. *Take them down now.*

The three ghouls scattered into the woods, running like wild dogs, snapping twigs and whisking past branches as they headed towards the northern end, where the other three stood waiting.

In the distance she heard a car starting. Next came the sound of a climbing car engine. It grew louder and then she saw a vehicle pull on to the road – a dark van. It came to a sharp stop and the doors slid open, then the deformed things rushed inside.

Two of the watchers from the woods followed, but not the tall one. He stayed where he was, looking, Darby thought, straight at her.

32

Darby saw him coming her way. Saw him take big, wide steps and turn his head in the direction of her bike, then look back at her.

He knows I'm hiding here in the dumpster, she thought.

The man broke into a jog. *Why is he coming in here alone? Why didn't he bring along the other freaks?*

He unzipped his sweatshirt. He reached inside and took out a handgun.

She measured the distance. Too far away to get off a clean shot. Too many trees in the way. She'd have to wait until he got closer. A few more steps and he'd be standing near the clearing. If he didn't stand down, she'd have to put him down with a shot to the thigh, maybe go for the upper-right section of his chest, away from his heart.

She looked down the MK's target sight as a bright, narrow beam of light appeared and started to move near the edge of the crater – a tactical light mounted underneath the barrel of a 9mm.

Glass shattered in the distance.

Darby didn't move or react, her gaze cutting to the direction of the sound. It had come from somewhere to her left. What was there? The other house. The one where the sniper had set up that night, the one that had been damaged by the explosion.

The man had heard it too. He stopped and was staring in the same direction. Staring and maybe wondering if the wind blowing through the big blast holes in the house had knocked something off a wall or table. Wondering, maybe, if she had brought someone with her. If he had been set up.

He shut off his tactical light. Turned back to the waiting van, took a step forward, then stopped again and glanced over his shoulder, looking back at her. Stared like he was about to come back.

No. He had decided to go back to the van. She watched him running through the woods, then across the street, and he entered the van's side door, which slammed shut behind him. The cool night air filled with the sound of tyres squealing, the rubber biting against the road as the van sped away, the sound growing dimmer until it died.

Darby lay there, heart drumming hard against her aching ribs, and she breathed in soot and ashes and the stench of charred wood. Thinking: *What in God's name did I just see?*

Ghouls, she thought. Bogeymen. Creatures that lived underneath the ground and came out only at night. Monsters that had come to capture her. At the last moment the wind had saved her. The wind blowing through the trees right now, shaking the branches and leaves, had knocked something fragile off a wall or worktop in the neighbouring house and it had shattered against the floor and scared off the lead bogeyman.

Had they really left? Or had they parked somewhere to wait? To watch the computer tracking her listening devices to see where she was going to go next? Maybe try and make another run at her?

Darby checked her watch. A few minutes past midnight. The Witching Hour. How appropriate.

She decided to wait for a bit to see if they'd come back. She used the time to plan.

She couldn't go back to her condo. It was bugged, for one, and it was possible these people she'd just seen had at least one person watching her building, waiting for her to return. The FBI too. The men she'd seen parked at the end of her street – she felt pretty sure they were feds. She needed a place to stay. That left her with only one option: a hotel.

Problem: hotels asked for IDs and a credit card. She didn't want that information in their computer systems. Someone with access to the right database could track her credit card. She needed to find a place that would allow her to register under an alias.

Her thoughts ran to Coop. He had a friend who was a manager for a Boston timeshare in McKinley Square called the Custom House. Sean Something. Grew up in Charlestown with Coop at a time when the small town was full of Irish gangsters and shady cops. They had all watched out for each other and she felt sure this guy Sean would watch out for her if she asked, bend the rules and allow her to register under an alias.

She also needed someone who could help her delve deeper into the significance of the Latin phrase tattooed on these creatures' necks. Harvard had a Divinity School. Latin and religious scholars. She made a mental note and checked the time. Quarter to one. Daylight would come in another four hours.

Darby turned her attention back to the woods, back to listening and watching.

Another hour had passed, and she had heard and seen nothing.

She decided to get moving.

Standing, pieces of wood and other bits of debris banged and clattered softly as they fell back into the dumpster. She pulled off the comforter and sheets, brushed off her jacket and, tactical belt in hand, hopped off and jogged back to her bike. She hung the belt across the seat and then went to the back to root around inside the small trunk.

She didn't have an evidence bag back there, but she did have a makeshift First-Aid kit with a small Band-Aid box. She took it with her on her way back to the crater.

Turning on her flashlight, she slowly ran the beam across the debris.

There. A smear of fresh blood on one of the walls. The ghoulish thing had cut its head and left blood.

Carefully she made her way down. She collected the blood sample using a piece of gauze and tucked it inside the box.

Climbing back out with her prize, Darby reminded herself to remove the Velcro-mounted tracking device they'd stuck on her bike before she drove away.

33

Considering that she was going to a place that housed life-threatening bacteria and viruses, Darby expected to find a huge building cordoned off by security gates, maybe armed guards roaming the perimeter or posted near or just behind the front doors. But the BU Biomedical Lab had been designed so it would blend in with the rest of the South End neighbourhood. Made entirely of brick, it sat on a corner of Albany, just another bland, non-descript building among the other industrial-type complexes that ran printing presses and offered legal services. Two exceptions: no sign or lettering advertising what the building was; and no windows on either the ground or first floors. Plenty of windows on floors two through six, some of them lit.

The stretches of kerb in the front and to the right of the building were bare of vehicles. Could be the hour; it was twenty minutes shy of 5:00 a.m., the sky beginning to break with a milky-grey, pre-dawn gloom. Most of Albany had plenty of available parking spaces. Darby drove to the front, flipped up the helmet's visor and found posted signs that prohibited parking. Violators would be immediately asked to move or risk being arrested. To enforce the threat, a pair of highly visible security cameras had been mounted above the front doors. One swept the street in front while the other watched the corner.

She suspected there were more cameras watching the perimeters. Given what was stored in there, the cameras had to have manual operators. There would be a security room where either rent-a-cops or army guys watched the streets day and night.

Darby took a right and drove around the corner. This side of the building had nothing but brick. No windows or doors. Security cameras observed the street. One whisked past her and, instead of completing its rotation, turned back to her. She drove to the end of the road, hooked another right and then stopped to look at the back. She saw a big steel door for a parking garage.

She drove to the next block, turned right again and again saw that the building's last side was exactly like the others, a fortress of brick.

A white, middle-aged man stood on the main street's corner sidewalk, smiling pleasantly and waving for her to come closer.

Security, she thought. She pulled up against the kerb and saw that this guy wasn't a hired hand from some rinky-dink security outfit. He made good money, and he had made a significant investment in his clothes: a simple dark suit with a notch lapel; a light blue shirt with a semi-spread collar that flattered his silver hair and complexion; and a dark, solid aubergine-coloured tie with a perfect four-in-hand knot. He looked like a news anchor ready for primetime.

She killed the engine.

'Good morning, Miss McCormick.' A soft, Southern accent. *Texas*, she thought. 'I'm Neal Keats, head of security.'

He extended his hand.

She left it hanging there. He withdrew it and said, 'Follow me inside. You can leave your bike here.'

'This is a tow-zone.'

'Only if we make the call. Besides, you won't be gone long. This will take only a moment.'

'What will take a moment?'

'You're here to get some of your questions answered, correct?'

'So is Sergeant-Major Glick finally available?'

'I'm afraid he's still detained, as is Mr Fitzgerald. But we have someone who is willing to talk to you.'

He smiled. He had invested a lot of money in his teeth. Perfect white caps. She didn't care for his greasy politician's smile or his calm voice and demeanour.

'Shall we head in?'

'Yes,' Darby said, matching his smile. 'We shall.'

Neal Keats, ever the Southern gentleman, held open the front door for her. She opened the second door herself and stepped into a bland-looking lobby with bare white walls and a tan linoleum floor. Dimmed halogen ceiling lights hung over an empty front desk made of light blonde oak and constructed in a podium-like fashion similar to the one in the Boston Police Department's lobby.

Standing to the right of the hall were two white men dressed in black suits. Big guys with thick necks and wrists and bodies like linebackers'. The sort of men you imagined could run through brick walls. The sort of men you wanted around for protection. Both stood with their hands behind their back, serious 'don't screw with us' expressions etched on their weathered faces. Their buttoned-up suit jackets had been taken out to accommodate their wide chests and broad shoulders. She didn't detect a bulge along their hips. If they were armed, they were wearing shoulder holsters.

Keats whisked past her. The two men didn't move. She followed Keats, and when she passed the two suits, they fell into step behind her.

It was a short walk. Keats stopped in front of an open white door and motioned for her to go in first. She did, entering a long, wide room strategically designed to hold the bulky security consoles and other surveillance and monitoring equipment. Banks of security consoles with dozens and dozens of closed-circuit TV screens trained on the building's perimeters and on the halls inside the lab took up the entire front wall. Everywhere she looked she saw glowing screens and flashing lights.

The crew manning the stations, a collection of men of various ages, all wearing shirt and tie, didn't turn to look at her. The small office to her immediate left — LAN MANAGEMENT, according to the plate hanging on the door – was empty.

'This way, Miss McCormick.'

She turned and saw Keats standing off to her right, motioning to another doorway, this one leading into a small, cluttered office with pressboard furniture. He let her go in first, then followed and pointed to a pair of cheap plastic chairs set up in front of a desk. He moved behind it but didn't sit.

'Please, have a seat.'

He waited for her to sit. Then he did and picked up the desk phone. A single light blinked on the unit. He pressed a button and the light stopped blinking.

Keats handed the phone to her.

34

Darby took the phone and said, 'With whom am I speaking?'

'Are you with Mr Keats right now?'

The voice on the other end of the line belonged to Leland Pratt. Even at this early morning hour, his voice sounded crystal clear. At the moment he was doing a good job of containing his anger, but it was there, waiting to explode.

'Darby?'

She didn't answer, too interested in Keats. He sat with his hands folded on his lap, staring at her from across the wide, messy desk. That greasy smile of his had disappeared, but he was obviously enjoying the show he had just arranged. His eyes were dangerously bright, as if he were containing himself, waiting for someone to give him the order to pounce.

'Yesterday evening, the United States Army came to my home and personally delivered copies of documents that you signed,' Leland said. 'Do you know the documents I'm referring to?'

'I do. Have you looked through them?'

'I have. The question is, have *you*?'

'Anything missing?'

'Darby, *if* you value *any* sort of career opportunity in law enforcement, I suggest you go with the two men Mr Keats has there with him. They'll escort you back to your home. Shower and dress in your Sunday best, understand? We have an early-morning meeting with Robert Chambers, the interim police commissioner.'

'What's the occasion?'

'You know full well what he wants to discuss with you.'

'The conditions of my re-employment or this business that took place in New Hampshire? Which is it?'

'I don't think you fully see the implications of your current situation,' he said, straining to remain calm.

She stood.

'And I'm through negotiating with you,' Leland said. 'If you choose not to work for me, that is, of course, your decision. But if you want –'

Darby pulled the phone away from her ear and, with her eyes on Keats, reached across the desk to hang it up. She walked around to the other side of the desk and sat on the edge, close to Keats, her legs touching his thigh.

She crossed her arms over her chest. 'How long have you been with the Secret Service?'

'Excuse me?'

She had to hand it to the guy: he had a great poker face. No look of surprise, he just cocked his head to the side, actually looking confused.

'The small hole in the left lapel of your suit jacket,' she said. 'You and the two linebackers guarding the doorway so nobody will disturb us? You all have the same small hole in the same spot. That's where you guys wear your SS high-level clearance pin or the other one when you're on protection detail, to let everyone know you're Secret Service.'

Keats chuckled, shaking his head. 'You have quite an imagination.'

'I don't think you're protecting me. If you were, you would have been a lot smoother than the two bozos parked at the end of my street. My guess is you're using me, watching me to see if I can draw these guys out.'

'What guys?'

'The ones who blew up the Rizzo house with dynamite,' she said. 'The ones I met tonight at the blast site.'

Keats's poker face didn't change. She let him chew on the silence, hoping he'd take the bait.

'I'm the head of security here, Miss McCormick. Sorry to disappoint you.'

'Okay, I'll play along. Who arranged the phone call with my former boss?'

'Sergeant-Major Glick. I'm just following his orders.'

'So let me talk to him.'

'He's unavailable.'

'When will he be available?'

'I wouldn't know. Maybe you should call his secretary.'

'Okay, let's head up to his office. I know it's early, but I don't mind waiting. Now that I'm unemployed, I can wait all day.'

'Let me ask you a question. What's your stake in all of this? Why not take your old job back?'

Because I know you're just another lying federal asshole. Because I know you're not looking for Mark Rizzo. Because I made a promise to the kid who had been abducted and turned into some sort of goddamn circus freak.

Darby didn't answer.

'Well,' he said, slapping his knees. 'My job here is done. Nice meeting you, Miss McCormick.'

He started to get up. Darby put a hand on his shoulder and pushed him back into his chair.

Out of the corner of her eye she saw one of the linebackers move to the office doorway.

'Prove me wrong,' she said to Keats.

'About what?'

'That you're not Secret Service. Empty out all of your pockets and let me see what you're carrying.'

Keats stared at her. Hard.

'Let's check out your wrists,' she said, 'see if we can find a microphone.'

She reached forward and clutched his left wrist, about to turn it around when Keats grabbed her forearm. The fabric of his suit jacket had moved and she caught the wink of the butt-end of a gun sitting inside a shoulder holster.

'I've been a gentleman up until now,' he said. 'But you're invading my personal space.'

'Get used to it.' Darby let go her grip and stood. 'I'll let myself out. I'll be seeing you around, I'm sure.'

35

Mark Rizzo had learned, years and years ago, to make peace with the darkness. As a child, he had discovered that all it did was amplify emotions, mainly fear. And pain. His father had been a man of little patience and a quick temper. Anything from a spilled glass of milk to a bad report card could set him off.

His father preferred the belt. Liked the ritual of it. He would stand – slowly, always slowly – and once on his feet he'd unbuckle it and then just as slowly pull the thick leather through the loops of his paint-stained jeans. Once it was free, he'd wrap an end around his big, meaty, callused fist. Usually, but not always, he'd just sit back in his seat and wait, sometimes an hour, sometimes a couple of days. Mark remembered when he'd been caught throwing a rock at a pigeon sitting on the garage roof for no reason other than he had hated the sight of it. The rock had broken a window and his father had waited a whole *month* to dish out the punishment, and that time he had worked the buckle into the mix.

And his father would always do it in the dark, always. The thing about the dark was that he couldn't see the strap. Mark would be torn from sleep by the end of the belt, and he'd hold up his hands, and the strap would keep coming until his father left, panting. Lying in the darkness of his bedroom, the pain always seemed greater, more intense. No matter how strong one's will, the mind couldn't grasp or manage pain. Anticipating the pain from the belt or buckle was far, far worse than actually receiving it.

Like now. The people who had him hadn't hurt him yet, but they would. They would. Because he knew they hurt people in this place.

Naked and trapped alone in this pitch black and dank-smelling darkness, sometimes awake, sometimes half asleep, they made him wait here locked inside this tiny prison cell where you couldn't stand. He sat or lay curled on his side, listening to the sounds drifting through the metal bars. Murmured voices praying to God. Pleading cries for mercy and forgiveness. He wanted to tell them to shut up. To stop. God didn't exist in this place – wherever this place was.

The screams were the worst part. Some were loud enough to wake God Himself from his slumber, and during those times he caught himself shaking the ancient cold iron bars locking this stone box, hoping they'd break. They wouldn't, of course, and he'd push himself across the cool, smooth floor looking for a place to hide, only to realize he was trapped, no place to run or hide. Nothing to do but sit here and use the time to try to steel his mind to whatever was coming. Because they were going to punish him. Drag it out for days, maybe even weeks.

He had seen it done to others with his own eyes.

Through the crying and whimpering, the soft but earnest praying, he heard the creak of hinges as a heavy door swung open.

Heard the *clink clink clink* of the keys.

Heard the soft scrape of footsteps, which suddenly stopped.

Now another pair of footsteps, urgent, running. They stopped and a voice said, 'I bring you news about the heretic.'

'Tell me, my child.'

That voice, Mark thought. *Oh dear God no.*

The first voice said, 'The heretic's family is guarded by six, possibly eight men. Five are inside the home; the other three are scattered between two cars to watch the roads.'

'And the heretic, has he returned?'

'No. He moves and hides.'

'I want only the girl. Take the girl and kill the rest.'

'Yes, Archon.'

The footsteps grew louder, heading his way.

Mark Rizzo didn't sit up. He turned on his side until the soles of his feet found the bars. If they came for him, he could fight with his feet.

The footsteps stopped. They were standing somewhere just beyond the bars, breathing.

A soft but muffled voice spoke:

'The time has come to pray for forgiveness, Thomas.'

'Stop calling me that.'

'Before we hear your confession, we have a question for you about the woman you invited inside your home.'

'I didn't invite her. Charlie did. Charlie called her.'

'Tell us why.'

'Ask Charlie. He was the one who called her.'

'What did you hide in your basement?'

'Hide?' he repeated, genuinely confused. 'I didn't hide anything.'

'The woman went back to your home tonight. To retrieve something from your basement. We had people watching her.'

He knew this to be true. They had people on the surface, people who would watch and do things. People who obeyed.

Mark – and that was his name, Mark. Thomas died a long time ago – Mark said, 'I don't know what you're talking about.'

'The punishment will be far, far greater if you lie to us.'

Mark Rizzo clamped his eyes shut, wishing he could transport himself, through sheer force of will, out of this place. He wasn't afraid of dying but what filled him with terror was how long it would take. How The Twelve stretched the torture over days until your heart gave out. And the devices they used, like –

A key rattled inside the lock.

Mark raised his foot, ready to kick. *Click* as the lock sprang free and he heard the weary creak of his door swinging open. A crackling sound and then he saw snakes of white and blue electric light sparking across a dark pole. Behind it, a ghostly white face with a stitched scar stretching from one temple, across the forehead and ending somewhere on the bald head.

Mark went for the head and missed. The pole hit him once, on the thigh, and the bolt slammed its way deep into his brain and his arms went flying and hit the walls and floor. The electrified pole hit him again and his head bounced against the floor as hands gripped him roughly by the ankles and dragged him out of his cell, his useless, flailing arms bumping against the iron bars. Feebly he tried to grab them and couldn't get his muscles to work and the pole hit him again and the electrical current exploded through his body and they dragged him out of his cell and into the corridor or whatever it was that lay in the darkness.

He was thrown on to his stomach, his hands yanked behind his back and his wrists shackled. He was dragged to his feet and then he heard a match being struck. He couldn't lift his head to see, but the flame flickered across the stone floor, revealing the iron bars of other cells. He saw a robe made of some thick fabric, like velvet, and, knowing who was standing before him, he started to tremble all over.

Fingers gripped his hair and yanked back his head.

The Archon, his onetime master, stood before him, his true face hidden behind a white-painted mask of wood carved to look like a devil or vampire. False black hair fashioned into a widow's peak on the top and false black eyes as round as buttons, the wooden nose long and hooked, chin shaved to a fine point and teeth carved into a frozen leer. The man's hands were covered with what looked like white gloves except the nail on the end of each finger had been shaved to a sharp point and painted blood-red. Mark watched as those points traced lines across his stomach and then came to a stop below his neck, near his throat.

'Your name is Thomas,' said the soft voice behind the mask. 'And you will tell me the truth. I have something that will help you find it.'

The figure moved away and Mark Rizzo looked down at the end of the long corridor, at the hooded figure lighting sconces on the wall. A single chair sat on the dank, grey-stone floor. A wide chair made of thick, heavy wood, every flat surface covered with thousands of razor-sharp spikes.

36

Darby, freshly showered and her third cup of coffee in hand, sat on the edge of her bed in her new residence at the Marriot Custom House. The manager, Coop's friend, Sean, had set her up in a spacious corner suite with a kitchenette and a separate living room that, along with the master bedroom, had a view of the Boston Waterfront. Sean had not only registered her under an alias known only to the two of them, but had given her a heavily discounted rate and told her she could stay as long as she wanted.

It was coming up on 1:00 p.m. She guzzled the last of her coffee, hoping it would sweep away the remaining cobwebs stubbornly clinging to the inside of her head. She had slept fitfully for the last six hours and wanted her head clear.

Standing, she picked up the cordless phone from the nightstand and carried it with her to the tall window – the air blowing through it was refreshingly cool, the sun warm on her face. She called Information and asked for Harvard's Divinity School, and, as she waited for the operator to connect her, her gaze drifted to the boats anchored in the water, to the people no bigger than dots on the pier lined with bricked restaurants, apartments and the ultra-expensive Westin Hotel, which took up most of the area.

After drifting through the automated choices, she finally got a real person on the other end of the line, a secretary who seemed both patient and eager to assist a Harvard alumna. Darby explained what she was looking for, and the woman suggested a professor named Ronald Ross.

Professor Ross happened to be in his office. The man agreed to investigate the historical and religious significance of the Latin phrase *Et in Arcadia ego*.

Her next call was to the Retired Boston Police Officers Association. The retired cop working the phone searched through his computer and gave her the information she needed on Stan Karakas: the former Boston Police detective had retired and moved to Darien, Connecticut. The man's address and phone numbers were in the system.

Darby wrote the information down on a hotel pad. She thanked him, hung up and called the Boston Police Department's main switchboard. The man who answered knew Darby and agreed to transfer her call to Jimmy Murphy's cell phone.

'Darby, my girl, I'd love to shoot the shit, but I'm about to hit the sack.'

'Just a quick question about the party you broke up last night at the end of my street, the corner of Temple and Cambridge.'

'The two guys in the Chevy Tahoe?'

'That's them. Who are they?'

'Feds from the Boston office. York and Blue. I didn't get their first names.'

'They tell you what they were doing there?'

'Surveillance – and doing a piss poor job, I might add. They weren't at liberty to say *whom* they were watching, so after we confirmed they were, in fact, federal agents, we sent them on their way. Anything else?'

'Sweet dreams, Jimmy. And thanks.'

Her lucky streak ended when she called Stan Karakas. His home number had been disconnected, and his cell phone was no longer in service.

For the next two hours, she worked the phone, giving her name and fake Boston police credentials to each person she spoke with, and by quarter past four she had hit a dead end. Stan Karakas was no longer among the living.

Karakas had moved around a lot during the last twenty-odd years. Connecticut, then Utah, Colorado, and finally Montana, where he had suffered a fatal heart attack at age sixty-nine, while fly-fishing. The news had been delivered to her by his widow, Nancy.

Karakas may have been the lead detective, but there were others who had put in a lot of man-hours. Darby remembered one, an Irish guy stuck with one of the most generic names on the planet: John Smith. She called back the Retired Boston Police Officers Association and found out that Smith had also retired but was still local, now living on the North Shore, in Nahant.

Darby called the man's home number. As luck would have it, he answered. She introduced herself and asked if he was available to talk.

'Sure,' Smith said. 'What's this about, if you don't mind me asking?'

'Charlie Rizzo. I'd like to speak to you in person, if

that's possible.' Cell phone transmissions were notoriously easy to pick up with scanning equipment readily available at stores like RadioShack.

'I can meet you at your home within the hour,' she said. 'Are you free now, Mr Smith?'

'All I've got now is free time. Sure, come on over. And call me Smitty, will ya? That's what everyone called me growing up, and hearing it now makes me feel less like a useless 72-year-old fart, you know?'

Darby locked up and went to the parking garage to grab her bike, wondering if her new friends had managed to follow her here.

A thorough inspection revealed no new tracking devices.

Still, they had to be close. Whoever – *whatever* – these people were, they were highly organized. A small army, she suspected. After what had happened at the blast site, they had most likely regrouped and discussed tactics. They knew she had found the original tracking devices placed on her bike and leather jacket.

Driving down side- and one-way streets, sometimes circling back around, she didn't spot any tails. Maybe they weren't following her. Maybe they thought she would return to her condo and were there now, somewhere close by where they could watch and wait.

Or maybe they would wait for night to fall and, hidden by darkness, try to capture her again or simply come straight at her and wipe her off the playing board.

37

Darby figured John Smith had either hit the lottery or robbed a bank, because there was no way a retired cop could afford this massive old Victorian home. It was situated on a cliff and had a sweeping view of the ocean. The driveway held a Mercedes and a Lexus, and some serious money had been spent on the landscaping in the front. Lots of fresh autumn flowers – enough to open a small nursery.

The man who answered the door was shorter than her, roughly five foot six. He wore a grey V-neck cashmere sweater with jeans and a pair of scuffed penny loafers. With his slim build and thick blond hair parted on the side and threaded lightly with grey, John Smith could easily have passed for someone in his late forties or early fifties. But the craggy face and saddlebags under the bright blue eyes gave away every moment of his seventy-two years.

Smith ushered her through the bright foyer and into a kitchen the size of a basketball court. He pointed to the mugs sitting in front of a coffee maker and said, 'Help yourself. Or do you want something a bit stiffer?'

'Coffee's fine.'

'I'm going to have myself a little poke. Don't think less of me.' He winked a rheumy eye at her and filled a highball glass with Bushmills. 'Let's go outside so I can smoke.'

He put on an L. L. Bean barn jacket and with his high-ball glass in hand – he had poured himself a healthy shot over ice – he took her to a living room with windows that stretched from floor to ceiling and overlooked the ocean. He opened a sliding glass door to a balcony. It stretched around the side of the house. Darby glanced over the railing and saw a private stretch of rocky beach and, to her far right, a part of the backyard where four puppies with stubby legs and round bellies sat on the warm grass, eagerly awaiting the petite older woman standing in front of them with their food.

'My third wife, Mavis,' he said. 'I thank the good Lord above for bringing her into my life.'

And her bank account, Darby added privately. There was no way a cop's pension could pay for a spread like this.

'People always think I married her 'cause of her money.' He turned to her, squinting in the last of the bright afternoon sun. In another hour or so it would be dark. 'You thought the same thing, am I right?'

'I don't know of too many retired cops who have waterfront views.'

'Look at you, being diplomatic.' He smiled at her, flashing a mouth full of crooked teeth turned brown and yellow from a lifetime of smoking and drinking coffee. 'Don't blame you for thinking it. Everyone does. In her former life, Mavis used to be a paediatric surgeon. She never married and spent all her free time playing the stock market. She owns the house free and clear. We don't hurt for money. I spend my time fishing and puttering around the house, and Mavis is a full-time foster mom for dogs, keeps them here until she can get them homes. What I got here?' He made a sweeping gesture with his hands. 'I consider this payback for all the shit I had to wade through.'

He held out a pack of Marlboros in a shaky hand. She politely declined and he pointed to a pair of weatherworn Adirondack chairs set up in the corner under a pale patch of sun.

Smith sat first, in the chair that faced the ocean. Darby moved her chair slightly so she could face him, but not enough to make him feel like this was an interrogation. She preferred watching people when speaking so she could watch their body language.

He wrapped his thin lips around a cigarette and plucked it from the pack. 'After you called, I looked you up on that Internet thing everyone uses, what's it called?'

'Google.'

He snapped his fingers. 'That's it. Mavis had to show me, of course, since the whole computer thing has sort of passed me by. But I can use the mouse to click on things.' He cupped a hand around the lighter, then sat back in his chair, inhaling smoke. 'You've had quite a, ah, *colourful* career with Boston PD.' A sly grin, and then he added, 'You know what we used to call people like you?'

'Trailblazers?'

'Shit magnets.'

The words were said without malice, but she couldn't tell if he was trying to bait her. She sensed he was building up to something, so she drank her black coffee and waited.

'It's an exclusive club,' he said. 'Yours truly is a charter member.'

He sipped his drink and made a hissing sound as the whiskey burned its way down his throat. 'I remember you now. It's the hair and green eyes. You came with the other lab rats to pick up Charlie's bike. You want to know what I thought?'

'I have a feeling you'll tell me even if I say no.'

'You're right. I said to myself, "What the hell is a such a pretty girl doing working in this shit?"'

'I like working in this shit.'

He chuckled softly. 'That's the other thing I remembered. You were really blunt. You were busting everyone's balls on procedural stuff, didn't care who you pissed off. The other lab rats you came with, they did their job and left. Not you. No, you stuck around and kept poking your nose into the case, asking us what we thought about this or that. You pissed the hell out of Karakas.'

Darby didn't answer.

'That surprise you?' he asked.

'No.'

'Why's that?'

'Most homicide cops like to steer the boat without any interference.'

'That, and they want the recognition. They want to be the ones to solve the case, get their promotion and names in the paper. Me?' He shrugged, took another sip of his drink. 'I couldn't've cared less. Putting the damn thing to bed was what mattered, and I got that same sense from you. All you cared about was finding that kid and bringing him home, which is why I suspect you're here.'

His gaze turned as sorrowful and rheumy as a bloodhound's. Then she understood. Smith believed her request to meet face to face had to do with her delivering the news of having come across either the boy's remains or some piece of evidence that would allow Smith mentally to put the case to bed. Homicide detectives didn't grieve the same way the parents of a missing child did – there was no way they should – but there was a strong emotional connection to the victim that was impossible to ignore. If the vic was dead, the case closed, you got some sort of closure. If the persons who did it were behind bars, you got the added benefit of a measure of satisfaction – enough to put the case on some shelf to gather dust and, God-willing, fade.

But cases involving missing children, when weeks turned into months and then years, you always kept a mental door open and periodically revisited it to see if there was something you had overlooked. You did it because those cases ate at you day in and day out, and the only way to stop that was to close it. To nail the goddamn coffin shut.

Smith took another drag of his cigarette and tapped it with a finger to flick off the ash.

'What happened to him?' he asked, curls of smoke drifting through the hairy nostrils of his bulbous nose.

'He was shot to death,' Darby said. 'I spoke with him before he died.'

38

Darby started with the phone call from Gary Trent. She summarized her conversations with the NH SWAT senior corporal inside the APC and the hostage negotiator, Billy Lee, inside the mobile command trailer. She went into great detail about the conversation she had with Charlie Rizzo inside the family's new home in Dover and then described what had followed after the explosion: the dead SWAT team members and the man she had captured, the thing with the egg-white skin and the missing tongue and the Latin words tattooed on the base of his neck. She explained to Smith what the words meant.

She told Smith about the sarin gas, the listening devices found inside her condo and the feds watching her at the end of her street. She left out what had happened during the early morning hours at the blast site and then later, at the BU Biomedical Lab, with the men she was sure were Secret Service. Her decision didn't have to do with trust; it was more to do with the fact that Smith looked like he was having a problem with everything she'd just told him. *Give him a moment to digest it.*

She waited for his questions. He had listened to her intently, and without interrupting. Now he lit another cigarette and stared thoughtfully at the small waves breaking across the shore below them.

Darby stared past his head, across the street at the nest of tall trees shedding their gold and red leaves. The puppies were still in the backyard, and she could hear their playful high-pitched barks and squeals behind the wind.

Smith leaned forward in his chair. He had smoked half of his cigarette. He opened his mouth to speak, then stopped. She waited.

'That's one hell of a story.'

'Agreed,' she said. 'But that's what happened.'

'Now I know why you insisted on talking face to face. If you had told me this shit over the phone, I would've hung up on you.'

'You read about it in the papers? I know the *Globe* covered it.'

'I'm a *Herald* guy, and I only buy it for the sports page. I stopped following the news . . . Christ, it's been years. First thing you learn as a cop is that almost everything that's printed or said on the news is about two per cent truth. The other ninety-eight per cent is bullshit spin. You really think it's him? Charlie, I mean?'

'I don't have the benefit of DNA or a fingerprint, so the rational part of me says no.'

Smith nodded, and took a long drag off his cigarette.

'My gut says the man I met was Charlie,' she said. 'The eyes were the right colour, and he was missing two nipples. He made it a point of showing them to me.'

He nodded again, more to himself than her.

'All this time . . .' He ran a big hand over his face, staring out at the darkening sky. 'If what you're saying is true, all this time that kid was alive and . . .' He took in a deep breath and cocked his head to her. 'You said his body was scarred.'

She nodded.

'He tell you from what?'

'No, but I think it was from being whipped.' She had thought about it on and off during the past week. The lattice pattern seemed right. 'It's only a guess. I forgot to mention he'd been turned into a eunuch.'

Smith glared at her, wide-eyed.

'Castrated,' she said.

'I know what it means, I just . . . you're *sure*?'

'Positive.'

He ran a big hand over his face. Then shook his head as if snapping out of a trance.

'This business with the face mask, what's that all about?'

'Don't know,' she said. 'Charlie didn't say anything about it. Does it mean anything to you?'

'First time I've ever heard about such a thing. Must have some sort of religious significance.'

'What makes you say that?'

'The tattoos on that guy's neck, the one with the missing tongue? You said they were Latin, right?'

'According to what I read on the Internet. I don't know their significance, so I sent them over to a Harvard professor to decipher their meaning.'

'You Catholic?'

'Irish Catholic.'

'My condolences.' He chuckled softly. 'They used to speak Latin during church services years and years ago, way before you were born – before I was born, probably. Makes me think you're dealing with some sort of religious cult.'

She nodded. The thought had occurred to her too.

'What did the army tell you?'

'They didn't tell me anything. Neither did the feds. I'm shut out from the investigation. My guess is that this thing is bigger than someone using nerve gas to kill a bunch of cops.'

'I'm not sure how I can help you here.'

'Tell me about Mark Rizzo.'

'He . . . Shit, you're talking about, what, twelve years ago? Truth be told, I don't want to revisit it. Don't look at me like that, you know what I'm talking about. You worked a missing person's case before, that Traveler creep, the one who came for you when you was a little girl and ended up snatching your friend.'

Darby nodded.

'So you know how that shit can linger if you don't find a way to turn it off. Because if you don't, you end up dragging it around like a ball and chain for the rest of your life. I can't really help you here. You'd be better off reading my case notes.'

'I don't have access to them.'

'You've lost me. You're not working with that CSU group?'

'No. It's been permanently disbanded. And, as of this morning, I'm no longer an employee at the crime lab. I'm looking into this on my own.'

'I hope to Christ you're not trying to recruit me. Because the answer's no. Besides, I wouldn't be of any use to you.

And I don't have them. Copies, I mean. Some homicide guys, they make copies of the cases they didn't get to solve before they go into retirement. They think they'll revisit one or two, you know, break it open or something. Not me. When I left, I shut the door behind me.'

'Was Mark Rizzo ever a suspect?'

Smith didn't pause to consider the question; he shook his head.

'Never,' he added.

'But you looked into him.'

'Of course we did. Him *and* his wife. It's the first thing you do when a kid is abducted or goes missing, because nine times out of ten the parents or a relative is involved. So, yeah, we looked into the parents, but they both had strong alibis. The mother was at home, the father working at the office. Everything checked out.'

'How far did you dig?'

'Well, if I'm to believe what you say, that the father was involved in his son's abduction, then I'd have to admit we didn't dig far enough.' He leaned back in his chair. 'Like I said, his alibi checked out. Marriage was solid.'

'Was he married before?'

'No. First marriage for both of them. He was a tax guy . . . I remember some incident involving one of his clients, guy pissed off about having to pay too much money to the government and thought Rizzo had bungled his tax return. So this guy, he went back to Rizzo's office and goes after him with a baseball bat. Police were called, so there was a report. We looked into it, thinking this guy har-boured a grudge all these years and *maybe* decided to get even with Rizzo by snatching the kid. I don't remember the guy's name, but I remember it came up empty.'

'Was Rizzo born here?'

He thought about it as he took another sip of his drink. 'I think so,' he said.

'I don't remember him having a Boston accent.'

'That doesn't mean anything. I know plenty of people who don't – people who've lived here their whole lives. Like you. You don't have one, and you grew up in Belham, right?'

Darby nodded. 'Where'd you hear that?'

'Didn't hear it, I read it. Online.'

'What about Mark Rizzo's extended family? Any brothers or sisters?'

'No. He was an only child. His parents died when he was seventeen. Some sort of car crash. I don't remember where or when.'

'Who raised him?'

'Haven't the foggiest. I can't even say I asked him the question. I don't know if the guy had any uncles or aunts either. And his wife, Judith? I don't remember anything about her except that she was a die-hard Catholic. Kept a pair of rosary beads in her hands at all times. That's the only thing that sticks out.'

He shrugged, showed her his empty hands. 'I don't know what else to tell you. The guy was as clean as a whistle – at least that's how he looked at the time.'

'Did the feds get involved in the case?'

Smith took another healthy slug of whiskey. 'They usually do with missing kids.'

'Only if they believe someone's been transported over state lines.'

'News got out fast that Charlie Rizzo had been abducted – that was the way it looked since we found his abandoned bike – and that's when the calls started coming. You know the ones I'm talking about. "I have Charlie and if you want to see him again put unmarked bills in a brown-paper bag on such and such a day." "I have Charlie and he's in a lot of pain." Shit like that. One call came in from someplace in the Midwest – Wisconsin, I think – and that's when the feds got involved. They helped us run down all the leads. They had the manpower and the resources.

'Almost every call came from a payphone, and they were all cranks. None of 'em knew specifics about the kid or how and where he was abducted. But we had to run them down. We got a shitload more when the Rizzos went to the press – you know, try to appeal to the kidnapper. Like I said, they were all cranks. Can I ask you a personal question?'

'Go for it.'

'You married?'

'No.'

'Kids?'

'Don't have the maternal drive. That, and the fact that I'm forty now, I'm pretty sure the factory's shut down.'

'You serious with anyone?'

Darby opened her mouth, then shut it, unsure of how to answer the question. *Yes, I'm in love with a guy I've known for fifteen years. There's always been an attraction between us, but I never acted on it because I didn't want the friendship to change. And just when I realized I couldn't ignore this attraction any more, he relocated to London. I haven't been over there to visit him because I'm afraid nothing more will come of it or, even worse, it will end our friendship, and, as much as I love him, I can't bear to lose that.*

'There's someone in my life,' she said. 'Someone serious.'

'Good. Spend as much time with him as you can. Get married and have babies. If you can't have them, be like Angelina Jolie and adopt a whole Rainbow Coalition or whatever. That's the shit that matters. That's what haunts you at my age, all the opportunities you ignored because of the job, because the job don't mean anything in the end.'

'It matters to me.'

'Your choice. Now, if you'll excuse me, I'd like to go spend some time with my wife. At my age, I don't have much time left.'

Smith got to his feet, his knees cracking. She was staring at the wrinkles on his face, about to get up, when his head exploded.

39

It was the worst pain he had ever experienced.

They shoved him down on the chair and Mark Rizzo felt the metal spikes stab through his flesh and muscle, shattering bones. He screamed and they strapped his wrists and ankles to keep him pinned and he kept screaming until his throat was raw. As bad as the pain was – and it was excruciating, never ending waves riding up his spine like bullets and tearing through the soft meat of his brain – he dug his fingernails into the wood and willed himself to keep still, because if he moved the razor-sharp spikes would move and they would tear and shred and break.

He sat there for hours, days, he didn't know. He had a clear memory of the two big men coming back into the room, the ones with the alabaster skin and ghoul faces, and in the flickering candlelight he could see that they weren't wearing any clothes or shoes and that their genitals were missing. They moved off to the sides, near the walls, and as he lost sight of them the Archon loomed into view and spoke in a whisper: 'What is your name?' And Mark heard another voice, this one in his head, and it was screaming *Don't give it to them: if you do they'll kill you, don't say it*, and he had hesitated, thinking over the pain, and the two ghouls with the scarred faces and bodies raised their whips.

The first strap hit him and he thrashed around on the chair and his voice came back and he howled, the sound loud enough to pulverize stone. They kept whipping him, the straps tearing out strips of flesh, and then one of them raked something hard across his shins and he vomited until his stomach was stripped and then, through the mercy of God, he passed out.

Delirious and drifting in and out of consciousness, he would sometimes open his eyes and see nothing but the awful darkness and wonder if the whips had blinded him. Now he opened them again and through his pain-soaked haze he could see candlelight flickering across a grey-stoned ceiling. They had removed him from the chair and placed him on his back on something cold and hard and wet.

The pain came back, roaring through his body, and his limbs shook and he felt straps biting into his wrists and ankles, his throat. His head bobbed slightly to the left and he saw a dark leather strap pinning the wrist of his broken hand against the edge of a long metal table. Blood – *his* blood – covered his naked body and pooled across the table's stainless-steel surface. He heard a dripping sound on the floor as he bled out and he wept, thinking, *I'm going to die.*

The Archon's voice echoed over the cold and dusty stones: 'What is your name?'

Mark Rizzo shut his eye, weeping. They were going to kill him and it didn't matter if he said his real name or not because they –

A bolt of electricity slammed through his head and

across his limbs, his vision exploding in white, and he couldn't see anything and his body bucked against the leather straps binding him to the table.

Then he fell back to the table and the pain was swept under a tingling numbness that fluttered back and forth across his limbs.

'Electroshock therapy,' the voice said. 'That was fifteen seconds. The next time it will be thirty.'

'Why are you doing this?'

'What is your name?'

He didn't answer and the electricity came again. When it was over, he couldn't move, felt his heart sputtering. Leaking.

'*Thomas*,' he screamed. '*My name is Thomas!*'

'Thomas what?'

'Thomas Howland.'

'Where were you born?'

'Tulsa, Oklahoma. My mother's name was Janice and she died of breast cancer and I went to live with my father, Duncan. His name was Duncan but everyone called him Chris. He was a painter. Painted houses.'

'You told me you prayed for him to die.'

'I told a priest.'

'And God. God was there with you in the confessional, Thomas. I heard your prayers, and I killed your father. I caused his ladder to fall, and I let him die. To punish him for what he did to you. And when you were living in a foster home, being abused, I heard your prayers and I sent an angel to bring you to a new family, to a mother and father who were kind to you. And how did you repay my kindness? You shot my family. You killed my angels while they slept and then you fled like a coward.'

His mind was spinning, flashing back to all those times he'd been inside the truck with his stepfather, a man named Ernest. Those long drives to other states and the hours spent in the truck waiting until Ernie gave the nod and then he would get out and approach the young boy or girl, use the speech he'd been given to lure them into the truck. Riding in the truck and trying hard not to cry because he knew the boy or girl sitting wedged between the two of them would disappear into thin air and then the time would come to move on to another state, move on to the next boy or girl, more states, more victims, always more victims.

'I'm not a murderer,' he said.

'You were a liberator,' the Archon said. 'My angel. I gave you the mark.'

He felt it rise up in him, the decades-old guilt over what he'd done. He had told no one, but his guilt had turned into the ulcers, high blood pressure and heart palpitations that eventually led to his first heart attack. The drinking that wouldn't take away the ghosts but reduced their voices to whispers.

'It took me a long, long time to find you the first time,' the voice said softly. 'Imprisoned in this body, I had to use man-made methods. And when I finally found you, in my kindness I gave you a chance to save your soul. I was willing to release your son, and what did you do?'

I saved myself, Mark thought. It was true. He *had* saved himself, yes, but he also knew that if he had done what was asked of him – if he had agreed to meet with them and go back to living in that dark, underground hell – they wouldn't have released Charlie. Charlie had seen too much. *They would have kept Charlie, tortured him as a way to punish me. If I had gone back, nothing would have changed. Nothing.*

But at least you would have been with him, another voice added. *Charlie wouldn't have been left alone with these people. You abandoned your son.*

'You wouldn't have released him,' he said.

The voice moved closer to his ear. 'You, a coward and monster, are calling me a *liar*?'

His eye flew open and he saw shadows on the wall, shapes coming together.

'You let him suffer,' the voice said. 'Your child. Your son. You let him suffer for your sins.'

'I've seen what you do here.'

'And what is that, Thomas?'

'You torture and kill people.'

'We prepare sinners for a good death, Thomas. They are here for the same reason as you. You are here to atone. To ask for forgiveness.'

'No.'

'Then you have much to think about.'

'You're going to kill me.'

'We want to *save* you, Thomas. Do you value your soul?'

He swallowed rapidly, deciding to go with it. Tell them anything they wanted to hear and then find a way out of this dungeon of horrors.

'Yes,' he said, licking his lips. 'Yes, I do.'

'Are you ready to confess?'

'Yes.'

They gathered around him, the black robes and faces shielded by hoods, and he confessed to everything.

'Thank you, Thomas.'

A soft kiss on his forehead. Real lips. The Archon had taken off the mask.

His eye automatically slammed shut, not wanting to see the face, and he shivered all over.

'You are forgiven.'

The electricity shot through him again. When it stopped, he was barely conscious, vaguely aware of his mouth being opened and a clear tube coated with Vaseline being shoved down his throat.

40

Darby stood in the late John Smith's living room with her cold hands buried deep in her jeans pockets. She had glass shards in her hair. Blood was smeared on her clothes, and she caught its coppery reek under the pervasive odour of cordite. Her face and hands and joints throbbed. She had been cut but not too badly. The paramedic had used tweezers to remove the glass shards from her face, then cleaned her wounds and applied some sort of antibacterial ointment but no bandages. She stood in front of one of the two floor-to-ceiling windows that hadn't been blown out by the gunshots and she could see her reflection, the crisscrossed network of fine red cuts and scratches along the right side of her face.

The adrenalin rush had long since dissipated, leaving her with a familiar but still strange hollow feeling. Numb, as if her organs had been shot full of Novocain. Her mind kept replaying what had happened in slow motion. Here it came again, the first part, and again she didn't turn away from it.

Smith sitting to her right and getting to his feet and then, a split second later, his craggy face exploded. Skin and blood blew across her face and she thought *exit wound*. She hadn't heard the gunshot and her mind registered two facts at once: *silencer* and *sniper*. The exit wound — Smith's face – meant the contact shot had hit him in the back of the head. Meant the trajectory of the bullet had come from behind him, from somewhere across the street and from someplace high, like the trees or a roof. Meant that she had been followed here.

Darby was already on her feet, turning away and scrambling for the sliding glass door. She had to get inside the house, the only safe place to hide. She heard a panicked voice calling out from the backyard: 'Smitty? Smitty, are you okay?' Smith's wife, Mavis. Darby yelled *gunshot* over the wind as she ran, yelled at the woman to get inside the house.

The second shot took out one of the windows. Glass exploded across her face. Darby put her hand on the sliding glass door, threw it open and tumbled inside as the next shot took out the glass door. It hit the far wall. She had the phone in her hand and, standing near the kitchen, called 911. Told the operator shots were being fired, shouted for back-up and an ambulance, gave the address and dropped the phone. Unzipped her jacket and reached for her sidearm and saw Smith lying on his stomach, the severed arteries in his neck spraying blood in fine mists while the large, gaping wound pumped blood in great spurts on to the balcony floor as his dying body thrashed and thrashed. She turned away, stumbling blindly through the large maze of rooms, looking for the staircase that would lead her downstairs and into the backyard.

'Miss McCormick?'

The voice belonged to a black patrolman standing guard in front of the broken windows – A. DAVIS, his nameplate said. He was one of the squared-jawed first responding officers, an ebony-and-ivory pair who had immediately sectioned her off here, inside the living room. Davis had stayed with her while his partner radioed for homicide and back-up. She hadn't been allowed to assist in the search for the shooter. She knew he was long, long gone, but she wanted to go out there and find the spot, as well as the spent brass casings. She wanted to be useful, not stand here with her thumb up her ass, waiting to speak again to John Lu, the Nahant homicide detective who'd caught the case.

'You need to use the bathroom?' Davis asked. 'Maybe get you a glass of water?'

I want the bottle of Bushmills Irish whiskey sitting on Smith's kitchen worktop.

'Water would be good,' she said.

'Stay right here, okay? Don't go wandering.'

She nodded and looked past the vacancy he left, at the two forensic techs from the state lab in Springfield taking detailed pictures of the former homicide detective. John Smith's headless body lay in a pool of cooling blood that had spread across the lit balcony floor and dripped over the sides. The techs had young faces and had good equipment and were doing a decent job of bracketing the shots.

The ocean wind blew against the house and whistled through the jagged holes left in the windows. When it died down, she could hear the murmured conversations as the techs spoke to each other. Heard the squawk of seagulls over the crackle of police radios and ringing cell phones.

The puppies were no longer barking. She assumed they'd been corralled somewhere away from the backyard crime scene.

'Dr McCormick.'

Not Davis; this voice belonged to the detective, Lu. She turned around and saw the thirty-something Asian guy holding a glass of water clinking with ice.

She took the glass and thanked him, noticing that he had called her *doctor*. She hadn't told the man she had a doctorate in criminal and abnormal psychology. Apparently Lu had made some phone calls. He probably knew her status with the Boston Police Department.

'Smith's wife?' she asked.

Lu shook his head.

'Too much blood loss,' he said. 'She died on the way to the hospital.'

The news didn't surprise her. Still, she had held out hope, and felt the loss at having it amputated twitch like a phantom limb.

After finding the stairs that led into the basement, she saw, through the windows, the backyard lit up by floodlights. Saw the frail woman with curly grey hair wearing a North Face parka lying sideways on the grass, screaming, her arthritic hands clutching the ripped meat of her bloody thigh. The puppies barked. They had gathered around the woman, four of them, maybe more, and they barked and licked her face and cuddled close to her body. And even in her excruciating pain, in fear and shock, Mavis Smith wanted to protect them. Tried to shoo them away towards the opened basement door underneath the balcony.

Darby found the light switch for the backyard lights and shut them off, knowing why the woman had been shot in the thigh: the sniper was using her as bait, trying to draw Darby out.

It worked. The woman screamed again. Darby tumbled against the grass fifteen feet away and ran. When she reached the edge of the backyard she turned and started firing blindly in the direction of the shots – the trees, the sniper had to be somewhere in those trees across the street, and she hoped the muzzle flashes would blind him momentarily. They had. With one hand she grabbed the parka's hood and kept firing as she dragged the screaming woman across the grass, kept firing until the magazine clicked empty. Darby locked the basement door and in the dim light stripped off the parka as the puppies barked outside, scratching their paws against the door, and the woman kept crying, 'I've got to call Paula, I've got to call Paula.'

Not two gunshot wounds but three. Mavis Smith had been shot in the chest, underneath her right breast. Darby used her belt as a tourniquet on the leg. Used a plastic garbage bag on the sucking chest wound, holding her fingers along three edges and keeping the fourth edge free so the chest could achieve its usual negative pressure state. She stayed with the woman, applying pressure as blood spurted through her fingers, urging the woman to stay calm. Mavis Smith whimpered 'Paula, I've got to call Paula' over and over again until the paramedics arrived.

Darby drank the water in one long, burning gulp, realizing her foolishness at having rushed blindly into the backyard. The sniper had had the advantage. He had been hidden somewhere in the trees and using a scope. She could have been shot. She could be lying dead on the ground right now while forensics took pictures of her body.

'How are the dogs?' she asked.

'Fine, not a scratch on them. We put them in the garage.'

'She kept talking about calling someone named Paula.'

'You told me that already.'

There was something off about Lu. Maybe the clothes had something to do with it. For some bizarre, unfathomable reason, the man had adopted the cartoonish attire seen in old American cop shows: a fedora and belted London Fog raincoat worn over a cheap navy-blue suit.

She held the empty glass by her side, wondering how Lu was going to play it. Only two choices: play it cool or come down on her hard.

'Any leads on the shooter?'

'We're canvassing the neighbourhood, speaking to people.' He sighed, then shook his head in frustration. 'So far, nobody's seen anyone heading into the woods carrying a sniper rifle.'

Darby stared at him. Did the man actually think someone would be carrying a fully assembled sniper rifle? Didn't he know that a sniper rifle was carried, disassembled, inside a small carrying pack that could be easily concealed underneath a jacket?

'What about spent brass?' she asked. 'You find any casings in the woods?'

'We found your shell casings all over the backyard.'

'I told you what happened. Three times.' There was no anger in her voice, just a calm, neutral matter-of-fact tone. 'What don't you understand?'

'You haven't explained *who* fired at you.'

'I don't know. I told you I didn't see him.'

'You said this person was using a rifle with a silencer and a scope.'

'That's right.'

'To know that, you must have seen him.'

'I'll tell it to you again,' she said. 'I didn't hear any of the shots. That means a silencer was used. To get off a head-shot in this wind, to shoot Smith's wife twice in the leg, you'd need a scope. To tear Smith's head off his shoulders you'd need to use a high-powered rifle and ammo. I didn't see any muzzle flashes, so this person was using a flash suppressor, a common piece of equipment on a sniper rifle. All of these facts *suggest* a sniper. I didn't say anything about *seeing* the shooter.'

'You failed to mention that you're conducting an investigation.'

'That's because I'm not conducting one. I came here to speak to John Smith, catch up on old times. We worked together.'

'So I was told.'

Darby waited for the rest of it. She didn't take her eyes off Lu.

'I made some calls to Boston and spoke to a man named Leland Pratt. He told me that you no longer work for the Crime Services Unit – or the lab, for that matter. He asked me to relay a message to you.'

'Can I borrow a pen and a piece of paper? This sounds important.'

'Don't worry, it's short. He said don't bother coming to the lab to collect your things. They'll be mailed to you.'

'That's wonderful. Tell him thank you.'

A thin smile, and then Lu said, 'Mr Pratt indicated that you've involved yourself in an investigation. Care to tell me what it is?'

Darby thought of an old Ben Franklin epigram: *One can keep a secret if two are dead.* The only person who knew the real reason for her visit was John Smith and, possibly, his wife.

'I told you. Catching up.'

Lu popped a cherry LifeSaver on to his small, thin lips. 'An officer will escort you downtown. I'll speak to you later, when you're ready to tell me the truth.'

'The truth about what?'

'This investigation you're involved in, these people who followed you here and tried to kill you.'

Lu held his hand in the air and motioned to someone over her shoulder. She turned slightly and saw a patrolman, a big white dude who hadn't bought a new shirt to accommodate his expanding waistline and ample chins, walking towards her, cuffs in hand.

She turned back to Lu and, laughing, said, 'You can't be serious.'

'I am.'

'What's the charge?'

'You're carrying an illegal firearm.'

'I have a licence.'

'Not any more. Boston PD has since revoked it.'

'When?'

'Today. Mr Pratt told me.'

'This is the first I'm hearing about it.'

'You can discuss the matter with your attorney,' Lu said. 'You can make the call at the station, after you've been charged.'

41

Darby rode in the back of the squad car with her hands cuffed behind her back. She used the quiet time to think.

Leland had told Lu she was involving herself in an investigation, so the question was: had Leland been told the truth about what had really happened to the Rizzo family? The feds had locked down that information, yes, but there was also the matter of her job offer from Leland on the same day she'd been released from the quarantine chamber. She didn't think it was a coincidence. She was willing to bet the feds had called the acting Boston police commissioner and put some pressure on him to get her back on the job until the investigation was over. Then the Boston PD could do whatever it wanted with her.

If Leland knew the real story about Charlie Rizzo and his family, he wouldn't have shared it with anyone. Leland knew how to keep his mouth shut. He was a good bureaucratic soldier, maybe one of the best.

When she reached the station, she surrendered her cell phone, wallet, belt, keys and gun holster. She had already given her sidearm to one of the forensic techs for bullet analysis. Standard procedure. Her items were dropped into a bag and she signed the inventory form.

After a thorough search, she was booked and fingerprinted. A patrolman escorted her to an interrogation room that smelled of BO and stale coffee. One of the overhead fluorescent lights hummed and flickered on and off.

The pudgy detective who came in had delicate fingers and an emerald pinkie ring. His brown hair, threaded with grey and white, had side-swept bangs that left little doubt he had punched a one-way express ticket to Gayville.

After he removed her handcuffs, he cuffed her to an O-ring in the centre of the table.

'You're joking,' she said.

The detective left the room without answering.

The scuffed desk had plenty of reading material: JIMMY MC WAS HERE!!!! TINA HERBERT LIKES BIG DONKEY DICK UP HER POOP-SHOOT. BOBBY K BLOWS HORSES. Someone had managed to write down all the lyrics to Van Halen's 'Running with the Devil'.

A clock hung on the wall: 9:20 p.m. She rested the uncut side of her face on her forearm and tried to get some sleep.

Sometime later, she heard the door open. She propped up her head and checked the clock: 10:33 p.m.

A new detective, this one a white guy with a big, pie-shaped face, dropped a pad of paper on the other side of the desk. He had bushy black hair and a thick moustache straight out of a seventies porn movie. Or maybe she was thinking this way given the high-grade erotica she'd just read on the desk.

'My name is Detective Steve Kenyon.'

Steve Kenyon, she thought. *Not a bad porn name. Steven Cannon would be better — or Cannon Kenyon, the Thunder from Down Under.*

He sat down, the chair straining under his considerable weight, and slipped a gold pen from his shirt pocket.

'You ready to talk?'

'Can't. I could go to jail. I signed forms.'

'Forms? What forms?'

'Legal forms. Had the United States Army insignia stamped on it. In gold.'

Up-and-coming seventies porn star Steve Kenyon looked confused.

'Call Sergeant-Major Glick,' she said. 'He's in charge of the BU Biomedical Facility.'

He rubbed his bushy moustache.

'That's in Boston,' she said.

'I know where BU is.'

'Good. Go and call him. I should warn you, he's a tough guy to get a hold of, so if he's unavailable, ask for a man named Billy Fitzgerald. He's supposedly their number two guy, but I don't believe it.'

'We're not calling anyone.'

'I can't answer any questions until you bring Glick or Fitzgerald here. I need their permission.'

'You need to play ball with us.'

'And you need to come up with a better tough-guy routine. Try using a deeper voice. That'll *really* make my ovaries quake in fear.'

He leaned back in his chair and crossed his arms over his chest. 'I heard you were a pisser.'

'You have questions, and I want to answer them. I really do. But I can't for legal reasons. Bring in Glick or Fitzgerald or anyone else from the place, and we'll answer your questions together, make it one big party here in Nahant.'

'I think you need some time to cool down.'

'You really should make that call.'

He stood.

'Speaking of which,' Darby said, 'I'd like my statutory phone call now. I'd like to speak to my lawyer.'

The holding cell was the size of a closet and held two bunk beds bolted to the wall. The opposite corner had a stainless-steel toilet built into a sink cabinet, one of those oh-so-clever advancements to save space in jail cells. It smelled of Lysol and urine.

Darby folded her jacket and, using it as a pillow, lay down on the bottom bunk.

She had spoken to her lawyer. He said not to worry; he could get the weapons charge dropped. But he couldn't do it until the morning, when he could get in front of a judge, so she was looking at spending the night in the Nahant Inn. Lu would be forced to let her go tomorrow – unless he manufactured some other charge. She wouldn't put it past him.

The weapons charge was a bullshit move. Lu had played it because he wanted in on the investigation. He had sniffed around and found a possible opportunity to advance himself, get transferred to someplace more exciting; with a better-paid job, he could stop buying used police costumes at the discount stores.

So now she had to play a mental version of the duelling gunslingers. She imagined Lu standing across from her on a gritty road in some dusty mining gown plucked straight out of a John Wayne Western. No need for guns on this ponderosa: the weapon used here was sheer stubbornness; it was a battle of wills to see who would buckle first. She wondered how much experience the man had with the most intractable people on the planet, the species known as 'Irish Catholic'.

Good luck, she thought, grinning. Darby closed her eyes and settled in for a long night.

42

Nahant PD's complimentary continental breakfast came early, at 6:00 a.m., served on a cardboard tray. Darby looked over the selection: soggy white toast, a mealy apple and powdered scrambled eggs, all of it wrapped under cellophane beaded with steam. She had settled on the apple when Detective Lu appeared.

His fedora and belted raincoat were gone, but he wore another cheap suit, this one black and made of some polyester-rayon blend designed to resist wrinkling and repel stains. The white shirt beneath it, though, was wrinkled. Was it the same shirt he had worn yesterday? Maybe. He had worn that atrocious-looking pink and purple striped tie yesterday, no question.

Lu, his hands deep in his pockets, jingled his keys and spare change as he stared at her through the bars. His eyes were bright and alert. Focused.

'Ready to play ball?'

'Sure,' she said between mouthfuls. 'You want to be the pitcher or catcher?'

'I was thinking of bringing you on as a consultant.'

'For what?'

'This case you're involved in.'

'You should loosen your tie. It's cutting off the oxygen to your brain, making you delusional.'

'I'm trying to help you here.'

'No you're not,' she said, tossing the remains of the apple into the toilet. 'You're here to make a last-ditch effort to find out what's going on because the case is about to be yanked from you, and you've just seen your lottery ticket go up in flames.'

A panicked anger flashed behind Lu's eyes.

'Who was it?' she asked. 'Feds or Secret Service?'

Lu said, 'What's the federal government's interest in what happened to John Smith?'

Darby grinned, letting him hang on the hook for a moment.

'Don't know,' she said. 'Maybe you should ask the feds or whoever's here.'

'The state of Massachusetts takes its gun laws very seriously,' Lu said.

'I'll take my chances in front of the judge.'

'I don't think the judge is going to look too kindly on the fact that you used hollow-point ammunition. Judges take that sort of illegal ammo very seriously, as I'm sure you know. But I'm willing to drop the charges if –'

'Talk to my lawyer.'

'The feds will use you. You're a fool if you think they're going to allow you into their investigation.'

'You're right. They won't. But that doesn't change the fact that you're an asshole.'

Lu stiffened.

'We're done talking,' she said. 'Let me know when my lawyer arrives.'

Lu didn't move away from her cell. He stood there,

red-faced and dejected, running through his options and trying to calculate his next move while knowing, deep down, he had lost.

A moment later, he turned and motioned for one of the guards. A patrolman came and unlocked her cell.

Lu slipped a LifeSaver past his lips. 'Your lawyer is here.'

Darby grabbed her jacket and followed Lu out of the holding pen and into a maze of busy cubicles. Phones were ringing everywhere, but the people seated at the desks or standing in doorways – even the ones huddling near the row of coffee-makers on the far side of the warm room – had stopped whatever they had been doing or saying to look at her. Some took quick glances while others stared.

'In here,' Lu said, holding open a grey-painted door.

Darby stepped inside the boxy conference room and came to a full stop when she saw who was seated at the table.

43

Her lawyer, Martin Freedman, was a squat, round man with a hawk-shaped nose, bald on top and uncombed tufts of salt-and-pepper hair feathered over small ears. Every time Darby met the man at his downtown Boston office, Freedman would have his liver-spotted hands resting on top of the battered brown leather portfolio he'd carried with him since law school. Freedman would always smile, flashing his capped teeth, and she could usually smell his cologne and spot a few stray dandruff flakes on the shoulders of his finely tailored suit jacket.

The man sitting at the table was tall and extremely fit and wore a black suit and dark blue shirt without a tie. He bore a striking resemblance to the insanely good-looking quarterback for the New England Patriots; but, unlike Tom Brady, this man had thick dirty-blond hair and the most interesting eyes she had ever seen: one a dark green, the other blue.

Her old partner, Jackson Cooper, rose unsteadily, his eyes widening with shock. At first she was confused, then she realized how she looked: face cut up from glass and wounds crusted with blood; her jeans and the front of her shirt and jacket matted and smeared with dried blood that had turned black and crusty. Blood and skin and hair and probably brain matter from John Smith's exit wound; blood from working on the man's wife as she bled out.

'Good morning, Dr McCormick,' Coop said. 'I take it those wounds I'm seeing aren't a result of your stay here.'

'No, they're not.'

Coop turned to Lu, who was still standing in the door-way. 'You can leave now, detective.'

The door shut with a soft click. Coop looked at her, worried.

'Since you're standing upright, I'm going to assume you're okay – physically, at least.' He had lowered his voice and was speaking quickly. 'You can tell me what happened later. Grab a seat. We don't have much time.'

'How did you find me?'

'Leland.'

'He *called* you?'

He shook his head. He had plunked back down in his chair.

'When you called and left me that voicemail, the number for the lab was on my Caller-ID,' he said, working a thick elastic band off a battered manila folder. 'So I assumed you'd been reinstated and went back to the lab and bumped into Leland. Fortunately, he came in early today. Unfortunately, he told me about what happened to you last night here in Nahant. We'll talk about that later, after you've spoken to your lawyer.'

'Is he here?'

Coop nodded. 'Right now he's talking to Lu and the sergeant,' he said. 'I ran into him in the lobby, told him who I was and why I was here, and he told Lu I was his legal assistant. We've got ten minutes. Sit down, will you? They've probably posted a guy outside to try and listen in.'

She pulled out the chair as Coop flipped through the messy stack of papers. Three months ago, those same hands had held her as the rain drummed against the walkway outside the front door of his home. He had pressed his lips against hers, hungry, as if he needed to steal something from her before he left; her heart was still beating in her throat when he pulled away. She saw him smile and she smiled back and then he said he had to go. Later, over the phone, he had told her he was never coming back.

But here he was sitting in front of her, the first time she'd seen him since he had left three months ago, and the adrenalin-filled joy surging through her body was slowly drowning in a piercing sadness, Darby knowing he hadn't flown halfway around the world and tracked her down to say hello.

'Take a look at this,' he said, slapping a sheet of paper on the table. The sound snapped her back to the windowless, hot room with its dingy white walls. His breath was stale and his eyes weary and bloodshot from the red-eye flight.

Darby looked at the sheet of paper and saw a laser-printed picture – a headshot of the smug army prick she'd met at the BU Lab, the one who forced her to sign the legal forms, Billy Fitzgerald. He wasn't dressed in combat fatigues or military gear, just a suit and a tie.

'You know him?' he asked.

Darby nodded, about to tell Coop when she realized they were pressed for time. 'I'll fill you in later. Who is he?'

'Special Agent Sergey Martynovich. He's a profiler for CASMIRC.'

She tried to chase the full title through a layer of hazy thoughts and came up empty.

'Sorry, but what's that again?'

'Child Abduction and Serial Murder Investigative Resources Center,' Coop said, flipping through the papers. 'They deal strictly in crime involving kids – abductions and disappearances, homicide and serial murder. Federal unit, works under NCAVC.'

Another federal-created acronym, but at least one she knew: National Center for the Analysis of Violent Crime, founded at the FBI Academy and managed by its Behavioral Science Unit.

Then Coop produced another laser-printed picture, this one of a man dressed in jeans and a black V-neck T-shirt standing on a sunny road with rolling fields behind him. He wore a shoulder holster but she didn't see a badge. He appeared to be scowling directly at the camera, looking downright *pissed*.

Her first thought was of a middle-aged Clint Eastwood: square-jawed; glowering and squinting under the sun; thick brown hair swept back from a high forehead. The man in the picture, though, was paler and packed much more muscle than the iconic movie star. This man had long, meaty arms and rock-hard biceps swollen with veins. Either he deliberately wore his T-shirt too tight to show off the definition in his upper chest and shoulders or he was simply just too big to fit into normal clothing. And he was tall – at least he seemed that way in the photo.

Coop said, 'Have you seen this guy?'

She shook her head. 'No, just Sergey what's-his-name. Who's this?'

'Jack Casey.'

'The former profiler?'

He nodded. 'Worked with the rock stars of Behavioral Sciences when it first started – Ressler, Douglas, you name it. I'd say Casey's a rock star himself, given what I've read about the guy in the past twelve hours. He worked a lot of high-profile cases but there are two that really stand out.'

'Miles Hamilton must be one.'

'Bingo. Did you know that Baltimore's favourite serial killer is about to get a new trial?'

'Something to do with the FBI lab botching evidence.'

'Not botched,' Coop said. 'Planted.'

'By who? Casey?'

'He worked the Hamilton case. That's public knowledge. What's also public knowledge is that Hamilton killed Casey's wife and the unborn child she was carrying.'

'Right. He tied Casey to a chair so he could watch,' she said, more to herself than to Coop. The Hamilton case had made national headlines, and the information was coming back to her in spurts, the first of which was the oddly fascinating fact that Miles Hamilton, the only child of a former Baltimore senator, was just a few weeks shy of nineteen when he killed Casey's wife. And just as oddly fascinating was the fact that Hamilton hadn't killed Casey. The serial murderer had left Casey tied to a chair while his pregnant wife bled out, then hopped in his car and drove to the airport. Police caught Hamilton as he was getting off a plane, on his way to his connecting flight to Paris, with a fake passport and a receipt showing the money he had wired from his father's vast bank accounts.

On the heels of those facts came another titbit she remembered about Casey, this one much more recent. Not that long ago the man had lived *and* worked here in the state of Massachusetts, on the North Shore, as Marblehead's chief of police. The reason she remembered this fact was that Casey had worked a particular case that had also made national headlines. A serial killer someone in the local press had dubbed 'The Sandman' was murdering families in their sleep. Only he deliberately left one family member alive each time. What had garnered the national attention was the Sandman's methodology: he waited until the police were gathered inside and around the house, then detonated a bomb.

Coop said, 'Casey retired after Hamilton was arrested. He spent a few years wandering around and then –'

'He came here,' Darby finished for him. 'The Sandman case, back in '99. You and I had just started working at the lab after it happened.'

'Right, but the thing is, Casey didn't work it alone. Rumour is he had someone helping him. Another former profiler.'

'Who?'

'Malcolm Fletcher.'

A brief silence followed the name.

Darby shifted in her chair. 'Does Fletcher have something to do with what's going on with me?'

'You'd have to ask the feds. Fletcher's prints weren't on

those sheets you gave me, but Casey's were. And this guy Sergey's. They both came back as a ten-point match.'

Coop hadn't jumped on a plane and flown all the way here to tell her that the feds and a retired profiler were involved in what happened to the Rizzo family. He could have emailed the pictures and told her all of this over the phone.

'What's the rest of it?'

'I'm consulting with IPS – Britain's Identity and Passport Service office. They're testing integration across the pond with IAFIS. The feds gave us access to their data, so your FedEx package comes along and I'm thinking, "Let's use a real-live demonstration, see if it actually works." So I processed the prints and fed them into the IPS database. Nothing comes back on our end, so it searches IAFIS and I get word of matching prints. I saw the time stamp. It's 2:00 p.m. my time. Keep that in mind.

'Now, unbeknownst to yours truly, my boss is inside his office speaking to the head of Behavioral Sciences. Here's what's interesting: the fed called my boss an hour *before* the prints came back, and he's grilling my boss about them, wanting to know where they came from, etcetera, etcetera.'

'The prints were coded.'

'Exactly.'

Darby nodded, not at all surprised. The feds ran and owned the national fingerprint database, and sometimes they put secret alerts on certain prints stored within the system. Case in point: Jack Casey. If an unknown set of prints that matched Casey's were to be fed into IAFIS, the FBI's head honchos would be the first to know, allowing the task force assigned to capture him to mobilize their people and equipment without alerting the inquiring law enforcement agency.

'My boss hangs up the phone,' Coop said, 'and, naturally, he comes looking for me. Needless to say, he's *quite* pissed at having one of his consultants feed a set of unauthorized prints into IAFIS without his consent.'

'I'm sorry, Coop, I didn't mean –'

He grabbed her hand. 'It's fine. *I'm* fine. I told him I wanted to try a real-live test, with real prints recovered from real evidence. I got a tongue lashing and that's it. Besides, if these prints hadn't been coded, my boss would have been none the wiser, and you wouldn't be in this mess.'

He let go of her hand.

Darby clutched it back. 'Thank you.'

He winked at her and said, 'Now this third print I found, it doesn't belong to Casey or to any other fed. This one's connected to an old case, a kid –'

The door swung wide open.

'Named Darren Waters,' Coop said. 'He's been missing for thirty-four years.'

44

The door banged against the wall with enough force to leave a mark. Darby didn't flinch. She sat still, her blood cooling.

Jack Casey was much older than the man she'd just seen in the pictures; he'd gone from the young Clint Eastwood to the older but still good-looking and still intimidating Clint: face weathered and wrinkled from too many years spent toiling in the sun; grey hair cut short and receding a bit around the temples. Casey was the same height as Coop, somewhere in the neighbourhood of six five, and, despite his age, the former profiler packed an amazing amount of solid muscle. The man looked as if he could lift a small car without breaking a sweat.

'You,' Casey said, pointing to Coop. 'Get out.'

Darby said, 'He stays, Mr Casey. Or should I call you Special Agent Casey?'

The man's gaze narrowed, surprised either that she knew his name or that she had the audacity to go up against his orders. Casey made his way to her, slowly, and when he reached her chair, he stared down at her, scowling. Unlike Army Boy Billy Fitzgerald, aka Special Agent Sergey Martynovich, the Secret Service agents and other men she'd met who had tried to intimidate her with their tough-guy glares, Casey was the real deal. He was struggling to maintain his composure.

Good, she thought. That gave her a tactical advantage. Angry people didn't think clearly. They made mistakes. They spilled secrets and painted themselves into corners.

'McCormick, right?'

'That's me.'

Casey put one hand on her chair arm. The other gripped the edge of the desk. He had big hands. Tanned, but rough and callused. A carpenter, maybe. Some sort of trade.

His brown leather jacket was unzipped, and when he leaned into her, she caught a glimpse of the shoulder holster. If he was back working with the feds, he certainly wasn't dressing like one: jeans, a black T-shirt and work boots.

'Listen to me carefully, sweetheart.' His voice trembled, struggling to speak clearly over his mounting rage. 'There are two federal agents posted outside this room. You are going to go with them. You are going to sit down with them and answer every one of their questions. If you give them any lip this time, if you so much as accidentally rub up against one, I am personally going to jam an obstruction of justice charge so far up your ass that you won't see daylight again.'

Darby sighed.

'It's a good threat. Honestly, it is.' Her voice was calm, a fact that irritated Casey. His crimson-coloured face, growing darker by the second, looked like it was going to explode off his shoulders. 'One small problem, though. You're going to have to put me in front of a judge, and you and I both know you don't want a judge or anyone else to know about this secret little investigation you're running – especially now, given your negligence.'

'My *what?*'

'Your negligence. Your people *neglected* to tell me that this cult or whoever they are would be following my every move. Your people *neglected* to tell me that they would try to capture or kill me. If I had known the danger, I wouldn't have gone to see John Smith. The man and his wife might still be alive.'

Casey swallowed, his eyes growing dangerously bright.

'And then there's the issue of those army documents I was forced to sign,' she said. 'You had one of your agents impersonate a US Army officer, and he forced me to sign – under duress, I might add – those forged documents.'

'Serious accusations. Going to be tough to prove.'

'I have in my possession a portion of the original documentation.'

Surprise flashed across Casey's face; his eyes widened, just a bit, before he caught himself.

'Three fingerprints were recovered,' she said. 'Yours and ones that belong to Special Agent Sergey Martynovich, the man who impersonated a US Army officer at the BU Biomedical Lab. The third print, though, was the most interesting one. A missing boy named Darren Waters, who's been missing for –' She turned to Coop. 'How many years was it again? Thirty-four years?'

'Thirty-four,' Coop said.

Darby whistled.

She looked back at Casey. 'How in God's name did a missing boy's fingerprints – a boy who has been missing *thirty-four years* – how did his fingerprints manage to get on those forged army forms?'

Casey didn't answer. Some of the heat, though, had left his glare.

'You'd better come up with an answer,' she said. 'Judges don't care for the silent treatment. And they don't look too kindly on federal agents who kick someone to the kerb to use as bait. The people I met at the Rizzo house? They followed me to the blast site.'

Casey tried to hide his confusion. 'When was this?'

Darby tapped the heel of her palm against her forehead. 'That's right, I forgot. You don't know about that because those two bozos you had parked at the end of my street, the ones in the Chevy Tahoe, York and Blue, they blew their cover. Too bad. If they hadn't, they could have followed me to New Hampshire. Maybe then you'd have in custody at least one of the six men I met there.'

Casey looked like he was going to make a move to grab her. Snap her in half like a dry branch, toss the broken pieces aside and then go after Coop, who was still seated and staring down at the table, a hand covering his mouth, she knew, to hide his grin. For reasons she never understood, he always got a kick out of it when she was on the verge of blowing a gasket.

'Doesn't matter,' she said. 'We'll discuss this in front of a judge.'

Darby sprang to her feet. The sudden movement caught Casey off guard; he stumbled back.

'See you at the courthouse.'

She moved past him, to the door. Had her hand on the knob and was turning it when Casey said: 'Those agents were sent there to protect you.'

240

Darby swung around and saw Casey standing with his back to her, his hands thrust deep in his jeans pockets.

'Who are these people?'

Casey didn't answer. Just arched his back and stared up at the ceiling.

'You can answer my questions now, or we can do it in front of a judge,' she said. 'A judge is going to ask you why I needed to be protected, and that's going to create all sorts of problems for you, the first of which is explaining that story you manufactured about the Rizzo home exploding from a meth lab. I was there, as you already know, and I saw the dynamite. I'll start there, then walk the judge through everything that's happened, ending with how I almost got my head blown off last night at a former cop's –'

'Enough,' Casey said, holding up a hand. 'Enough,' he said again, this time in a softer, tired voice. 'You've made your point.'

He turned around and faced her. Blew out a long stream of air. 'Fine,' Casey said. 'We'll talk, but we'll do it alone.'

Coop stood, knowing full well she'd fill him in later. He collected his papers. 'I'll wait for you outside, Miss McCormick.'

Her focus never left Casey. The man's gaze was still pinned on her but he wasn't looking at her. His attention had drifted inward.

The door shut.

'Let's hear it,' Darby said.

45

'Start with the people I met at the Rizzo house,' Darby said.

Casey sat on the edge of the desk. 'I should mention that everything we talk about right now is confidential.'

'I assumed it was.'

'Glad to hear it. Because if any of this information gets leaked, after the Bureau is done with you, I'm going to use every favour I've accumulated over the years to bury you. I don't take too kindly to being blackmailed.'

Darby laughed. 'That's what you're calling this?'

'You've put me in a position where I have no choice but to talk to you. It's the only way I can get you off my back. You've already done enough damage –'

'Stop right there.' Darby felt her anger ride up her spine like a bullet and she stormed over to him and got in his face.

She stared straight into those piercing blue eyes expecting to find something cold and hard. She was taken aback by what she found: a sad weariness, a man who appeared to want nothing more than to go home, lock the doors, unplug the phone and bury himself in his bed.

'Let's get one thing clear right now,' she said. '*I* didn't ask to be put in this situation. The New Hampshire SWAT team commander called *me*. I went into the house and talked to Charlie Rizzo – and it was him, there's no question in my mind. I risked my life, and you and your people kept me locked inside that goddamn quarantine chamber when you knew full well I was no longer a health risk.'

'That was done to keep you protected.'

'Bullshit. You needed time to bury the story about what really happened up north.'

Casey crossed his arms over his chest. 'What do you think the public's reaction would have been if news got out about an attack using nerve gas?'

'A terrorist attack,' she said.

'Exactly. It would have been like 9/11 all over again. Every news outlet from across the country would have been camped out in New Hampshire to report around the clock on an attack on American soil using nerve gas. You were an investigator. You know what it's like trying to work a case while reporters are trying to crawl up your ass. So I came up with the meth lab scenario. Very plausible, happens all the time.'

'How'd you get the locals to sign off on it? Did you have your people pose as army officers? Have them sign forged documents and threaten them with the Patriot Act?'

'Using sarin gas is an act of domestic terrorism,' he said. 'That was our way in. We had to take over the investigation in order to keep your name out of the papers.'

Bullshit, she thought. There was more to it than that.

'From day one,' he said, 'my goal was to keep you safe.'

'But these people somehow still managed to find me.'

'Yes, I know.'

My phone. She had left her iPhone in the lap of the thing with the egg-white skin. All of her information was stored inside that phone. Everything. *They must have found it when they cut him loose from the tree.*

'When did you plant those listening devices inside my condo?'

Casey looked genuinely surprised. 'You found bugs in your home?'

'Only one, as far as I know,' she said. 'On my kitchen phone. Sloppy job, so it was easy to spot.'

'We didn't do it. I'd like to take a look at that, with your permission.'

'Tell me why you used me as bait.'

'I wasn't using you as bait.'

'Then why would you send me out there without telling me about these people? That they would be watching me?'

'We kept your name out of this. We thought there was no way for them to find you. The mobile command trailer? The tapes were still there and we pulled them.'

'And the body in the ambulance?'

'Gone,' he said. 'They shot the EMTs. I put people on you as a precaution.'

'Federal agents or Secret Service?'

'Both.'

'When were you going to tell me?'

He didn't answer.

'How long?' she said.

'How long what?'

'How long were you going to have people watch me?'

'As long as it took,' he said.

'Because you know these people.'

'Let's just say I've had . . . experience.'

Darby waited for the details. Casey didn't offer any.

'I want it all out on the table,' she said. 'Right now.'

'If I tell you, will you go to a safe house?'

'No.'

'That's the only way I can protect you.'

'I've seen your people's talents in action. No, thanks.'

'You're not getting it.' Some of Casey's anger resurfaced. He slid off the desk and stared down at her. 'I'm trying to protect you. I've been trying to keep you safe all this time but you keep kicking me in the goddamn face.'

'Then you shouldn't have lied to me.'

His expression softened slightly. 'This group has been – they're dangerous.' He paused, then added, 'Very dangerous. I can't stress that enough. You need to go with the agents to the safe house. Please.'

Casey had delivered the words without the usual cornball melodrama seen in bad TV shows. He said them almost painfully, and she would have forgiven the cheesy pregnant pause – a lame attempt to let the seriousness of his words sink in – if it wasn't for the way he was looking at her right now, this odd, almost paternal expression.

'What do you want?' she said. 'A hug?'

'You don't understand –'

'I understand perfectly,' she said. 'I tried to bait them at the blast site. They installed tracking devices inside my jacket and on my bike. I thought I was being followed by one, maybe two of these people. Turns out they brought six, three of which I wouldn't even classify as human.'

'What are you talking about?'

She told him about hiding in the dumpster, about watching the three people standing on the edge of the woods. Told him about watching these three through her night-vision goggles when the ghoulish-looking creature scrambled to the edge of the crater holding a stun baton. Told him about the thing scrambling down into the crater and into the basement and then coming back up and making that creepy squawking sound in the night air.

Casey should have refuted what she had just said, maybe excused himself and then returned with two psychiatric orderlies holding a straitjacket clinking with buckles. But he didn't say anything, didn't seem at all surprised.

'Why did they want to capture me?' she asked.

'I don't know, which is why you're going into seclusion for a while.'

'You're a bad liar.'

'Come on, let's go.'

'I'm not sitting in a safe house with a bunch of low-grade feds who got stuck babysitting me.'

'What are you going to do? You can't go back to work.'

'I'm going to find Mark Rizzo.'

'He's already dead. If he isn't, he's on his way.'

'Then I'll keep digging.'

'Small problem,' he said. 'You're no longer in law enforcement.'

'Neither are you, but here you are, plucked out of retirement and running the show. Why?'

He didn't answer.

'I've already uncovered evidence,' she said.

That got his full attention.

'What sort of evidence?' he asked.

'I'll turn it over after you bring me on board.'

'To do what?'

'To assist in the investigation,' she said. 'I've seen these people up close. And if you're worried about protection, then move me into the inner circle. I'd be safer, sticking close to you since –'

'Deliberately withholding evidence is a clear charge of obstruction of justice.'

'It sure is. And you can get me locked up for it too.' She snapped her fingers, then added, 'Oh, but then you're back to your original problem of having me speak in front of a judge, and you're not going to allow that to happen. And I'm not going to sit around a safe house waiting for these people to find me – and they will. They found Mark Rizzo, and my guess is they're also looking for you.'

She waited for Casey to speak, to refute what she had just said, but he only sat there, staring.

'I think I know why you're here,' Darby said. 'The *real* reason you're here.'

46

'I've read about you,' Darby said. 'Followed you in the papers and on the Internet.'

'You shouldn't trust the press,' Casey said with a wry, tired grin.

'So you're saying you didn't plant that fibre evidence at Hamilton's house.'

'I'm assuming you have a point to make so let's hear it.'

'After the Hamilton case, you retired from the Bureau. Then, years later, you came back to police work – as a detective here, in Massachusetts. You worked the Sandman case. With Malcolm Fletcher.'

No reaction from Casey.

'Miles Hamilton,' she said, 'has been gearing up for a retrial for the past few years, and there's been no word from you. The Bureau has stated in the press that you moved out of the country. That they had no idea of your whereabouts or how to get in contact with you, yet here you are, surrounded by federal agents and heading up an investigation. Want to know what I think?'

'Sure, why not?'

'I think you've been in the country the whole time. I think you've been living under an alias and I wouldn't be surprised to learn that the Bureau helped you because they don't want you to take the stand in Hamilton's retrial. And

I think you have some sort of history with this religious group or cult or whatever you call them. I think they've been looking for you for a long, long time. I think you've been moving around a lot. I think you remarried – you have a faint white line on your ring finger, but you're not wearing your wedding band – and I'm willing to bet you have at least one child. I think that, given what happened to your first wife and your unborn daughter, you agreed to come out of exile and make a run at these people because that's the only way you can keep your new family safe.'

Casey stared at her, his body very, very still. It reminded her of the way the air turned just before a thunderstorm broke.

Darby said, 'I don't think they'll make a run at me again, at least in the short term. Right now, they're too busy planning. They're going to try to find a way to bait us. My guess is they'll come after you since I don't have anyone they can use against me. My parents are dead. I don't have any brothers or sisters. I'm not married, and the only person I care about is the man you saw sitting here at this table.

'So you have a choice to make. You can bring me inside your inner circle, where I can help you out, or I can do it on my own. Either way, I'm going to get in front of this. I'm not going to spend my time sitting in some safe house. And I'm sure as hell not going to spend the rest of my life living under different names and hopping from state to state praying to God that these people don't find me.

'Ball's in your court,' she said. 'How do you want to play it?'

Casey weighed the question on his cold scales. The only sound came from the hum of the overhead lights.

Then he looked down at the scuffed floor between them. Looked at it as if something expensive and rare had shattered there and was lying in pieces.

He let out a rush of air through his nose.

'You're right,' he said.

His expression had changed. Become more haggard.

'Okay,' he said. 'I'll bring you on board. Probably better that way. I can keep a close eye on you.'

'And Coop. That's the man who was sitting in here with me, Jackson Cooper. He stays next to me. That condition is non-negotiable.'

Casey thought about it for a moment, then finally nodded.

'Now let's talk about Darren Waters,' she said.

Casey rubbed his eyes. 'He was abducted in July of '76. He lived in Washington – the state, not the city. He was four when they took him. Mother put him down to sleep and the next morning he was gone. He suddenly reappeared in the summer of 2001.'

Darby ran the numbers in her head. *Disappears in 1976 when he's four, then reappears in '01, which puts his age then somewhere in the neighbourhood of twenty-nine, which means now he's –* Jesus *– thirty-eight years old.*

'Police in Reno, Nevada, picked him up,' Casey said. 'He was rooting through a restaurant dumpster. Wasn't wearing a stitch of clothing. An employee came out, tried to shoo Waters away from the dumpster, and the guy ended up with two broken arms and a concussion. Police came and Waters was just sitting there eating scraps. It took three policemen to take him down.'

'And the police knew to call you?'

'No. The Bureau asked me if I'd be willing to consult.'

'The Bureau found out because his fingerprints had been coded.'

He sighed. 'Yes, we had his prints coded. I was called and asked if I'd be willing to consult and talk to Waters because of my prior experience with these people.'

Darby wanted to know more about Casey's experience with 'these people', but decided to stick with Waters for the moment. 'How do you know they were the ones who abducted him? No, let me guess. He had a certain Latin phrase tattooed on his neck.'

Casey nodded. '*Et in Arcadia ego.* Literally translated, it means "Even in Arcadia, I exist" – the "I" being Death. We believe it's a reference to someone who once enjoyed the pleasures of life and has now been transformed in death. That's all we know.'

'Waters didn't shed any light on it?'

'His tongue and vocal cords had been removed.'

Darby flashed back to her first encounter with the pale-faced creature with the missing tongue and teeth and said, 'Did he have a black plastic device sewn into his back and above his spine?'

'No.'

'Where's Waters now?'

'Someplace where they can't find him.'

'Not even his parents?'

'They died in a car crash, a couple of months after Waters

251

disappeared. Police think the father ran the car off the road on purpose. I read the reports and I'm inclined to agree.'

'How did his fingerprints wind up on your forged army forms?'

'I had a Bureau lawyer draft up the forms so they'd look legitimate. I had them with me when I went to see Waters, and he –'

'Why did you go to see him?'

'To make preparations to move him to another hospital. The Bureau moves him every couple of years. But, with what happened in New Hampshire, I wanted to move him again as a precaution. I wanted to oversee everything myself so there'd be no mistakes, no way to find him.' Casey sighed. 'Darren Waters grabbed the forms from me and took them over to his table and his crayons and markers.'

'You're telling me a 38-year-old man thought you had, what, brought him a colouring book?'

'Physically, he's an adult. But he has the mentality of a child.'

'What happened to him?'

Casey blinked away whatever image had appeared in front of his eyes. He was about to speak when the door swung open.

47

Darby turned and saw the army man she had met at the BU Biomedical Lab, Billy Fitzgerald, aka Special Agent Sergey Martynovich. The man had traded his army fatigues for a stylish navy-blue suit.

He came into the room alone but didn't shut the door behind him. She saw a mass of dark suits and ties huddled outside, an unknown sea of faces except for one: the well-groomed man she'd met at the BU Biomedical Lab, the head of security, Neal Keats. The man towered over the other agents and wore an earpiece, his gaze locked on Casey.

Security, she thought. *A standard-issued fed, maybe Secret Service.*

'Sergey,' Casey said, 'I've decided to let Dr McCormick into the investigation.'

'And Jackson Cooper,' she said.

Casey nodded. 'And Jackson Cooper.'

Sergey didn't so much as glance at her, but she caught the hardness in the man's gaze, a single-minded determination fighting like hell against a mounting horror.

'I have the plane in the air, with the lab people,' he said. 'Everyone we need is on it. Brightest minds and the best equipment.'

'What's going on?' Casey said.

Sergey's voice was calm now, like a doctor steeling himself before handing over a terminal diagnosis to a patient. 'You need to stand here and listen to me. You need to hear all of it.'

'Tell me now.'

'The bastards found the safe house. Taylor – *wait*, Jack.'

Sergey had blocked Casey's path. Pressed both hands against Casey's chest and pushed like a man keeping a stone statue from toppling over. Casey was a good foot taller than Sergey and three times as wide and doing everything in his power to shove the agent aside and then race through the blockade of suits crowding the doorway. Darby could only think, *You're going to need more bodies.*

'Taylor and Sarah aren't there,' Sergey said. 'Did you hear me? Taylor and Sarah *aren't there.*'

'The implants, you said –'

'The satellites locked on to their signals. We got a blip in Connecticut and then the signals vanished, we don't know why yet.

'Now listen to me, Jack. *Listen.* The plane's going to touch down in Florida at any minute. I've been on the phone with the Sarasota police. They're at the house now, and they promised not to go inside the house until our people arrive. We're going to get the crime scene fresh. The forensic guy you like, Drake? He's going to go into the house. Alone. He's going in with a video camera. We're going to have it linked up to a secured satellite link and you're going to be able to see and hear everything inside the techs' van. We're setting up the equipment right now. We're –'

'*Are you out of your goddamn mind?* I'm not staying here –'

'Listen to me, Jack. *Listen.* They're bringing your wife and daughter here. *Here.* The Boston office received a phone call from a young girl claiming to be your daughter. Came in a couple of hours ago. I heard it. They patched the recording to my phone. It's her voice, Jack. Sarah's. It didn't sound doctored or spliced together. It was *Sarah's* voice, Jack, I'm certain of it.'

Something – maybe the relief of knowing his wife and daughter were alive, or maybe just the hope of it – made Casey back off. Sergey's hands dropped and fell to his sides. His olive-skinned forehead shone with perspiration.

Casey, to his credit, forced himself to stay in the room. His attention retreated inward, but the fear and worry and panic were all still there, radiating off him like waves of heat.

'Sarah gave an address,' Sergey said. 'It's local. She said you have to go there alone. Just you, no federal agents or Secret Service.'

Darby glanced back to Keats, thinking she was right about him, about his being Secret Service.

Casey said, 'And do what?'

'Wait for her to call. She said she's going to call. At one.'

Darby checked her watch. Quarter to nine.

'I think Taylor's with her,' Sergey said. 'I heard crying in the background. Sounded like a woman.'

48

Darby spoke up for the first time: 'What's the address?'

Both Sergey and Casey snapped their attention to her, startled, and glared at her as if to say, *Who the hell are you and how did you get in here?*

'No. 62 Mason,' Sergey said. 'The house —'

'Is where the Rizzo family lived in Brookline,' Darby finished for him.

Sergey nodded.

'Who's there now?'

'Family named Hu,' he said. 'Two daughters, ages six and nine.'

Darby saw the knowledge in the man's eyes and said, 'They're dead.'

'I can't say that for sure, not yet.' A visible sadness swept through his voice and body. 'We pulled the family's records, got their numbers and started making calls. Father hasn't shown up for work and daughters haven't been to school.'

'How long?'

'Three days.'

'Mother?'

'Works from home.' Sergey flicked his weary gaze back to Casey. 'I haven't sent anyone to scope out the house yet. I wanted to get your input first since you know these people better than anyone else.'

Fear rose in Casey's eyes and the man tightened his jaw against it. She sensed most of the people here were afraid – afraid that their lives could possibly be at stake. But they didn't know how to hold the terror. They didn't have Casey's experience, and she sensed they were looking to him not only for direction but also for guidance as to how to act. And Casey knew it. He stood steady on his feet, thinking over the rising swells of fear for his wife and daughter, and looked away from the gazes.

A cell phone rang. Sergey reached into his pocket and took the call. Motioned to Casey to give him a moment.

Casey turned to the desk where she had sat with Coop and ran the big fingers of one hand along the edges.

Darby needed to say what came next. Casey probably already knew it, but the words still had to be spoken out loud.

She went over to the door, shut it and then returned to him. He was still running a hand across the edge of the desk. She could hear Sergey whispering in the corner, murmured voices and ringing phones coming from somewhere beyond the wall.

'Special Agent Casey –'

'Jack,' he said, absently. 'I'm not a federal investigator any more.'

'But you were one once, Jack, so you know you can't go to the house.'

'They won't kill me. Not yet.' His voice sounded flat. Detached. 'They're going to send me a message first.'

'They already did. The phone call from your daughter.'

Casey shook his head. 'That was to get my attention.

257

Now they'll give me a demonstration of their intentions. Why else would they deliberately pick the Rizzo house?'

'They left something there for you to find. Something they want you to see.'

'Right.'

'Have they done something like this before?'

'What's that?'

'Have they contacted an investigator?' she asked. 'Taken a family member?'

'Or, in my case, an entire family.' He shook his head. 'This is a first.'

'The Rizzo house is in a rural neighbourhood. Lots of trees, lots of places for a sniper to hide. You go there, you could get your head blown off the moment you step out of the car. Or they have the house rigged with an IED, get you and all of us out of the way.'

Casey didn't answer.

'The Sandman did that, remember?'

'Nothing's going to happen,' he said.

'How do you know that?'

'Because I'm a special case.'

She waited for him to explain.

When he didn't, she said, 'Why are you a special case?'

'They've tried to kill me,' he said. 'Twice.'

'When?'

'First time was in late 2001. Darren Waters was at a private treatment facility, but I had found one more suitable for his . . . condition. We moved him to a safe house while we made arrangements, setting up an alias for him, and this group found us and tried a stunt like the one they pulled at the Rizzo house. Waters survived. I did too, along with Sergey.'

Casey placed two fingers underneath the edge of the desk.

'Second time was about five months after the Sandman case,' he said. 'I had moved away and remarried under a different name. Somehow they found us. We made it out of that one okay, but I reached out to the Bureau for help – my wife was pregnant – and they offered to put us into sort of a . . . I guess you could call it a special witness-protection programme. Only a handful of people know about it.'

'People you know and trust?'

'I know where you're heading, and no, I don't know these people, nor can I say with any confidence that I trust them. Could this group have people on the inside? Maybe.'

'Probably,' she said.

'Computers are a more likely bet. Everything's stored on them now. You know your way around them, you can sit somewhere halfway across the world and find people's lives like this.' He snapped his fingers. 'Get in and out without leaving a trace, usually.'

'You know they're good with computers?'

'No, I don't. That's what's infuriating about this group. We don't know much of anything. They snatch kids and they disappear – the kids *and* the group.' He lifted the corner of the desk with his fingers. 'We know they've been doing it for at least four decades, maybe even longer, but we don't know *why* they're doing it.' The desk legs hung two inches above the floor. 'One of them escaped, and for all practical purposes he's a vegetable. Oh, and the best part is that anyone who gets close to these people winds up dead.'

He let go of the desk. The legs slapped against the floor as he turned to her.

'Now I hope you understand the reasoning behind all this subterfuge,' he said. 'I wanted to keep you far away from this. Now you're in the middle of it and you can't go back to an ordinary life. You realize that, don't you?'

'I'll go to the former Rizzo home,' she said. 'I've been in there, I know my way around.'

'Didn't you just tell me that one or more of these people would be watching to –'

'I can get inside the house without being seen.'

'And how, exactly, are you going to do that?'

'Simple architecture,' Darby said. 'They won't see me coming, I guarantee it.'

49

Darby started with the most important part – how she was going to get into the house undetected – when Sergey snapped his phone shut.

'Plane touched down,' Sergey said, and then went on to explain how federal lab technicians were now riding inside a van, on their way to the safe house in Sarasota. The tech Casey liked, Drake, had already set up the equipment needed for the video feed.

'You know those small lights you can wear on your forehead?' Sergey said. 'The one attached to the straps, looks like a miner's light? Drake's going to be wearing something like that, only instead of a light it'll have a video camera. We just tested it out, got a crystal-clear picture. What he sees, you'll see. What he hears, you'll hear. It'll be like you're walking in there –'

'How many?'

'Just Drake. Nobody else –'

'The agents you had guarding my family,' Casey said. 'There were eight of them, right?'

Sergey nodded.

'And?' Casey prompted.

'All dead,' Sergey said. 'I don't know what went wrong yet, Jack, but I swear we'll –'

'Is the video feed set up?'

'In about an hour.'

'Van out front?'

Sergey nodded. 'Now, about the Rizzo house, I'm thinking –'

'Talk to her, she's already got a plan, a solid one.'

Then Casey whisked past them, and Darby saw the ghosts of his dead wife and unborn daughter hanging in the man's frightened eyes. She watched him open the door and push his way past the bodies, wondering how much violence and suffering a person's mind could take before it broke him.

The door shut and Darby looked at Sergey, expecting to see some of that brash cockiness she'd witnessed at the BU Lab when the man had played the role of the army officer, Billy Fitzgerald, the second-in-command of the facility. She didn't see any, but he straightened, puffing up his chest as he took in a deep breath. With Casey no longer in the room, Sergey was going now to give her the lay of the land, take this moment to lecture her about who was in charge around here. He came up to her and she was surprised to find what looked like compassion swimming in his tired brown eyes.

Darby said, 'You have a problem with me being here, let's get it out on the table right now before we get moving.'

'I wish you weren't here, but not for the reasons you think. I'm assuming Jack told you why he wanted you kept inside the quarantine chamber.'

She nodded.

'He was adamant about that – about not wanting you

anywhere near this,' he said. 'Truth be told, I wanted to bring you into the fold from the beginning, after we found out what had happened at the Rizzo house. I told Jack you'd seen these people up close, for one, and with your background and experience, I argued it would help to have a pair of fresh eyes. I've been working this thing far too long now.'

'How long?'

'Since they took my son.'

He saw the confusion on her face and said, 'Jack didn't tell you about Arman?'

'No.'

'They took him when he was five,' Sergey said. 'Came into the house in broad daylight and shot my wife when she answered the door. Fifteen years ago, this happened. Arman would be twenty today.'

'I'm sorry.'

'My fault. I should have . . . I was a young hotshot profiler full of drive and ego and thought I could crack this group. Maybe you can help me now. Let's hear this plan of yours.'

She told him. The man listened to her intently, without interrupting, and when she finished, he thought it over for a moment and then nodded.

They discussed equipment next, Darby giving him exact names and specifications.

'I can do that,' Sergey said. 'Okay, let me make some phone calls. I'll meet you out front in a few minutes.'

'What about the gun charges?'

But he had already opened the door and run off. The

crowd blocking the doorway had dispersed, and when she emerged into the bullpen she saw that it had gone back to normal, everyone working the phones or their computers, people flipping through case files, people moving in and out of doorways, everyone busy.

Coop stood off to the side, waving to her.

'Freedman here?' she asked.

'No, he left about an hour ago. Gun charges have been dropped. Didn't take much time since it was bullshit to begin with.'

'I've got to get my stuff from inventory.'

The cop seated on a stool behind the grille rose slowly from his chair and then took his sweet goddamn time to collect the envelopes storing her wallet, keys, cell phone, belt and shoulder holster. She was without a sidearm. Her MK23 had been confiscated by the state's lab techs for testing.

Two men, mountains of pale flesh poured into black suits, blocked her path to the front door. They wore ear-pieces and she could see the outline of their Kevlar vests underneath their shirts.

'You need to wait here, Miss McCormick,' one of them said. 'You too, Mr Cooper.'

Bright light poured through the glass front door leading into the warm lobby. From where she stood she could see the hard blue sky, cloudless, the sun bright and strong. She moved closer and then saw part of a black sedan parked a few feet away from the entrance, the driver's-side window down, a Secret Service man seated behind the wheel, talking into his wrist mike.

One of the lobby's Secret Service agents held up a hand and said, 'Back up, Miss McCormick. We'll tell you when it's safe.'

She nodded and took a step back. Breathed deeply and smelled the coppery stench lining her nostrils. John Smith's blood, his wife's blood. Her fingernails and the callused parts of her palms and fingers were stained near-black and she saw John Smith's face exploding into bone and hair and skin. Saw Mavis Smith, remembered the feel of the woman's blood spurting out against her fingers – and then the enormity of it hit her, how she'd be forced to live her life going forward, under constant guard, her every movement scrutinized. Travelling from state to state, from safe house to safe house, switching names and identities, living on the run until this group was found. Until every one of its members was arrested or dead.

But how many were there?

The question swelled inside her as a fragment from her conversation with Casey rolled through her head and made her skin turn cold. These people were lurking somewhere beyond these walls, waiting. Watching and planning and sharpening their knives. Cleaning their guns.

Coop placed a hand on her shoulder and some of the cramping tension inside her chest and shoulders loosened. He led her to the far corner and they turned their backs to the agents so they could have some privacy.

He kept his hand on her shoulder when he leaned in close and said, 'You okay?'

She nodded. Coop's eyes searched her face. The green one was the most interesting. Flecked with tiny specks of gold you could see only when you stood this close. She felt his hand and she could smell him and thought, incredibly, under the circumstance: *So this is what it's like to find your other half in this world.*

'I'm fine,' she said. 'Thanks again for coming.'

'Anytime, Darbs.' He grinned, picked something out of her hair and tossed it to the floor. 'You could use a shower at some point. I'm just saying . . .'

'How long can you stay?'

He shrugged. 'It's open-ended. Family emergency, I told my boss. He said to take my time. The Brits are good about holidays – that's what they call vacations over there.'

'Let me start at the beginning,' Darby said.

50

Darby had finished explaining last night's conversation with John Smith when word came down it was time to move.

The Secret Service agents escorted them to an over-sized black van parked a few feet away from the main doors. They stayed close, holding their arms, and in the space of a few steps, she saw a scattering of Secret Service agents guarding the area. Saw them standing on street corners. Caught a flash of one with a pair of binoculars on the roof across the street, saw another standing guard near the side door of another black van. Casey was in there, clamping down on his fear as he watched a man hundreds of miles away searching the blood-splattered walls, floors and bodies for evidence, clues to help him find his wife and daughter before they joined the dead.

She stepped up inside the van, Coop moving right behind her, and saw Sergey sitting hunched forward at a small desk, phone pressed against his ear and his forehead resting on the heel of his palm as he listened to someone on the other end of the line.

The side door slammed shut and the van started rolling, slowly at first, then gaining speed. The warm interior, lit from the half-dozen computer screens, blinking lights and a small desk lamp next to Sergey, had that pleasant new-carpet smell.

This was no cheap five-and-dime surveillance rig. Looking around, she saw the new encryption packs developed by the CIA on the wall-mounted phone. The wall behind Sergey contained another desk, this one longer, with an array of forensic tools, each one bolted to the surface: dual-slide microscope, a scanning electron microscope and portable mass spectrometer. In the back, to her left, was a locked metal gun cabinet.

Darby checked her watch. It was coming up on 10:30 a.m.

Sergey rose halfway out of his seat and reached up to the wall to hang up the phone.

'That was the woman you asked me to speak to, Virginia Cavanaugh,' he said, plopping back down in his bolted chair. 'You were right about the tunnels.'

Coop said, 'Tunnels?'

She hadn't told Coop about this part. She had run out of time when the Secret Service agents came for them.

Sergey turned to the computer monitor on the desk, grabbed an edge and swung it around to show them the screen holding an aerial satellite photograph – a close-up roof shot of the Rizzo family's former Brookline home surrounded by dozens of trees in full autumn bloom. Darby got out of her seat and knelt, grabbing the edge of the desk for balance.

'Here's the Rizzo house,' she said, and then traced her finger diagonally across the wooded area, stopping less than a quarter of a mile away, on the roof belonging to a sprawling three-floor mock-Tudor home. 'This belongs to a woman named Virginia Cavanaugh, the Rizzo family's old neighbour. An old Prohibition tunnel runs between the two houses.'

Coop said, 'And you know this from, what, your old days as a bootlegger?'

'When I worked Charlie Rizzo's case, someone, a detective or patrolman, I forget which, told me the Rizzo and Cavanaugh houses were owned by some big Irish family who made all of their money in lumber. When the Great Depression hit, the money started to dry up, and this family had something on the order of twenty kids and grandchildren.'

'Small family by Irish standards.'

'True. So this small but enterprising Irish clan turned to the one known commodity available to them at the time. Hint: it's not growing potatoes.'

'Then I'd have to say bootlegging.'

'Correct. Prohibition was in full swing, so they manufactured moonshine and beer in their basement and then rolled the big barrels across the tunnel to where the Cavanaugh home now sits. Now ask why.'

'Why?'

Darby grinned slightly, enjoying the easy banter she had with him, missing it. For a moment it took the grief and severity of her previous conversation with Casey and Sergey and muted it.

She returned to her seat. 'The Cavanaugh home used to be the site for this Irish family's lumber company. They used the house as an office and sold their lumber there, so it was a perfect spot to pick up the illegal booze. Trucks pull into a lumberyard all the time, right? But in the driveway of a home, not so much.'

Coop raised his hand. 'Question. How do you know this tunnel is still in service?'

Darby turned to Sergey.

'Virginia Cavanaugh,' Sergey said. 'Woman's in her eighties and told me her home – the aforementioned site of the lumberyard – has stayed in her family for the past three generations. They will it free and clear to the surviving family members, the only stipulation is that it can't be sold.'

'Clever,' Coop said.

'Cavanaugh told me her uncle took her through the tunnel once, you know, part of a history lesson or something,' Sergey said. 'As far as she knows, you can still walk through it, but you won't know until you're actually there.'

Darby said, 'So she agreed to let us in.'

Sergey nodded.

'What about the other part?' she asked.

'No problem there,' Sergey said. 'I think it gave the old bird a thrill, getting a call from the FBI to help assist an investigation. That plus I don't think she's real fond of her neighbours.'

'What gave you that impression?'

'She called them "chinks".'

Coop said, 'That's one clue, sure.'

Darby leaned forward and with her eyes on Sergey said, 'Tell me the rest of it. How Casey found this group.'

'The short version is this,' Sergey said. 'When Casey was working as a profiler, he was sent to consult on a series of abductions that occurred in and around Los Angeles over a seven-year time period. This was back in '81. Eleven victims, all kids. The youngest was six, the oldest twelve. They came from different backgrounds – poor parents, rich ones, middle class – and the racial backgrounds were different. Black, white, you name it. Each boy or girl was snatched somewhere outside their home, and each abduction was quick and clean, no witnesses.

'Reviewing the cases, Jack discovered that each vic was the youngest family member. Eleven victims, many of whom had older siblings, and each vic was the youngest. What were the odds? That was the only unifying thread he found.'

The wall phone rang. Sergey took the call, listened for a moment then said 'Okay' and hung up.

'On the ninth abduction,' he said, 'the one near Chino Hill Park, a witness saw a van pull up next to a kid riding his bike. Kid's name was Mathew Zuckerman. He's ten, pretty good-sized boy for his age, lots of weight, and the van pulls up to him and pauses just a moment and then speeds away, leaving the bike bouncing across the dirt road.'

'So you're talking two people,' Darby said. 'The driver and whoever was in the back of the van.'

'At *least* two people. The boy wasn't light, so you'd need at least two to pull and lift the kid from the bike that fast.'

'And that's when Casey came to the conclusion this was a group rather than a single serial killer.'

Sergey nodded. 'That was his theory, yes. Now the detective who caught the Zuckerman case, he was this young guy probably looking to make a name for himself because he forced the forensic guys to collect and bag into evidence every piece of trash along the entire stretch of road. We're talking about a good mile before you can turn. Thank God this guy was that thorough; otherwise he wouldn't have found the empty syringe tube.

'The state lab did a good job with the people and resources they had, and Jack convinced them to send everything to our lab, including the bike. We managed to lift a print off the tube and got lucky. The print, we later discovered, belonged to a ten-year-old boy named Francis Levin who disappeared on his way home from school in '54.'

'Wait,' Darby said. 'Your fingerprint database wasn't operational until '99. How did Levin's prints get into the system?'

'When Casey stopped working the original cases, a different task force took over before it was finally blended into CASMIRC. Any only or youngest child who was either abducted or who disappeared under mysterious circumstances – the task force made sure that hard copies of their prints were on file. When the IAFIS database went operational, the task force simply loaded and coded their prints.'

'So you didn't find out Levin was behind the abduction until '99.'

'Correct. We don't have prints for every missing kid. We got lucky with Levin because the police had lifted prints from his bedroom after he was abducted.'

'Was Levin one of the California abductions Casey investigated?'

Sergey shook his head. 'Levin was born and raised in Oregon. Jack had Behavioral Sciences pull up every missing person case where the vic was either an only child or the youngest child in the family, and the entire West Coast lit up like a Christmas tree.'

'How many kids?'

'Eighty-six,' Sergey said.

Coop mumbled, 'Jesus.'

'And that's just the West Coast,' Sergey said. 'This group or cult – I still have no idea what to call them – they've been travelling across the country all this time, snatching the youngest child of families.'

'How many?' Darby asked again.

'The last time I checked,' Sergey said, 'the number was just over three hundred.'

51

Darby's gaze dropped from Sergey's face to the tops of the man's polished black Oxfords, her head dizzy with calculations.

Francis Levin disappears in '54 and shows up in '81 when he snatches this kid named Zuckerman and Levin's prints are found on a syringe. That's twenty-seven years. And now Casey is here and he's saying the same group is responsible and that's fifty-six years, they've been snatching kids for at least fifty-six years.

Sergey was saying something to her.

'I'm sorry, can you repeat that?'

'I said the only thing we know with any degree of certainty is that they abduct the youngest child of the family. For example, Charlie Rizzo. We know he was the youngest member of his family, so when he was abducted, we made sure his prints were entered into the IAFIS system. Now, I'm not suggesting *all* of these missing kids who are the youngest family members can be attributed to this group, so that three hundred number could be lower.'

'Or much, much larger,' Darby said. 'There's collateral damage, the people they killed, like John Smith and his wife.'

And your wife, she added to herself.

'Yes,' Sergey said, 'you're correct. But I'm focusing on just the missing children. The fact is we don't know anything about this group. Who they are or what they do. Why they snatch the youngest kid from the family.'

Darby was thinking of what Charlie Rizzo had said to his father – *Tell her,* Daddy. *Tell her what you did* – and said: 'The parents of these missing kids, you mean to tell me you found absolutely nothing in their backgrounds?'

'Nothing that can tell us why their kids were taken, no.'

'I find that hard to swallow.'

'I do too. But, still, it remains that these could simply be random abductions. You're more than welcome to take a look at the case files.'

'What about bodies?'

'Not one. Whatever happened to them, we don't know. The cases are unsolved.'

'Casey – Jack – told me he was called back when Darren Waters was found.'

'You mean when he reappeared,' Sergey said. 'We asked Jack to come in and consult, since Waters was one of those cases that lit up on the West Coast – only child, snatched from home, etcetera. So we took Waters into custody, brought him to what we thought was a secured location –'

'Where this group somehow managed to find him.'

'Yes.'

'How?'

'Followed would be my guess.'

'How, though?'

'You don't think they knew this guy escaped?' Then, as if reading her mind, he said, 'I see. No, I don't think it was an inside job. Nevada police, they didn't know who Waters was, so they ran his prints, and we had all of those coded. Techs operating the IAFIS computers didn't have security access for that particular code, and neither did the guy who ran the department at the time. So the prints got bounced upstairs, and that's when I got called. And if you think I had something to do with my son's abduction, you're wrong. These bastards tried to kill me when Jack and I had Waters at the safe house.'

He pulled up a trouser leg. A chunk of his calf muscle was gone, as if a shark had got hold of it and ripped the flesh free.

'Hollow point,' Sergey said. 'Shattered my tibia and the exit wound blew out most of my calf muscle. Almost bled to death. I don't walk with a limp any more, but I can't run, and anytime it rains or snows, the leg throbs like a mad bastard.'

He let go of the fabric. 'We investigated the inside angle and couldn't find anything.'

'How secure is your fingerprint database?'

'Very secure,' he said. 'We checked into that. No break-ins.'

'Ever had one?'

'If we did, I don't know about it.'

'And Darren Waters was never able to shed any light on these people or how he escaped?'

Sergey shook his head. 'He can't speak or write. Well, he can write now, but on a first-grade level.'

'Jack mentioned something happened to Waters but didn't tell me specifics.'

'This group gave Waters a transorbital lobotomy – a rather crude one. You familiar with the procedure?'

Darby nodded, wishing she didn't know the details about the barbaric operation popularized in the US by Dr Walter Freeman, who, through the mid fifties, had used the 'ice pick' procedure on thousands of schizophrenic inmates and, later, on depressed housewives and 'unruly' children. The patient was given 'electroconvulsive therapy' – shocked with electricity until unconscious – and then an ice pick was inserted into the upper eyelid. A hammer tapped the tip past the nasal cavity bone and into the brain's frontal lobe, where the pick severed neural pathways. Some patients survived, but a good majority died or were left with severe disabilities. And almost every one had been reduced to a childlike state devoid of any personality.

'Darren Waters,' Sergey said, 'is severely handicapped – mentally and physically. He lives in a constant state of fear. He's medicated most of the time.'

'With what?'

'Thorazine.'

'Why? He a danger to other patients?'

'Sometimes,' Sergey said. 'Mostly the poor son of a bitch screams about the monsters coming through the walls to eat him.'

A voice echoed over a speaker: 'Arrival in five minutes.'

Sergey gripped the armrests. 'We better get you dressed and ready.'

52

The van came to a stop a few minutes later. Sergey opened the back doors and Darby saw a cracked parking lot; a dumpster and trees that shook in the wind were on its edges. He shut the doors just as quickly to give her some privacy to get dressed.

Coop had stayed behind. He sat hunched forward on the bench with his elbows resting on his knees and rubbing his hands. He stared at his fingers.

She had stripped down into her Hanes bra and boy shorts when he said, 'You ever get tired of it?'

Darby slipped into the pair of black trousers Sergey had laid out for her. 'Tired of what?'

'Rushing in where angels fear to tread.'

She put on a long-sleeved Nomex shirt to keep in her body heat. Tucked it into her trousers and, smiling, said, 'Someone's got to do it.'

Coop didn't return the smile. 'Why you, though?'

She shrugged, tying her hair behind her head. 'Because I'm good at it.'

'At violence.'

'At doing what's right,' she said. 'What's eating at you? You pissed at me for bringing you into this?'

'Par for the course.'

'So what's eating you?'

He didn't answer. She worked a black polypropylene thermal balaclava over her head.

'Charlie,' she said.

Coop looked up at her.

'He wanted to expose these people,' she said. 'You heard what Sergey said about all those missing kids?'

He nodded, like he agreed with the point but not the method.

Darby tossed him her key ring. 'Tell Sergey to go and search my place for the listening devices. And tell him to take my machine and listen to the voicemail where I'm talking to one of these people from the Rizzo house, the one I tied to the tree who later escaped. He'll know what I'm talking about.'

'Sure. Anything else?'

'Yeah, one last thing. The other night, at the blast site, one of these . . . things cut itself inside the basement. I collected a blood sample. It's in a Band-Aid box in my bike trunk. . . . What's wrong now?'

'I'm worried about you, Darby. At some point, your lucky streak is going to run out, and when it does, I don't want to be there to see what's left.'

Darby opened the back doors and Coop's parting words drifted away in the bright, warm sunlight flooding the back parking lot behind a police station.

Virginia Cavanaugh, a thin-boned, grey-haired woman who could have passed as a Catholic school nun – severe-looking and dressed in bland cashmere sweater, blue polyester slacks and black orthopedic shoes with Velcro straps – stood next to her sensible tan-coloured Buick LeSabre, the trunk already popped open. Darby looked at the woman and saw a home with plastic-covered furniture, bed sheets folded in tight hospital corners.

Sergey had already explained to the woman what she needed to do. Cavanaugh didn't ask any questions because there wasn't any need. Her part was simple. All she had to do was drive back to the house, go back to watching the TV or reading or whatever she did to pass her days.

Darby lifted the trunk lid and found that Virginia Cavanaugh had some compassion in her. The woman had placed a pillow and blanket inside her clean and tidy trunk.

Darby climbed inside. Sergey handed over a rucksack containing the equipment and tools she had asked for and then shut the lid. A moment later the car started, and the Cavanaugh woman drove smoothly back to her home.

53

Darby kept track of time in her head. Twenty seconds shy of ten minutes, she heard a garage door open. A moment later the car came to a stop and then the motor shut off. The garage door came down, and under the grinding sound she heard the latch for the trunk pop free.

She climbed out with the rucksack and followed the woman up a set of stairs and inside a house with tall, white-painted walls and furniture covered in plastic, the uncomfortably warm air smelling faintly of cigarette smoke and burned bacon.

The basement was cavernous and cool, the walls lined with the kind of dark wood panelling made popular in the early seventies. All that was missing was a shag rug and a lava lamp. Darby turned the corner and saw a rolled-up oriental rug and, just beyond it, in the middle of the floor, a big square trapdoor made of ancient wood. The ladder was made of wood too, and descended maybe ten or twelve feet to a dirt floor.

'They'd pull their booze barrels up by ropes,' Virginia Cavanaugh said with a shake of the head. 'Obviously there's no electricity down there. I'm assuming you have a flashlight stored in one of those big pockets of yours.'

Darby ripped open the middle pouch of the tactical vest and came back with a small but sturdy MagLite.

'Are you expecting trouble over there? You look like you're dressed to go to war, and that foreign gentleman Searchy –'

'Sergey,' Darby said.

'My Lord, you're a *woman.*'

Darby suddenly realized the woman couldn't see her face, just her eyes.

'Remember what he told you. Stay here inside the house in case he calls – and if someone else calls, remember not to say what's going on. We don't need any sightseers, okay?'

A nod, and then the woman said, 'The door on the other side is similar to this one, but there's no ladder, just a dirt ramp. They'd roll the barrels right down from the basement, from what I was told. As I told Mr Sergey, I have no idea if the new owners carpeted over the area or bolted it down or whatnot. The previous family, the Rizzos, I know they just had a rug over it like I do, but they didn't allow the children to play down there, obviously.' She smoothed the ends of her sweater. 'Poor thing what happened to that boy. Charlie. He was taken, you know.'

'I know.' Darby swung her legs over the edge.

'Disappeared into thin air, and they never *found* him. Gave me the shivers for a long time, thinking about that happening in such a nice neighbourhood as this.'

Darby made her way down the ladder, feeling the wooden slats straining underneath the weight of her boots.

'I'll be upstairs,' the woman said. 'In the living room watching my TV shows in case you should require my assistance. Just don't sneak up on me, please. I don't hear so well, and I scare easily.'

'Will do.' Darby reached the soft, dirt bottom. 'Thanks again for your help, Mrs Cavanaugh.'

She turned on her flashlight.

The tunnel was maybe five feet high and just as wide and very, very long. There wasn't enough room to stand down there, but then it hadn't been created for that purpose. She imagined the men – and possibly women and children – hunched forward as they rolled barrel after barrel of illegal moonshine and beer underneath the now-rotting sheets of plywood covering the ceiling, the barrels' edges bumping against the wooden support slats lining the dirt walls every eight to ten feet. They hadn't done it in the dark. Nailed into the wood slats she saw old, rusted hooks for kerosene lamps.

Darby adjusted the mike hovering near her mouth and said, 'Can you hear me?'

'So far, so good,' came Sergey's reply over her earpiece.

'You'll probably lose me once I start moving. I'll contact you once I'm inside the basement.'

Hunched forward, Darby moved across the bumpy dirt floor, breathing in the odours of rotting wood and must and dampness, her breath steaming slightly in the cold air. She had dressed in full assault gear: boots, a bulletproof vest underneath the tactical vest that was loaded down with equipment and a gas mask. With the rucksack gripped in her gloved hand weighing another twenty or so pounds, she was sweating heavily by the time she reached the end of the tunnel.

Virginia Cavanaugh had been right about the dirt ramp. It stretched up to the same trapdoor on the opposite end of the tunnel. Darby crawled her way up it, then dropped the rucksack and leaned on her side. She placed a gloved hand on the wood and slowly pushed. It lifted about two inches before she heard the soft rattle of metal – a combination padlock.

From the sack she took out an eyehole camera. She turned on the unit, saw a bright glow of green ambient light on the monitor before the camera lens adjusted to the darkness, and then snaked the tiny pinhole camera through the edge and examined part of the basement. Boiler and hot-water tank and boxes, lots of boxes and plastic storage containers. Mark Rizzo's wood shelving had been stripped off the walls. She found the door leading into the next part of the basement – the finished part the family had used – and was relieved to find it shut.

Now, the lock.

She grabbed the SWAT-grade bolt cutter, pinched the padlock between its sharp steel teeth and with a single squeeze snapped it. Rather than working on fishing it out with her hands, she snapped the other half and then collected the broken pieces and tossed them into the dirt.

Slowly she lifted the door, hoping the old hinges wouldn't squeak. She grabbed the rucksack and lifted it slowly too, not wanting to make any noise, and set it down on the concrete floor. She snaked the pinhole camera underneath the door and checked out the basement. Clear.

'I'm in,' Darby whispered into the mike.

'Don't take any chances,' Sergey said. 'Use the gas mask.'

She tucked the pinhole camera unit into one of the cargo pockets in her trousers. Secured the gas mask across her face and grabbed the final piece of equipment from her rucksack: a small, handheld device that could monitor the frequencies given off by listening devices and pinhole cameras. She strapped it underneath the forearm of her left hand.

Sergey had given her the same sidearm as the one used by the FBI's Hostage Rescue Team, a fifteen-shot Glock 22 equipped with .40 S&W cartridges. She removed the sidearm from its holster, threaded the silencer, and held the sidearm out in front of her as she moved into the basement while stealing glances at the monitoring device. Right now the light meter was yellow. If it spiked anywhere into the green zone, that meant listening devices and/or cameras had been installed, and then she'd have to go back through the tunnel and meet with Sergey to discuss whether or not they should risk using jamming equipment.

Darby threaded her way through stacked boxes and plastic containers scattered haphazardly across the floor, past a couch and a TV hooked up to a video-game system, and then turned the corner and stepped over what seemed like hundreds of Lego pieces covering the Berber carpet.

The monitoring unit stayed yellow.

Upstairs, a steady hum of motor. It sounded like a dryer. She moved up the carpeted steps and stopped when she saw the opened door. Looked past it and into part of the kitchen with yellow-painted walls and hardwood oak floors. Moved up the final steps and checked the visible areas and didn't see anyone. She reached the doorway and over the hum of the dryer heard a steady *tick tock, tick tock*. Turned the corner and checked the blind spot behind the door – clear – then swivelled to her left and looked down a foyer, the hardwood glowing with slats of sunlight. The monitoring unit stayed yellow, didn't flicker once.

She passed through the kitchen, cleared the dining room and then, turning a corner, stared down the sight of her gun into the living room and found the source of the ticking: a big grandfather clock standing proudly on the wall between two windows. The living room was clear. Five steps and she stood near the end of a stairwell. Checked the front door across from it and didn't see any wires. She had wondered if the front door might have been wired to an IED.

The rooms felt hot – incredibly hot. She backed up into the dining room, and saw a thermostat, a digital model with the home's exact temperature displayed in black and white on the tiny LED screen: 95 degrees.

The dryer clicked off. Back inside the kitchen now, she checked the sliding glass door standing to the left of a gas fireplace. No wires there and the monitor strapped to her wrist remained yellow. And everything she had seen was neat and orderly. No sign of a struggle, nothing disrupted, it was as if the family living here had packed up their car and gone out for the day.

Tick tock. The sound inside her head now and itching

her skull. One final place left to search: the hall past the basement door. She moved down it, saw that it led to a small bathroom and a garage door.

Tick tock. It was too goddamn hot in here. She decided to leave the garage alone for now and made her way quietly back to the dining room, to the thermostat. She pressed the up button. The temperature didn't go any higher. It had been set at maximum.

Tick tock. She was sweating and something wasn't right.

Why the hell . . .

Tick.

. . . had the temperature . . .

Tock.

. . . been set so high?

Tick.

THUMP.

BWEEEEEEEP.

The sounds were coming from upstairs.

54

Darby had her gun raised, pointed up at the first-floor hall of beige-coloured walls. Lots of sunlight up there – the bedroom doors must be open, she thought, and she saw at least one opened door past the banister of decorative white spools. It was a bathroom. She shifted her stance and caught sight of a blue shower curtain hanging on a metal rod.

She made her way around the lower railing, noticing that the thick burgundy runner was the same as the one in the Rizzos' Dover house. Then she stood in the foyer waiting for the sounds she'd heard to repeat – the soft thump of something solid bumping into a wall or floor. Like a body. A body shifting around in a hiding spot.

But that other sound, that nasal squeal . . . her mind tried to identify it, this foreign sound, and came back empty-handed.

The first-floor layout came back to her: the bedroom Mark Rizzo had used as a home office was to the right of the top step. Across from that was the master bedroom, and at the opposite end of the hall, two more bedrooms. The twins had used the one on the left, the bigger of the two.

Darby took the first step, aware of her shadow against the wall, aware of the blind corners waiting for her up there. Another step and Coop's parting words about her luck having to run out at some point came back to her, and the warm feelings his presence had created vanished, swept away by the tide of adrenalin washing through her pounding heart, while her mind was racing, trying to identify that *goddamn* sound, where was it coming from and what the hell was it?

She turned the corner and saw the last part of the stairs. Saw no one, just more beige walls and two opened doors. She moved up the steps quietly, listening, then swung into the doorway on her immediate right, Mark Rizzo's old home office. The blue-striped wallpaper that had covered the walls was gone now, replaced with bright blue paint. A nursery. A half-assembled crib in the corner, the instructions and other parts waiting to be installed lying on a dark throw rug.

The monitor strapped to her arm didn't flicker once.

Moving inside the master bedroom, she found the bed made and folded laundry sitting on top of a long bureau waiting to be put away. The master bath was empty, the big jacuzzi still there, clean, just like everything she'd seen downstairs. Everything up here clean and tidy, no sign of a struggle, and the air felt just as hot, if not hotter. The thermostat on the wall just outside the bathroom doorway also read 95 degrees.

Bweeeeeeeeeeeeeeeeeeeek.

Scattering sounds followed, both noises coming from the other end of the hall.

Darby moved out of the master bedroom with her gun raised and checked the next bathroom and found it empty.

After a quick glance over the banister to look into the foyer – clear – she moved against the far wall and looked into the bedroom where Charlie Rizzo had once lived. Instead of *Star Wars* bed sheets and Darth Vader posters hanging on the scratched white walls, she found a room painted a deep yellow, almost gold in the sunlight. Across from the end of a bed covered with a purple comforter was the closet door, painted white now and covered with Polaroid-type snapshots of a frightened young woman.

Darby looked away, her gaze dropping to the fingers of blood that had soaked the carpet near the bottom of the closet door. She turned away from the images and swivelled around the doorway of the other bedroom, found bunk beds with tangled sheets and more Lego pieces scattered across a tan carpet. Curtains covered the windows and she heard the wind slapping against the house and shaking the panes of glass as she moved inside to check the closet. The twin doors were already open, the tiny walk-in area holding children's clothes.

Three quick steps and she moved across the hall and stepped into the gold-coloured bedroom with her gun raised and got a closer look at the pictures.

Eight or so had been tacked to the wood, and each one featured the same young woman with lightly tanned skin and long blonde hair tied behind her head with a red elastic band. A teenager, Darby guessed, looking at the terror on the young girl's face – Jack Casey's daughter. Had to be Sarah Casey. Darby saw the resemblance in the face, the same blue eyes and the same angular nose with the small bump on the tip.

Here was a close-up photograph of duct-tape wrapped around the girl's wrists. Darby saw chipped red nail polish on the long, slender fingers, and she looked up at another picture, this one a snapshot of the teenager's frozen scream. One snapshot showed the tape around her mouth and another showed blood smeared across a white T-shirt, the fabric strained as if being pulled.

Scattering sounds from behind the door, like dry twigs scraping across wood.

She gripped the doorknob knowing that whatever waited for her behind it was dead. Casey had told her this group would send a message and as she turned the knob she prayed to God the man was right, that she'd wasn't about to find his daughter's body.

Darby threw open the door as she stepped back, raising her gun.

A nude body covered with bloody red welts and missing patches of skin sat on the floor of the closet, underneath bright and colourful clothing draped across hangers. Not a woman, not Casey's daughter. Male, one with wild, curly black hair matted with dried blood and sweat. Darby looked at the face, expecting to see Mark Rizzo, and found it covered by some alien-looking spider the size of a dinner plate. It reminded her of the face-huggers from the *Alien* movies. This thing had a long, pale, cylindrical body, and its eight spiked legs were gripping the man's swollen and bloody cheeks while a pair of big red mandibles or pincers or whatever the Christ they were called were busy feasting on the few remaining scraps of soft meat left in the eye sockets. And it had inserted its backside into the gaping mess of the lips and was pumping away as if it was laying eggs.

Darby backed away, bile shooting up her throat, and saw more spiders – Tarantulas and smaller, quicker ones – crawling across the body and into the darker recesses of the closet. Another one of those big, pale, ugly things sat on a shoe rack, its oily black eyes staring at her. Then it let out that awful alien scream, like it was going on the attack.

The spider jumped into the air with a frightening speed and as she leaped back she felt it land on her vest with a considerable thump. She moved to swat it away with a quivering hand but the spider had already bounced off her chest. Darby stared after it, cold dripping through her limbs like pieces of ice as she watched it scurry underneath the bed to hide.

55

If Jack Casey had seen the pictures, his face didn't show it. Darby thought the man's face didn't show much of anything, just a perfect stillness as if his flesh had been replaced by concrete.

He sat at the long dining-room table with Sergey and another man, a fed, who wore a pair of headphones and studied a small laptop hooked up to a white cordless phone. It had been removed from the kitchen wall and brought in the room.

They had shut off the heat and opened the windows, but everyone was still sweating.

Sergey checked his watch. Ten minutes till one. Darby knew the time because she could see the stove's digital clock from the archway where she stood.

She heard the front door opened and then shut softly.

Coop came into the kitchen. 'We need to talk about the spiders,' he whispered.

Darby nodded, knowing that the bedroom was infected, that the pair of Boston medical technicians had dressed head to toe in biohazard gear to collect the spiders from the body before hauling it away. One of the spiders was a deadly Black Widow. She knew because she had collected it from the body, had seen the distinctive red hourglass on its tiny, black-rounded belly before dropping it inside a collection jar.

Coop said, 'Leland isn't going to let his people into the autopsy room with those things still crawling around on him.'

'I know. That's why we're going to do it.'

'Do what?'

'Examine the body.'

'Why us?'

'The FBI's lab people are tied up in Florida, so I offered to examine the body.'

Coop's face drained of colour.

'Don't like spiders?' she asked with a grin.

He didn't have a chance to answer. The house phone was ringing.

Darby moved back to the archway and saw Sergey picking up his headphones. Casey looked at the phone but didn't pick it up. It rang three times before the man seated in front of the laptop gave Casey a hand signal.

'Hello . . . Yes, this is Jack Casey.'

Casey didn't speak, just listened, his face as unreadable as stone. Darby watched him as she counted off the time in her head.

Twelve seconds later, he pulled the phone away from his ear.

Silence. Sergey's face was ashen. The other man stared at his computer screen. Casey placed the cordless phone back on the table as if it were made of delicate crystal and then stood, knees cracking. Darby followed him with her eyes until he disappeared somewhere inside the living room. Sergey got to his feet as the front door opened, a Secret Service agent saying something about moving back.

Darby pulled out the seat next to the only man left, a fleshy white guy with a shaved head that looked shiny under the chandelier's bright lights.

'Couldn't get the trace,' the guy said, shaking his head. 'Wasn't on long enough.'

'You heard what was said?'

The man licked his lips, nodding. 'His daughter was on the phone. Crying. She told her father that she'd left a gift for him in the upstairs bedroom, something that he had to see.'

'I'll meet you in town,' Sergey said to her after he came back inside the house. 'I've got to make some phone calls first, to our Boston office. They're going to send over an ERT – Evidence Response Team – to process the bedroom.'

'Call Boston PD,' Darby said. 'You can use their lab.'

'It's a thought.'

'This group, have they ever done something like this before? Contact you and leave a body with evidence for you to find?'

'No, this is a first. And that bothers me. They're planning something.'

'While psychologically torturing Casey.'

Sergey nodded, but his eyes had grown distant.

'The pictures upstairs . . .' Darby said.

'It's Jack's daughter.'

'Has he seen them?'

He nodded.

'How old?'

'Twelve,' he said, glancing at his watch.

'Where's Casey?'

'On his way to the morgue. He wanted to be there – wants to keep busy.'

'I need to stop by my house first and grab my forensic kit.'

'It's already at the morgue. I'll have someone drive you.'

Sergey had half turned to walk away when she said, 'About the spiders: we need to get them identified so we can have the appropriate anti-venom on hand in case one of us gets bitten here or at the morgue. It's a liability issue, and the guy who runs the place, Ellis, he's got a permanent hard-on when it comes to anything that's a liability.'

A long tired sigh and he rubbed his eyes with the heels of his hands.

'Okay,' he said. 'I'll head in and handle it.'

Darby went back to the kitchen. She stripped out of her thick white coveralls and gloves, balled everything together and stuffed it in a biohazard bag.

Casey's Secret Service agent, the Southern guy she knew only as Neal Keats, stood at the front door.

He read the question on her face and said, 'Mr Casey wants me on you now.'

'And your name?'

He smiled. 'Why, Neal Keats.'

'You used your real name as cover? What if I called the BU Biomedical Lab and asked to speak to you?'

'They would have forwarded your call to my cell phone. Mr Cooper's already in the car, the black Lincoln Navigator parked at the kerb. I'll escort you.' He moved his right hand close to his mouth and spoke into the wrist mike. 'Bringing out PIA.'

Darby said, 'PIA?'

'Pain in the Ass. Fitting, don't you think?'

Keats had opened the door, about to bring her out, when her cell phone rang. The Caller-ID listed the incoming number as 'unknown'.

'McCormick.'

'I see that Mr Casey has left,' said a garbled male voice on the other end of the line. 'Since you've become quite cosy with him, Dr McCormick, I'm going to elect you to be the messenger.'

She looked up and down at the handful of cars she could see parked along the street.

'And you are?'

'Listen carefully. I have someone who wants to speak to you.'

Darby didn't interrupt the hysterical woman on the other end of the line.

When the call ended, Darby took in several deep breaths to calm her racing heart.

56

The big black Lincoln Navigator drove them to Boston in a wail of sirens and flashing lights. Coop sat next to her, silent, the two of them protected by bulletproof glass, and they watched the cars parting in front of them, trying to manoeuvre to the shoulder to give the Lincoln room to move.

She didn't tell him about the call, not yet, wanting a moment to process it. And for some reason her thoughts kept sliding back to John Smith. She'd seen him stand up and then his face had been blown apart. Saw it again. A post-traumatic reaction? Maybe. But there was something . . . off about it. Something that didn't quite gel. She closed her eyes and tried to chase it through the waves of exhaustion, but lost sight of it completely when the vehicle came to a hard stop that made her buck against her seatbelt.

Through the tinted window and through the darkness outside she could see the familiar rectangular brick building sitting on the corner of Albany Street. Keats waited until he got the all-clear signal, then he drove to the front, stopping in front of a pair of Secret Service agents. They opened the door for her, and then Keats and another agent – one of the big linebackers she'd seen at the BU Biomedical Lab – quickly ushered her and Coop through the building's twin tinted-glass doors and into the lobby of the Commonwealth of Massachusetts Office of the Medical Examiner. They stayed by their sides as Darby walked with Coop through the long, bland institutional corridors lit up by fluorescent lights.

Two other Secret Service agents had been posted outside the autopsy suite, along with a federal agent who had a big black rolling suitcase parked next to him.

An agent with a crooked nose busted from too many fights stepped forward. 'Dr Ellis asked me to tell you to make sure you wear the Nomax gloves and the hoods with the face shield.'

Darby thanked the man, then headed into the locker room with Coop. She started pulling the gear they needed from the shelves. Keats, she saw, stood outside the door.

'I'm going to need to pick up some clothes,' he said, stripping out of his suit jacket. 'The only thing I packed was my passport.'

'I'll take care of it. You can stay with me.'

They dressed quickly and quietly. She headed to the door and saw him smiling.

'Feels like old times, doesn't it?'

She nodded and kissed him once, lightly, on the lips. 'Thanks again for coming. It means a lot. And I'm sorry I dragged you into this.'

'If the roles were reversed, would you have done the same thing for me?'

'In a heartbeat.'

'Then save the Irish Catholic guilt for something else,' Coop said, opening the door and moving across the hall to the autopsy suite.

57

Darby followed Coop into the room and found the pair of stainless-steel gurneys empty, the metal surfaces glinting underneath the bright lights. Nobody in here except for her and Coop – and the spiders.

They sat inside sealed specimen jars, on the long metal shelves that were mounted above the sinks. At least a dozen jars, each one containing a single spider. Most of them were big, some the size of a man's fist. A handful lay still at the bottom of their jars while the others were busy exploring, fluttering their long, hairy legs against the smooth glass.

But there was one that dwarfed the others, the massive, pale, ugly, alien-looking spider/scorpion hybrid with over-developed fangs and legs so ridiculously long it had to be placed in a small fish tank – the same face-hugging thing that had jumped at her and that she'd seen on the face inside the closet at the Rizzo home. It scampered around like it was on fire, its legs, with their spiked, needle-like hair, furiously digging through the inches of sand at the bottom of the tank. Two bricks had been placed on the tank cover.

Coop leaned in close and said, 'That thing looks like a vagina with legs.'

'I'll make sure I introduce the two of you.'

The spider/scorpion hybrid thing started smacking its hairy, oversized pincers together, making that skin-crawling, high-pitched hissing sound she'd heard in the bedroom: *Bweeeeeeeeep!*

She heard footsteps clicking across the floor behind her and turned to see an older man with a black pompadour shiny with something like Brylcreem. The clothes hanging on his reedy frame – white shirt, chinos and a tie – were all wrinkled and gave him a slovenly appearance, as if he'd plucked them from the bottom of his laundry basket.

'Beautiful, isn't she?' their new companion said, gawking at the creepy thing hissing in the tank. 'I've *never* come across one of these Solpugids before.'

'Sol what?'

'*Sol-pu-gid*. That's their proper name, but they're also referred to as Wind Scorpions, Sun Spiders or Camel Spiders. You can tell it's a Solpugid by its long body with its tactile hairs – and the enormous mouth pincers. I think this lovely lady might be a new species. I've got my fingers crossed.'

She didn't like the way he beamed with excitement, like a kid who had discovered a treasure trove of Christmas presents hidden underneath the tree skirt. And the loving way he spoke about this thing, in the sort of tone reserved for the discovery of a soul mate, convinced her this guy was off his rocker. No wedding ring on his finger. What a surprise.

She knew almost everyone who worked in this building and had never seen him before.

'I'm sorry, and you are?'

'Nigel Perkins, from the University of Massachusetts,' he said, extending a hand. Darby shook it. 'I specialize in arachnids. Special Agent Martynovich sent me to identify the specimens.'

Darby nodded, impressed. Sergey had not only found someone incredibly quickly but had also got the man to hop to. Apparently FBI credentials opened a lot of doors. Fast.

'Mr Perkins, if you're going to attend the examination, you need to get dressed.'

The man looked perplexed.

Darby pointed to her uniform and said, 'You need to wear one of these. There's a locker room across the hall. You'll find everything you need in there.'

Coop, a clipboard gripped in his gloved hand, stepped up next to her as Perkins hustled out of the room.

'Who do you think is creepier?' Coop asked. 'Perkins or your friend in the fish tank?'

'I'd say they're equal.'

The freezer door opened. Two men dressed head to toe in white coveralls, face shields and thick blue gloves wheeled a bloated corpse into the autopsy room. The person manning the bottom end of the gurney was Jack Casey. She couldn't see his face but his size gave him away. He had wedged his body into a pair of coveralls that looked like they were about to split.

When the second man turned and started backing up the gurney next to the autopsy table, she got a good, clear look at a pair of wild and busy white Andy Rooney-type

302

eyebrows. Dr Samuel Ellis, the new head of the medical examiner's office. His face was a mottled red, the sure sign he'd just had a heated argument. Probably with Casey. The former profiler's face, she saw, also looked flushed. She wondered what the argument had been about – probably turf-war bullshit, she thought. The body should have been waiting for them on the autopsy table. Ellis, bland and dour, had probably put it in the freezer and scheduled it for sometime tomorrow. The man placed a lot of importance on proper procedure, and he was *very* protective about who he let into his autopsy rooms – and, make no mistake, he considered everything inside this building as *his*.

The two men transferred the body to the autopsy table. Darby found her kit, the bright orange toolbox she kept in the bottom of her closet, sitting on a worktop, waiting. She opened it and took the items she needed from the top shelf – the forensic light, the long tweezers and a handful of glassine bags she used for trace evidence.

Perkins came back into the room, his gloved fingers fumbling with the face shield, trying to attach it to his suit. With a heavy and theatrical sigh, Ellis darted around Casey to give Perkins a hand.

Casey paid no attention. He seemed to have dissociated himself from everyone in the room. When she reached across the body and handed the bags to Coop, the former profiler's cold blue eyes remained fixed on the body, studying it not with a sense of loss or revulsion but of opportunity.

Darby moved to the top of the table to begin her examination.

58

The body's swollen, decimated face was a mess of purple and red contusions and gnawed-off sections of flesh, some so deep she could see bone. She doubted an ordinary spider could do this kind of damage, but that screaming thing locked in the fish tank didn't seem like any run-of-the-mill arachnid. She was willing to bet its enormous finger-sized pincers could snap a stick in half.

She turned to Perkins, who stood anxiously by her side. He looked a little white in the face, his skin already beaded with sweat.

'Your first time seeing a dead body, Dr Perkins?'

He nodded, kept nodding.

'If you think you're going to be sick, either step outside or, if you don't think you can make it, use one of the trashcans.'

'And,' Coop added, 'don't forget to pull off your face shield. You don't want any blowback.'

Using her tweezers, she pointed to a section of gnawed flesh on the victim's face and said to Perkins: 'That Camel Spider, can it cause this kind of damage?'

'If the man was dead, then yes,' Perkins replied. 'They do have to eat.'

'Do these spiders generally attack people?'

'Camel Spiders? No. Oh no. That's a misconception.

They're solitary, nocturnal creatures. They don't like direct light, as you can see by the way it's squirming and screaming inside the tank. They prefer darkness and shadows.'

'One of them jumped at me.'

'Well, yes, they can do that when they're trying to hide. They're not aggressive – or venomous. A Camel Spider could *not* have killed this man. Now this mark right here –' Perkins leaned over the body and pointed a gloved finger at a black ulcerous blister oozing with pus. The wound covered most of the victim's right forearm. 'This is definitely a spider bite. Given the extensive tissue damage, the colour and size of the blister, I'd say this one is the culprit.'

From the shelf Perkins grabbed a specimen jar holding a furry brown spider with a body the size of a deck of playing cards. Its long, needle-like legs tapped against the glass. Darby noticed a violin-shaped mark on its cylindrical-shaped back.

'This is a Brown Recluse,' Perkins said. 'Very poisonous. It injects haemotoxin, which produces the distinctive wound you're seeing here on this man's arm. The ulcerous opening on the man's forearm occurs within twenty-four hours after the initial bite.'

Darby felt sweat gathering under her coveralls. 'Is the bite fatal?'

'A single bite? No.' Perkins, thankfully, placed the jar back on the shelf. 'The haemotoxin kills the cells and tissues at the bite and slowly spreads. That being said, the bite, if left untreated, can lead to fever and vomiting and, in rare cases, coma and death. That occurs within two or three days. Now, granted, I'm not a medical doctor, so I can't tell you when this man died. But I can tell you he was bitten multiple times by several different venomous spiders.'

Perkins traced a gloved finger above a series of red and purple welts of various sizes that started at the victim's shoulder and ran across his chest, legs and pubic area. One appeared to have bitten him on a testicle. It was black, swollen to the size of a grapefruit. She found several more bites on the soles of the man's feet.

Perkins said, 'Almost all of the spiders in these specimen jars are what you would classify as poisonous or deadly. I was surprised to find a pair of Tunnel Web Spiders – the Sydney species. Sydney as in Sydney, Australia. Their bite is *extremely* painful, and their venom carries atraxotoxin, which disrupts neurotransmitters. The victim experiences muscle twitching, severe nausea and vomiting.'

'Are they common in the US?'

'No, absolutely not.'

So someone smuggled them in here, she thought, and made a note on her clipboard for Sergey to check customs logs, see if anyone was caught trying to bring venomous spiders into the country.

'These spiders,' Perkins said, 'live in dry, hot climates. They wouldn't survive long in this cold.'

'In the house where I found them the heat had been cranked up to 95 degrees.'

'The one at the far end is a Black House Spider. Not toxic, but the bite causes deep pain and plenty of sweating and vomiting. Not only are those babies very quick on their feet, they're highly aggressive. If you disturb them, they go on the defensive. Dr Ellis, when you run your toxicology reports, I'm sure you'll find several different kinds of venom inside this man's system, as I said.'

'Enough to kill him?'

'Oh, yes, most definitely. And it would have been a *horrible* death. Once, while I was in El Salvador, I was bitten on the hand when trying to collect the Pink-Bellied Spider. Not only was the pain incredible, I couldn't stop vomiting – and this after I was administered an anti-toxin. Whoever did this used these lovely creatures to inflict an unbelievable amount of pain and suffering.'

Darby switched on her forensic light and, moving closer, started examining the face for trace evidence. The eyes had been eaten, and deep inside one of the hollow sockets of rotted and frozen meat she discovered a small black spider with a body the size of a pencil eraser.

She gripped it with the tweezers, watched the legs struggling in the air, seeking purchase. Coop had a jar ready. She dropped the spider in it, and after he closed the lid he handed the jar to Perkins.

'That's a Black Widow,' Perkins said. 'There could be more in the eye sockets, the ear and nasal cavities. They're tiny, as you can see, and they're very good at hiding. Be very careful if you find one – if you find any spider, for that matter. Dr Ellis placed the body in the refrigeration unit or whatever you call it, and I can tell you spiders don't care for the cold, puts them in an aggressive mood.'

'Excuse me.' Ellis's voice. 'I'd like to remind everyone here that I *strenuously* object to conducting this examination now, as we don't have the appropriate anti-venom on hand. Mr Casey assured me that vials are being collected and will be flown here and hand-delivered, courtesy of our federal tax dollars, so if one of you should happen to get bitten, the federal government will be assuming the liability. Do I have that right, Mr Casey?'

'You do.'

'Are you sure? Did I leave anything out?'

'Evidence that we collect will be sealed and given to a courier to be brought back to our lab.'

Darby thought of the man she'd seen standing next to the suitcase.

'Anything else?' Ellis prompted.

'Yes. Thank you, again, for assisting us.'

Casey's voice had that odd, detached tone again, as if he had departed his body and left someone else to pull the puppet strings.

Then, to Darby, he said: 'See the puncture wounds running along the sides of the back?'

'Yes.' Bright and red, they oozed blood.

'They cover the victim's entire back, legs and buttocks.'

Darby looked up and across the body. 'Any ideas?'

'No,' Casey said, 'but the puncture wounds all look the same, and there's . . . there's an order to them, as if he had been forced to sit on something sharp.'

'What about the welts on the front of the torso?'

'Whip marks,' Casey said. 'Most of the wounds are pretty fresh, so this couldn't have been done too long ago. The marks along the wrists and ankles are consistent with restraints, probably leather. Whatever they did to him, they had him strapped down.'

Using the tweezers, Darby parted the hairs on the man's head. Her other hand held the forensic light. She moved it over the scalp, searching for evidence and, now, spiders. She immediately found a series of tiny welts.

'Spider bites,' Perkins said.

Darby kept searching, wondering if the spiders had been dumped on the victim to ensure immediate bites – or if he had simply been locked inside the closet with them crawling around in the dark. Both thoughts were equally disturbing.

Perkins seized the upper part of her arm, his gloved fingers digging into the meat of her bicep with a strength that surprised her.

'*Stay still.*'

She did, and out of the corner of her eye watched as Perkins's hand came back from underneath her right forearm, clutching a black spider the size of a matchbook. Squat, black and incredibly hairy, it squirmed in the air, its oversized fangs exposed.

'An Australian Recluse,' Perkins said, carrying it to a specimen jar. 'Very fast and very poisonous.'

Darby blinked the sweat away from her eyes and then quickly gathered herself. Coop stood across from her, on the other side of the table. She looked at him and said, 'We'll need close-ups of the wounds on the scalp.'

He nodded and grabbed the camera. She pointed to the first wound, which was a few inches beyond the hairline, then moved away to give him some room. It would take him a minute or two to set up the shot. She used the time to take a quick look around for any more stray creepy-crawlers.

There were none on the table – at least none that she could see. She checked behind the victim's head and, failing to find any, searched the ear canals with a new and brighter flashlight. Clean. Same with the man's nasal cavity. Nothing in there except a forest of fine black nasal hairs.

Now the mouth. Fortunately it hung open, frozen in place by rigor. She had to break the jaw to get a better look.

The victim's mouth, throat and the soft smooth pink cheek lining had multiple abrasions and contusions. She dipped her tweezers inside the mouth and prodded around the victim's tongue for stray spiders. She inserted her tweezers down the throat and hit something hard.

Coop said, 'What is it?'

'I don't know. Someone hand me the forceps.'

Ellis said, 'I should be the one who –'

'Sam, just give me the damn forceps.'

She needed a brighter light. She reached up and grabbed the plastic arm belonging to one of the autopsy lights. She turned it on and pivoted the circular dish with its intense, bright light near the face. It took her a moment to find the right angle to illuminate every inch inside the victim's mouth. Something was definitely lodged in the throat.

Ellis slapped the forceps against her waiting palm to make sure she knew he wasn't pleased at playing lab assistant. She caught the grin on Coop's face before turning her attention back to her work.

Grabbing the object was easy. The forceps had found purchase immediately, but dislodging the thing in question from the throat was another matter. Whatever it was, it had been shoved a good way down the victim's oesophagus. It took a few minutes of delicate, almost surgical manoeuvring before she could move the item into the intensely bright light. A USB drive and a small, severed finger, bound together with a red elastic hair-band.

59

The finger belonged to a woman. The long fingernail had chipped red polish on it.

Sarah Casey had worn the same red nail polish, the same red elastic hair-band, in the pictures tacked to the bedroom closet. The blood on her T-shirt had come from the severed finger and she hadn't been screaming in fear in those pictures; she had been screaming in pain.

Darby placed the finger and USB drive on the dish Coop had waiting.

'I want to get this printed,' the former profiler said, his voice trembling.

Coop said, 'I'll do it.'

Casey moved away from the table and she said to Coop, 'The second you're done printing that finger, put it on ice and then have one of the feds or Secret Service take it over to Mass General to give to Dr Izzo.'

'That the guy who fixed Dale Brown's finger?'

'That's him. Izzo managed to reattach it because we put it on ice.'

Coop darted away. Darby looked at Ellis and said, 'I need two buccal swabs, the ones with the brushes.'

'They're in the same place they always are,' he said, pointing across the room.

'I know. I need you to get them for me.'

Ellis gave another theatrical sigh as he moved to get the packets. He came back a moment later, ripped open one and handed her a long plastic rod with a tiny white scrub brush on the end. She stuck the brush inside the victim's mouth, scrubbed the frozen cheek lining, then removed it and placed the brush inside the sterile plastic cylinder Ellis had pinched between his fingers.

The first sample she could use for PCR-ready DNA identification. The second buccal swab she could save in case further DNA identification was needed.

The samples collected, she grabbed the kits she needed to collect fingernail scrapings. Ellis assisted without any further bitching and moaning. He had even got into the spirit of things by picking up Coop's clipboard and making notes.

Darby turned off the bright autopsy light. Switching to a forensic light with a green filter, she searched the victim's mouth for trace evidence, finding a small fibre – possibly a rug fibre, judging by its size and shape. She dropped it into the glassine envelope Ellis had waiting.

There was more. A single blond hair, which was sadly missing its DNA-packed root bulb. A black speck that could have been a piece of leather, stuck behind the back-right molar. She prised it out carefully with the tweezers.

Dr Ellis leaned over the body. 'Is that a bumblebee?'

'It's definitely a bee,' she said, 'but not an ordinary one.'

'And you know this how?'

'It doesn't have the usual yellow or red bands. The body is entirely black and the eyes are abnormally large. Dr Perkins, hand me one of those specimen jars on the shelf across from you . . . No, the next shelf, the bottom one. Thank you.'

313

She dropped the bee into a specimen jar, and then she ran her forensic light back and forth inside the victim's mouth, searching the crevices between the lip and gum line, and caught a faint glow from the corner of her eye.

Darby turned, blinking and moving the hand holding the flashlight. The glow had vanished.

Something *was* there. She had seen *something* on the soft lining behind the man's lip.

Darby moved away from the body, grabbed the UV forensic light and turned back to the victim's mouth, examining the smooth cavity between the teeth and cheek. Nothing glowed. She turned the light slowly, trying different angles and then different light sources. She had seen something, she knew she hadn't –

There, on the soft area behind the bottom lip, the labial sulcus: a bright fluorescent glowing shape now visible to the naked eye. She fumbled around for the best angle and distance, and then had to steady her head in order to see it fully:

Out of the corner of her eye she saw Ellis leaning in for a closer look.

'What in God's name is that?' he asked.

'Looks like some sort of symbol. Where's Coop?'

'He's in here. Hold on.'

Darby didn't know what the symbol meant, but knew it had been tattooed into the skin using some sort of ink invisible to the naked eye. She thought about the stamps used at nightclubs, amusement parks and some kids-themed restaurants. A hand was stamped with a fluorescent but invisible ink as the person entered. Then, if they had to exit the place and come back in, the person placed their hand underneath a black light, which illuminated the stamp and let the business know the person had already paid the entrance fee. That ink washed off and eventually faded. The ink on the lip had been tattooed into the skin. In a hidden area.

Coop stepped up on the other side of the table and leaned in across the body for a closer look. She showed it to him and then they talked about the best way to photograph it.

'We don't have that kind of equipment here,' he said.

'What time is it?'

'Quarter to six.'

'Call Ops, have them page ID.'

He used the wall phone in the autopsy suite to call Operations. Boston lab techs, as well as those who worked for ID, the separate section that dealt with forensic photography, had to live within a certain radius of Boston so they could report to a crime scene or the lab within an hour.

Dr Perkins calmly asked her to step aside. She did and watched the man use a pair of long tweezers to grab a small brown spider trying to crawl its way out of the victim's mouth.

60

Coop helped her to photograph the front torso and to diagram the wounds, searching each one for trace evidence. Darby kept stealing glances at the vic's mouth to see if anything else had decided to crawl out.

They found a lot of fibres on the wounds and body, a lot of dirt. On the vic's shoulder she found a dried white blob; it appeared to be candle wax. They collected blood samples and made detailed diagrams of each wound, noting its location, length and size.

'I need to make a quick phone call,' she said.

Standing in the back, she took off her face shield, picked up the phone and called the direct number the Harvard professor had given her.

'Professor Ross, this is Darby McCormick. We spoke earlier.'

'Yes, yes, of course. The Latin phrase.' The man sounded as though he was fighting a cold. 'I've made some notes for you.'

'I was told it's a reference to someone who once enjoyed the pleasures of life and has now been transformed in death.'

'That would be a correct interpretation, as some believe the phrase was spoken by Death, a reminder for one to enjoy the pleasures of earth. Other scholars believe *Et in*

Arcadia ego is an anagram for another Latin phrase that means "Begone, I keep God's Secrets." I don't know how much information you need. I don't want to bury you in it.'

'I want to send you a symbol I found, see if it ties into this phrase in any way. Would you be willing to take a look?'

'Of course,' he said, sounding positively delighted.

'Do you have a fax machine?'

He gave her the number. She wrote it down on a piece of paper and took it with her down the hall to Ellis's office. Inside, she removed a sheet of paper from his printer tray, drew the symbol and faxed it to the Harvard professor with a note saying to call her immediately if he knew anything.

Stepping back inside the autopsy suite, she saw that ID had arrived. She didn't recognize the faces of the two men behind the face shields. Coop showed them the tattoo and then left the table to give them room to work.

Darby followed him to the corner. Her eyes felt dry and gritty, like sandpaper, and her head had begun to feel thick and sluggish from lack of sleep. She thought of the photographs of Sarah Casey, of the young girl's severed finger, and that helped to keep the haze at bay.

'Where's Casey?' she asked.

'He left with the fingerprint card.'

'Where?'

'To Ellis's office, I think.'

'I was just there. I didn't see him.'

'That guy that was standing outside, the one with the

suitcase? He has a fingerprint transmitter. And he's a courier. That bee you found? I saw Casey hand it off to him.'

'That was, what, two hours ago?'

'That finger belongs to Casey's daughter, doesn't it?'

'I think so,' she said.

'I saw the wound. Up close. Judging from the marks, I'd say it was snipped off with something like a bolt cutter.'

Jesus. 'What about the USB drive?'

'He took that too.'

'*Before* it was fingerprinted?'

'Casey said that other guy was going to take care of that.' He held up an apologetic hand. 'Hey, don't give me that look. His show, his rules – remember?'

She did. She did remember, and she was going to have to have a discussion with Sergey about the former profiler. Jack Casey was a force of nature, a genuine cult of personality; she had the enormous reverence with which Sergey and the others treated the man – maybe out of simple respect, maybe because of his background as a profiler and his service to the Bureau. But he had an emotional stake in this case now, and he needed to be removed – not from the case but from calling the shots.

And there was something else at work, something that she couldn't quite identify. Something that reminded her of rotting floorboards found in a derelict house. Something *unsafe*. And the others had sensed it too. She had noticed how none of them stood too close to him.

ID had finished with the pictures. They agreed to go back to the lab and print out copies. Darby asked them for duplicates. After they left, she used a desk phone to call

Sergey. She told him about the tattooed symbol and explained why she had called in ID to take the pictures. She didn't have to tell him what she had found inside the victim's throat; Casey had already called him. He said he'd meet them at the lab shortly and then abruptly hung up.

Coop helped her turn over the body. They kept at it, fighting through their exhaustion, talking to each other so they didn't miss anything. Checked over each other's work and, wanting a fresh set of eyes, asked Ellis to look over everything.

Darby checked the clock as she stripped off her gloves. Twenty to eight.

She grabbed her kit, about to leave to allow Ellis to begin the autopsy, when Perkins insisted on doing a thorough inspection of her clothing. Spiders, especially some of the smaller ones, he said, could find all sorts of places to hide. She stood holding her arms out by her sides while Perkins checked every fold and crevice and corner. When he finished, he turned to Coop.

Darby went across the hall to strip out of her gear and found Keats still posted beside the door. She unbuckled her face shield.

'Where's Casey?'

'He left,' Keats said.

'Where?'

'Don't worry, he's safe.' Keats nodded towards the locker-room door. 'You should go on and get dressed. We'll take you and Mr Cooper to your hotel. You look like you could use a shower.'

Coop came into the locker room a moment later. She

had dressed first, told him she'd wait for him in the hall, and when she opened the door she saw Sergey heading her way, his phone pressed against an ear and heels smacking against the polished floor.

61

Sergey's hair had been blown silly by the wind and his face had a thin veil of oily perspiration that made his olive skin look both pale and damp underneath the light. Darby saw fresh coffee stains dotting his white shirt and pinkish tie, probably from trying to guzzle a cup during the bumpy car ride here.

'Prints came back,' he said just as he reached her. 'Vic is Mark Rizzo. Boston PD had logged his prints into the system, along with those of his wife and the twin girls.'

'Standard procedure when a child disappears or is abducted,' Darby said, aware of the weary sadness seeping through her. It was now official. Mark Rizzo was dead. 'We have them on-hand for comparison purposes when we examine evidence. What about the finger? Is it . . .'

'Yeah. It's Sarah Casey's.'

Darby nodded, as if confirming it herself. She had suspected this, of course, when she'd seen the chipped red fingernail polish. Now it was confirmed. The severed finger that had been stuffed down the vic's throat – Mark Rizzo's throat – belonged to Jack Casey's daughter.

She recalled a part of her first conversation with Casey, back inside the Nahant PD: *They won't kill me. Not yet*, he had said. *They're going to send me a message first.* She thought, *His daughter's severed finger.*

Sergey spoke slowly: 'Jack had his daughter printed as part of one of those child-safety programmes they do in the schools. This was a few years ago. After what happened to my son, I convinced him to load her prints and DNA into our system in the event these people ever targeted her.'

'Did ID call you about the pictures?'

He nodded. 'I just sent someone over there to collect them.'

'I need to speak to Casey.'

'He's on the plane.'

'Where's he going?'

'Nowhere.' Sergey answered the question before she could ask it. 'It's our plane, the one we sent to Florida. It touched back down at Logan.'

'You brought your forensic people back?'

'Not all of them. I left a few at the safe house.' Sergey moved the hair out of his eyes. 'We had eight agents down there – four inside the house, the other four doing a perimeter watch, okay? The ones outside, we think were taken out from a distance. Silenced weapons, nobody heard a thing. The four we had inside the house, all headshots, and not one of them had pulled his weapon. I watched the video feed on the way over here. Way the bodies were found? It was like they had fallen asleep and then someone came up and shot them.'

'Nerve agent?'

'Don't know anything yet. If they used it, I don't know how they managed to get it inside the house. Maybe the outside A/C units. Put the gas in there.'

Coop came out of the door, shrugging into his suit jacket.

Darby said, 'I was told Casey took the USB drive?'

Sergey nodded. 'It's on the plane. We processed it for prints before we let Jack look at it.'

'What's on it?'

'A video. That's all he'd tell me. He hasn't let anyone watch it yet.'

'We need to talk about Casey,' Darby said, 'his involvement.'

Sergey waved a hand, cutting her off. 'I know where you're going with this, and, yes, I agree. He's been emotionally compromised, and he can't be the one calling the shots. You won't get any grief from him. That being said, I want to – *he* wants to stick close to this. You can't blame him.'

'I want to see the video.'

'You will. Later. First, we need to get you two settled.'

Sergey pointed to a pair of agents hovering a few feet away. 'These men will take you to the hotel. Shower, get something to eat, take a few hours to unwind. Don't argue, you need some time away from this so you can look at it fresh, okay?' He glanced at his watch. 'Let's make it ten. No, eleven. Give you some time to unwind before the meeting. Go and grab some sleep, decompress.'

Sergey turned to leave.

'Hold up,' Darby said. 'I talked to Jack's wife.'

He spun around on his heels, nearly tripping. 'When?'

'After you left, one of them called my cell phone and put her on the line. She told me Jack has to hold a press conference. They want him to –'

'A press conference? For what reason.'

'Do you know who Budd Dwyer was?'

Sergey shook his head, showed her his empty hands.

'Budd Dwyer,' Darby said, 'was a politician from Pennsylvania accused of receiving bribes. Day before his sentencing, he calls a press conference. Has three of his staff members up there with him, and he hands each of them an envelope – letter to his wife, one for the governor and an organ donor card – and when he's done he places the barrel of a .357 Magnum in his mouth and blows his head off.'

'They want Casey to commit suicide on national TV?' Sergey said.

'First they want him to shoot Darren Waters.'

'And if he doesn't commit murder and suicide, then what?'

'His wife said these people were going to mail her and their daughter to us,' Darby said. 'In pieces.'

The Secret Service agents led them to a different SUV, this one a Ford Expedition. Keats took the wheel and his partner had a cryptic conversation over a phone hooked into a big box mounted in the console.

'I need to pick up some clothes from my condo,' Darby said.

'I'll call and check,' Keats said.

His partner made the call, hanging up less than a minute later.

'You're cleared,' he said.

'Cleared?' Darby repeated. 'Cleared of what?'

'ERT found a cyanide gas canister mounted underneath your bed. Remote-controlled device.'

'When was it set to go off?'

'Didn't have a timer on it, just a cell phone. You call and it lets out the gas. Pretty sophisticated construction too, from what we were told.'

Darby sank back in her seat, her jaw snapping shut.

Cyanide gas. Also known as Zyklon B when it was used in Hitler's gas chambers and in the gas wagons that rounded up gypsies and homosexuals and killed them on the spot. And now these people that no one knew, these people who belonged to a group that didn't have a name – they had wanted to turn her bedroom into a gas chamber. If she had gone back home instead of calling Coop's friend for that room at the Custom House . . .

But you didn't.

No. No, she hadn't. But it got her thinking back to what Coop had said about her lucky streak having to end at some point because that's what lucky streaks did. They always did.

Coop was leaning forward in his seat and Keats was saying, 'No need to go to a store. We've already purchased some clothing for you.'

'I hope you didn't buy me tighty-whities,' Coop said. 'I'm a boxer man.'

'I didn't do the shopping. Someone from the office did. A woman.' Keats gave Coop a hard, stern look in the rear-view mirror and added, 'I don't shop for clothes for guys.'

Coop laughed. 'Where you taking us?'

'Four Seasons.'

'How romantic.'

'Hotel offers us several security advantages. They cater to visiting diplomats, our bozo politicians and other types.'

Coop eased back, turning to her with a grin on his face, trying to break the sombre mood.

'Four Seasons,' he whispered. 'Ooo-la-la.'

Keats went up with her to her condo. The FBI's Evidence Response Team was there, making a mess of her rooms – moving furniture, rugs and all of her bureau drawers. Black fingerprint powder covered every surface. All the lights had been turned on and when she stepped inside her bedroom she found her bed torn apart, the mattress propped up against a wall and a guy wearing a particle mask and an FBI windbreaker spraying a Super Glue mist against the metal bed frame. Two young guys stood on her porch dusting her sliding glass door and she caught flashlight beams crisscrossing through the darkness, searching the postage-stamp-sized backyard she shared with the ground-floor tenants.

She didn't ask what else they had found; she'd get the details later from Sergey. She opened the folding doors to Beacon Hill's version of a walk-in closet: a small space of carefully crafted shelves designed to maximize every last inch of space. She threw clothes into a suitcase, about to close the doors when she saw the bulky white shopping bag sitting on the top shelf. She hesitated for a moment, then grabbed the bag and stuffed it inside her suitcase.

A quick trip to the bathroom to grab her toiletries and then she was hauling her suitcase down the winding staircase. No sign of her neighbours. She wondered if the feds had evacuated the building as a precaution.

Back to the car and half an hour later it stopped.

When her door opened again, she saw a man dressed in what looked like a military uniform – a cream-coloured commander's hat, dark navy-blue trousers and a matching long overcoat with gold bars on the sleeves and above the breast pocket. He stood under a roof heater a few feet away from a pair of gold-plated doors, the entrance of the Four Seasons Hotel.

The doorman grinned and welcomed them to the Four Seasons. Either the man hadn't noticed the earpieces worn by the Secret Service agents or he was simply used to seeing such things, as the hotel, she knew, hosted a wide variety of foreign dignitaries and rich Middle Eastern types who often travelled with bodyguards.

Keats didn't bother with the check-in and escorted them through a regal lobby full of warm, earth-tone colours – the brown and cream rug, the blond wood panelling and chairs and sofas arranged around pillar-type stones holding pots bursting with freshly cut flowers. She could see why people held lavish weddings here, why businesses held conferences meant to impress their staff and clients. The area gave off a distinctly powerful but elegant vibe.

They took the elevator to the top floor. She followed Keats and the other agent, who'd been assigned to Coop, down a quiet, carpeted hall. A moment later Keats dropped her suitcase in front of a small alcove separate from the rest of the rooms. Darby saw the bronze-plated sign mounted on the wall next to the door: GARDEN SUITE.

'I'll be posted outside your room,' Keats said. 'For obvious reasons, we prefer that you dine in. We'll come for you at eleven, so take the time to unwind, sleep, whatever.'

Coop picked up her suitcase. Darby remained in the hallway for a moment.

She rubbed a hand across the back of her neck. 'If for some reason you need to come in and get us, could you do me a favour and, uh, you know . . .'

'Knock?'

'Yes. Knock.'

'Of course. A gentleman such as myself always knocks first, then waits.'

'I'd appreciate that, thanks.'

Keats cracked a thin smile. 'Enjoy your stay.'

62

Darby's first thought was that she had stepped through a time portal and into the top floor of one of those old historic mansions she'd once seen in Newport, Rhode Island. The space was immense, with Victorian-inspired sofas, chairs and heavy curtains; the only modern flourish was the soft lighting that glowed like candlelight across the cream and beige striped wallpaper. The warm air smelled of lavender – fresh lavender and not some sort of chemical scent, and it was coming from a huge bouquet of fresh-cut lavender sprinkled among white and red roses set up on the table.

She looked around, taking in the immense space and the adjoining kitchen – there was a kitchen in here, an actual kitchen – and she half expected some butler or maid from a Jane Austen novel to come waltzing into the room and tell her the duchess was ready to receive them.

She turned and walked, dragging the rolling suitcase behind her, into a master suite almost as big as her condo. Tall ceilings, and two lamps on cherrywood nightstands bracketing a king-sized bed. Coop stood next to the bed, going through the packages of clothes that had been left on top of the thick white velvet comforter.

Darby parked her suitcase at the foot of the bed and he held up a package of Hanes briefs.

'Tighty-whities. What am I, ten?'

'Let's make a rule,' she said, slipping out of her leather jacket. 'No talking about the case.'

'Fine with me. I could use a break.'

'You want to crash?'

He shook his head, picking up a package holding a blue dress shirt. 'I'm too wired to sleep. All I want is a long, hot shower.'

'You mind if I go first?'

'Not at all. It'll give me time to raid the mini-bar.'

The bathroom, made of black and white marble, had a jacuzzi with windows overlooking the public garden. She could see the old lantern lights glowing around the street and in the distance as she undressed.

Hopping inside the shower, she wished she could stay under the hot water until it ran cold, but she didn't want to waste time. She wanted to spend every available second with Coop. A part of her felt guilty for having these feelings right now, given the day's gruesome events. It seemed wrong, almost abnormal. She was tingling with excitement and anticipation, and Casey was drowning in fear and terror.

Coop was here, and she was alone with him – alone in one of the world's most luxurious and romantic hotels, and she planned on taking full advantage of it. As life had demonstrated to her time and time again, there was no such thing as planning or waiting for the perfect moment, or mood. You had to watch out for it, and when it came along, you had to seize the opportunity or lose it, and there was no way in hell she was about to miss out on this one.

Stepping out of the shower, she debated whether or

not to blow dry her hair. Conscious of time, she towel-dried it, combed it back and, still damp, pinned it up in a loose chignon using hair grips. She took her time with the eyeliner, eye shadow and lip gloss.

First she slipped into the special lingerie she had picked out for this moment, along with the dress and shoes. She generally shopped for clothing only out of necessity, and when she did she often chose practical, comfortable items. She never had that girly-girl need to be up on the latest fashions, but she had her own sense of style, and she liked to get all dressed up when the rare occasion demanded it.

Coop almost exclusively dated girly-girls who, after a hard day of shopping, liked to unwind by hitting the clubs. The brighter ones managed to string words together in full sentences but often tired out after a few minutes of conversation. Darby knew she beat every one of them in the brains department and knew, with the right clothing, she could compete with the best of them. With that goal in mind, over the summer she had purchased two items, which she knew, at least from her limited experience of shopping through the sales racks at Banana Republic and J. Crew, had cost a small fortune: a heather-grey, 1920s-inspired cocktail dress with a scooping neckline and plunging back made of silk-chiffon; and a pair of black Magrit heels adorned with crystal satin bows.

Darby checked herself in the mirror. The dress was cute – sexy but sophisticated. Sort of a modern Audrey Hepburn, especially with her hair pulled up, although she doubted the style icon would have worn peep-toe platform shoes with four-inch heels.

They'd look stunning with just *the lingerie*, she thought.

Darby smoothed out her dress and eased the bathroom door open.

Coop was still standing by the bed, sorting through his new clothes – trousers, jeans, socks, packaged dress shirts and tees. He had taken off his shoes and shirt. She looked him over in the soft glow of light coming from the lamp on the nightstand. The white tank top hugged the curves of his broad and well-defined chest.

He had been hunched over the bed when he glanced up at her. Any doubt she may have had about her plan vanished when she saw his slack-jawed expression.

Coop straightened, eyes widening. He suddenly seemed self-conscious at the way he was gawking at her. His gaze cut to the nightstand, where he picked up a glass of what appeared to be Scotch.

'Well,' she said after a moment. 'Aren't you going to say anything?'

'You look amazing.' He swallowed, then added, 'You always do.'

'Thank you.'

He took a slug of Scotch and wiped at his mouth with the back of his hand.

Darby walked up to him and placed her hands lightly on his chest. In her heels, she was almost eye level with him. She could smell the alcohol on his breath.

She ran her fingers up his chest and across his shoulders. Gripped him gently by the back of the neck and pulled him closer and kissed him once, lightly on the lips.

'It unzips in the back,' she whispered. 'Like this.'

She heard the hitch in his breath when her dress fell to the floor. His throat flushed when he saw what was lying underneath the dress.

Coop cradled her face in his hands, and as he kissed her she reached across his back and pulled up his tank top. He raised his hands and she yanked it over his head and tossed it into the air. Her hands went back to his body, palms and fingers sliding across the smooth hardness of his chest. *He feels like he's made of marble*, she thought, and pressed herself against him.

They kissed more slowly, more deeply. Coop's warm, strong hands slid down the small of her back. His fingers moved underneath the elastic band of her panties and gently squeezed her buttocks. She let out a soft moan, feeling him growing hard against her, and realized how much this moment matched the fantasy she'd been nursing since the moment he left for London.

'One question,' she whispered.

'What?' The word thick in his throat.

'Shoes on or off?'

'On,' he said, swallowing. 'Definitely on.'

She kissed his neck. His breath caught again and she kissed his chest, slowly, and she heard his beating heart and the way his breath was now coming sharper and faster as she slid her hand over the bulge mashing against the smooth fabric of his trousers. She undid his belt buckle. His hands gripped her arms and she unbuttoned his trousers. They dropped to the floor, and his eyes slammed shut and his head arched back when she ran her fingers inside his boxers.

'Darby . . . I . . . I . . .'

His words trailed off. His eyes flickered shut and she ran her fingers back up his chest and cupped his jaw.

'Coop.'

When he looked at her, his eyes seemed wet, on the verge of tears. Was he crying?

'I love you,' she said. 'I always have, and I always will.'

'I know.'

He *was* crying.

'I know you do,' he said. 'But I can't. I'm involved with someone else.'

63

Darby was vaguely aware of Coop standing in front of her, eyes bleary, but she wasn't *really* in the room with him, her mind having separated itself from her body. She'd seen this kind of moment played out in TV shows and romantic comedies endless times – and always in a highly clichéd and melodramatic fashion, with the scorned or rejected woman turning on the waterworks while crumbling into the role of a poor, pathetic victim. And every time she saw such a scene, a part of her would want to shout at the screen: *Get your shit together, stop blubbering and say or do* something.

Watching such a thing unfold from the comfortable and safe distance of a chair, though, was a whole galaxy away from actually experiencing it.

Coop wiped at his face, then scooped his trousers off the floor, but instead of putting them on, he sat on the edge of the bed and leaned forward – probably to hide his erection, which was still prominently displayed.

Well, at least you managed to turn him on, a critical voice chimed in. *At least you did something right.*

His elbows propped on his knees and hands dangling between his legs, he took in a long draw of air, his voice shaking when he spoke.

'I'm sorry, Darby.'

She opened her mouth, ready to speak – wanting to speak – but her brain had somehow disengaged itself from her tongue.

'I planned on telling you,' he said. 'I was just looking for the right moment.'

She found she could move now. She turned away from Coop and caught her reflection in a mirror mounted above the bureau across the room. She saw herself standing there in a $300 set of lacy thong panties and low-cut bra, and $600 shoes. Clothes she had bought specifically for him. When she saw the wounded, vulnerable look on her scarlet red face staring back at her, she turned away again, cringing, hating herself for it. For this.

She scooped up her dress from the floor and walked to the bathroom, numb. She shut the door. That sickening process of sinking back inside one's skin had started, and when she saw what was waiting for her – the hurt and anger and everything else mixed with it lying there like the proverbial lump in her stomach – she turned away from that too, by doing what she did best, the only thing that had never failed her: she got busy.

Dressed in a clean pair of jeans, socks and a black tee, the well-worn boots back on her feet and giving her back some sense of who and what she was, Darby opened the door and walked back into the bedroom.

Coop was standing now, near the windows. He had put on his trousers, buckling them, she supposed, to prevent her from further temptation. His tank top, though, was still on the floor.

'I'm sorry, Darb.'

'You've already apologized,' she said, working her arms through her shoulder holster. 'Saying it two, three or a hundred more times doesn't make it any more effective.'

She was surprised – surprised and glad – at how calm she sounded.

'What's the lucky lady's name?'

Coop didn't answer. She didn't care, busy looking around the room, trying to figure out where she'd left her jacket.

And then it came to her, the thing that was slightly off about the evening on John Smith's balcony. She looked at Coop standing on the other side of the bed and slightly to the right. When Smith had stood, he hadn't been standing directly in front of her but off to the side. The sniper would have had a clear shot at her but instead had shot Smith. Why had John Smith, a retired police detective, been shot first?

'Amanda,' Coop said.

'What?'

'Her name is Amanda.'

'That's it? Just a one-word name, like Bono?'

'Amanda Jones. She owns a PR agency in London.'

'Congratulations.'

'Look, I should have told you this before –'

'I humiliated myself,' she finished for him.

'You didn't humiliate yourself. You think I didn't want to –'

'Fuck?'

'That's not what I would have called it.'

'I'm proud of your self-restraint. I really am. Normally

you deliver bad news to your victims after you're done screwing them.'

'Nice.'

'Hey, I'm just repeating what you've told me.'

'What just . . . I'm sorry I let it go on for as long as it did,' he said, pronouncing each word as if she were some autistic child who had trouble grasping the nuances of human emotions. 'I let it go on because I do, in fact, care about you. Deeply. You've been a close friend, and I'd be lying through my teeth if I didn't admit that I've always wondered what it would be like if you and I got together – and I don't just mean physically. I mean long term. White picket fences and all that stuff.'

She didn't want to hear this. She moved to the door.

Coop sprang from around the bed and blocked her exit.

'You're one of the most beautiful women I've ever met – and, let's face it – probably the most unique,' he said. 'But, for whatever reason, our timing was off. I left for London and you decided to stay here.'

'I decided,' she said flatly.

'Yeah. You could have come over to London at any time to –'

'I was a little wrapped up here, Coop, with my own problems.'

'What about all those times we spoke on the phone?'

'What about them?'

'Not once did you mention or remotely *hint* that you wanted to take what we had to a different level.'

'Neither did you. And, as I recall, *you* were the one who

kissed me. And when we spoke later, right before you boarded your flight, I told you how I felt.'

'No, you didn't. Your exact words were, "Coop, before you go, I just wanted to say . . ." and then nothing.'

'Did you forget the part where you said, "I know. I feel the same way for whatever it's worth." When I said, "It's worth a lot" and you ran to the plane to get away —'

'Darby, you never came right out and told me how you felt until now.'

She stared at him, dumbfounded.

'Why the hell did you wait for so long? If you had —'

'I can't believe this,' she said, feeling the anger starting to seep through. *Careful*. 'I can't *believe* you're trying to pin this on me.'

'I'm not trying to pin *anything* on you. Jesus! I didn't say anything because I didn't want to change what we had. I love you too much to —'

'Enough,' she said, pushing him aside and moving into the living room. 'It's starting to sound like some bad romance novel.'

'Where are you going?'

'To work.'

She found her jacket draped across the back of a chair.

'You might as well try to book a flight back home,' she said, putting on her jacket. 'There's no reason for you to stick around.'

'So that's how you want to solve the problem between us? By running away?'

She zipped up her jacket. 'It's a trick I learned from you.'

Coop crossed his arms and studied the tops of his feet.

'You should get back home. Back to Amanda.' She removed all of the cash from her money clip and tossed it on the floor in front of him. 'That should cover part of your plane fare. Let me know the rest and I'll drop a cheque in the mail.'

His face jumped up, sparks of anger in his eyes.

'Thanks again for coming, Coop.'

She had reached the door when he called out to her:

'I waited, Darby. For *you*. Don't get pissed at me because you're the one who blew it.'

She fumbled for the doorknob. When she opened the door, she found Keats standing with his back to the wall so he could watch the hall.

She shut the door behind her and said, 'I need to go back to the medical examiner's office.'

'They expecting you?'

'Not yet,' she said, reaching for her cell phone. She had missed a call – Ronald Ross, the Harvard professor. He had left her a message.

Keats was looking at the door.

'Mr Cooper's not joining us,' Darby said, dialling the answering service for the Boston medical examiner's office. 'He's going back home. To London.'

64

Settled inside the back of the SUV, Darby played the message from Ronald Ross. The Harvard Divinity professor wanted to discuss the symbol she had faxed him earlier this afternoon. He left three numbers – office, cell and home phone.

She asked Keats for a pad of paper and a pen. He took his eyes off the road for a moment, then grabbed something from the console and handed it back to her – napkins and a bottle of water.

'What's this for?'

'Your mascara,' he said. 'It's smeared all over your face.'

No wonder the people inside the Four Seasons had given her such strange looks. Jesus. She took them, twisted off the plastic cap and dumped the water on the napkins, spilling some on her lap and not caring, feeling more angry than embarrassed. Angry at herself for letting her guard down like that. For exposing herself and crying like . . . well, like a girl.

She wiped at her eyes and cheeks, the napkins coming away black, and caught Keats watching her in the rear-view mirror.

'You okay?' he asked in that soft and soothing Southern drawl.

'Never better.'

'Anything I can do to help?'

'No.' *Unfortunately*, she added privately. 'But thank you.'

'Toss everything on the floor back there. When you're through cleaning up, I have a leather writing pad you can use. Pen's clipped inside, a real nice one too, so don't go losing it on me.'

Ronald Ross answered his home phone on the fourth ring. He sounded like he had been asleep.

'I just got your message,' she said. 'Sorry if I woke you.'

'I dozed off on the couch. You did me a favour.' A grunt and then he cleared his throat. On the other end of the line she could hear the click of his heels echoing across a floor. 'I made some notes on this symbol you sent me. I assume it's connected to a case you're working on.'

'You assume correctly. I can't give you specifics.'

'I understand,' he said. 'What do you know about Gnosticism?'

Darby thought about it for a moment, looking out of the side window at the surrounding traffic, and again wondered if she was being followed and watched.

'It's something to do with pre-Christianity, I think.'

'Okay,' Ross said, like he had expected this. 'Let me start with a simple definition. Gnosticism is derived from the Greek word *gnosis*, which means "knowledge". The religion dates all the way back to early Jewish and Christian sects, and its doctrine, simply put, is that there are two gods. The first is a lower, imperfect god, called the Demiurge, who created the material world. The second, the Supreme God of Truth or the Supreme Father God, is a transcendent god and does not care about human affairs. The Demiurge believes he is supreme despite his imperfect creations – the world, mankind. The Demiurge employs servants, called Archons, who roam the world, enacting their own will.'

Darby finished writing in her quick shorthand, then said, 'Which is?'

'Nothing.'

'You mean the Archons are nihilists?'

'No. Archons provide their own order. Their own laws and justice. They are capable of mercy, but by and large they are jealous, wrathful creatures possessed by a singular will and capable of great destruction. The symbol you sent me, it's a bastardized version of a Gnostic baptismal cross developed centuries ago by a medieval group who had roots in Gnosticism. Those twelve spikes? Each one represents an Archon. The circle is a representation of earth.'

She thought about Charlie Rizzo's odd-looking black medieval tunic. 'What's the name of this group?'

'It doesn't have a specific name. But this group believed that symbol represents one who is basically a slave to an Archon.'

'Is Gnosticism an actual religion or is it a cult?'

'An actual religion,' Ross said. 'It was essentially wiped out by the end of the fifth century. What we know about it comes from the Gnostic library discovered in Nag Hammadi, Egypt, in the forties, and then, in 1970, the discovery of the Gospel of Judas in El Minya. It's a Gnostic gospel written by Jesus's Gnostic followers, and the pieces that have been recovered claim to be a documented conversa-

344

tion between Judas Iscariot and Jesus. Judas is believed to be the only disciple who was taught the one, true Gospel, by Jesus.

'Now, according to the canonical Gospels of the New Testament — Matthew, Mark, Luke and John — we know that Judas betrayed Jesus. The Gospel of Judas claims that Judas was acting on the orders of Jesus, which, taken from the Gnostic point of view, makes sense. Jesus wanted to be released from his spiritual prison, and Judas acted as the catalyst. So you have –'

'Sorry to interrupt,' Darby said. 'I appreciate the history lesson, Professor, but I need something along the lines of evidence. Something that can lead back to this group or cult or whatever they are.'

'I understand. The short answer is no, I don't have anything to give you other than historical background on Gnosticism. But I can tell you more about this symbol you found. I know you can't get into specifics of the case, but let me ask you this: the person who bore this symbol, did he murder someone?'

'As far as I can tell, no. The man was a husband and father.'

Tell her, Daddy, Charlie Rizzo had said. *Tell her what you did.*

She wrote on her pad: *Mark Rizzo alias?*

'Historically speaking,' Ross said, 'Archons crave power and destruction. They're not sent here to do God's work but rather to fulfil their own needs and desires. Archons want the world to bend to their will. They achieve that through inflicting both physical and psychological pain and suffering. Through the destruction of one's soul. Forgive the cliché, but think of them as monsters masquerading as human beings.'

Darby finished writing and looked up, reminded of Jack Casey. Then she saw, a few blocks away, the medical examiner's office.

'I have to go, Professor Ross. Can I call you back?'

'You can, but there's no need. That's about all the information I have at the moment, anyway. I can send you my notes if you'd like.'

'That would be great.' She gave him her private email address. 'I appreciate your taking the time to do this.'

'If I can be of any further assistance, don't hesitate to contact me. You have my numbers? I left them on the voicemail message.'

'I have them. And I may take you up on your offer. In fact, I may have an associate of mine call you. Keep your cell phone handy.'

Darby hung up as the SUV came to a sudden stop in front of two Secret Service agents, one black, the other white, both tall and young and looking like they could bench press a car.

'They'll take you in and bring you back out when you're done,' Keats said.

The black guy opened her door and his partner reached inside and gripped her arm. She left the pad on the backseat, not wanting to carry it with her, and with the two men flanking her jogged to the building's front doors.

Dr Ellis wasn't happy about being summoned back to work at such an hour. He stormed across the lobby and without a hello or nod swiped his laminated ID across the keycard reader to let her in, the agents sticking close.

Walking through the halls, she called Sergey.

'You got a pen?' she asked when he picked up.

'Always do.' He sounded exhausted. 'What's up?'

She gave him Ross's name and cell number. 'He's a professor at Harvard's Divinity School. I just got off the phone with him. He has information on that symbol I found tattooed on Mark Rizzo's lip. I want you to bring him in on this.'

'I already have someone at Langley. Cryptography's working on it right now.'

'Then have them coordinate with Ross. This is the guy's area of expertise. Trust me, we need him.'

'Okay, fine. Where are you?'

'At the ME's office. I'll explain everything when I get there.'

Darby hung up and ducked into the locker room. She dressed quickly.

The black agent followed her inside the autopsy suite. His partner stood guard outside with his back to the door, watching the hall.

Until you find the people who belong to this group or cult, a voice whispered in the back of her head, *this is how you're going to spend the rest of your life.*

Ellis wheeled out John Smith's body, the cadaverous skin covered with frost.

Darby turned to the agent and said, 'Hit those lights, would you?'

The exit wound had destroyed most of John Smith's

face. Using alcohol swabs, Darby cleaned the blood away from what was left of the man's lips and examined the tissue. She didn't find any trace of the symbol.

She decided to examine the rest of the body.

The symbol had been tattooed on his chest, just above his dead heart.

65

Darby saw the big, familiar sign welcoming her to Boston's Logan Airport. A moment later Keats accessed a private gate leading to a brightly lit stretch of tarmac holding a small fleet of private planes – a couple of jumbo jets used to shuttle around rocks stars but mostly smaller, sleeker models.

The Lincoln Navigator came to a stop and she saw a new pair of Secret Service agents dressed in heavy winter coats standing guard at the bottom of a set of portable metal steps leading up to the main door of the biggest plane here – a Boeing 747, she guessed, given its size and shape. There were no markings or printed words on the side of the plane, nothing to indicate what kind of aircraft it was.

Keats asked her to stay in the car for a moment. He got out and jogged over to the other two agents to have a private conversation.

What had happened back at the hotel was painfully fresh in her mind but she had managed to tuck it away by keeping busy. Focused. Now, waiting alone in the warm silence of the car, the wind roaring outside, wanting to blow everything clean, her thoughts flashed to Coop and she wondered if he was waiting for her to return or if he had said *screw it* and left to catch a flight back to London.

She pictured him inside the airport talking to Amanda what's-her-name, making plans for when he returned in between exchanges of 'I miss you' and 'I love you'.

Keats came back and opened her door, and when she stepped out the wind slapped her face, which thrust Coop into the back of her mind (but not too far back; she could still see his face, and his anger, and hear him say: 'I was the one who waited for you.'). Keats didn't hand her off to the agents. He took the metal staircase and she followed, the railing cold beneath her hand and the wind whistling past her ears.

She stepped inside a semi-dark cabin. Two men dressed in white were fast asleep in the first rows of seats, paramedic kits resting on the floor near their soft-soled white shoes. The remaining four rows of leather seats were empty, and another Secret Service agent stood in front of a closed door that, on an ordinary plane, would separate the first-class passengers from the commercial herd.

But this plane wasn't ordinary. The door, made of heavy steel, had a magnetic lock that required a code.

Keats punched in the code, and, as he held open the door for her, he said, 'Sergey's on the lower deck. Go straight down and you'll see a set of stairs to your left. Take them all the way down. I'll join you in a bit.'

Darby thanked him and stepped into a luxury cabin worthy of the president's private plane, Air Force One. The first section, with beige carpeting and soft lighting coming from several lamps, had comfortable leather chairs and seats. They were empty, as was the leather chair bolted to the floor behind a nicely sized executive mahogany desk. Thick pale curtains covered part of the plane's windows. The others had blinds, all drawn, and on one she saw a presidential seal.

Maybe this *was* Air Force One. Not the current one the president used but possibly a retired model that had been appropriated by the Bureau. Made sense. She remembered Sergey saying the plane stored lab equipment and a place this size could certainly accommodate a full-sized forensic lab.

The next part of the plane appeared to be a conference room. More empty leather sofas and chairs; more empty desks, only these were much smaller than the one in the previous room. A flat-screen TV hung on one wall, tuned to CNN. Anderson Cooper's lips were moving but no sound came from the speakers.

Making her way to the back, the warm air smelling of coffee and stale food, she wondered if Casey, Sergey and the others slept here. Probably, as the plane clearly served as the base of operations. The place was packed with high-tech equipment, secured phones and computers, video-conferencing monitors.

Darby passed what she guessed had to be the 'presidential bathroom' – gold fixtures and a roomy shower. She turned on the light and stepped inside to examine her face in the mirror, saw blotches of mascara. She ran the hot water and scrubbed her face with soap and several paper towels.

A high-pitched scream came from somewhere deep in the plane.

66

Darby straightened, water dripping down her face as she listened to a young woman crying and pleading for help.

Darby grabbed the hanging towel and quickly dried her face. A final check in the mirror and then she moved out, heading down the aisle on her far left.

The young voice screamed a single word:

'*Daddy.*'

Jack Casey sat in the gloom, his back to her and his attention focused on a flat-screen monitor mounted on the wall across from his chair. The film playing on the screen had been recorded by a video camera equipped with night vision; his daughter, Sarah, was bathed in a green ambient glow of light. She wore the same clothes as those in the photographs – jeans and a white tee smeared with her blood – and she stood shaking and crying behind some sort of prison cube made of Lucite or Plexiglas.

She wasn't in danger of suffocating – several holes had been drilled through the walls for air – but she was in danger of being bitten by the dozens of eight-legged creatures crawling above her.

The spiders moved and scattered across a separate rectangular cube mounted against the ceiling. The people who had captured her had installed a sliding bottom, one operated by a lever situated outside the young girl's clear cell.

A scarred, grimy hand clutched the lever. With a flick of the wrist, the ceiling – well out of the girl's reach – would disappear and drop the venomous spiders down on her.

Darby's mind filled with images of Mark Rizzo's body. Saw the necrotic bite on the man's forearm caused by a Brown Recluse. She saw at least one on the screen, and another one that Perkins had identified as a Tunnel Web. *Their bite is* extremely *painful,* Dr Perkins had said. *Their venom carries atraxotoxin, which disrupts neurotransmitters. The victim experiences muscle twitching, severe nausea and vomiting.*

Sarah Casey pounded on the clear plastic, screaming at her father. Her right little finger was gone, severed above the knuckle. *There's going to be no way to attach it,* Darby thought, approaching the empty chair next to the profiler. Too much time had passed, for one, and, given the blackened stump on the swollen right hand, she suspected, with a nauseating intensity, that the wound had been crudely cauterized with something like a blowtorch to stem the bleeding. If it had, the nerves had already been damaged.

Casey had a highball glass on his lap. He wasn't drunk – not yet, his eyes were too clear when he looked up and focused on her – but he was well on his way. He had put a serious dent in the bottle of whiskey sitting on the table to his left. The bottle was more than half empty.

Casey picked up the remote and paused the video. He seemed to be waiting for her to say something. She felt like telling the man how deeply sorry she felt about what was going on. No, he wouldn't want that. Stick to business.

'Did Sergey tell you about the tattoo I found on Mark Rizzo's lip?'

He nodded.

'I found another one tonight,' she said. 'On the chest of the former cop who worked on the Charlie Rizzo investigation.'

'The cop from Nahant who got shot?'

She nodded. 'John Smith.'

'Interesting.'

Clearly – understandably – Casey's attention was on the video. On his daughter. She decided not to fill him in yet on her conversation with the Harvard professor.

Darby took the empty chair. 'Sergey told me this video was on the USB drive.'

'Yep.'

'Anything else?'

'Just this. The USB drive is downstairs. The computer whiz kids are scraping through it right now, seeing if they can find some digital fingerprints or something. Another group is analysing the video frame by frame, trying different light sources to see if anything jumps out.'

He polished off the rest of his drink, the melting ice cubes rattling in the glass. He reached for the bottle, and Darby glanced at the image frozen on the screen: Sarah Casey pounding on the clear plastic, lips stretched back in a howl of pain and terror.

'How much time does she have?' he asked, pouring himself another drink.

'That's a question you're much better suited to answer, isn't it? You know these people –'

'I meant her finger. How much time until a surgeon can reattach it?'

'I'm not a surgeon.'

'But you knew enough to send my daughter's finger over to Mass General.'

'Six, maybe eight hours.'

'And if, by some miracle, my daughter was found right now?'

She didn't see a point in sparing the man the truth. 'I think the time has passed.'

'Why's that?'

'The wound's already been cauterized. The nerves need to be healthy in order to reattach the finger.'

Casey nodded, kept nodding, his face not registering any emotion.

'Dr Izzo told me the same thing,' he said after a moment. 'He called me an hour ago, said the window of opportunity is now officially shut.'

She told herself to keep her voice gentle, and she did. 'If you already know this, why did you ask me?'

'To see if you'd bullshit me,' he said.

'So this was, what, a test?'

Casey didn't answer. He swirled the booze around, the ice cubes tinkling against the glass, and looked around the cabin. 'This plane's an old Air Force One, one of two that's been refitted to combat the war on terror. State-of-the-art technology on board. Had to fight the Bureau to let us use it. These people we're after, they fall under the domestic terrorism label, don't you think?'

She nodded, sensing he had a point to make. She crossed her legs and waited.

'I look at all this technology and see the one thing it

can't do: understand or figure out a person's motive,' he said. 'I'm not just talking about serial killers or this group who have my daughter and wife right now. I could be referring to anyone. Like the housewife who wakes up one day after thirty years of marriage and just decides to pack up and leave her husband and kids. You can never know what truly goes on in somebody's mind. You learn that pretty fast when you work in the Monster Factory. That's what they called Behavioral Sciences in the early days.'

Casey took a long sip. He wiped his mouth with the back of his hand. She watched his face in the dim green glow of light coming from the TV screen.

'Before I went to work there, I was a cop in Michigan. This one case, this guy calls 911 and says he murdered his family. My partner and I get the call, and when we get there the front door is cracked open and the second I step in I see the blood covering the walls and the floor. We go inside with our guns raised and find this guy sitting at his dining-room table eating dinner and reading the newspaper. He greeted us – *thanked* us for coming, and then tells us his family is in the basement.

'He killed them one by one, starting with his wife in the morning. Picks up the youngest from nursery school, brings him inside and shoots him in the back of the head. Guy makes himself lunch and waits for the next one, the ten-year-old. He gets shot the moment he walks in the door, doesn't even get a chance to take off his jacket. The thirteen-year-old has soccer, so the father goes and picks him up after practice, brings him home and shoots his son just as he's going up the stairs. Guy didn't tell us this.

I found out after the fact, after we studied the splatter patterns and drag marks on the carpet.

'I went into the basement myself. They're all sitting there, the wife and her kids, they're sitting on a couch watching a Disney movie in the VCR. *Bambi*. Guy said it was the family's favourite movie. He went down every hour and a half to rewind the movie and play it again.'

'He tell you why he killed his family?'

'Nope. Guy died on death row without telling a soul.'

She sensed he had more to say, and waited.

A nearby plane took off, its engines vibrating through the cabin and her seat.

Casey said, 'The first guy I caught, Tommy Barber? He broke into houses, bound, raped and tortured women and their families. Recorded everything too. Guy had quite the little home-movie collection. Tommy's a quadriplegic now, serving a life sentence in Angola. I shot him in the spine.'

No sympathy in his tone, just matter-of-fact, as if he were narrating some instructional video.

'Charlie Slavick,' he said, looking up at her, his gaze level and cool, 'put boys inside dog crates and tortured them. I beat him to death with a hammer.'

'And Hamilton?'

'He's alive.'

'I know,' she said. 'Did you plant evidence?'

'I did.'

'And then what?'

'Then I went to work on how to kill him. And the only thing I regret is that I couldn't do it.'

'Maybe you'll have a second chance when he's released,' she said.

Casey regarded her for a moment, wondering if she was being serious or glib.

'I'm assuming Sergey told you I talked with your wife,' Darby said.

'He did. If we don't find my wife and daughter, I'm going to go ahead with the press conference.'

'Wait, you're not seriously thinking of –'

'No. No, of course not. Confessing on live TV and killing Waters isn't going to save my family. If I knew it would for certain, I'd do it in a heartbeat. I'd turn the gun on myself if it would save them, but there's no way these people are going to let Taylor and Sarah go. They won't kill them – there's no fun in that.'

His words came out sounding rote, and his face remained, as ever, expressionless.

'They want me to suffer,' Casey said. 'They've already given my wife a transorbital lobotomy.'

Darby felt cold all over, sitting still as she watched Casey pick up the remote from his lap and point it at the screen.

67

He played the video from the beginning.

A black screen followed by a low hiss from the speakers. Then a male voice said: 'Property of the Federal Bureau of Investigation, case number 489765, item number 86. This is a copy of the original video.'

On the TV screen Sarah Casey stumbled around her cell, her nine remaining fingers feeling their way through pitch-black darkness. The spiders, Darby noticed, weren't visible on camera – not yet – but she could hear their soft thumping sounds as they bumped into the walls of their cage. Casey's daughter had heard the sounds too. She paused every few seconds to glance up and listen carefully, alert to the danger waiting several feet above her head.

The camera lens didn't waver. *Must be set up on a tripod*, Darby thought, switching her attention past Sarah Casey to the stone walls beyond the young girl's clear cell. Ancient and craggy, they reminded Darby of the ones she had seen in historical churches in Paris – walls that had never seen sunlight, dusty and smooth. The colouring, though, was uneven. Splotches of black and lighter colours covered the walls.

Now the camera lens panned back and the spiders were visible to the viewer but not to Sarah Casey. She bumped into one of the smooth walls and screamed. Darby watched the grimy hand grip the lever for the bottom of the spider cage and the green glow of night vision disappeared, giving way to a steady bright spotlight shining from somewhere on top of the video camera.

Sarah Casey held her hand up to the sudden burst of light. Her cheeks were swollen and shiny with tears, her breathing so fast and sharp she seemed on the verge of hyperventilating. Her hand moved away from her face and, blinking, she saw whoever was standing behind the camera and screamed. She bumped into the back wall and heard the sounds above her head and looked up and saw what was up there and screamed again.

Now came the part Darby had already seen: the young girl pounding on the translucent barrier of her prison cell and screaming for her father. The girl sinking into a corner, wailing, her gaze darting between the spiders crawling above her head, the person holding the lever and the person or persons standing behind the video camera. A flapping sound came over the speakers and Sarah Casey turned to the camera. She blinked several times, wiping away the tears from her vision, and when her eyes focused they widened for a moment and she choked out a single word:

'*Daddy.*'

Sarah Casey disappeared as the camera cut to a new shot, this one also in night vision but from a different angle, the lens pointed down at another person, a middle-aged and almost model-perfect woman with prominent cheekbones, long blonde hair and long legs strapped down to a crude-looking operating table. Darby saw leather straps biting into the woman's ankles and wrists and thought about the abrasions she'd found on Mark Rizzo's body and wondered if he had been strapped down to the same table.

'My wife,' Casey said in a dead voice. 'Taylor.'

His wife's shoes and socks had been removed but not her shorts or tank top. A thick leather strap had been placed across her forehead to keep her head steady. Her eyes, wide and frightened, searched vainly through the darkness.

Seconds passed and nothing happened. Darby looked at these walls and found them to be nearly identical to the ones she'd seen surrounding Sarah Casey's cell – the same dry round stones, the same blotchy colouring, the same cracks and fissures in the mortar. Only here Darby found a black shadow to the far left. Maybe part of a doorway. Darby could see only the bottom quarter of it.

Then she saw a black-robed figure step over to the table. His head wasn't visible and the woman didn't seem to hear him, and she couldn't see the man's hand as it came up from underneath the table, the fingers gripping a long, slender metal instrument shaped like a nail.

Darby felt beads of sweat pop out along her hairline and from the corner of her eye she looked at Casey. The green light glowed across his weathered face, and his eyes were steady as they watched the screen, his lips parting not to speak but to take another drink.

The robed man on the screen moved to the top of the table. Taylor Casey didn't see him. The camera zoomed in on her face and then she screamed and bucked against her restraints as the man's thumb shoved back her upper eyelid.

Darby's stomach dropped and she forced herself to watch but the screen went black. Then the woman's screams exploded over the speakers.

She wasn't aware that a phone was ringing until she saw Casey leaping out of his chair.

Darby rewound the DVD to the black spot she'd seen on the far left of the screen. She still couldn't see anything, then rewound the DVD again, this time pausing on the black spot. She stood, feeling cold and more than a little shaken, and moved closer to the TV screen.

She couldn't make out much, just the faint outlines of several shapes that could be nothing more than grainy marks left over from the DVD transfer.

'Sergey wants to talk to us,' Casey said. 'He told me you think I should be removed from this case.'

Darby opened her mouth to speak but Casey cut her off.

'I don't blame you for thinking it,' he said. 'You're right. I'm too close to this, obviously.'

'If you find one or more of these people, what are you planning on doing?'

'Arresting them, of course.'

'That's too bad.'

'Why's that?'

'Because I plan on killing them,' Darby said. 'Every last one.'

68

Darby summarized her conversation with Ronald Ross as she followed Casey into another dimly lit room, this one an area of bunk beds that reminded her of an army barracks, only these beds unfolded from the walls and came with seatbelts. She trailed behind the man as he made his way down a set of stairs. Casey got off on the next floor and opened the door to a room lit by soft and elegant lighting.

The long cabin seemed as wide and as long as a football field and had both the look and feel of downtown Boston's Harvard Club – dark wood panelling on the walls, worn brown leather club chairs and small mahogany tables. A well-worn oriental rug of deep burgundy, forest green and dark brown hues covered the entire floor. Despite being inside a plane, this space was as regal and luxurious as the Four Seasons' banquet hall; only this space was being used to host the missing and the dead.

Darby gaped at all the young faces captured in black and white and colour – the faces of children, hundreds of them, each one staring at her from the photographs tacked to the wall-mounted corkboards that filled almost both sides of the plane.

The photographs had been arranged by year. To her right, a corkboard with a label at the top that read: '1945 to 1972?' Filling almost every square inch of that space were old and fraying Polaroids and black and white pictures. Each child had a name. Each one had a question mark written next to it. These kids had been abducted from Washington. The next board, this one labelled '1973 to 1975', had photographs of abducted and missing children from Oregon. The next one was dedicated to California. She read the years printed on the label: '1976 to 1981'.

The time Casey got involved, she thought. Then, on the heels of it, came another one: *Washington, then Oregon and California. The West Coast.*

She swung her head around to her left, to the area near the door, and saw two tall and wide corkboards filled with colour photographs of more recent victims – 2009 and 2010.

She moved forward, slowly, taking in the photographs of more missing children from the previous years and thinking, *It's like the Traveler case all over again, hundreds and hundreds of photographs of missing victims spanning decades.*

But Traveler had predominately hunted women. Teenagers, women in their twenties and thirties – there had even been a handful in their late forties or early fifties. The women, she had discovered later, hadn't been carefully selected; they were victims of opportunity, snatched from the streets while walking to their home or car, and each one had been killed inside Traveler's underground dungeon of horrors.

But *these* bulletin boards and *these* pictures contained pictures of young children – both boys and girls from different races and backgrounds. What had Sergey told her? In each case Casey had discovered the abducted child was the youngest member of the family. There was a careful selection process at work here, a singular reason that united all of the hundreds of gap-toothed smiling kids staring at her in this grisly shrine.

She counted the pictures underneath the boards labelled 2009 and 2010. Three victims – two boys and one girl – abducted from New Hampshire, Massachusetts and Vermont.

In 2007 and 2008, eleven kids had been snatched from Tennessee and North and South Carolina. Before that, from 2004 to 2006, this group had focused on Arkansas, Mississippi, Georgia and Alabama.

Something itched in the back of her mind, something about the states, how they –

They surround each other, she thought. New Hampshire and Vermont bordered Massachusetts. In the 2007 and 2008 abductions . . . she could see the map of the US in her mind's eye now, the states drilled into her memory courtesy of the nuns at St Stephens School. Tennessee . . . the right-hand portion of the state bordered both North *and* South Carolina. Same with the abduction cases from 2004 to 2006: Alabama was the central state, bordering Arkansas, Mississippi and Georgia. This group (another difference between the Traveler case: there was a *group* of people at work here, not a pair of serial killers), *this* group worked in a tight cluster.

She turned to Casey, saw that he wasn't standing next to her. He was behind her, his hand gripping a doorknob.

'Clusters,' she called out to him. 'They work in a tight cluster of states.'

'I know.'

'So the state that borders all the others must work as their base of operations.'

'That's the theory,' he said, motioning for her to hurry along.

She whisked past him, through the open door, and stepped into a private conference room decorated with the same rich wood. All of the eight leather chairs arranged around the table had seatbelts.

Special Agent Sergey Martynovich sat at the far end, a phone tucked against his ear, his other hand holding the edge of a computer screen. It had been bolted down to the table so it wouldn't fall, as had the other device sitting in the table's centre – a wireless conference phone made of black and silver and shaped like some sort of sinister-looking spaceship.

He hung up and said, 'Tom Geary from Langley's calling. They're setting up the video-conference stuff on his end right now. Jack, did Darby tell you about her conversation with a Harvard professor named – she did. Okay, good. Now let me bring you both up to speed with what we have so far.'

Sergey looked at her and said, 'The recording of that person from the Rizzo house you had on your voicemail? After you left, they came and untied him. You can hear their footsteps and one of them says, *Vos es tutus, custodio.*' He glanced down at his notes. 'Its loose translation is "No harm will come to you, guard." The blood swab from the crater has been loaded into CODIS. We're not hoping for miracles there, just an ID. That's all I've got.'

Casey said, 'What about the GPS implants?'

'Still silent.'

'They were operating fine when I left Florida.'

'I know. It's . . . the technology is still somewhat new, Jack. It's not perfect.'

The silence grew in the room. Sergey glanced at her with a grim smile.

'Your friend Coop is on his way back home. First class,' he said. 'We had him booked under another name. We have an agent who will meet him at Heathrow and escort him home.'

'Thank you.'

More silence. Sergey seemed relieved when he heard a knock on the door. It opened and a woman dressed in a professional navy-blue suit came inside and with both hands placed a bulky case on the table. Big and square and made of black plastic, it looked like something used to house a power tool.

The woman undid the hinges and flipped the top open. Lying in the foam was an aluminium gun with a fine metal tip. She looked at Darby and said, 'Right or left arm?'

Sergey waved his hands. 'Sorry, I forgot to tell her. Darby, we're going to put a chip in your arm. It's very small, sits right below the skin.'

'I don't see the point,' Darby said, 'as it doesn't seem to be working.'

Sergey placed his hands together as if in prayer. 'I'd feel better if you did it. It'll only last a week and then we'll take it out.'

Darby shrugged. She took off her leather jacket and shirt, glad that she had worn a tank top underneath. A swab of alcohol and then a slight sting and it was over. The woman placed a Band-Aid on her arm, collected her stuff and left.

Casey said, 'This guy from Cryptography, you tell him what's going on with me?'

'I gave him the background stuff,' Sergey said. 'No specifics.'

'When he calls, tell him I'm not in the room. That way he won't be inclined to hold anything back. I'll listen from the corner.'

Ten minutes passed.

Darby said, 'I want to examine the USB drive.'

'We have people doing that right now,' Sergey said. 'Computer geeks. They're looking for what they called "digital fingerprints". Every computer leaves them behind, they said, so we're going to see if we can track down these people that way.'

'I want to hold it in my hands.'

Sergey thought it over for a moment, then shrugged and picked up the phone.

'Can I ask why?' he said as he punched in numbers.

'It feels . . . off. Wrong. The finger, the USB drive – they're risking exposure,' Darby said. 'They're too clever for that.'

The USB drive arrived ten minutes later. Darby held it, twirling it around in her fingers when the conference-room phone started ringing.

69

Sergey picked up the phone and listened, looking at the web-type cam set up on top of the computer monitor. A moment later, he glanced at Casey and nodded, and Casey got out of his chair.

Sergey hung up and pressed a button on the alien-spacecraft speakerphone. 'Tom?'

'I'm here,' replied a deep, baritone voice.

Casey moved away as Sergey swivelled the monitor around to her.

On the screen she saw a freckle-faced older man with pale skin and shocking bright red hair that, for some strange reason, he decided to wear long, like he was stuck in the seventies. The boyish face didn't match the deep voice.

Sergey pulled out the chair next to her.

'Tom,' he said, sitting, 'this is Darby McCormick, the one who found the symbol tattooed to the victim's lip. She's got security clearance, so there's no need to hold anything back.'

'I don't see Mr Casey,' Geary said.

'He's not here.'

'Okay. Probably better this way. The news isn't good.'

Darby glanced to the corner where Casey stood and saw the defeat reach his face. Casey had been hoping the symbol would lead to something solid – the proverbial needle in the haystack.

Geary said, 'I just got off the phone with the Harvard professor, Ross. He informed me he spoke to both of you individually and gave you the background information he has on the symbol and how it relates to this Gnosticism business.'

Darby nodded. Sergey said, 'Correct. What did Cryptography uncover on the symbol?'

'Nothing,' Geary said. 'We've never come across it – this is the first time anyone here has seen it. Good call bringing Ross in on this. If it wasn't for him, we'd still be looking.'

Darby looked at the USB drive. It was encased in plastic, and, as she moved it around in her fingers underneath the light, she saw several small scratches and scuff marks.

Sergey said, 'What about connecting this symbol to a group or church that practises Gnosticism? Any luck there?'

'I'm afraid not. Like I said, nobody here has come across this symbol, and since it's not listed in any of our computer systems, we don't have any way to connect it to an individual church, group or radical cult. I'd rule out churches, though.'

'Why?'

'Gnosticism – the actual religion – isn't something that's hidden in the shadows. There are thousands of Gnostic churches in the US alone. The religious aspect is, in many ways, no different to Catholicism.'

'Small difference,' Sergey said. 'The Catholic Church isn't going around the country abducting kids.'

'True,' Geary said. 'They're too busy molesting them.'

Darby reached into her jacket pocket for her pen knife.

'Given what you've told me about the case,' Geary said, 'I'm thinking you're dealing with some underground movement or splinter cell.'

'Or cult.'

'Possibly. The tattoo on the lip gives it that whole secret society vibe.'

'What about these Archons Ross mentioned? Has that word come across your radar screen?'

'No. This is the first time anyone here has heard it.'

Darby worked the blade into the USB's plastic seam to prise the case apart.

Geary said, 'As for what Ross told me regarding Archons – and I'm reading his words here – they want the world to bend to their will, their law, their order. They achieve that result through inflicting both physical and psychological pain and suffering – in this case, on Jack Casey. You said he has a history with this group.'

'He does. A long history. They've been looking for Jack for a long time.'

'Then if you believe Ross's historical literature on Archons and how they fit into Gnostic doctrine – that they are the servants of a divine being, hell bent on acquiring power through human pain and suffering – then this group, cult, splinter cell or whatever they call themselves or whoever they think they are, I think it's safe to say they won't release Casey's wife or daughter. I think – and Ross agrees with me on this – I think they'll deliver on their promise of mailing pieces of his family to you.'

'And if Jack delivers on his promise and holds the press conference?'

'That's more your territory than mine. You've dealt with the group longer than I have, so you know more about them than I do. Given what you told me, they want Casey. The family is just a means to an end. They know you can't watch or protect him for ever either. They'll wait and plan, and when the moment presents itself, they'll take him and he'll most likely vanish like the others. As for the man's wife and daughter, I wouldn't hold out much hope of seeing them alive again.'

Darby popped the plastic case off the USB drive, then worked the pen knife's blade to prise open the metal case hidden underneath.

'So what you're saying, Tom, is that you've got shit.'

'That pretty much sums it up, yeah,' Geary said. 'Ross told you about the symbol, what he thinks it means?'

'He said the person who wears it is a slave to an Archon.'

'Correct.'

'We found the same symbol tattooed on the chest of a former Boston cop about an hour ago. A cop who worked the Charlie Rizzo investigation.'

Darby put the pen knife on the table and opened the metal case with her fingers, thinking about John Smith leaning on the balcony railing of his home, proud and smiling at what he had achieved, his wife taking in rescue dogs.

'What did he say?' Geary asked.

'He's dead.'

'Finding one or more of the people connected to this group is going to be your best bet, I think, of finding where Casey's wife and kid are being stashed.'

'Provided they'll talk.'

'I don't have anything that can help you, Sergey. I'm sorry. You know what you need.'

'Evidence.'

'That's right. Something that will lead you to them. Any leads there?'

'Maybe. There's someone who –'

Darby seized Sergey's arm and said, 'That lead turned out to be a dead end.'

Sergey whipped his attention to her. Darby made a cutting motion near her throat with her hands, signalling for him to stop talking. Then she pointed to the dismantled parts of the USB drive scattered on the table.

Darby looked at the monitor screen and said, 'We don't have anything to go on, Mr Geary. Nothing at all. Thank you for your time.'

She got out of her seat and cut the signal before Geary could do any more damage.

70

Sergey gripped the edge of the table, staring at a small microphone attached to a battery that had been hidden inside the USB. The listening device had been glued down to keep it from moving, the mike affixed underneath the USB's tiny heat vent so it could eavesdrop on conversations like the one they'd just had.

Casey had seen it too. He had moved out from the corner and now stood behind Sergey, leaning over his shoulder. Both faces were pale, slick with perspiration.

'We're screwed,' Darby said.

Both men looked up at her.

'No evidence, no leads,' she said, the frustration clear in her voice. 'Every avenue we've explored leads to another dead end.'

Casey nodded and played along: 'We still have the USB drive. The computer guys –'

'It's a wipe,' Darby said. 'No digital fingerprints. There's nothing on the video that can help us. We won't find them that way.'

'What about the safe house? They had to have left something behind.'

'I read the report. They found nothing. I'm sorry, Jack, but we don't have any evidence. These people are too smart at covering their tracks.' A long, tired sigh, and then Darby said, 'I need a break, grab some coffee.'

'I think we could all use one,' Sergey said, standing. 'Let's meet back here in fifteen.'

They regrouped in the adjoining room, in the far corner near the corkboard holding the yellowing photographs for the missing children from 1945 to 1972.

Darby took the lead. 'It's minor damage.'

Sergey's jaw dropped. '*Minor* damage? They just overheard that entire call. And that USB drive has been floating around from person to person. It's been sitting on desks inside the lab where people have been talking about evidence. Jesus.'

Sergey pinched the bridge of his nose between his fingers. Casey, arms across his chest, stared at the children smiling at him from the board.

'There's nothing we can do. It's over,' Darby said. 'But it's still a lucky break.'

Casey spoke. 'Radio frequency.'

'Exactly,' she said. 'All we need to do is find out what radio frequency that listening device is set to and track it down. You have that kind of equipment on board?'

'I'm not sure,' Sergey said. 'Let me talk to our tech guys.'

'Wait, before you go, what were you about to say before I cut you off?'

'I have a potential lead. Our forensic entomologist identified the bee you found and called a conservation biologist from the University of Connecticut, this guy named James Wright. He's on the phone, holding.'

'Any other place where we can talk to him?'

'No, not at the moment. We have only one of those conference-phone units set up.'

'Get the USB drive out of there,' Darby said. 'Pack it away someplace where it can't do any more damage and then meet us back at the conference room.'

Darby took her original seat. Casey leaned against the wall with his arms folded across his chest and Sergey sat on the edge of the table next to the conference-room phone.

Sergey pressed a button. 'Mr Wright?'

'Still here,' replied a nasal and reedy voice.

'I'm sorry to have kept you waiting, sir. Thank you for holding.

'Mr Wright, I have two people sitting with me right now: Jack Casey and the person who discovered the bee, Dr Darby McCormick. She's also one of our special investigators. I've told them who you are and how you came to us, so in the interests of saving time go ahead and summarize what you told me about the bee.'

'The bee,' Wright said, 'is a silver-haired species known as *Epeoloides pilosula*. They're very rare in New England. In fact, we thought the species was extinct. The last time one was spotted was in Needham, Massachusetts, back in 1927. Then, a little over a year ago, I discovered one here in Connecticut, in the south-eastern part of the state – in a power line corridor, of all places. That's what made my study so controversial. I won't bore you with the details, as I know you're pressed for time, but suffice to say people think these power line corridors – or transmission corridors, as they're more commonly referred to – are disruptive to the environment. When you carve out a section of forest, you don't expect to discover, decades later, a rare species of bee that was generally considered extinct to be thriving underneath power lines, of all places.

'But that's exactly what happened – and is still happening. Because of the excavation, and the considerable care taken to prune trees to a height that won't disrupt the power lines, we are, in essence, re-creating what I guess you could call a meadow in which dwindling insects like bees can thrive as well as other animals and plants. Needless to say, most of the conservation groups are up in arms about this.'

Darby said, 'What about Massachusetts? Have there been any confirmed sightings?'

'It's possible these silver-hairs are thriving somewhere in Massachusetts, but, if they are, no one has reported it. I spoke with several of my New England colleagues – we're a small group – and not one of them has any documented sightings of *Epeoloides pilosula*. As far as I know, the transmission corridor here in Connecticut is the only area where these silver-hair bees have been discovered.'

'Do they or can they live in someplace like a basement or cellar?'

'I'm not sure I understand your question.'

'Would these bees seek shelter in someplace like a house? We're already well into autumn, and my understanding is bees can't thrive in cool weather.'

'Ah, now I see where you're heading. As I'm sure you're all well aware, we've been experiencing several climate changes in the last decade. Warmer winters and sometimes we don't even *have* a spring, we head right into the start of summer. And several times since the start of October, we've hit temperatures in the high seventies, so it's not uncommon to see bees and other insects during these periods.

'Now, to answer the question about their seeking shelter inside a house, the answer is no, absolutely not,' Wright said. 'This species feeds on yellow loosestrife. It's not a houseplant but rather one that lives outside and grows in shady banks or wetlands. That's where I discovered my *Epeoloides pilosula*, feeding on the yellow loosestrife. And I should note that the bee you found was, in fact, dead.'

In her mind's eye Darby pictured Mark Rizzo being dragged across the woods, across dried pine needles, leaves and now this bee making its way into his mouth.

'This transmission corridor,' she said. 'Where is it?'

'Off Route 163 in south-eastern Connecticut,' Wright said. 'You can access it easily from the highway, and you can drive down the path since it's . . . I'd say, oh, roughly three hundred feet or so wide.'

Darby had no intention of driving down it. 'How isolated is this area?'

'I'd say very.'

'Any old homes or buildings in the area? Cemeteries?'

'Nothing but miles and miles of woods.'

'Any of it excavated?'

'Not to my knowledge, but then again I can't say I've explored the entire area.'

She turned back to Sergey. He didn't have any questions and looked at Casey, who shook his head.

Sergey said, 'Mr Wright, I'd like to ask you to stick close to your phone in case we have any additional questions.'

'Of course, of course. You have all my numbers?'

'I do. Again, thank you for your help.'

Sergey hung up and said to Darby: 'Let's hear it.'

'Hear what?'

'This plan you've got cooking.'

71

'First,' Darby said, 'tell me how many people you have on this plane.'

Sergey checked his watch and then leaned back, hands stuffed in his pockets. He shut his eyes and bit his bottom lip, hissing in air.

'Could be . . . maybe twenty-five or so.'

'That number include Secret Service?'

'No,' he said. 'Doesn't include support staff either, like the pilot.'

'I'm going to need to examine each person on this plane to see if they have this tattooed symbol. And we should check the bodies in Florida, the Secret Service agents –'

'Okay.' He ran his fingers through his hair. 'Okay, Jesus, I'll set everything up. We'll do it here in the conference room.'

'You should call the pilot too. Tell him to warm up the engines.'

'Where are we going?'

'Connecticut,' she said. 'We need to search the woods.'

'You think these people are hiding out in the woods.'

'This group has been moving around the country for several decades. The bulletin board shows that they're somewhere here in New England.'

'No, we *believe* they could be somewhere in New England. The New England kids who disappeared, they're the youngest family member, which adds them to our working list.'

'Fine. What we *do* know is that they have to be holed up someplace close by. They came to Portsmouth, New Hampshire, and after they blew up the house they waited around the area to follow me. They killed John Smith. They planted Mark Rizzo's body at his old home, along with Sarah Casey's finger and the USB drive with the listening device. To do all this, they have to be somewhere in the area. Southern Connecticut is about two, two and a half hours away.'

'And you think they've got, what, some little cottage somewhere near that transmission corridor?'

'No, I think they live underground.'

Sergey glared at her, his eyes dry and bloodshot. Casey's gaze had narrowed.

'The tracking chip in my arm,' Darby said. 'Could you get a signal if I was somewhere underground?'

'Depends on a number of factors. How deep you are, if the walls are shielded.'

'Anything new on Taylor or Sarah Casey's signal?'

'Still quiet.'

'So maybe you can't track them because they're somewhere underground.'

'Or maybe this group discovered the tracking chips and removed them.'

'Where were they installed? Left-upper arm?'

Sergey nodded.

'I think they're still in there,' Darby said. 'On the video,

I looked at their arms and didn't see any type of lacerations that would indicate the tracking units had been removed. Another thing I noticed were the walls. They're made of uneven stone. Boulders and rocks, all shapes and sizes. The kind you find in the ground. Common rock, in other words. And the walls in both rooms, the stones were smooth, not shiny. No dampness.'

'I'm not following you.'

'Water, even a small amount, if it gets into a basement, what happens?'

'You get mould.'

'Exactly. Basements are sealed tight with OPC – Portland cement. It's made primarily of concrete, mortar and stucco. Seals in any type of moisture. You've got blood in a basement, you're going to get mould. The walls in the video had cracks and fissures in the mortar. Perfect places for moisture to come through, but the stones were dry. That means another type of mortar was used.'

Casey said, 'Lime.'

Darby nodded. 'Lime mortar was used in Ancient Rome and Greece. It wicks away any dampness from the wall and it evaporates. But if you get a lot of dampness, over time, it creates an irregular, almost mottled appearance – what's called "limewash". You find it in old cellars in England but not here in the States. Taylor and Sarah Casey are locked inside the basement of some old building.'

Sergey said, 'That happens to be sitting in the woods.'

'We might find the remnants of, say, an old church, but I doubt it,' she said. 'This place is hidden. It has to be. The people I met at the blast site? The ones I saw crawling around the crater and the thing I tied to the tree, the one missing its tongue? You think they're living in a suburban neighbourhood? Going to the grocery store and the movies?'

Sergey pulled out his chair and sat, casting a weary glance at Casey.

'And then consider what they did to Mark Rizzo,' she said. 'Those puncture wounds on his back – he was tortured first.'

'Using what?'

Darby showed him empty hands. 'Don't know. But Ellis completed his autopsy, so I can tell you at least this much. Rizzo's stomach was infested with spiders – the smaller ones. Ellis found at least two dozen, each one of them poisonous.'

Sergey blanched. 'How . . . How is that even possible?'

'Mark Rizzo had multiple abrasions and cuts on the back of his mouth and throat. My guess is that they shoved a tube down his throat. That's the only way the spiders could have entered the man's stomach.'

Casey showed no reaction. Sergey, swallowing, looking like he was trying hard not to vomit.

'My point is,' she said, 'if they tortured Rizzo first, what better place to do it in than some underground cavern or basement located in the woods, where they didn't have to worry about anyone hearing them? I'll guarantee you something else. Wherever this place is, they buried the bodies not far from it.'

'What bodies?'

'This group has been collecting kids. Either they're killed or they die naturally. You've got to dispose of the bodies someplace. What better place to do it than a mass grave site surrounded by miles and miles of woods?'

'So you want me to fly to Connecticut based on a bee sighting.'

'A rare bee,' she said. 'One that's believed to be extinct.'

'Agreed, but that bee could've just as likely come from someplace else – someplace closer to Boston. You heard Wright. He said one was sighted here in Needham.'

'Back in '27.'

Sergey looked at Casey and said, 'I'm leery of flying out to Connecticut now. I want to see what develops here with the radio frequency. I talked with our tech guys onboard, and they said we don't have the tracking equipment we need. So I called the Boston office. Their tech department does, so I sent the USB drive over there.'

'How long?' Darby asked.

'It's going to take some time.'

'We need to go to Connecticut.'

Sergey rubbed his face.

'Okay,' he said, through his fingers. 'Okay, let's say these people have some underground place where they're hiding. That Taylor and Sarah Casey are there. We take off right now for Connecticut and then drive to the woods, it's still going to be dark. How do you suggest we search the woods?'

'Call your Connecticut field office and ask them to get us a helicopter with thermal-imaging equipment that can penetrate the ground.'

'And if they hear a helicopter, panic and decide to cut their losses and start shooting?'

'It's a risk. I realize that. But the circumstances don't change whether we leave now or in the morning.'

'And if something happens here –'

'You have people – trained people – who can handle the situation,' Darby said. 'If something happens while we're in the air, we can always turn around. But if there's a chance that Sarah or Taylor Casey or any other victim is somewhere out there in those woods, we need to act on it. Now.'

Sergey drummed his fingers against the pad of paper.

Casey, stoic through the whole discussion, cleared his throat.

'I agree with Darby,' he said, sounding surprisingly calm. 'We need to go.'

Finally, Sergey stood and called the pilot. Casey kept his gaze focused on the table, his face a waxy pallor under the bright lights.

72

It was time to hold the examinations in the conference room. They talked briefly about how to go about doing it. Darby didn't need to retrieve her kit because Sergey brought her the forensic lights she needed.

Casey unbuttoned his shirt. He caught the surprised look on her face and said, 'Never assume.'

Both Casey and Sergey were clean. As the plane's engines warmed up, Casey came back with the Secret Service agents. There were seven on board, including Keats. Casey asked each man to come inside the conference room alone. Darby examined Keats first, while Casey and Sergey stood near the door, their palms resting on their guns, ready to pull them if she gave them the signal.

Keats was clean. He was told what was going on, then opened the door and invited his men in. He told them to submit their weapons and they did so without complaint, handing them across the table to Casey. Then Keats told his men to strip out of their shirts. They did, and they all passed.

An announcement came over the speakers to prepare for takeoff. Darby buckled in and waited impatiently for half an hour until the big Boeing levelled off to cruising altitude.

Casey collected the groups and Darby did the exams, checking upper and lower lips, checking necks and chests.

The only tattoos she found were those belonging to two embarrassed women – 'tramp stamps', as they were called, a butterfly and some Indian design located on their lower backs, right above the waistband of their trousers.

Casey escorted her upstairs to cockpit. The two pilots passed.

Next he took her to the lower deck. Deep in the belly of the plane a small army of federal agents worked in a mobile lab, hunting for evidence underneath the bright overhead lights. They were huddled around white worktops and workstations, studying computer monitors and printouts. They scurried around each other, grabbing phones and pens and laptops, their faces anxious and sweating and tired from lack of sleep and surviving on adrenalin.

She followed Casey across a clear path that divided two distinct areas packed with banks of desks and workstations, leading to half a dozen or so doors. Casey opened the middle one. A guy somewhere in his thirties but with grey hair and a liquorice-coloured scar on his chin sat wedged behind a tiny white desk, the only furniture in the immaculately neat and windowless space. He swivelled the computer screen around so they could see it.

An autopsy room. Eight male bodies drained of blood and stiff with rigor lay on stainless-steel gurneys, their white skin covered with frost from their time spent in the meat locker. Sergey had told her they'd been shot in the back of the head, and she saw the same exit wounds on each fore-head and face. Today's date and a running time in bold white filled the bottom-right-hand part of the screen.

Casey punched a button on a speakerphone. 'Drake, it's Jack. Can you hear me?'

'Yeah. We're ready. I've got Hein here with me, manning the camera.'

'Go ahead, let's see what you've got.'

Someone picked up the camera – Hein – moved to the middle of the room and stopped next to a gurney holding an older male with fine grey chest hair and packing a considerable amount of weight around the midsection. His torso had been washed and Darby could hear water dribbling into a sink.

She looked at the star-shaped exit wound. A crater now stood where the man's left eye had been, the resulting trauma taking out his nose and shredding most of his upper lip.

'It's a mess,' Drake said over the speakers, 'but we managed to find it.'

Darby watched as the man's gloved fingers pushed the ragged strips of flesh together. Now came the black light and she saw the tattoo, the same as the one on Rizzo and Smith.

Drake said, 'His name is Richard Govornale. Forty-six, been with the Secret Service for fifteen years. Immaculate record, from what I was told. Secret Service has investigators here right now, but they've pretty much shut us out.'

'Sergey's talking with their lead guy, Baxter.'

Drake said, 'I took apart the outside A/C units and found a cyanide canister, a remote-controlled thing operated by a cell phone. Canister's empty. They pumped in enough cyanide to make them pass out and then came in and started shooting. Never seen anything like this in my life. What the hell is going on, Jack?'

Casey handed her off to two young guys who looked like they had just graduated college seconds ago, their bright and eager faces ready to tackle anything the world threw at them. Their names were Louis and Gerrad, and they worked for the FBI's Video Enhancement Unit. They had hunkered down in one of the other white rooms, this one just as cramped but designed with an L-shaped worktop so the two men could be side by side, talk and compare notes.

The tall, bony one, Louis, handed her an envelope and said, 'The pictures you wanted.'

'I want to take a look at something specific on the video,' she said. 'There's a black spot behind the surgical table, what could —'

'Right, right, I know exactly what you're talking about. I'll show you.'

Gerrad said he was going to the galley for coffee. Just as well. There wasn't room for three people in there. Darby took a seat and, looking at the computer monitor, saw a close-up, frozen frame of Sarah Casey's face.

Louis's hands flew across the keyboard. Windows menus popped on the screen and disappeared as Louis worked the mouse, pausing every moment or so to hit a key or type in a command. The video whooshed by and then stopped on the spot where she'd seen the blackened area.

Now Louis enlarged it. He pressed a series of buttons and applied what she guessed was some sort of light filter. The blackness disappeared and she saw an archway made of human skulls, their hollowed sockets looking down on Jack Casey's daughter.

Darby leaned forward. 'I can't make out what's beyond the archway.'

'Just give me a minute . . . There.' He got out of his chair to give her a better view.

A wall constructed of legs and arm bones stacked on top of each other, like logs. She could make out the curved ends of tibias, more skulls, hundreds and hundreds of bones, maybe thousands.

Louis said, 'You have any idea what that place is?'

'Some sort of ossuary would be my guess.'

'A what?'

'A place that holds the bones of the dead. Can you print out a copy of this?'

'Already did. It's in the package I gave you.'

'What else did you find?'

'Some shadows that still need to be enhanced,' he said. 'We've got to examine each frame. It's a painfully slow and tedious process. There's nothing we can do to rush it, unfortunately.'

'What about audio?'

'Sent by courier to our actual lab,' Louis said, sounding both sad and apologetic for some reason. 'Stuff the audio guys use is too bulky to fit in here, plus they need the actual source and not a digital copy. You've been doing this a long time?'

The question took her off-guard. 'Doing what?'

'Investigating cases like this.'

'Yes. A long time.'

She stood and saw Louis standing with his hands behind his back, staring down at the computer screen, mournful and solemn, as if it had turned into a coffin.

Darby went off to search for either Casey or Sergey. Twenty minutes later she found both men on the top floor of the plane – Sergey seated behind the former presidential desk, rubbing his forehead with one hand, the other pressing a phone against an ear.

Casey sat in a chair, gazing out of the window at the rolling clouds floating on the black sky. She approached him, trying to take his measure, trying to see if there was any evidence he was about to crack. Whatever he was feeling, he was keeping it well hidden. Guarded.

She handed him the stack of pages.

'What's this?'

'Pictures of where your wife and daughter are being held,' she said gently. 'If we're going to strike out into the woods, I think we should go to see Darren Waters before we do so – show him the pictures and the video, see if he can tell us where this place is.'

'He can't speak. He doesn't have his tongue, remember?'

'I remember. I was assuming that after all this time he was taught to read and write.'

'He suffered too much brain damage when they gave him the lobotomy. He knows sign language and some basic words and that's it.'

Casey's voice was stripped of colour – stripped of everything. She then realized that the flat tone she kept hearing in his voice wasn't an ability to disconnect from what was happening. The man had nothing left. If he didn't find his family, he'd find a way to eat his gun.

'Where did you move him?' she asked.

'Here. On the plane. Only safe place we could think of.'

'I'd like to speak to him.'

Casey stared at her for a moment, considering the question.

'It's not going to help,' he said.

'What would you suggest I do, then?'

Casey handed her the pictures. 'He's in the back.'

'Anything I need to know?'

'Yeah. Keep the lights off.'

73

The two sleeping paramedics Darby had seen upon entering the plane were posted outside a door, its window dark. They were playing cards – poker, by the looks of it – and they didn't look up at the bumping sounds coming from beyond the door.

'You here to perform another strip search?' This from the pudgy one with the goatee and man boobs that could fill a B-cup bra. The plastic nametag pinned to his chest read ROY.

'I'd like to speak to Darren Waters,' Darby said.

'He can't talk.'

'I know. I was told he could write, though. Simple words.'

'What's that in your hand?'

'Pictures.' She had already sorted through them, taking only the ones showing the skulled archway and boned wall.

Another bumping sound and then Roy's partner, a black guy with thick glasses and a short grey Afro, picked up a King of Hearts from the deck.

'What's he doing in there?' Darby asked.

'Exploring,' Roy said. 'This is his first time on a plane. He's been acting a little skittish.'

He folded his cards and tucked them in his breast

pocket as he looked at his partner. 'I'll keep these here, Avis, and we'll continue my winning streak when I get back.'

Darby blinked in surprise when she saw the pudgy guy pick up a pair of night-vision goggles.

'Darren don't care for light,' Roy said. 'Throws a fit if you go in there and turn it on. So he may not want to look at your pictures, and there's nothing I can do to force him, okay? I wear these night-vision goggles as my eyesight's for shit.'

That got a soft chuckle from the black guy.

'Darren,' Roy said, 'knows some basic sign language, so if he uses it, I'll be able to see and interpret it for you. Remember, he's got the mentality of a toddler, so use simple, direct words.'

Darby nodded. 'Anything else I need to know?'

'Don't look upset when you see him, he's very sensitive to that. It'll get him upset, and we can't really give him anything to calm him down. Guy's got Graves' disease and, on top of that, a bad ticker. Play it cool and calm and he can be a teddy bear.'

Roy cracked open the door. 'Hello, Darren. It's me. Roy. Your friend.'

A thump of footsteps and then a moan creaked through the darkness.

'Do not be scared,' Roy said, enunciating each word. 'I am coming in to say hello. I have a friend with me. A nice lady. She wants to meet you.'

Roy put the night-vision goggles over his head and stepped in first, Darby following into the semi-dark cabin.

It had a window, and the flashing lights on the wing parted the darkness and revealed that the furniture had been removed. She could see the holes and bracket marks left on the carpet, the paper and crayons and clothes. Hospital smocks, she guessed, along with dirty socks and a pair of soft-soled white sneakers with Velcro straps.

To her left was a small room, its door removed, and she could make out a tangle of bare, crooked limbs trying to hide.

Roy grabbed her upper arm and gave it a small tug to keep her from moving forward.

'Darren,' Roy said, his voice kind and gentle. 'Come out and say hello to my friend.'

The limbs unfolded – she still couldn't see him – and then Darren Waters plodded out of the room backwards, nude, a Frankenstein mess of deformed bone. He was severely hunched from osteoporosis, and she could make out the crooked vertebrae bulging from the deathly pale skin covered with row after row of round, welted scars. They covered his back, buttocks and thighs, and she thought of the puncture wounds she had found on Mark Rizzo.

Darren Waters kept his face pointed at the corner wall, out of view.

'Do you feel shy?' Roy asked.

Waters bobbed his head up and down, up and down. He rocked back and forth.

'How about we all sit down and colour?' Roy asked. 'Would you like that?'

'*Aye-ah*,' Waters garbled, and turned. She caught a flash of a crude scar the size and thickness of a bicycle tyre left from his castration, and most of his right ear had either been chewed or torn off.

Waters plodded over to the crayons. He was about to sit when he noticed her and then decided to come over for a closer look.

'This is my friend,' Roy said, and she felt his finger dig into her arm. 'Her name is Darby.'

'Hello, Darren.'

Jagged scars the colour of jelly and smaller, neat ones left from a scalpel were slashed across a face of missing eyebrows. Goitres, the result of his Graves' disease, covered his neck and half of his left cheek. His nose had been broken she didn't know how many times and what was left was a pulpy, crooked mess. He tried to smile but the lips twitched. No teeth, just like the thing with the egg-white skin she had tied to the tree.

He snatched the envelope from her hand and then retreated to the corner, making some sort of nasal but gleeful sound as he went to work tearing off the paper like it was a Christmas present.

The pictures spilled across his lap. He picked up one, turned it over and looked, then tossed it aside and went after another one. Darby watched him do it six or so times before his head darted up, his hand waving a sheet at Roy.

'It's a picture,' Roy said.

Waters performed some sort of sign language, then picked up one of the photographs and held it close to his face.

'Then you need to turn on a light,' Roy said.

Waters kept shaking his head.

Darby felt Roy release his grip. He reached into his trousers pocket, came back with a small flashlight, placed it on the floor and sat next to Waters in the corner.

'Darren, would you like to use this?' Roy asked, tapping the floor where the flashlight lay.

Waters tilted his head to the side. He made some signs again and his gnarled fingers scooped it up.

'You're welcome,' Roy said. 'Can my friend Darby sit with you?'

'*Aye-ah.*'

She sat next to Roy. Waters turned on the flashlight and she felt her stomach slide south – not from fear of seeing his ghoulish face with its scars and lumps but more so out of anger and piercing sadness. This group had abducted Waters at four, tortured and beaten him over decades and turned him into this ghost of a human being.

Why in the name of God did they do this to you?

'Darren,' she said.

He looked up from the picture.

'Do you know Mark Rizzo?'

No reaction.

'Can you tell me anything about this?' She pointed to the picture in his hand, the one showing the archway formed from human skulls.

No reaction.

'Do you know this place?'

Water picked up a blue crayon and began colouring one of the skulls.

'Too many words,' Roy said to her. 'Darren knows only basic language.'

'Darren,' she said kindly.

He looked up, tilted his head to the side.

'This,' she said, tapping the picture. 'Where?'

She pointed down. 'Below the ground?'

He didn't understand.

'Darren, can I use a crayon and paper?'

He didn't understand and looked at Roy, who used sign language. Darren nodded and handed her a piece of paper and his box of crayons.

She drew a quick, crude picture of an outdoors scene dotted with trees and flowers. Below it, she drew a tunnel; inside it, a floor and the archway.

She put the drawing on the floor. Pointed to the picture of the archway he was colouring and then pointed to the one she had drawn.

Waters brought his hands together, kissed his palms and then made waving motions with his hands, like rising flames of fire.

A voice came over the speaker: 'Darby McCormick, report to Situation Room 102.'

Darren Waters pressed his hands over his deformed ears.

After she stepped outside with Roy, she said, 'That sign language at the end, what was he trying to describe? Hell?'

Roy shook his head.

'Heaven,' he said.

74

Her face flushed, Darby opened the door to the situation room and found three men dressed in SWAT gear picking up weapons from the table.

Casey wasn't here, but Sergey was, leaning back in a leather chair with his legs crossed. He had loosened his tie and was eating peanuts from a bag, reading a stack of papers.

'What took you so long?' he asked, a half-grin cocked on his face.

'I had to ask someone for directions.' She nodded to the papers on his lap. 'That Ross's stuff?'

He nodded. 'Religious theory on Gnosticism, stuff about these Archons. They like to bend people to their wills and wage war. Creates unity.' He shook his head. 'Load of useless mystical propaganda created centuries ago.'

'And this group, for whatever reason, has bought into it.'

'Sure looks that way. And none of it is going to do us any good.'

He tossed the stack on the table, ate another peanut. 'I've got guys checking on customs logs to see who's tried to import any of the spiders Perkins put on his list. No hits so far, but we've only just started.'

'I didn't know you carried SWAT on board.'

'Former Hostage Rescue guys, on loan to us. Your stuff

is in the back. They could use an extra body, and with your training I figured you wanted in.'

'What about transport?'

'You're going to love this.' He crumbled his bag into a ball and threw it into the trashcan bolted against the wall. 'It's a Huey, a Bell UH-1H, one of the new ones with a four-blade rotor system and dual GE engines. Powerful but quiet. And it's got just about every piece of equipment we need to stage a military coup or mount a search and rescue.'

'How did you score that?'

'Pure luck.'

'What about ground support?'

'SWAT, local police and ambulances,' he said. 'Jimmy Blackstone from the Connecticut field office is overseeing everything. Good guy, he knows what he's doing. He's going to go in quiet when he gets close to the transmission corridor. He's going to have to wait for us to scout out the terrain first.'

'We know anything about the terrain?'

'Woods. Lots and lots of woods. We're going to fly in and scope it out using FLIR thermal imaging. Never seen it in action before.'

'It's good, unless you're going into an area with fog or poor visibility, like tree cover.'

'FLIR won't pick that up?'

'Depends,' she said. 'It'll probably pick up warm spots as opposed to hot spots – the thermal image of the target won't be entirely clear.'

He broke out in soft laughter.

'What?'

'You are one goddamn remarkable woman, you know that?' He raised his hands, still laughing. 'I mean, Christ, how many women look the way you do and can kick the ass of every guy in this room and also know the specs on FLIR?'

She smiled back, and it eased some of the tension. 'Thank you.'

'You're welcome.' He stood and pointed across the table to a guy with a shaved head and a square jaw. Marine, she thought. The only thing he was missing was a cigar jammed into his mouth.

'That's Knowles,' Sergey said. 'He's heading up the operation, and he'll brief you.'

'You said "we" a moment ago. Are you coming along?'

Sergey nodded. 'Jack too. He's already dressed.'

'Does Casey have SWAT training?'

'He has training.'

'That's not the same thing, Sergey, and you know it.'

'Of course I know it. Jack knows it too. But he wants to be on the ground if you find his wife and daughter.'

'You think that's wise, given what's on the video?'

Sergey knew what she meant. She saw it in his eyes.

'Jack's not stupid, Darby. He knows the score. If the bodies of his wife and daughter are in those woods, he wants to be the one to bring them home. And that's the least I can do, given what the man's put on the line for the Bureau.'

Darby nodded. 'Any news on their signals?' she asked.

'Nothing.' He shook his head, sighing. 'Sandwiches and stuff are on the table in the corner. Dig in now. You could be in for a long night.'

The FBI helicopter was perfect. Two sliding aft doors had enough room to allow two to three people to rappel from either door. The cabin, specially lengthened, had an internal rescue hoist and passenger seats that, if detached, could accommodate the six stretchers stored in the back.

Right now there was plenty of space to spread out. Darby took a rear seat, the pleasant roar of the engine throbbing through her limbs. The men filed inside, along with Casey. She didn't look at him. She didn't want to see whatever might be on his face, didn't want that in her head right now.

Sergey had climbed in next to the pilot. The team leader, Knowles, slid both aft doors shut, then pounded twice on the wall behind the pilot.

The copter lifted off the ground. ETA was thirty minutes. Nobody spoke.

Having already checked and prepared her weapons, Darby closed her eyes and meditated, wanting her mind clear for whatever was waiting for them in the darkness.

75

Knowles's gruff voice barked across her headset: 'Mount up, people.'

Darby stood, crouching forward, and grabbed an O-ring on the ceiling for balance.

'Our FLIR picked up a collection of warm spots,' Knowles said. 'These images aren't clear because of our current distance from the site and because of the tree cover. We don't want to risk flying in for a closer look and alerting anyone who may be down there waiting for our arrival. These warm spots aren't moving.'

Nobody said it but everyone was thinking the same thing: bodies. *Buried* bodies. A possible mass grave site.

'Bravo One, McCormick and Farrell,' Knowles said. 'We're dropping you south of the target. Proceed ahead a thousand metres to what appears to be a clearing. Bravo Two, Clark and Reggie, we'll drop you north of the location. All of you are to treat this as though you're stepping into a potential hot zone. In other words, be aware of traps. Take nothing for granted. We'll be monitoring the area and radioing updates. Make sure you all do the same. Questions?'

There were none.

Knowles gripped the side door handle. Darby reached down and grabbed the thick rope with her gloved hands.

The aft door slid open. Cold wind rushed inside the cabin and the engine roared against her ears as she moved to the opened doorway, which looked out on a black sky peppered with bright stars. She affixed the rope to her harness, threw the dangling end out of the copter and stepped outside, on to the railing. Got her boots planted firmly and, gripping the rope, leaned backwards into the air, waiting for her partner, Farrell.

She gave her zip-line a final check. Looked good. She flipped the night-vision goggles down across her eyes and in the bright ambient green glow of light saw that Farrell had got himself into position. A bend of the knees and she pushed herself off the railing, falling through the awful dark, her stomach jumping with anticipation and worry.

She kept her grip steady as she whisked past leaves and tree branches. She saw the rushing ground, slowed her descent and hit it softly. She released the rope, and as it climbed back up and into the air she noticed she could barely hear the copter above the wind whistling through the trees and shaking the branches.

Her partner hit the ground a moment later, a little more roughly. He stumbled and she had to help him release his zip-line.

Standing behind a tree, she scanned the surrounding area, saw nothing but trees and leafy ground. They searched the flat and bumpy areas ahead, and then the trees and ground and boulders for any moving shapes.

She hand-signalled to Farrell and he nodded and stepped out from behind a tree. Up came his HK submachine gun with a silencer and flash suppressor. They fell into step with each other, their backs nearly touching, and moved forward in a two-by-two formation, checking the ground before each step, the dark forest lit up by their night-vision goggles, the wind camouflaging the sounds of twigs and branches snapped by their boots.

It was slow work. Several minutes later she heard Clark from Bravo Two whisper over her headset: 'Command, this is Bravo Two. We've discovered a path east of the clearing. Permission to investigate.'

'Permission granted,' Knowles replied. 'Proceed, Bravo Two.'

Ten more minutes and up ahead she spotted the clearing she had been instructed to reach.

Definitely man-made. Someone had removed the trees and stumps in a space roughly the size of a basketball court, the ground covered with snapped branches, some looking as if they had been stabbed into the ground and –

Darby took another few steps before hand-signalling to Farrell to stop. She pointed ahead to the clearing and Farrell looked down the length of her arm and she heard him mumble, 'Jesus.'

She called it in: 'Command, this is Bravo One. I have a partial visual on the clearing. I'm seeing at least three hands sticking out of the ground. They don't seem to be moving, but I won't know until I get a closer look.'

A short pause, and then Knowles replied: 'Acknowledged. We don't have a visual so walk us through it. Proceed with caution. I repeat, proceed with caution.'

You don't have to tell me twice, she thought. The whole

scene smacked of a Grand Guignol performance, only she wasn't dealing with theatre of the macabre. These hands belonged to real people, not actors. These people weren't pretending to be dead, they *were* dead.

Jack Casey's wife and daughter flashed through her mind and Darby wondered with a sickening dread if one or both had been buried somewhere up ahead. She advanced slowly, a single word worming its way through her thoughts: *trap*.

These people worked too hard to remain hidden in the shadows — and had done so successfully — so why would they bury their victims with their hands sticking out of the ground for us to find?

Two tight, bright beams emerged at the opposite end of the clearing — the path Bravo Two had mentioned. She could see Clark and Reggie sweeping the beams of their tactical lights across the ground.

Clark's voice spoke over her headset: 'Command, we've come across a hatch of some sort. It's covered in . . . a camouflage blanket you could call it. It's made of these fake leaves, like the kind my wife buys at craft stores. I don't know how else to describe it.'

Darby reached the edge of clearing and saw a sea of hands sticking out from underneath the dirt — there were dozens of them hanging in the air, lifeless.

'Hatch is locked with a padlock and chains,' Clark said. 'The chain's got some slack so I think we can lift it up enough to take a look and see what's down there.'

Darby glanced at the path. The black guy, Reggie, lifted up the hatch — a big door mounted against the earth, the top covered by a camouflage blanket of fake leaves. She heard a rattle of chains as the door rose about a foot and then came to a jarring stop.

Clark, down on his knees, moved his tactical light through the foot-long gap.

'There's a ladder,' Clark said. 'Goes down to a hall made of stone.' Coughing and gagging sounds followed, and then he said, 'Christ it reeks like an outhouse. I'm seeing candles inside lanterns and they're hanging on the stone walls.'

Darby thought about the walls behind Sarah Casey's Plexiglas cell as Knowles said, 'Anyone down there?'

'Negative, Command. If we're going to go down there, we'll need bolt cutters.'

'I've got them,' Darby said. 'Standby, Bravo Two. Command, I've reached the clearing.'

Darby clipped her weapon to the front of her vest. Straight ahead she spotted a set of hands, the thin wrists bound together by rope, the fingers crooked, broken.

She flipped up her night-vision goggles. She covered her mike as she leaned into Farrell and said, 'Give me some light.'

Farrell turned on the tactical light mounted underneath his HK and focused the beam on the bound hands. Darby leaned forward and grabbed the wrists. She pulled hard, then staggered and tumbled sideways against the ground.

76

'Bravo One,' Knowles said, 'what's your status?'

Darby sat up. 'Command, I'm holding a set of hands that have been severed at the forearms. Someone just stuck them in the dirt.'

'What about the body, any sign of it?'

'Stand by.'

She got on her knees, moved to the spot where she had pulled the hands and dug through the earth.

'Command, I'm not seeing a body, just several bones.'

'And these other hands? Any survivors?'

'Unknown. Farrell and I will split up, check each one and see who's alive. There're at least a dozen or more here.'

'Bravo Two, assist Bravo One and search for survivors.'

Farrell moved to her left. Darby walked to the next pair of hands, grabbed the wrists and this time pulled up a body. Down on her knees, she stripped off her gloves and then brushed away the dirt from the neck and checked for a pulse on the cold skin.

Standing, she turned on her tactical light and saw a shaved, scarred head. The emaciated body was covered with fresh and old scars, fresh and healing wounds – and there were no eyes, the sockets scorched and blackened as if they had been burned away. Like Charlie Rizzo, like Darren Waters, this victim had been castrated.

She swiped her forearm across her forehead. 'Command, this is Bravo One. I have one male vic, deceased.'

Clark had pulled up a body and was checking for a pulse. His partner, Reggie, was kneeling on the ground, digging.

She moved on to the next set of hands when Clark said, 'I have a young female vic, deceased, with blonde hair.'

Darby felt as though her stomach had been rolled across shards of glass. *Please don't let it be —*

'It's not Sarah Casey,' Clark said. 'Vic appears —'

Screaming cut through the air and she whipped her head around, bringing up her weapon. In the beam of her tactical light she saw Reggie writhing on the ground, his gloved hands working furiously at something wrapped around his knee — the clawed metal jaw of what she was sure was a bear trap. It had clamped around his left thigh and shin, trapping his leg at a 90-degree angle. His knee had been spared. *He must have knelt on the ground and triggered the trap's spring with his knee.*

Clark had bolted over to help his partner. Darby ran too, Reggie's screaming and painful blubbering as loud as gunshot reports against her ears. The hands sticking out of the ground were bound by rope at the wrists. She dropped to her knees and helped Clark prise away the trap, her bare fingers slipping across the rusty metal jaws slick with blood.

Out of the corner of her eye she thought she saw the bound hands move. Darby turned to them and saw moving fingers.

Reggie slid his shredded mess of a leg out of the trap. Darby got to her feet, wrapped her hands around the wrists and pulled.

77

A dirty oxygen mask covered Taylor Casey's mouth and nose; a tube ran from the bottom of the mask into the ground. Her body swayed, limp and useless, and Darby pulled her out of the hole and laid her back against the solid ground. She checked for a pulse, found one and removed the mask.

Blood bubbled from her nostrils and the woman's left eye and her entire forehead were swollen. Darby remembered the video, snapshots flashing through her mind – the woman strapped to the operating table and her eyelid being pulled back and the grimy hand holding the long, surgical ice pick – and she yelled over the awful howling:

'I have Taylor Casey, need immediate EVAC.'

'Stand by,' Knowles replied.

Darby stood perfectly still by the woman's body as new sounds filled the woods: the rattling of chains and thumping. She turned along with Clark, who had his HK back in his hands. He swung the tactical light in the direction of the noise – it was coming from the path – and she saw a tangled mess of pale arms reaching out from underneath the hatch. Hands gripped the edge of the hatch, trying to push it up. Emaciated bodies and scarred faces with shaved heads and frightened eyes, *oh Christ* there were dozens of them fighting to escape through the gap and they were screaming and howling.

'Command,' Darby yelled. 'We're going to need additional support. We have people trapped down here, underneath a hatch.'

A spotlight came from high in the air directly in front of her, from the fast-approaching Huey, and it lit up the clearing. In the space left by Taylor Casey's body Darby saw skeletal remains, bones and skulls stacked on top of each other.

The Huey hovered over the treetops, its engines drowning out the awful howling. Leaves kicked up and spun around her in the powerful wind, and she caught sight of a shadow rappelling down a rope. Looked up and saw the heavy orange stretcher swinging underneath the copter's black steel belly, being lowered by a rescue hoist.

Now Farrell screamed over her headset, his voice nearly drowned out by the copter's engine. 'Command, this is Bravo One. We have a possible IED situation.'

Darby turned around holding the woman's limp body and almost dropped her when she saw Farrell standing at the edge of the clearing, his hand gripping a nest of multi-coloured wires that ran in different directions, each one disappearing underneath the ground where she stood.

Clark had Reggie on his shoulder and was making his way around the edge of the clearing, heading to where Jack Casey now stood. Darby, wary of any additional bear traps, backtracked.

Knowles said, 'Can you disarm it?'

'I have to find it first,' Farrell said, staring down at the wires in his hand like they were a puzzle he could solve.

Casey had already unbuckled the straps for the stretcher.

He wore a combat helmet but not night-vision goggles, and his face was pinched into a fist, his eyes wet. He took his wife from her hands. Darby held the stretcher to keep it steady and Casey's face broke when he saw her. His stomach hitched and the tearing sound that erupted from his mouth rode down her spine like a bolt and made her want to turn and run.

Casey didn't seem to know what to do with his hands. She went to work buckling the straps around his wife while Reggie sat on the ground, hissing in pain and putting pressure on the bleeding wounds of his shattered leg. Clark helped secure the rope to Reggie's harness and then he secured himself.

Darby reached around her back for the bolt cutters.

'I'm coming with you,' Casey yelled, and his face nearly broke again. 'My daughter could be somewhere down there. If she is, I want to be the –'

The explosion came east of their position, a low, thunderous boom from deep within the ground. She heard trees splitting and the night sky bloomed with dirt and rock and wood.

The helicopter started to climb, while Reggie and Clark tried to climb up the swinging ropes. Casey turned to look at his wife's stretcher, saw it dangling in the air and almost seemed to want to grab it, as if he could keep her safe. Darby took his arm and pushed him north, screamed at him to run like hell.

A second explosion, closer, like God's mighty fist had punched up from underneath the ground, sending up earth and stone and splintering trees high into the air. The copter's searchlight crossed through the woods directly in front of her and she sprinted, trying to see the terrain up ahead, trying to commit it to memory. Branches whisked past her face and her hands released the clips of her tactical vest so she could cast off the additional weight. Another explosion and the force of it rocked the ground and she stumbled sideways against a tree. Darby regained her balance quickly and sprinted, as debris rained down through the woods. BOOM, another explosion, too close, from the clearing packed with bones, it had to be. The shock wave slammed into her and sent her spinning into darkness.

78

Darby's eyes opened to a tunnel of bright light, the heavenly kind people reported in near-death experiences. She didn't see God, though, just a big hand holding a medical penlight directly above her right eye.

The light shut off and the hand moved away and she saw slants of revolving blue and white and red lights moving across a scratched white metal ceiling. A helicopter roared somewhere outside and when it died she heard beeping sounds and, from the south, voices.

She found she could turn her head and she did, to her right, and saw IV lines and Jack Casey. He lay next to her, unconscious, an oxygen mask strapped across his swollen, bloodied face. Nose broken and left ear mangled. A steel frame had been mounted across the front of his torso so he couldn't move – it was a Stryker frame. You put someone in that when you suspected possible paralysis and didn't want the body to move.

She wiggled her toes, felt them move along with her fingers and arms. She craned her head – a pain like nails being hammered through her skull – and saw her body lying on a simple stretcher. Her boots had been removed but the rest of her clothing, torn and dirty and bloodied, remained. Her wrists were strapped. Two more straps covered her chest and she saw one across her thighs. They had strapped her down to keep her body from moving in case she had suffered a spinal injury.

The pain turned into a jackhammer and before she sank back down to the pillow she saw the back of the ambulance, the open doors revealing patrol cars, fire trucks and other emergency vehicles parked on wild grass twisting in the wind, while above a pale milk-coloured sky filled with smoke.

Someone jumped on the back bumper and she heard heavy footsteps.

Sergey's face hovered above her own. The man looked beaten down, broken, but he didn't have a single scratch on his face. Good. The copter had made it out.

It took great effort to speak.

'Taylor,' she said in a hoarse whisper.

'En route to the hospital. You're going there too, in a moment.' Sergey touched her hand, squeezed it. 'You're fine. Probably a concussion and that's it.'

'Three.'

'Three what?'

'Third one. I keep this up I'm going to end up like Muhammad Ali.' She licked her lips. 'The listening device.'

Sergey hadn't heard her. He leaned closer and she asked him about the listening device she'd found inside the USB drive.

'The Boston techs couldn't track it down,' he said. 'My guess is they shut down their listening post from their car or wherever they were hiding.'

'Hatch?'

'Gone. Blown apart, have no idea who or what was down there.'

Sarah, she thought. Had Sarah Casey been trapped somewhere beneath that hatch?

'Same with the mass grave site where you found Jack's wife,' Sergey said. 'Explosion blew it apart, scattered shit everywhere. We've started the recovery effort, collecting body parts, evidence, whatever we can find. We almost didn't get out of there.'

'Farrell?'

'Banged up but okay.'

She looked at Casey. Sergey answered the question.

'I don't know,' he said. 'The Stryker frame's a precaution. When they found him, he was unconscious. Could be a severe concussion or something more serious, we won't know until he gets to the hospital. That's where you're both going. Keats is going to be there with you. Keats and some of his men. They'll keep an eye on you and Jack.'

'I'll come back and help you search.'

Sergey didn't answer. He had already left.

An EMT, a doughy, bald man with cheeks red from the cold, came into view and she saw him knock twice on the side of the ambulance. It drove away a moment later, sirens wailing.

The EMT moved in the space where Sergey had knelt and checked the machine beeping somewhere behind her. A moment later he checked one of the straps binding her wrists to the gurney.

'Too tight?' he asked.

She nodded and looked up at the ceiling, drowsy. The EMT loosened the strap, then cupped her hand in his own.

She lifted her head slightly. It wasn't the EMT who was holding her hand; he had moved to the other side of the gurney to shoot something inside her IV line. It was Keats. He was kneeling by the end of the gurney and his eyes were damp.

'Sorry,' he said.

She swallowed, trying to get some moisture into her mouth. 'Not your fault.'

'I'm sorry,' Keats said again, and this time he lost it, broke down and started to cry. 'They made me do it. They have my son.'

A bolt of fear exploded through her and then died as the drugs floated through her system.

'They said they'd give Luke a lobotomy,' Keats wailed. 'He's only eight, and they said they'd turn him into a vegetable like Jack's wife unless I brought you to them and I had to . . . I'm sorry, I had to do it, God forgive me, I'm so, so sorry.'

Darby struggled to stay awake and Keats wailed as if he were about to burst apart at the seams. The EMT clapped a hand on the Secret Service agent's shoulder, leaned in close and told him not to worry. Luke was alive and everything was going to be okay.

PART THREE
The Wheel

79

Darby couldn't remember how she had arrived at this place, wherever this place was, or who had brought her here. She remembered lying in the back of the ambulance and Keats crying and then she had drifted away. When she woke up, all she saw was this cool, pitch-black darkness that smelled of mildew, dust and decay. She had been stripped of her clothes, her wrists shackled with chains that extended somewhere above her, bolted to the ceiling. Her ankles had been shackled too, but she could move if she chose.

She did, the first day, stumbling around in the darkness with her chains, her fingers and palms sliding against smooth stone. A hole dug in the floor to use as a toilet. She felt thick iron bars mounted inside a small, rectangular space. The same darkness was out there but with sounds of life – jagged breathing, crying.

Several times she had called out for Casey. He didn't respond. Either he was somewhere else or he was dead. She had tried calling for Sarah Casey and received no answer.

Sergey and the FBI had to be looking for her – and Casey, Keats had said they wanted Casey too. A package deal in exchange for Keats's son, Luke. She didn't know about Casey, but she still had a GPS unit installed in her arm. The FBI hadn't come so she assumed they couldn't lock on to her signal, which meant she was being held somewhere underground. She didn't know where – for all she knew she could be halfway across the world. But Sergey and his men had to be looking for her. And what had happened to Keats? Had they spared his life and left him to spin some bullshit story about how she and Casey had disappeared – or had the Secret Service agent disappeared too?

Darby lay in the dark with questions revolving in her head and heard whispering voices asking God for help and strength. Prayers for mercy and forgiveness. The voices never stopped.

Darby didn't pray. She didn't sit around trying to wish the situation away. She was here, trapped, but sure of one thing: she had to find a way to survive. If she was going to live, she would have to be the one to save herself.

She had no idea how long she'd been shackled in here. At least a day but probably longer. Two, maybe, possibly three. The darkness pressed against her and her mind kept demanding answers. She couldn't provide any so it reacted, of course, with its natural primitive response: fear. And each time it came, each time she felt it flutter through her stomach and limbs and start to close around her throat, she didn't push it away, didn't try to talk it away. She embraced it. *I'm shackled in some dungeon-like cell, so, yes, I'm scared. There's no food or water and I'm starving, so, yes, I'm afraid. Every inch of my skin is exposed, and when they come, they could hurt me like they hurt Mark Rizzo and Charlie and everyone else that came before them, so, yes, I'm terrified, because I don't want to be hurt. I don't want to suffer.*

But that would come later.

The first part of their plan, whatever it was, had to do

with fear. They wanted her to be trembling in fear when they came. That was why they had locked her in here in the dark. They had stripped off her clothing to make her feel vulnerable. They had denied her food and water because hunger did extreme things to the mind. Her mind didn't know what was happening or going to happen so it busied itself conjuring up all sorts of gruesome scenarios. She acknowledged all of these things but she also knew she had to steel herself against them. Conserve her strength and, more importantly, her sanity. Fear clouded the mind, prevented you from seeing opportunities. She had learned this first-hand, during the time she'd been imprisoned inside Traveler's dungeon of horrors. She had survived that and she would survive this.

So she occupied her time with things she could control – her body, her mind. She kept her body limber. Stretched. Did push-ups and sit-ups and when she finished she meditated to clear her head. *Show no fear*, she kept telling herself. *That's what they want to see from you, that's what feeds them. No matter what happens, don't give them what they want. Keep the fear at bay and you'll find a way out of this. These people are not divine beings. They bleed like the rest of us.*

The first one came as she lay asleep. She awoke to the sound of a key in a lock and she sat up as the door swung open.

No shoes clicked on the floor, no sound. *Bare feet*, she thought.

She sat stock still, listening to the clicking sound of metal chains.

The sound stopped.

Clink clink near her ear and she didn't move.

Clink clink somewhere directly in front of her face and she felt warm drops on her stomach.

Clink clink and her heart hammered inside her chest as something cold and hard and wet slithered up the inside of her thigh. She didn't move and it travelled up her stomach and across her breast and over her shoulder and disappeared.

The door shut and then she was left alone. She touched the liquid on her stomach and held it up to her nose: she smelled blood.

The door opened again, sometime later. Several people this time.

She stood against the wall and listened to the soft foot-steps. She could feel them surrounding her, could hear their breathing.

One of them moved closer and pressed the edge of something hard against her lips. She jerked her head and heard a splash of water.

'Drink,' a deep but muffled voice said.

'No.'

'You need to conserve your strength. To keep your head clear for the choice you are about to make.'

She clamped her lips shut.

'We could make you.'

Say something? No, not yet. Wait and see.

She stood, defiant, lips pressed together. *If only I could see them, see how many there are . . .*

Something was placed on the floor in front of her and she heard them retreat.

'You will learn to do what we ask,' another voice said, and then the door shut.

No, she told herself, *I won't.*

She found what they'd left on the floor: a thick wooden bowl holding cold water. She rooted her fingers around inside the bowl, but felt only its smooth surface.

She lifted it up to her nose and couldn't smell anything. Didn't mean it wasn't poisoned. Anything could be in there. Drugs. LSD.

Or just water, her mind said.

She put the bowl back on the floor. Her tongue and throat swelling with thirst, she picked it back up and with two hands smashed it against the floor. Heard it split. She brought it high over her head and kept smashing it. All she needed was one piece with a pointed end.

She found one and scurried to the door to wait. They must have heard the noise and would come to investigate. *Pray for one*, she thought. *Just one.*

Nobody came.

She kept waiting and nobody came.

Sitting back against the floor, she inserted the jagged end of the piece of wood into the keyhole for the manacle around her left wrist. These locks had to be old; they wouldn't be complicated. A simple spring mechanism, she figured. She moved the tip around inside the keyhole until the wood snapped. She gathered the other broken pieces, sharpening their ends against the stone. Put one into the keyhole, took a deep breath and tried again.

80

Darby woke to the sound of chains. Hers. They were moving.

The metal shackles bit into her wrists as her arms were jerked above her head. The chains kept climbing and the chains attached to her feet were moving too, sliding down the tiny holes inside the floor.

She wrapped her hands around the chains above her head and pulled with all of her strength. Her fingers and palms, cut and tender from the long hours of trying to sharpen the pieces of wood and pick the locks, started to bleed and she couldn't maintain her grip. The chains kept rising, and, as she had been without food and water for days, her strength evaporated.

But not her will. No, her will to fight was still there. She had to conserve her strength for when the opportunity came and this wasn't it.

Her feet dangled above the floor, arms stretched high over her head.

She closed her eyes and breathed slowly to calm her pounding heart. Time passed and the muscles in her arms and shoulders and back strained and cramped, but she kept her breathing steady, her mind clear. Pain was created in the mind. Pain could be controlled. It could be managed.

The door opened and she kept her eyes closed.

A click of footsteps this time and they stopped in front of her. She heard a match being struck.

'What did you do with the bowl?' a muffled voice asked. 'We know you broke it.'

She didn't answer.

The footsteps left, stopped, then came back.

'You put them in your toilet,' he said. 'How ingenious.' Soft laughter. 'Open your eyes.'

She kept them shut.

'Open your eyes.' He stood by her side now. 'I shall not ask again.'

She didn't and heard another match being struck.

Clink clink.

She gulped air and her body stiffened with fear.

The pain can be managed.

A whistling sound . . .

I can manage the pain.

. . . and hard strips of metal were raked against the back of her thighs. Her eyes flew open and she hissed back a scream, shaking on the dangling chains and casting shadows in the flickering candlelight.

The person who stepped in front of her wore a black theatrical cape made of what looked like thick velvet over a dark suit with a silk crimson scarf. His face – his real face – was hidden underneath a white mask of wood shaped to resemble the devil, maybe a vampire. The mask was scratched and peeling in several spots, especially along the long wooden nose, and a couple of teeth were missing from its wide grin. False black hair shaped into a widow's peak on the top, and tiny black marble eyes. *Grand Guignol at its finest*, she thought.

A white-gloved hand with red fingertips sharpened into points held a carved wooden handle; at its end was an O-ring with three chains, each made of seven links.

'A chain scourge. A rather wonderful invention. The first time I used one was in a castle in Nuremberg and I fell in love.'

'Is that what you're doing here?' Darby said through gritted teeth. 'Creating your own little private Hitler-inspired army to take over the world?'

A tired sigh from underneath the mask. 'The time for creating war has passed. Unfortunately. I don't like it up there any more. The surface. I don't like what we created. It's become . . . evil. Unmanageable.'

'But you keep going up there to snatch children. Why?'

'Because I want to,' he said matter-of-factly. 'Because I can.'

He hit her again with the chains, this time across the shins. Sparks flew across her eyes and her body shook as she clamped down on a scream, refusing to give in to him.

'I can create a lot of pain,' he said. 'And pleasure.'

Darby didn't answer, concentrating on his voice. It was calm but she detected something else, something in his choice of words. He had said 'I can create'. Not *we*. *I*. The leader?

He traced his fingernails down across her stomach. 'You're very beautiful, and your bone structure is excellent. Good hips. Now that I'm seeing you in the flesh, I may have to reconsider my original intentions and use you for breeding.'

The nails moved up her stomach. 'We should start soon, as I fear my time in this body is limited.'

'Are you an Archon?'

'The first. Iadabaoth,' he said, unsurprised, more interested in continuing his examination of her body.

'I understand there are twelve of you. Where are the other eleven?'

'Here and there.'

The man folded his arms across his chest and placed a hand underneath his chin, his nails clicking across his wooden cheek.

'We need to discuss ovulation.'

'Sure,' she said. 'Tell me when you get your period and I might be able to help you out.'

Darby started laughing. Laughed so hard that tears spilled from her eyes.

'I can make you unspeakably ugly,' the man said.

'Like Charlie?'

'Yes.'

'Now I know why you wear the mask. You must be *one* ugly fuck.'

He cupped a hand over her heart. Left it there for a moment with the side of his head pressed against her stomach.

The nails dug into her skin and the mask tilted up at her.

'You *are* a true knight warrior. I could rip your heart out right now and eat it in front of you and yet you show no fear. Remarkable. Truly remarkable. I can't remember the last time I encountered one of your type. Well, well, this *does* present a rather unique opportunity.'

'Better get to it quick, then. We know who you are.'

'I'm sure you *think* you do.'

'We know about the tattoo.'

The Archon didn't answer.

'The one on the upper lip,' Darby said. 'We found them on Mark Rizzo and John Smith.'

'Ah. The mark of the trusted servant.'

'To you?'

'To all of us. John Smith belonged to another. Thomas Howland was mine. The one you knew as Mark Rizzo. He helped bring me the children. Lots and lots of them to play and experiment with.'

Charlie's voice echoed inside her head: *Tell her, Daddy. Tell her what you did.*

'What's with the mask?'

'I prefer it.'

'Why? What are you afraid of?'

'Afraid?' A tremor in his voice. 'What makes you think I'm afraid of you?'

'The masks and the costumes,' Darby said. 'This whole Dungeons and Dragons thing you've got going on down here.'

The gloves came off. Darby saw long, soft fingers. He worked at the edge of the mask and lifted it off his head.

A woman. Shaved head and pale egg-white skin threaded with veins and a pair of cold ice-blue eyes that looked liquid in the candlelight. But definitely a woman. You could see it in the cheekbones and lips. No eyebrows and the voice was wrong. The voice belonged to a man.

The Archon smiled and Darby saw shark's teeth, tips sharpened into daggers.

'Satisfied?'

Darby didn't answer.

'You haven't asked about Mr Casey and his daughter.'

'They're here?'

'Yes. Most of them, anyway.' The woman clasped her hands together. 'Which one do you want to live? Do you have a favourite?'

'Both.'

'You're going to have to kill one.'

'I don't think so.'

'The one you pick shall decide your fate. You can contemplate this while we affix the obedience device to your back.' The Archon held up the device Darby had seen on the spine of the toothless, tongueless thing in New Hampshire – a black plastic box with a series of spiked metal ends. 'You will do what you are asked or you will suffer incredible pain.'

The mask came back down. The Archon left the room.

The door shut. Darby heard a creaking sound coming from somewhere outside and then the chains loosened and she collapsed on the floor, the whip marks throbbing and a pins-and-needles sensation sweeping across her limbs.

'You will,' a strange voice whispered in the darkness. 'Believe me, you will.'

Time passed. Had to be at least two days, Darby thought. The welts on her thighs and shins had started to scab over.

She lay in the dark, thinking.

Planning.

Dreaming.

The next time the door opened, one of them came in holding a candle and a bucket. Darby saw a bar of soap and a washcloth floating on the full pail of water.

'Wash,' he said. He wore a robe and a hood covered his face. He was barefoot.

'Which Archon are you? Tinky Winky or Dipsy?'

'Wash.'

She picked up the bucket and started to wash herself, not an easy thing to do with the chains, and the Archon or whoever he was standing there, watching.

After scrubbing her hair, she dumped the rest of the water over her head and then threw the bucket at him. He wasn't prepared. It bounced off his face before he could catch it and he staggered, catching himself on the wall to keep from falling.

He stood up, slowly. His hood had fallen slightly and she still couldn't see his face. It was hidden behind some sort of fencing mask made of black mesh. She saw the part where the bucket had dented it.

He took the bucket and the candle and left her there in the dark, cold and wet and dripping.

Only one came through the door. Holding a candle and something else. She didn't see it; he tossed it to the floor.

Clothing.

'I hope you're taking me out someplace nice,' she said.

He unchained her. 'Dress.'

She picked up the clothing. Black cloth trousers and a black tunic. No shoes. The fabric felt greasy. Used.

He didn't watch her this time. He placed the candle on a ledge high on the wall, well beyond her reach, and shut the door him.

It seemed to open a moment later, just as she had slipped into the tunic.

A small robed figure with a hood came in holding a tray of food. Nuts, an apple, water in a big plastic cup.

The door shut and Sarah Casey placed the tray on the floor.

Darby thought about moving the hood away from the girl's face, then decided against it. Sarah Casey had no idea who she was.

'Sarah,' Darby whispered, her gaze on the door. 'Is that you?'

Sarah Casey removed her hood to get a closer look at Darby. Her eyes were glazed over, either from shock or drugs, maybe from a combination of both. She had a fading bruise on her cheek and what looked like a burn mark.

'I'm a friend of your father,' Darby whispered. 'Is he here?'

The girl didn't answer. She licked her lips and swayed slightly on her feet.

Jesus, they drugged her.

'Who are you?'

'My name is Darby McCormick. I'm working with your father. Is he . . . Can he walk?'

Sarah nodded, pursed her lips. 'My mother . . .'

'Tell me about your father, where they're —'

'My mother here?'

'No,' Darby said, not seeing the point of telling her the full truth. 'And keep your voice down. Where are they keeping you?'

'Far away.'

'I don't understand.'

'This place is big. Lots of corridors and tunnels, lots of floors.'

'Do you know where we are?'

'Hell,' she said. 'We're here to pay for our sins.'

'Listen to me.' Darby kept her voice low. 'I will find a way to get you out of here. I promise, but I need —'

'You're lying.'

'No. No, I'm not. Look, your father and I, we were working with people. The FBI. They're looking for us right now. It's going to take some time. I need you to be strong and brave for yourself and for —'

'You're the one.'

'The one what?'

The girl's eyes grew wider. 'You're going to kill me.'

'No. No, I'm not going –'

'You are. They told me. You're going to kill me tonight in front of the others.'

'What others?'

'The children. They have children down here and these . . . people who look like ghosts. They're all chained in the great hall, where they're going to watch you kill me.'

'I'm not going to kill you, I promise. Don't walk away. Have you eaten? Here, take some of this food.'

The door opened and two people with lobotomized stares and ghoulish features limped into her room, barefoot and wearing torn sarongs. Their skin, heavily scarred and emaciated, was leached of colour. They held stun batons. One held a key ring.

A robed person came in and hauled Sarah Casey away. He didn't lock the door. It stood open and Darby stared at it, thinking, when she heard the crackle of electricity.

The stun baton hit her waist. Her legs collapsed and the baton hit her again, causing her to fall headfirst against the wall. The baton remained pressed against her waist and she shook violently, chains bouncing against the floor. One of them grabbed her ankle and unlocked the manacle, the fetid odours baked into their scarred skin making her gag.

The baton was withdrawn and, as they rolled her on to her stomach and shackled her wrists, she knew her opportunity had come. She lay there limp and useless, and they grabbed her by the arms and lifted her to her feet.

She was dragged out of the door and down a long, candlelit corridor with a dirt floor and the walls on each side stacked with skulls. She passed an archway and saw a dirt floor leading down and then it disappeared as they led her into another hall, this one narrow and made of bleached and dusty brick. They were close to her now and, suddenly moving her feet behind their knees and arching her back, she threw them off balance. The one to her left fell to the floor, taking her down with him.

She lay on top of him and smashed the back of her head against his face, breaking his nose. Not much room to manoeuvre, but the one now on top of her had no idea how to fight at close quarters. He seemed confused. Scared. His neck was inches from her mouth and without hesitating she sank her teeth into the thin, foul flesh and bit down hard like a rabid dog, tearing. An arterial spray of blood exploded against the wall and the thing howled, a ragged sound, and she slammed her forehead into his nose, pushed him to the side and got to her feet. Rolled back against the dirt floor, swept the chains from underneath her legs, brought her hands up as the bottom one scurried to his feet, clawing the walls for purchase and slipping on the blood. A quick snap of the neck and the bleeding thing dropped. The other one tried to scrabble away and she wrapped the chains around his neck and went to work on strangling him, some boy who had been brought to this place and turned into a monster.

With the things dead and lying on the floor, she found the keys. Four of them. She tried the first one and it worked.

Darby wiped her bloody mouth on her sleeve and ran.

82

A sepulchral tomb of twisting halls leading left and right and forward, some lit by sconces holding candles, some dark, almost every wall lined with bones. Some dirt floors dipped down and some rose, and Darby paused at each one, thinking about Jack Casey and his daughter and the decision she would have to make.

Up, she thought. *Towards the surface.*

She ran with the keys gripped in her fist to keep them from jingling and each hall led to a circular area of dirt, some with barrels decorated with skulls and bones and holding water. She saw no one and heard nothing but her ragged breathing.

Another circular area, one that held a granite sarcophagus placed in front of a stone altar. Latin words and phrases cut into the dusty stone and she recognized only one, the name on the sarcophagus: Iadabaoth.

To the right of the altar, a staircase made of ancient brick. She saw it curved and led only one way, up. She climbed it, her bare feet sliding across the smooth stone, and it seemed to go on for ever. It was cool and dark in here, musty and dank, and she was sweating. She paused when she heard the screaming.

Not screaming. Roars of approval and delight and triumph, like a Red Sox crowd at Fenway Park on opening day. Darby kept climbing, only more slowly, eyes wide and searching the cool and musty-smelling dark, the roars growing louder.

The staircase ended and led to another smooth-bricked hall. She found a ladder. Ahead, maybe twenty feet, an archway lit up by candlelight coming from somewhere far below. No floor beyond the archway, just the candlelight and the cool air throbbing with roars and screams. She moved towards it, had to see, needed to see, and when she reached it she got on her hands and knees and looked down and down.

A great hall, full of manacled children and the manacled pale things with shaved heads and scarred bodies, a crowd of at least a hundred down there. Some were shackled to the walls; others were shackled by only one wrist, and they picked up rocks and threw them at the person in the centre of the big space: Jack Casey, his massive body tied to a giant, raised wheel that was opposite his kneeling daughter. Sarah Casey had been chained to some contraption that wrapped around her throat, the stiff metal bars leading to rings that encircled her knees. Hooded figures stood behind her and others were gathered near their leader, the Archon Iadaboath, sitting high on a perched throne.

Darby stared at the sailing rocks; the roars were like slaps across her face. Even from this height she could see the tears on Sarah Casey's face, the look of abandonment and hopelessness on Casey's. He had been broken. Shattered. Physically and mentally. He looked dead on that wheel – a medieval wheel used as a torture device.

St Catherine of Alexandria had been tortured on such a device, and when the wheel broke, they beheaded her on a guillotine.

Darby looked at the table set up at the end of the Archon's throne, a table stocked with strange and ancient torturing devices. She saw a metal-framed helmet with blades on each side that sat right above the ears. Saw spiked instruments and whips and metal vices used to crush bone. Collars lined with metal teeth.

You can't save them, a voice said.

She knew that, logically. She couldn't take them on without weapons. Without a small army at her back. And yet she didn't move, because the crowd gathered below was waiting for her to enter the room – waiting for her to kill Casey or his daughter. Or both.

You can't take on these crazies by yourself. You'll need help.

Yes. That made perfect sense. She couldn't do this by herself, but if she left now, what would happen to Casey and his daughter? They could be dead by the time help arrived.

If you want to save them, you need to save yourself first. You're their only chance for survival now, so get moving.

Darby backed away and climbed the cold metal ladder that stretched high into darkness. At the top she found a hatch.

It was locked.

Panic fluttered through her limbs and then vanished when one of the keys worked on the padlock. Darby pushed the hatch open and climbed outside, into woods lit up by a bright moon.

She eased the hatch shut and started moving through the cold air, telling herself she had done the right thing. She hated running away – she had never run from anything in her life – but she knew this time she had no choice. She breathed in the cold air, trying to ignore the primitive part of herself that rejoiced at being free. At being alive.

83

Darby ran.

The wind was cold and raw and kept shaking the tree branches and limbs high above her head. Most of the terrain was flat, nothing more than freshly shed leaves, and she kept running straight, figuring, at some point, she'd hit either a road or a clearing.

She covered a lot of ground and had a lot of speed despite the fact she was barefoot. Then her thoughts became consumed by traps – trapdoors and bear traps hidden underneath all these leaves, things with steel jaws and clawed metal teeth ready to tear flesh and snap bone – and she traded pace for caution. The Archons would have planned for something like this. Get a foot stuck in a trap, and she'd be dragged back under the earth and set up on one of those operating tables for an amputation, maybe even an emergency lobotomy.

Were they already out here looking for her? By now they had discovered the bodies. They knew she had the keys. They were searching every hall, every room, every hidden area. The staircase. She imagined one of them poking his head out of the hatch, looking around and seeing her footprints in the damp earth. Saw him climbing out and releasing the ghouls, sending them off into the woods like dogs to follow her scent, and she knew she couldn't slow her pace and ran faster.

The woods never ended; like something from a nightmare, they stretched on and on.

She ran until she was rubber-legged. She paused and leaned forward, gripping a tree as she sucked in air, her hair wet and matted against her face. Her skin felt hot and wet but her mouth was bone-dry and she couldn't get any moisture into it.

She pressed on, jogging this time. She had almost given up hope, thinking she would die out here of dehydration, her flesh picked apart by crows and animals, when she saw a path straight ahead and bolted for it.

Not a path but a dirt road that broke into different directions, some leading into new sections of trees. She looked up at the sky and searched for the Big Dipper. There. The Pole Star was located directly off the Dipper's top and she turned slightly to her left. Now she was facing north, the way the road led. She took it, noticing how the air had turned cooler.

She smelled the salt in the air before she heard the ocean.

The road wound its way around a cliff. Looking over the edge, she saw water lit up by the moonlight, the spent waves creaming against the rocks, and then they disappeared, lost in a blizzard.

She jerked backwards, blinking. No snow. She could see perfectly well. A hallucination. What had caused that? She hadn't drunk their water. What? Her heart was thumping erratically and when she touched her face it felt as dry as her tongue. Dehydration? Or had that bucket of water she used been laced with something?

Looking off to her left, she could see endless water. To her far right, more water lapping against cliffs and a half-standing lighthouse sitting on a small island.

The area directly above the lighthouse was a field of broken boulders. No choice but to go down.

She had made it halfway when she saw some stairs cut into the rock. She took them down, relieved to see she didn't have to swim to reach the lighthouse. But she had to wade through water cold enough to turn bone to ice, and it rose all the way up her legs before she reached the next set of stairs. She stumbled up them drunkenly, her head pounding by the time she reached the top.

The door was locked. She went to try a key and found she was no longer carrying the key ring. She had no memory of having dropped or lost it.

It took four blows of her shoulder to knock it open.

A winding metal staircase, the wind howling above her. She found a storage room in the back, the wooden shelves stripped bare.

Shivering, she took the stairs, her breath pluming and then disappearing in the cold air.

Halfway up she found another room with an upended cot and an old AM radio covered in rust. Warmer in here than outside. She shut the door, heard the wind whistle through the gaps and cracks, and turned over the cot. She lay down on her back and stared up at the black ceiling, thinking.

Where was she? Had to be somewhere on the East Coast, okay, but where? Some sort of island? She hadn't seen any homes or cars. Nothing but woods and the ocean and this lighthouse.

Despair pressed against the walls of her heart and she closed her eyes and ignored it. Think of a plan. Wait for sunlight. Pray for a bright day and then head out of here. There has to be something here. Those people had brought her water, and Sarah Casey had brought her food. There had to be a grocery store somewhere near by. Darby switched back to Sarah Casey and wondered about the girl and her father, praying that they were still alive – still had the will to live. Jack Casey had had it crushed out of him, but his daughter – would she still cling to it if something happened to her father? What would she do if her father died? The question hung in Darby's mind as she drifted off to sleep.

She dreamed that Coop had rescued her. He came with an army of helicopters that soared above the lighthouse, men rappelling down ropes and carrying guns.

Coop sat on the edge of her cot and nudged her awake. 'I came back for you,' he said. 'I found you.'

He took her in his arms and kissed her cheek and hair and held her as she let it all out, dry sobs at first, then the rest of it, the worst part, and she wailed into his neck and screamed into his chest, wanting to purge it from her heart.

When she pulled herself away, she saw Jack Casey's face pulverized and blood running from his nose and ears. His eyes.

'Luck always runs out,' he said. 'You have to come back home now.'

*

Darby sat up in the dark and saw light creeping underneath the door. Heard footsteps.

'Miss McCormick? Miss McCormick, you in here?'

She crept to the edge of the door and opened it slightly, looking down the winding staircase. In the bright sunlight saw a man dressed head to toe in black peering through the target site of an HK sub-machine gun. His partner was standing right behind him, SWAT in bright white letters on his back.

How had they found – the GPS transmitter in her arm. Sergey or the feds monitoring the signal had found it and sent people here.

She had to scrape the words from her dry throat.

'Don't shoot,' she said, her voice a whispery rasp. She came out of the doorway with her hands raised. 'Don't shoot.'

The one in the back turned to her, then dropped his gun and said, 'Jesus.'

84

The SWAT officers draped her arms across their shoulders and carried her out of the lighthouse. The wind slapped her face and blew her hair, and the bright sun pierced her eyes as she looked up the weathered cliff and caught sight of a Coast Guard helicopter.

'It's hidden in the woods,' Darby croaked. 'A hatch. Jack Casey and his daughter. Underground. Need to help them.'

They didn't answer and she realized they couldn't hear her.

She tried again when they brought her inside the helicopter.

'Jack Casey and his daughter.'

They guided her on to a stretcher.

'Below us,' Darby croaked. Christ, how her throat ached. It felt raw and dry and nearly swollen shut. 'Go to the woods and find the hatch, hurry, not much time.'

Darby felt a cool alcohol swab brush against the back of her hand. She turned and saw a Coast Guard officer, a woman, hovering by her side. Darby looked over the woman's shoulder, at the two SWAT officers who had turned away. They had heard her, she was pretty sure. She could see them running towards the woods, the trees shaking in the breeze on a beautiful autumn day.

Darby moaned when the IV needle slipped into her hand.

'Sorry,' the woman said. 'It's your skin. You're dehydrated. We need to get fluids into your system.'

Darby needed to be sure they had heard her. She beckoned the woman closer and told her about the hatch, Casey and his daughter, everything.

The woman straightened, looking confused and frightened. 'I'll tell them.'

'Where am I?'

'Black Rock Island. It's off the coast of Maine.'

'Stay.'

'I will. Don't worry, I'm not going anywhere –'

'No. Stay here. On the island. I need to go back there. I need to see.'

'There's nothing out there, hon. Nobody comes out this way.'

'Don't take me away' was the last thing Darby said before she drifted off.

Coop came as the sun started to set.

Darby saw him standing near the edge of the woods. She sat up on the stretcher, the IV line still in her arm, and lost sight of him for a moment. Her head was spinning but not as badly as before and she leaned back against the cabin wall.

The aft door slid open and Coop popped his head into the copter, his face washed in the sunset's deep gold and purple hues.

Not Coop but a federal agent with a similar face and haircut.

'Special Agent Martynovich wanted me to tell you he's here.'

'The hatch?' Her throat was still raw but most of her voice had come back.

'They found it. He's about to go down, and he said he'll talk to you once – What are you doing?'

'Coming with you.' Darby slid the IV needle out of her arm. She found a bandage and covered the wound.

'Miss McCormick, you're not exactly dressed for the weather,' he said, looking at her hospital scrubs and bare feet stained with dirt. They had cleaned her up and dressed her while she had slept. 'It's getting pretty raw out.'

'Grab that.' She pointed to one of the bulky orange Coast Guard jackets hanging on the wall.

'What about shoes?'

'I'll manage,' she said. 'Come on, let's get going before it gets dark.'

She found Sergey pacing in front of the hatch.

'I don't know anything yet,' he said. 'We discovered the hatches about an hour ago and –'

'Hatches? There're more than one?'

'Two. One here, and one in the southern part of the woods. Before I sent anyone down, I wanted the air tested. I'm glad I did. It tested positive for sarin gas.'

Darby thought about Casey and his daughter, the people she'd seen chained to the walls, and felt a sick and hollow pit in her stomach.

'I was told what's down there is an ossuary created back

in the early eighteen hundreds,' he said. 'When the cemeteries on the mainland flooded, they brought the bones here to this island and created this space to honour the dead. There's some old church up there, what's left of it. The locked cells and some of the other things we found, they're probably new. The locals say nobody comes out to this rock.'

'Jack and his daughter are down there. I saw them.'

Sergey nodded, kept nodding. 'I couldn't send anyone down until we had the proper masks and clothing. I'm waiting for mine to arrive, and then I'm going down.'

'You didn't have that stuff on your plane?'

Sergey kicked a tuft of grass with the tip of his shoe. 'The plane's been grounded. My boss and the pencil pushers he works for have decided to conduct an internal audit of this investigation. When we found your signal, I had to make other travel arrangements.'

'Why did they shut down the investigation?'

'Because I've lost too many people – Jack and his daughter, and now Keats. The Secret Service agent has vanished, along with his wife and son, Luke.'

'Keats didn't disappear.' Darby told Sergey what had happened with Keats in the back of the ambulance.

Sergey looked at the hatch and said, 'Did they bring Keats here with you and Jack?'

'I don't know. I didn't see him. Just Jack and his daughter. In the great hall.'

'The what?'

'The great hall. That's what Sarah Casey called it. I know where it is.'

'There's no need for you to go down there, I'm sure they'll –'

'The place is a maze of tunnels. I'm going down. Don't argue.'

'Then you're going to need to be properly dressed,' he said, and barked a request for another suit and gas mask into his radio.

85

Halfway through the tunnels, Darby got dizzy. Not from whatever was in the air; she wore a gas mask, as did everyone who was down here. The dizziness came from dehydration. Her body hadn't bounced back yet and she had ignored it, pushing herself too fast; her body was now pushing back. Sergey had to hold her arm the rest of the way.

They walked into what Sarah Casey had called the great hall and found it packed with bodies. A hundred, maybe more, it was impossible to tell. Dead from sarin gas.

Casey was no longer tied to the wheel. The device that had held his daughter lay on the floor, spotted with blood.

Sergey glanced around the room packed with bodies. 'I can't . . . This is . . .'

Darby moved to her right and searched through the bodies for Jack and Sarah Casey.

She didn't find them.

She was thinking of the smiling faces of those missing children in the photographs when she turned around and saw Sergey studying the metal device Sarah Casey had been forced to wear around her neck: the rusted O-ring with four metal rods leading to a horizontal one with two half-moon rings.

'I didn't find Jack or his daughter,' she said. 'You?'

'No, nothing here.' Sergey's voice was muffled behind the gas mask. 'This thing is called the Scavenger's Daughter. I first saw it, along with some other torture devices, when I toured the Tower of London. Henry VIII used it: prisoners would be forced to kneel with their chins on their knees, and then they'd be locked into the device, which crushed them into a foetal position.'

Darby looked away, her eyes wet. They settled on the steps leading up to the throne where the masked Archon had sat, watching the spectacle.

'Lot of pain,' Sergey said. 'Cracked ribs and collapsed lungs, and if enough time passed, the capillaries would burst and blood would start pouring from every orifice of the body. I pity the poor son of a bitch who had to endure this.'

She turned back to him as he leaned the device against the Catherine Wheel, its thick wooden spokes splattered with blood – Jack Casey's blood.

'Jack,' she started to say, and her throat closed up.

Sergey gave her his full attention and she told him about what had happened in this room, everything she had heard and seen.

A tall man dressed in a biohazard suit stepped inside the room and waved to Sergey. She went with him, and they followed the man down through the dirt-floored tunnels lined with bones and skulls.

The man stopped halfway down one tunnel and then fell to his knees and faced a grille. No, not a grille – the iron bars of a cell. She saw an ancient padlock flecked with rust.

The man shone the beam of his flashlight on whatever was inside and she also fell to her knees and looked, saw the tiny cell holding a tangle of broken limbs and dirty skin covered with fresh abrasions and welts from whippings – Neal Keats, the Secret Service agent, curled into a foetal position and hugging his dead son fiercely against his chest.

Epilogue

86

Darby woke to sunlight and the squawk of seagulls.

She sat up in the bed and checked her watch. It was early, just past six. She pulled the covers off and padded across the room in her bare feet to the rear window overlooking the ocean. The binoculars sat on the bureau. She picked them up and examined the shore.

After her hospital stay, three short days that felt like a lifetime, she helped Sergey and a federal team consisting of fifty people, most of them forensics, search every corridor, tunnel and room. When Jack and Sarah Casey's bodies didn't turn up, she braced herself for the fact that they would bob to the surface of the ocean at some point. The currents from Black Rock Island hit the beach near her rental home in Ogunquit, so she checked the shoreline every morning, at noon and then in the early evening before it got dark and she had to lock herself inside the house.

No bodies this morning, but she could see only part of the beach from her house. She'd have to walk the rest of it to be sure. She put down the binoculars, went back to the bed, grabbed the Glock from underneath the pillow and took the nine with her to the shower. She had already put out the next day's clothes, laying them on top of the toilet tank.

After she locked the door, she wedged the chair underneath the knob.

Dressed in heavy winter clothes, her hair blown dry and tucked underneath a Red Sox baseball cap, she checked the upstairs rooms first, Glock in hand.

Finding nothing out of the ordinary – all the closet doors were open, the windows locked tight – she headed downstairs and started with the front door. Locked, alarm still on. Living room, spare bedroom and bath clean. All the windows locked. She wound her way into the kitchen, found everything neat and tidy, just as she had left it. She relaxed a little but kept the gun in her hand as she started to make coffee.

She found the picture when she went to put in a new coffee filter.

It was a recent one, showing Sarah Casey huddled in a corner and clutching her knees tightly against her chest. Fresh cuts and bruises on her shins. Her head had been shaved.

Darby tripped on the way back upstairs to retrieve a pair of latex gloves and an evidence bag.

The restaurants in Ogunquit's downtown area catered to the lunch crowd, so most of them were closed. Darby hit the gas stations and found a payphone next to an air pump at a Mobil Station, its windows sprayed with fake snow and decorated with Christmas garlands.

Sergey was back in Washington. She called his cell, woke him up and told him about the picture.

'Bring it to our Boston office,' he said after she finished. 'Give it to Tina.'

Tina was the name of the federal agent who handled Sergey's mail. Darby had met the woman only once, when she drove to Boston at the beginning of the month to deliver the letter and stack of pages she'd written for Coop. Tina had forwarded the package to Sergey, who had delivered it to Coop's London address. When it came to Coop, she didn't want to take any chances.

She hadn't talked to him since he'd left but knew he was safe. Sergey had placed people on him, and she had called him every three days, like clockwork, to get a status report.

Coop had no way of getting in contact with her, and she hadn't called him. She thought about him, wondering what he was doing right now, if he still thought of her.

Sergey was speaking.

'What's that?'

'I said I'll send some forensic people to your house,' he said. 'What are you going to do now?'

'I'm already on my way to Boston.'

'I meant after that.'

'Pack and move.'

'Where?'

'I don't know yet.'

'You want me to bring you into federal —'

'No,' she said. 'No, I don't want that.'

'You still checking the beach every morning for bodies?'

Darby didn't answer. A car had peeled into the station and her hand reached inside her jacket.

The car, an old blue Volkswagen Beetle, parked at one of the pumps. She watched three college-aged guys stagger out, their faces pinched with hangovers.

'You there?' he asked.

'I'm here. How do you know about the beach?'

'I have people watching you too.'

Her jaw clenched. 'Since when?'

'Since you decided to embark on this plan or whatever it is you've got locked in your head. I know about your beach walks, how you watch it every morning from your window. I know about the boats you chartered during the first month to see if any bodies bobbed to the surface.'

'We should check the tunnels again.'

'We've checked them a dozen times. Each time we brought you along, remember?'

'But we haven't really explored every inch of the island. There could be –'

'Jack and his daughter aren't there.'

'Then they moved them someplace else. You have any leads?'

'Darby, you need help.'

'I'll be fine on my own.' But the words died on her mouth. One of these people had broken into her house, bypassed the alarm code and left Sarah Casey's picture in her coffee-maker. They had been watching her and found her. Maybe they were watching her right now.

'I'm talking about your head,' he said. 'You're exhibiting classic signs of post-traumatic stress disorder.'

'What's the status of that EMT? Have you found him yet?'

Sergey didn't answer, and she spoke into the silence.

'I gave you his description. He spoke to Keats, remember? I told you –'

'His name is Peter Grange,' Sergey said. 'He's thirty-six years old and single.'

'When did you find out?'

'A while ago.'

'When were you going to tell me?'

Sergey didn't answer.

'Do you have him in custody?' she asked.

'No. He disappeared. We know he's not one of the bodies we found in the ossuary.'

'So let me help with the investigation. I can –'

'The Bureau has enough people working on it.' He sounded so incredibly tired. 'The guy's gone. We're never going to find him.'

She squeezed the receiver, wanting to take it and smash it across Sergey's head. Knock out that loser thinking and help him get his priorities straight.

'Darby, you're going to have to deal with this.'

'I'd deal with it much better if you'd let me into the investigation.'

'There is no investigation. Not any more.'

She felt a cold space in her stomach. 'Since when?'

'Since about a week or so ago. The suits upstairs, they decided to pull the plug on it for the time being. Those bodies we found, most of them were identified and –'

'I know. It's all over the news.' She had followed it in the papers and on TV. The FBI was getting heat about not having found this cult sooner, with the media resurrecting

461

the ghost of Waco and drawing comparisons with that botched operation.

She also knew that Sergey's son was not among the dead.

'We put in a lot of manpower, a lot of time and even more money,' he said. 'The suits and bean-counters looked at the bottom line and decided that finding and identifying those bodies, bringing them home to their families – that was a victory. They put all the information about this group into the open. Forwarded all our information to police departments while the press is hot and it's fresh in everyone's minds. This group is on everyone's radar screen now.'

'And Casey and his daughter? Are they still on *your* radar?'

There was a long pause on the other end of the line.

'I consider Jack a friend,' he said. 'Keep that in mind when you hear what I'm about to say.'

She heard a hitch in his voice. He cleared his throat and said, 'Have you considered the fact that both he and his daughter are dead?'

'They're alive.'

'You don't know –'

'Last week you told me Taylor Casey received a phone call from her daughter.'

'Yes. Yes, I did say that. But we don't know for sure that her daughter was on the other end of the line. Taylor Casey received a phone call that lasted twenty-two seconds. And you remember I said I couldn't trace it.'

'You said it was Sarah. Taylor told you her daughter

called crying, asking her mother when she's coming to get her.'

'Darby, the woman was *lobotomized*. She has permanent and severe brain damage. She doesn't know what day it is. She thinks Jack is coming in any minute to pick her up.'

'I want to talk to her.'

'No. She's being moved to another private facility – the same place we're taking Darren Waters. They'll both be well taken care of. You need to stop this obsessive thinking.'

'Sarah Casey is twelve years old.'

'And my son was five when they took him.'

Darby propped an arm up on top of the payphone and looked out at the cars whisking by on the highway, the sun warm on her face.

'My son isn't coming back,' Sergey said. 'I've come to grips with that. I won't lie to you, it's not an easy process. For a while there I was a member of the living dead. But I've got past that now, and yes, there are still days when I wake up and wish I could go back and do things differently. But I can't. Sad fact of life but there it is. That day is gone, and my son's gone. You've got to start letting this go.'

Her eyes were burning. Wet. 'And do what?'

'Live,' Sergey said. 'Coop has been calling me. He wants to know where –'

'Don't tell him.'

'He wants to talk to you.'

'No. I can't risk it.'

'You can't hide for ever.'

'Don't tell him,' she said, and hung up.

*

Darby delivered the picture to the Boston office and then checked herself into the Four Seasons. The room she had shared with Coop was occupied, so she picked out the cheapest room, raided the mini-bar and got drunk.

That night, she dreamed of men and women rising from the surf under a moonless sky, their ghoulish faces and bloated white bodies picked apart by fish. They crept across the sand dragging their chains and she was so tired she didn't hear them enter her room.

She woke with a start. Her Glock was lying next to her, and she picked it up and searched the rooms.

Sweating, she sat on the couch in the small living room, her Glock aimed at the door.

87

Sergey called two days later, a few minutes after midnight.

'Where are you?' he asked, and Darby heard him give a sigh of relief.

'Back at the rental house. Packing. I just got here.'

'My guys lost sight of you.'

'I've been moving around.'

'If you're scared, the offer for protective federal custody –'

'I'm going to do this on my own.'

'Good. Good for you. The offer is there if you ever need or want it. You need any help packing? I can send some people there. They can drive you to wherever you're going.'

'Thanks, but no. I'm all set.'

Sergey paused. She sensed he had something more to say. She stopped packing and sat on the edge of the bed, her attention drifting to the windows filled with the black night sky.

'The picture's a wash. No prints on it, no prints on the coffee-maker or your rental unit either.'

'I figured as much.'

'They're bringing in fresh eyes from ISU to take a look at the case,' he said.

'And you?'

'I'll be taking some time off. After that, we'll see.'

So they had pushed him aside, probably dangled a golden parachute in front of him if he promised to step down.

'What about you?' he said. 'What are you going to do now?'

'I don't know.'

'You ever thought about coming to work for us?'

'The Bureau?'

'ISU. There's been some internal talk. The new guy who's going to be heading up the profiling unit asked me about you, and I passed along my recommendation.'

Darby didn't know what to say.

There didn't seem to be anything left to say.

'Good luck, Sergey.'

'Thanks. You too. Stay safe and call if you need anything.'

'Before you go –'

'Yeah.'

'I never had an opportunity to tell you how sorry I am about your son. I hope . . .'

'I know,' he said. 'I do too. Maybe one day.'

'If you find anything out about Jack and Sarah, anything at all, please call me.'

'You still think they're alive, don't you?'

'I do.'

'Why?'

'Because they want him to suffer. That's what keeps these people alive – it's their nourishment, what feeds them.'

Sergey didn't say anything after that, and they exchanged goodbyes and promises to keep in touch.

Darby carried her bags downstairs. The inside lights were off, but she had left the back porch lights on and she could see well enough. She told herself she didn't need the lights. She would be fine.

The plan was to go home, get settled and then take some time to figure out her next step.

She put the bags down by the front door. She didn't need to call a cab. She had sold her bike for an ancient but sturdy Honda Accord. The transmission was a little shaky. All she needed to do was get home and then she'd dump it.

She stared out of the window at her car parked in that endless night and wondered what was waiting for her.

Heavy footsteps thumped across her back porch. She ducked into the hall and got into a shooter's stance.

A fist banged at the door.

'Darby?' Coop yelled. 'Darby, you in there?'

Sergey. The son of a bitch had told Coop where she was.

'Darby?'

'Hold on.' She unlocked the door.

Coop took a step forward, stopping when he saw the gun in her hand. He raised his arms slightly.

'You going to put that away?'

'Yeah.' She blinked as she backed away. 'Yeah, sorry, come in and lock the door.'

He did and they stood there, staring at each other.

'Who told you?' she said. 'Sergey?'

He nodded. 'He's worried about you. I am too. I got your package.'

Her face felt flushed, her throat tight. 'I just wanted you to know what had happened after you left.'

'And in case something happened to you.'

She didn't answer. She could hear the surf pounding outside the windows.

'You didn't have to come,' she said.

'I know I didn't. I came because I wanted to.'

'You bring Amanda with you?'

'No. No, I came alone.'

She licked her lips and her eyes stung when she said, 'She's not going to like this, your making emergency transatlantic flights to make sure I'm okay. Not a good way to start off an engagement.'

He moved closer and cupped her face in his hands and her throat seized and when he smiled she started to cry.

'It's okay,' he said, holding her. 'Shhh, it's okay.'

Darby buried her face in his chest and she cried the love she'd been carrying for him all this time and she cried for Jack Casey, knowing he was alive, living somewhere underneath the earth, locked in some dark place alone and thinking of his daughter, trying to find a way back to her.

Acknowledgements

Writers are great at coming up with ideas, but it takes a talented cast of people to shape the story. Much like a movie production, these people work 'behind the scenes'. They do all the heavy lifting, in my opinion, and don't get the recognition they deserve. If you liked the book, then you should thank the following people:

My agent, Darley Anderson, and his talented staff: Camilla Bolton, Kasia Behnke, Madeleine Buston and Zoe King.

My editor, Mari Evans, who always shows tremendous insight. And thanks to everyone at Penguin UK who helps with everything from the covers to selling the books. Nick Lowndes keeps me organized and on target for publication. I am *extremely* grateful to have a brilliant copyeditor by my side, a remarkable woman named Donna Poppy. Nothing slides by her, and she isn't happy until I get things right. If something was missed, please blame yours truly.

My wife, Jen, and my good friend Mark Alves are my first readers and always give me great feedback. Thanks also due to Gregg Hurwitz and John Connolly, two great writers who always let me bounce my ideas off them (while showing infinite patience and understanding). My good friend Maggie Griffin is always a great sounding board. This book also owes a debt of gratitude to Lee Child. I won't explain. He knows why.

This book is a work of fiction. That means I made everything up.

UNCOVER THE DARBY

1

'A scary, breakneck ride with thrills that never let up'

Tess Gerritsen

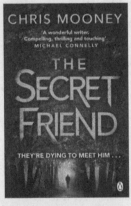

2

'Chris Mooney is a wonderful writer. Compelling, thrilling and touching'

Michael Connelly

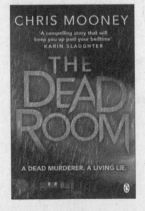

3

'This will keep you up past your bedtime'

Karin Slaughter

McCORMICK THRILLERS

'An exceptional thriller writer.
I envy those who have yet
to read him'

John Connolly

'If you want a thriller that
will chill your blood, break your
heart and make your pulse race,
Chris Mooney is your man'

Mark Billingham

'One of the best thriller
writers working today'

Lee Child

dead good

*For all of you who find
a crime story irresistible.*

Discover the very best crime and thriller books on our dedicated website – hand-picked by our editorial team so you have tailored recommendations to help you choose what to read next.

We'll introduce you to our favourite authors and the brightest new talent. Read exclusive interviews and specially commissioned features on everything from the best classic crime to our top ten TV detectives, join live webchats and speak to authors directly.

Plus our monthly book competition offers you the chance to win the latest crime fiction, and there are DVD box sets and digital devices to be won too.

Sign up for our newsletter at
www.deadgoodbooks.co.uk/signup

Join the conversation on: